BAYOU BRIDE

BOBBI SMITH

ZEBRA BOOKS
KENSINGTON PUBLISHING CORP.

The book is dedicated to my two favorite radio personalities—Michelle Kent and Paul Grundhauser.

A special note of thanks to my friends at The Difference—Cathy, Mary, MJ, Mary Lew, Sherry, and Tookie and to my friends at G & S Printing—Gary, Janet, and Mike.

ZEBRA BOOKS

are published by

Kensington Publishing Corp.
475 Park Avenue South
New York, NY 10016

First printing: February, 1991

Printed in the United States of America

"NO!" SHE CRIED . . .

But it was too late.

With unerring precision, Nick's lips found hers and began to plunder their softness. It was a fiery kiss, an explosion of wonder that rocked them both. Gently he urged her closer, and instinctively they molded together, full breasts to hard-muscled chest.

For one long, sweet moment, Jordan let herself enjoy the embrace. But just as she was about to loop her arms around his neck to melt even closer to him, her sanity returned. She couldn't allow this to happen!

"No!" she said, backing away from him. She was afraid of what he was making her feel, and she had to fight it.

"Jordan?" Nick frowned, startled by her reaction and by his own. That one long kiss had left his body throbbing with excitement.

"How could you?" she cried. "You told me this arrangement would be *in . . . name . . . only!*"

Nick's gaze hardened. "You needn't worry, Jordan. I'm a man of honor."

Not worry, indeed! Jordan was still tingling all over from the effect of Nick's caresses. She took a deep breath and stood on tiptoe to look into his dark, passion-filled eyes. "It's not your honor that's worrying me," she whispered.

ZEBRA ROMANCES FOR ALL SEASONS
From Bobbi Smith

ARIZONA TEMPTRESS   (1785, $3.95)

Rick Peralta found the freedom he craved only in his disguise as El Cazador. Then he saw the exquisitely alluring Jennie among his compadres and the hotblooded male swore she'd belong just to him.

CAPTIVE PRIDE   (2160, $3.95)

Committed to the Colonial cause, the gorgeous and independent Cecelia Demorest swore she'd divert Captain Noah Kincade's weapons to help out the American rebels. But the moment that the womanizing British privateer first touched her, her scheming thoughts gave way to burning need.

DESERT HEART   (2010, $3.95)

Rancher Rand McAllister was furious when he became the guardian of a scrawny girl from Arizona's mining country. But when he finds that the pig-tailed brat is really a voluptuous beauty, his resentment turns to intense interest; Laura Lee knew it would be the biggest mistake in her life to succumb to the cowboy—but she can't fight against giving him her wild DESERT HEART.

Available wherever paperbacks are sold, or order direct from the Publisher. Send cover price plus 50¢ per copy for mailing and handling to Zebra Books, Dept. 3311, 475 Park Avenue South, New York, N.Y. 10016. Residents of New York, New Jersey and Pennsylvania must include sales tax. DO NOT SEND CASH.

Prologue

Up River From New Orleans
Early Spring, 1849

Attorney Aaron O'Neil was a man of mild, good-natured temperament but today his normally calm expression was tinged with urgency as his driver finally turned the carriage into the long, tree-shrouded drive that led to the Kane plantation — Riverwood. They were here . . . at last! The cold, soaking, miserable rain that had begun soon after they'd left New Orleans had slowed their progress considerably, and though the trip had really taken only two hours, to Aaron it had seemed an eternity. As he waited for the carriage to travel the last half mile to the house, the message he'd received that morning from Charles Kane kept repeating itself in his mind.

Come at once . . . There is a matter of utmost importance that must be dealt with immediately and in the strictest confidence . . .

Aaron was filled with dread as he thought of the letter he now carried in his waistcoat pocket. It was not like Charles to make such an unusual request, and for that reason Aaron had immediately canceled all his appointments and made the trip. Something must be wrong . . . terribly wrong.

As the carriage neared the main house, Aaron let his sharp-eyed, bespectacled gaze sweep over the immaculate grounds of the pillared, white-washed brick mansion and then beyond to the greening fields and well-maintained outbuildings. He searched for some clue to the problem behind the cryptic note, but as far as he could tell there was nothing amiss. Outwardly, everything appeared normal.

Riverwood was one of the most successful plantations in the area, and it looked it. Charles had done a marvelous job of carving his own empire out of the Louisiana wilderness, and now with his son, Dominic, working at his side, it would likely remain a most productive operation.

"We're here, Mr. Aaron," Slidell, his driver, announced as the carriage drew to a halt before the house.

Aaron climbed down as soon as his driver opened the door. He thanked Slidell distractedly as he paused in the slow drizzle to take a long look at the beautiful house. The magnificence of Riverwood never failed to impress him. With its huge columns, wide galleries, and perfectly landscaped lawns, it looked as if it belonged on Mount Olympus, and Aaron wondered, not for the first time, if Charles didn't really consider himself God here. Certainly, all who worked with him knew it was not wise to cross him. Though he was a fair and generous man, he wielded much power and authority and was not afraid to use it.

The rain quickened. Aaron would have liked to remain there taking in the glory of the place a moment longer, but he was forced to seek shelter on the gallery. He mounted the steps quickly, removing his spectacles and drying them as he went. He was pleased to find the Kane family's butler, Weddington, already at the door, holding it wide and smiling in warm welcome.

"Come on inside out of this nasty old weather, Mr. Aaron," Weddington said. "They've been expecting you."

"They? Oh, is Dominic here, too?" Aaron asked as he entered the main hall and allowed the servant to take his damp cloak.

"No, sir. Mr. Nick isn't at home right now," the butler answered quickly, and then just as quickly turned away from Aaron, acting almost as if he was afraid he'd said too much.

Aaron frowned as he put his spectacles back on. Since the death of Charles's wife, Andrea, many years before, it had only been the two men, father and son, living at the plantation. So, if Dominic wasn't the one with Charles, then who was? Curious, he hurried to follow Weddington down the hall. The servant gave one short knock at the study door and then opened it for Aaron to enter.

"Thank you, Weddington."

"You're welcome, sir," Weddington replied as he quietly shut the door behind him.

"Aaron . . . I'm glad you could come . . ." Charles spoke from where he stood. There was no lamp lighted in the dark, wood-paneled study, and he remained a tall, broad-shouldered silhouette against the rain-spattered, floor-to-ceiling casement window behind his desk.

"You know you have only to ask and my time is yours," Aaron replied, taking a step into the room. There was something strained in the way his friend was holding himself so rigidly upright, and he wanted to move even closer in order to read his expression in the gloom of the room.

"You know Dr. Michael Williams, don't you?" Charles asked, gesturing toward the wing-backed leather chair before his desk where the physician was seated.

"Dr. Williams?" The doctor's presence startled Aaron, and he glanced nervously in his direction. "Yes, yes, of course. Good to see you, Michael . . ."

Williams, a tall, thin, studious-looking man of fifty, rose from where he'd been seated to shake his hand. "Aaron."

The perfunctory greeting done, the attorney's glance slid back to Charles. He hadn't seen him in almost a month, and, standing this close to him now, he could see the difference in his appearance and it shocked him. Charles Kane had always been a vibrant, active man, and the change in him was dramatic. Aaron wondered how it was possible for his hair to have turned almost completely silver in such a short period of time. Deep lines of fatigue were etched in the planter's face, and there was a soul-shattering weariness in his eyes that had never been there before.

"Charles, what is it? What's wrong? I know you wouldn't have called me out here unless it was serious. Is Riverwood in trouble?" Aaron knew that, next to his son, the plantation was the most important thing in Charles's life. He lived and breathed for Riverwood.

A sad smile carved its way across his craggy features. "I wish it were as simple as that, Aaron," he said with a slow sigh. "Please, sit down, and I'll explain everything."

Charles settled into his own chair as his two guests sat in the matching wing-backed chairs before him.

"I asked you to come this morning because I knew Michael would be here."

The lawyer glanced from his friend to the doctor seated beside him. "I don't understand . . ."

"There's a change I need to make in my will, and I need to have it executed right away."

"Your will?"

"Yes, you see, Michael's informed me today that there's no hope. I have less than a year to live, and I have to do something about Dominic."

"Wait . . ." Aaron held up a hand in immediate denial of what he'd just been told as he riveted the physician with a challenging look. "What do you mean, he's got less than a year to live?"

"I'm sorry, Aaron, but there's nothing more anyone can do. Charles has already seen the best doctors in the country."

"What is it?"

Charles lifted a troubled gaze to his friend's face. "It's my heart, Aaron, and there's no real point in discussing it further. Suffice it to say that I've done everything humanly possible to beat this thing, but for the first time in my life I've come up against something I can't defeat . . . or buy." A bitter smile twisted his mouth as a flicker of painful emotion shone in his eyes.

"Charles . . . I . . ."

"Don't say anything, my friend. I'm dealing with this the best way I can, but there is something I must do. I have to make that change in my will."

"Why?" Aaron countered, forcing himself to concentrate on business. "I thought you were completely satisfied with what we laid out last year."

"A year ago I thought I'd live forever," he responded brusquely. "Now, I know I won't."

"What do you have in mind?" He couldn't imagine what Charles wanted to alter. In the original document, he'd left everything to Dominic, and deservedly so.

"I want to add this single clause . . ."

Charles handed him up a neatly written paper, and Aaron quickly scanned it. When he was finished, astonishment showed plainly on his features.

"You can't be serious. This is blackmail . . ."

"I prefer to think of it as an inducement," he replied. "Michael says I may last a year, but we really don't know. I could have even less time, and I can't afford to sit by and watch my son waste his life."

"Does Dominic know about your condition?"

"No, but I intend to tell him just as soon as he gets back . . . from wherever the hell he went!"

"He's gone?"

"Again," Charles stated flatly. "He left a week ago with scarcely a word. I was riding the fields, and when I returned he'd already gone. He told Weddington he had to go out of town for a few days and that he'd be back as soon as he could. Period. I have no idea how to reach him, and this isn't the first time it's happened."

"Was it some kind of emergency, maybe?"

"Who knows? Even when the boy's here, half the time he's out carousing until all hours."

Aaron wanted to remind Charles that, at age twenty-six, Dominic was no longer a boy, but he didn't want to anger Charles. It was obvious that he

10

was upset by what he considered his son's rakish ways. "He's a young man, Charles. As I recall, you've told me about some wild times you yourself had in your youth. Aren't you being a little rough on him? I've seen him work right by your side for days on end to help save the crop, and he's a miracle worker where your horses are concerned. Riverwood boasts the best stables in six parishes because of his efforts."

"That may be, but he still spends too much time drinking and gambling with his friends."

"You know Dominic loves Riverwood as much as you do," Aaron chided.

"That's precisely what I'm counting on," he declared as he pointed at the paper Aaron was still holding. "If this is what it takes to make him settle down, then I'll do it. I'll do whatever I have to do to guarantee Riverwood's safety. I can't risk his losing everything I've worked so hard for. This is his heritage. It's time he grew up and accepted his responsibilities."

"But not like this . . ." Aaron read the short, concise paragraph out loud.

"In order to validate this will and so claim his inheritance upon my death, Dominic Kane, my son, must make a suitable marriage by six months from today, March 15, 1849. Should he fail to do so by September 15 of same year, I declare that upon my demise all my worldly possessions shall be sold and the money given to the church in loving memory of my wife, Andrea. Signed, Charles Kane."

He looked up, hoping to see doubt in his friend's

expression, but there was only stony determination mirrored there. "You won't change your mind?"

"I can't. Too much depends on this. I won't be able to rest easy until I know that he's settled down."

Aaron studied Charles's implacable features a moment longer, then acquiesced without another word. Charles hadn't asked him for his opinion. He wanted him to do his job, and being the professional he was, Aaron knew he would, even if he didn't agree with it.

"When do you plan to tell Dominic?"

"I'm going to have a long talk with my son just as soon as he returns." He looked disgusted as he thought again of his absence.

"I'll see to the changes right away, then, and get a copy of the revised document back to you within the week. Will that be satisfactory?"

The planter nodded, satisfied. "That'll be fine."

Much later, after both Aaron and Michael had taken their leave to return to town, Charles stood alone once more at the window in his study. Staring out across his flowering gardens and the lush fields beyond, he poignantly recalled how he and Andrea had fought so hard to tame the land, to make it what it was today. He remembered how proud they'd been when they'd moved into their first house—the small two-room cabin that had been their home for several years before the crops had started to pay off and they'd managed to build the mansion. He remembered the joy they'd shared at the birth of their son, and sorrowfully he remembered, too, how ten years later Andrea had died of the fever as he'd held her in his arms.

A deep, lonely longing filled Charles, and he drew a ragged breath. Since that day sixteen years ago when he'd lost Andrea forever, he'd dedicated himself completely to raising his son and to building up Riverwood in memory of his beloved wife. Soon, however, Nick would have to take over, and he wondered if his roguish offspring could find it in himself to settle down and handle the full responsibility.

Charles reflected on his own misspent youth and knew that Aaron had been right. In his younger years he had been just as wild as Nick, but finding and falling in love with Andrea had been the making of him. Right now, he saw Nick making no effort to meet the right kind of woman to marry. Perhaps if Nick married, he'd become the fine man Charles always knew he could be. He hoped so . . . With a heavy heart, he turned away from the rain-drenched landscape, wondering all the while where his errant son was, how much longer he'd be gone, and how he was going to react to the ultimatum when he did return.

Chapter One

Night was falling across the land. Two undetected figures, one male, one female, tied their three horses to a tree and then moved off through the thick undergrowth. The girl, her trim figure disguised in baggy, dark-colored clothing, her long raven tresses tied back in a single braid, led the way. They knew that the element of surprise was the only thing they had on their side, so they were careful not to make any noise as they made their way to the hilltop that overlooked the large hacienda spread out in the valley below.

Halfway to the top, the young woman paused and glanced back to make sure her companion was keeping up. She was surprised to find him close behind her, moving through the tangle of foliage with such predatory male grace that she wondered suddenly if he were not accustomed to being in such untamed surroundings. There was an aura of danger about him now that she hadn't been aware of before. Her gaze went over him quickly, taking in his broad shoulders and lean, dark-clad body and the gun he wore low on his hip with casual ease. His hair was as black as a moonless night and his

15

tanned features were strong, almost hawkish. She imagined that many women thought him handsome, but in truth she knew that it was the sense of power he exuded—and not any classical perfection in his outward appearance—that drew women to him. He would make a formidable foe to man and woman alike, and she was glad he was with her tonight. Perhaps, just perhaps, their daring plan would work. The fear that too much time had passed, though, haunted her.

She started off once more and didn't stop again until they'd made it to the crest. After reaching the best vantage point from which to study the layout of the buildings below, she sought cover in the thick greenery.

"You're sure this is where they're holding him, Anna?" the man asked in a low voice, his gaze riveted on the scene below as he joined her.

"I'm as sure as I can be, Nick," she replied quietly. "But it's been over two months . . ."

"I know." His voice was flat as he worried about his friend, American agent Slater MacKenzie, held captive in the compound below.

"That night they came for Slater, I was in my own room down the hall at the hotel. There was screaming and fighting . . . I came running out to help just as they were dragging him and Francesca away."

"Francesca . . ." Nick groaned the name of Slater's beautiful Cuban wife. "You're sure about her . . ."

Anna nodded, her eyes filled with sorrow. "The word came the day after the attack. She was killed . . ."

Nick's expression grew bleak for a moment, then

16

turned grim.

"I followed them here," she continued, "and I believe they're keeping him locked up there, in that house." She pointed to a small, windowless out-building where two heavily armed men stood guard.

"Why didn't they just kill him?" Nick glanced at her as he spoke, wondering how his friend had gotten involved in this. It wasn't the first time Slater had needed his help. There had been several times in the past when he'd had to bail him out of trouble, but this was the first time he was likely to end up getting killed from one of his adventures.

"The Peninsulars *are* evil and vicious," she said, filled with hatred for the Spanish-born ruling class. "Armando Carlanta, the man who had Slater brought here and is responsible for Francesca's death, is probably the worst of the lot. But though they are cruel and greedy, they are far from stupid. It would be no small thing for them to kill an American agent. Slater's wife's death he could explain away as an unfortunate accident, but an agent's death would be investigated. Besides, Slater's more valuable to them alive. They want names from him—the names of other agents working in Cuba and the names of those of us who oppose Spanish rule and are willing to fight for our freedom. God knows what they've done to him to make him talk . . ."

"What was he doing that got him in so much trouble?"

"You don't know why he was here?" said Anna in surprise.

"No. I don't work with Slater. I'm just his friend, someone he can trust."

She studied him closely for a moment and then

17

answered, "Slater's been trying to encourage the native Creole landowners to push for independence for our country. For that reason alone, the Peninsulars feel they have to put an end to his efforts. A revolution in Cuba would mean they'd lose everything, and they are not about to give up the riches and power they hold so dear."

"How did you get mixed up in all this?" Nick was curious. He knew little about her, only that she was the one who'd written him to come to Slater's aid.

"I am one of Slater's contacts here in the city," she explained.

"How did you know to send for me?"

"He always told me that if anything happened to him, I should contact you. I'm glad you came. I'm just sorry it took so long to get the message to you."

The grateful look she gave him spoke volumes, and Nick knew in that moment that she was in love with Slater.

"So am I. We'll get him out of there just as soon as we can, but I think we'd better wait until it's completely dark before we make our move."

"We'll have to hurry once we free him. The ship I've arranged for your escape will only wait for you at the rendezvous point until dawn. If you're not there by sunup, they'll leave without you."

"What happens if we don't make it?"

Anna's expression turned grave. "There will be no safe place for you on the island. Carlanta is the devil himself! He knows everything that happens here . . . Everything . . ."

"But what about you? If we make the ship, are you coming with us?"

"No, I can't."

"Why?"

"I must stay here. My home is here and my family. I care for my elderly parents. They have no one else."

"But if this Carlanta is as bad as you say he is, won't he come after you?"

"No. I'll be safe. He thinks women are stupid," she scoffed. "I'd be the last person he'd suspect to have helped Slater escape."

Nick nodded in the growing night. He was about to say more when the sound of voices below drew his full attention. The two guards were now standing together, talking in low tones, their vigilance relaxed.

"This is no job for a man. A woman could do this," Juan complained as he threw open the door and took a quick look inside the hut. There was just barely enough light left to let him see their gringo prisoner. He lay on the dirt floor against the opposite wall, his battered and bruised face swollen nearly beyond recognition. His hands were tied behind him, and his ankles were bound. They had yet to remove the gag that had been used to muffle his screams during the hours of torture Carlanta had put him through. "He's not going anywhere. Why do they need both of us to watch him?"

Emilio gave a curt laugh as he shrugged his shoulders. "He's supposed to be one dangerous hombre. I hear Carlanta never broke him, not even when he told him of his wife's death."

"Does he look very dangerous to you right now?" Juan derided. "I've seen newborn babes more threatening than him."

Slater didn't move as he listened to their bragging talk, though he felt a driving urge to kill. When the

19

guards closed the door leaving him locked in the impenetrable darkness once more, he renewed his relentless struggle to free himself. He had been trying to work his hands loose ever since they'd brought him here, but the ropes were so sturdy and so expertly tied that he was beginning to fear that his efforts were useless.

Still, Slater knew any activity was better than just lying there waiting. He wasn't sure just how much more of Carlanta's torment he could stand. His strength was failing him, and his thoughts were becoming disjointed and confused. He couldn't remember how long it had been since the night when they'd come for him or how long it had been since his captor had told him of Francesca's death. Days? Weeks? Months? He didn't know any more. He couldn't be certain of anything now, not even day or night.

Outside, Juan gave Emilio a joking jab in the ribs. "What do you say I sneak off for a little while? My Maria is waiting for me. I could have a little fun and be back before anyone even notices I'm gone."

Emilio's expression was knowing. "I don't care, but what if Carlanta comes out to check?"

"He won't," he assured him. "He hasn't checked on us since that very first night."

The other guard grinned, intrigued by the possibility that he, too, might get the chance to slip away a little later. "Go ahead, then. I'm sure I can handle this alone. The only danger in standing guard here is the danger of falling asleep."

"This shouldn't take too long," Juan chuckled as he clapped him on the back. "I'll be back."

Emilio watched until his friend had disappeared

into the deepening darkness, then he circled the building once more to make certain that all was secure. The truth of the matter was, he wasn't as concerned about the security of the cabin as he was about the possiblity that some of Carlanta's other men might have heard them. Confident that Juan's secret was safe, Emilio was just starting back around the corner, intending to stand by the door, when suddenly he was struck from behind. Before he knew what had happened he felt his knees buckle and the ground come up to meet him. As painful reality faded into deep, dark oblivion, he was vaguely aware of the sound of the door being opened and his prisoner freed.

"Slater?" Anna whispered his name as she pushed the door open and entered the small hut. Rushing to his side, she dropped to her knees beside him and removed his gag. Without thought, she pressed a desperate kiss on his lips.

"Anna . . . ?" Slater was confused. "How did you manage to get past the guard?" he asked quickly in a raspy voice.

"I sent for your friend, Nick. He came," she told him breathlessly as she drew back and freed her knife from her belt. She made short business of the knots at his wrists.

"Nick's here?" His thoughts began to clear. For a moment he'd feared that Anna was alone, but now that she'd told him Nick was there he knew a glimmer of hope. The minute his hands were free he tried to sit up, but the weeks of little food and nightmarish torture had sapped his energy. Only with Anna's help was he able to sit. He watched as she hurried to untie his ankles.

Just then, Nick came through the door, dragging

Emilio's inert body with him and dumping him on the ground. He turned to his friend and was horrified by the sight of him. Slater was a strong, vibrant man, but Carlanta's systematic, savage punishment had taken its toll. Nick feared he might not even have enough strength to walk.

"Slater! God, are you all right?" Nick asked, racing to his side.

"I will be once I get my hands on Carlanta! He killed Francesca!" Slater told him feverishly as he gripped his hand and stared up at him. He was nearly out of his mind from physical pain that had been inflicted on him and from the emotional agony of learning of his wife's senseless death. He wanted to go after the man responsible.

"No, Slater," Anna interrupted angrily, unwilling to let him sacrifice himself. "There is no time. Besides, I've never known you to be stupid. You would be one man, two if Nick goes with you, against hundreds of Carlanta's best, most well-armed men. It would be suicide."

"I have to . . ." He looked to Nick, feeling what little strength he had left fading.

"No, you can't go back. Right now, we have to get you out of here while we can. Anna's made arrangements to get us off the island, and we have to go."

Defeat ravaged Slater, for he knew they were right.

"Let me tie up the guard and then we'll get out of here."

Nick took the discarded rope that had been used to tie Slater's ankles and quickly restrained the guard, then he gagged him. That done, he hurried to help Anna get Slater to his feet. It took Slater a

22

moment to get his equilibrium, and he swayed unsteadily when he stood. He took a last glance around his prison.

"I'm glad you came," he told them huskily.

"I'm glad you're alive," Anna said with heartfelt meaning. Though she'd always known he belonged to another, it hadn't stopped her from falling in love with him. It had been a painful, unrequited love, but she hadn't minded. To her, Slater was the most wonderful man in the world, and if she was destined only to be his friend, so be it.

"Thank you, Anna." Slater was grateful, knowing that without her help, he would have eventually been killed by the powerful Peninsular.

Anna gazed up at Slater adoringly. Though not as tall as Nick, Slater still topped six feet. He was more solidly built, his chest wide and deep and heavily muscled. His hair was dark brown, but the sun had burnished it with golden highlights. Before Carlanta's beatings, his features had been strong and rugged, showing a great strength of character, and she knew he would look that way again once the swelling and bruising were gone. His vivid green eyes had always had the ability to set her pulse racing with just a look. She knew he was not as handsome as Nick, but there was something about him that was so elemental and so very male that it left her wanting him always.

Anna fought back the surge of emotion that threatened to overwhelm her at the knowledge that he would soon be out of her life. She told herself that it was enough that he'd survived. When you loved someone, you wanted what was best for him, and she knew it was most important that Slater leave Cuba. Still, she was unable to end the contact with him just yet, and she kept her arm around him as they started from the cabin.

"I was beginning to get a little worried," Slater said to Nick. He tried to smile, but his swollen lips only twisted in what resembled a grimace.

"You know I always show up when you're in trouble."

"This was more than the average trouble this time, Nick," he said solemnly.

"We'll talk about that later. Right now, we've got to get to the horses waiting at the top of the hill. Anna's arranged passage on a ship, and we have to make it to the rendezvous."

A moment later they were retreating up the hillside to where they'd left their mounts. Luck was with them. Though they were forced to move more slowly than they liked because of Slater's condition, they made their escape unnoticed. By the time Juan returned nearly an hour later, Nick, Slater, and Anna were miles away, heading at full speed for the ship.

When they reached the secluded cove, two hulking, unsavory-looking sailors were waiting for them.

"Hurry and get in the skiff," one of them ordered gruffly. "Captain Curtis doesn't like this waiting."

"Shut up, you. Your captain was well paid for his effort. They will go when they are ready," Anna snapped defiantly, her agony at losing Slater fueling a fierceness in her she'd never known.

The sailor fell silent. He would have liked to throttle her, but the presence of her two companions discouraged him. He stood sullenly by while he waited for them to say their farewells.

Nick spoke to Anna first. "Thank you, Anna."

"You're welcome, Nick. Make this final trip

safely."

"We will, because of you." He moved away to join the sailors, leaving the two of them alone for a few minutes.

Slater stood in the moonlight staring down at the young woman who had risked everything to save him. She was a lovely girl, and he cared for her a lot. With a gentle hand, he touched the smooth curve of her cheek.

In a heartfelt move, she pressed a fervid kiss to his palm. "I'll miss you, Slater MacKenzie," she whispered.

"And I'll miss you. You'll be careful?"

Anna nodded, but couldn't look up. Tears filled her eyes, and she didn't want him to see. But he grasped her chin in a tender grip and lifted her face so he could see her. With great care, he pressed a sweet kiss on her forehead.

"There's something I want you to have . . ."

"What?"

"In my room, hidden behind the painting on the wall opposite the window, is a small key. It's to a metal box I left with Mañuelo Pineda. Just show him that you have the key and he'll give you the box."

"But why? What's in it?"

"Something that will help you," he promised, then turned and made his way with a slow, painful tread to join Nick in the boat. "Take care of yourself, Anna."

Anna watched as the sailors pushed the small craft into the water. She stayed on the beach until the ship disappeared from sight into the Caribbean night. Only then did she let her tears fall.

Anna made the trip back to Havana and immediately went to claim Slater's key. It was exactly where he'd said it would be. Grasping it tightly in her hand the whole way, she went to Pineda's and got the box, then went straight to the privacy of her own room before opening it. With shaking hands, she unlocked Slater's mysterious present and lifted the lid. A gasp of surprise escaped her at the sight of all the money Slater had stowed there.

Joy filled Anna. Because of his gift, she would never have to work another night in the cantina. In a silent prayer, she thanked God for Slater's kindness, yet the sweetness of the moment was tempered by the terrible, empty ache in her heart. She loved Slater MacKenzie, and there would always be a part of her that wished he'd given her the key to his heart instead.

Nick knew that Slater didn't want to leave, but they had no other choice. As pleased as Nick was that their escape had gone so well, his satisfaction vanished the moment he discovered that the *Sea Demon,* the ship Anna had arranged their transport on, was a slaver.

They slept on deck for the balance of that night rather than try to seek rest below, for the stench of filth and disease clung to the vessel. Slater's sleep was restless, filled with agonizing dreams of Francesca and bloody visions of Carlanta and his men. When he awakened, shaking from the power of his nightmare, Nick was at his side.

"What is it? What's wrong?"

"Damn!" Slater swore as he sat up. "It's all my fault! If it hadn't been for me, Francesca would still be alive!"

"Slater, you're wrong! It wasn't your fault. There was nothing you could have done. You were caught, just like she was. You had no control over anything."

"I swear to you, Nick, one day I'm going to go back and find a way to get even with Carlanta!"

"How will going back to Cuba and getting yourself killed help anything?" Nick demanded. "She's dead, Slater," he added gently. "You're going to have to let her go . . ."

"God," he groaned miserably, "will the pain of missing her ever go away?"

"In time . . ." was all Nick could say. "You just need time."

"I hope you're right," Slater answered, and then fell silent.

Dawn finally came, and with it, their first full day of exposure to life on a slave ship. Nick had always known that slaving was an ugly business, but seeing the abuses of it first hand brought it home to him even more forcefully. As a slave owner himself, he was not opposed to the institution. He was, however, opposed to brutality in any form, and there could be no denying that the illegal smuggling of slaves was an atrocity. Hundreds of blacks had been crowded into the dark, dank, barely ventilated bowels of the ship with scant food and water for the duration of the trip from Africa to America. It was a wonder to Nick that any of them survived the horror of the voyage.

Slater, too, was all too familiar with the terrible abuses of the slave smugglers, and he had no use for any of them. He had dealt with their kind before and knew just how ruthless and murderous they could be—all in the name of profit. This encounter, however, held even deeper meaning for him, for after having spent endless weeks in Carlanta's power being restrained, beaten, and starved, he could readily identify with the captives held belowdecks.

Late the following afternoon Nick and Slater stood at the rail of the *Sea Demon* gazing out across the gulf. Slater was still weak, but feeling a little better now that he was free. They knew it would be at least several more days before they made landfall in Louisiana, and they couldn't wait to reach their destination.

"Captain! Ship sighted! North by northeast!"

The hue and cry raised by the lookout captured Nick and Slater's full attention. They scanned the horizon in the direction the sailor was pointing, and saw the distant hulking outline of what looked to be a lumbering government ship heading their way.

Captain Curtis, a big, brutish man with a full flowing black beard and emotionless, icy blue eyes, raced to the side with his spyglass to get a better look. His expression hardened as he focused on the oncoming vessel's flag. It was a U.S. Navy ship, and he knew why it was there.

"Damn," he swore. Turning away, he raced to the helm and ordered his helmsman, "Turn her into the wind, Mr. Givens! Full sail!"

The sails of the schooner snapped as they caught the stiff afternoon breeze, and Curtis continued issuing terse directives, ensuring that the *Sea Demon*'s course led away from the government vessel. He kept watch to see if the other ship meant to give chase, and to his disgust, he found that it did.

"It's a patrol boat," he snarled viciously. "We'll have to outrun them!"

"Aye, aye, sir," his men replied, knowing how much was at stake.

When the *Sea Demon* had been commissioned, her owner had directed that she be of the sleekest, fastest design, and she was showing her worth right now as she cut through the water with daring speed and grace. In this business, fleetness made the difference between success and failure, and failure meant not only the threat of prison but also financial disaster for the owners as well with the loss of the cargo and the forfeiture of the ship itself.

Curtis grew more and more pleased as the minutes passed. His usual confidence was returning as the *Demon* pulled steadily away from the menace of the U.S. ship. It was the lookout's second warning that jolted him and let him know the true seriousness of his situation.

"Captain Curtis!" the man yelled in panic. "There's another vessel, sir! It's closing on us from due west!"

"Hellfire, man!" the captain cursed as he caught sight of the rapidly approaching brig. "Why didn't you spot her sooner?"

"The sun was at her back, sir. I couldn't see her at first! She's traveling mighty fast, Captain. I don't know if we can get away from this one!"

"Change course, due south! Now!" Curtis was furious. In all the years he'd been running slaves from Africa to America, he'd never been cornered before. He had a reputation as a man who delivered on schedule, and it enraged him to think he'd finally been trapped.

"But what if they fire upon us, sir? That schooner's faster than we are! He'll catch us within the hour!"

Curtis turned a baleful eye to his helmsman. "I can tell how quickly the ship's coming, Givens. Just do as your ordered and leave the rest to me."

As he debated with himself over the best course of action, thoughts of Luther Radcliffe hounded him. Radcliffe was the agent of the *Sea Demon*'s owners, and he was one of the coldest, most money-hungry bastards he'd ever met. Curtis knew better than to disappoint him; yet he also knew that there would be no escaping the two American ships. If he was boarded by the U.S. authorities he would lose not only the slaves but also the *Demon*. Nothing, absolutely nothing, was worth losing your ship over.

Gauging the angle of the sun and the number of hours left until dark, Curtis made his decision. He would do what Radcliffe had told him to do should this situation ever arise. As much as it angered him, he would sacrifice his cargo and his lucrative profit to save the ship. They would lose this time, but at least they'd still be in business.

Chapter Two

Nick and Slater kept out of the way as the crew of the *Sea Demon* slammed into action. Time passed in a blur as events unfolded quickly. The swiftly moving government brig altered course and managed to block the slaver's way south, giving the bigger, slower U.S. ship time to move in and close the trap. It was almost completely dark when Curtis, in frustration, ordered his vessel brought to a stop.

"I wonder what he's up to," Nick remarked to Slater. "It's too late for them to board us now, but why else would he leave us sitting here dead in the water?"

"He's probably going to wait it out until morning. If there were only one ship, he might have had a chance of slipping away tonight, but not with two. There's no way he can get away from both of them, especially not when one is as quick as that brig," Slater told him. He knew that when the U.S. authorities boarded them at first light, the blacks being held down below would be freed. For the first time in ages, he began to believe that there might be some justice in the world.

They watched the approaching government ships in silence, then settled down in an out-of-the-way place on deck to wait for morning.

Captain Curtis paced his cabin in agitation. As soon as it was nightfall it would be time to begin. The moon would be late rising tonight, and so he calculated that he had until midnight to do what needed to be done. He'd sent for his first officer, Mr. Jones, and when the single knock at the door signaled his arrival, he curtly bid him enter.

"Yes, Captain, you wanted me?" the dark, rugged-looking first officer asked as he entered the room. He had been at sea for most of his forty years, and it showed in the way he carried himself and in his weatherbeaten features.

"I have a job for you. It needs to be done quickly and quietly."

The first officer frowned. He knew they were in trouble with the authorities, but he had no idea what was on his captain's mind. "Yes, sir. What is it you want me to do?"

As Curtis gave him his instructions, Jones grew more and more shocked. Though not a particularly moral man by any stretch of the imagination, he was horrified by his orders. "Sir . . . are you sure? I mean, there are over five hundred of them . . ."

"Are you questioning me, Mr. Jones?" Curtis bristled. His word was life and death on this ship, and he didn't like to be challenged in any way.

"No, Captain." The first officer went rigid at the reproach.

"Good," he responded with smooth sarcasm. "Then carry on. Execute in groups of fifty. You should be able to handle that many without major incident."

"Yes, sir."

"See to it at once."

"Aye, Captain."

Jones quit the cabin and made his way up on deck to recruit men to help him. He told them ahead of time what they had to do so there would be no hesitation once they were ready to start. One crewman balked momentarily, but was silenced when he saw the ominous glint in Jones's eyes. The sailors knew the fires of hell couldn't be any worse than a lashing with a cat-o'-nine-tails wielded by the first officer. Swallowing any fear of eternal damnation that might have haunted them over the deed they were about to do, the men prepared to carry out his orders.

Within minutes, the first group of fifty blacks had been roused from their squalid quarters. After checking to make sure their leg irons were intact, the crew prodded them topside with the promise of a few minutes of fresh air.

At the first officer's direction, only a single lamp stood burning near the helm. Otherwise the area was shrouded in blackness to ensure that their terrible deeds would go unwitnessed. They couldn't afford to be seen.

Unaware of the fate awaiting them, the chained captives — men, women, and children alike — filed eagerly up on deck. They were generally brought outside once each day, and they assumed they were being allowed out now to make up for the time they'd missed earlier. Many of them were growing weak and sick from the heat and stench below, and they were thankful for the reprieve. The blacks paid little attention to the crew as they were lined up along the rail. They didn't notice that the sailors were carrying guns this time. They were too busy enjoying the sense of freedom being on deck gave them, and the sweet, fresh smell of the night sea air.

"Tie an anchor weight to that big man's ankle chain down on the end," Jones ordered emotionlessly.

Jones' unusual command brought Nick and Slater to their feet as one of the sailors hurried to do his bidding. They watched worriedly as he attached the heavy weight to the cruel iron clasp that cut mercilessly into the raw flesh of the captive's leg. They hadn't been concerned until they'd heard his directive, and watching the scurrilous activities going on now, they suddenly had an ominous premonition about what was about to take place.

"What's going on, Jones?" they demanded, approaching him where he stood slightly apart from the others.

"Gentlemen, I suggest you do not concern yourselves with things that are not your affair," he told them coldly. Then ignoring them completely, he continued following through with his captain's deadly plan. "Now, men."

With silent deadliness, the sailors unexpectedly clubbed the first few men on the chain. As they dropped to the deck unconscious, they were thrown roughly overboard. The weight of their bodies, along with the continued violent prodding of the crew, dragged the others after them. High-pitched screams of terror erupted as the women and children fought to keep from being forced to jump to their deaths in the pitch black waters of the Gulf.

"My God!" Nick and Slater were stunned for an instant. Neither man could believe that the *Demon*'s captain would be so callous as to order the murder of hundreds of men, women, and children just to save his ship, but he had. They quickly regained their senses and lunged for the sailors in an attempt to stop the slaughter.

When the struggling blacks saw white men fighting white men, they knew a glimmer of hope until Captain Curtis' deep booming voice ended the fracas.

"Get those two out of here!" he commanded. It infuriated him that his two passengers were the instigators of the trouble. He had come up on deck to see how Jones was progressing and had found near bedlam instead.

The crewmen descended on Nick and Slater with a vengeance, pummeling them for their interference. Slater was clubbed viciously from behind as he battled with a sailor, and he fell unconscious to the deck. Three other sailors overwhelmed Nick and beat him soundly. Nick kept trying to get back up and keep fighting, but the crewmen were determined to keep him restrained. They twisted his arms behind his back, and holding him immobile, dragged him on his knees before the captain.

"You'll pay for interfering with the running of my ship, Mr. Kane," he snarled.

Overwhelmed by what he'd witnessed and realizing, to his horror, that there was more to come, Nick protested in a slurred voice through bleeding lips, "You can't just throw them overboard!"

Curtis turned on him with murder in his eye, "I can do whatever I please on this ship. I am her master."

"But it's murder!" he insisted, defiant even in the face of defeat.

"Murder, sir?" the captain approached him, his eyes narrowed evilly. "Who's to say? When the authorities board tomorrow, there will be no blacks in the hold . . . no evidence of any wrongdoing . . . and no witnesses."

Nick's stomach lurched sickeningly as he realized that what he was saying was true. Curtis couldn't be stopped. He was God on the boat. "You no good bastard . . ." he swore.

In an act that was pure pleasure for him, Curtis kneed Nick viciously in the chest. He watched with sadistic enjoyment as Nick doubled over and hung limply between his captors.

"I've killed men for less, Kane! Remember that!"

Nick heard his words as if from a great distance as the blackness of oblivion swelled and roiled around him.

"You want these two thrown overboard, too, Captain?" one of the sailors holding Nick asked.

"No. There would be too many questions if they disappeared. Take them below and put them in my 'special place.' Leave them there until after the other ships have gone tomorrow."

"Aye, aye, sir."

As Nick and Slater were carried off, the rest of the crewmen resumed their gruesome duty. The balance of the first fifty slaves were tossed over the side, their pitiful cries echoing eerily across the darkened sea. Within a matter of seconds they were dead, dragged beneath the surface by the weight of those who'd gone before them.

* * *

36

When he regained consciousness Nick thought he was in hell. He was surrounded by darkness and by the overpowering, oppressive stench of human filth. Excruciating pain seared through his side as he tried to move, and nausea welled up within him. In a desperate attempt to figure out what had happened and where he was, he levered himself up.

"Slater?" He was surprised when his own voice sounded like a hoarse croak. "Slater, where are you?"

There was no answer to his call, and he was forced to grope around for his friend. He found him lying close by and, for a moment, feared he was dead. Only when he rested a hand on his chest and felt its regular rise and fall, was he relieved Slater was only unconscious.

The agony in Nick's side was fierce, and he felt certain that a few of his ribs were broken. He sat back to catch his breath and to wait for the pain to let up.

When the pain finally lessened, Nick began a search to discover where they were and how they could get out. His efforts provided only scant knowledge. The room, if it could be called that, was boxlike, measuring only about four and a half feet high by six feet across. It was completely windowless and had only one way out. He tried to force the single door open with what little strength he had, but several futile attempts convinced him that it was securely barred from the outside.

Collapsing back against the rough wall near Slater, Nick drew a few strangled breaths as he agonized over the murders taking place somewhere above him. His own helplessness to prevent the killings enraged him, but he knew there was nothing more he could do right now. He vowed silently to himself that one day he would see that someone paid for the massacre.

A low groan came from Slater a few minutes later, and Nick felt a little better knowing his friend was going to be all right.

"What the . . ." Slater growled as he came awake to find himself engulfed in total darkness. For an instant he almost panicked, thinking himself back with Carlanta, but the sound of Nick's voice calmed his fears.

"Welcome back to the land of the living," Nick remarked dryly.

"I'm not so sure about that. What the hell happened?" His head was pounding so violently that he could barely think. He blinked into the darkness, trying to focus his eyes, but there was nothing to focus on.

"I think one of the sailors got you from behind."

"Oh," he grunted, then closed his eyes once more and lay unmoving, wishing the agony would go away. When it didn't, he gathered his strength and pushed himself up to a sitting position. "What about you?"

"I've got a couple of cracked ribs and a bad headache, but I'll live. It seems our illustrious captain has made us his captives," Nick explained.

Slater said nothing for a moment, waiting for the pain in his head to ease. "Where are we?" he asked finally.

"My guess is Curtis wanted us out of the way, so he had us thrown in some kind of secret compartment way belowdecks. I'm sure he wants to keep us safely stowed until the government ships are gone."

"Have you tried to find a way out?" Slater asked

38

with a great sense of urgency, still wanting to do something to try to stop the murders.

"There's a single door on the other side of me, but it's barred and locked from the outside. If you've got the strength, it might give if we both try at the same time."

"Let's do it," Slater said as he made his way slowly through the cramped, malodorous quarters to Nick.

Though Nick's chest felt like it was on fire and Slater's head was killing him, they gave no thought to their injuries. They only knew that they wouldn't be able to live with themselves unless they did everything in their power to save the slaves. Horrible images of men, women, and children being callously murdered stayed with them as they sought out the door and jammed their shoulders against the solid, portal over and over again.

Curtis had known what he was doing when he'd ordered the two men hidden in his "special place." The room was as close to soundproof as it could be, and the door had been specially reinforced to prevent a breakout. It didn't give an inch despite their frantic efforts.

Exhaustion claimed Nick and Slater, forcing them to realize that their attempts were useless. They fell back weakly against the wall to rest, cursing their entrapment.

"I hope to hell the government officials find something when they board," Nick swore angrily.

"Don't get your hopes up. Curtis and Jones aren't about to take any chances. They'll get rid of anything and everything that might even be remotely construed as evidence. The only thing they won't be able to get rid of is the smell, and that's not proof

39

enough," Slater told him.

"I've always known smugglers were ruthless, but I had no idea they were capable of doing something this vile."

"This ship means everything to Curtis and to its owners. They'll do whatever they have to to save it. They'll willingly sacrifice the blacks because they're the lesser of the two investments."

"All for money . . ." Nick was filled with revulsion. "I'm going to see that Curtis pays for this!" he vowed.

"He was only following orders," Slater pointed out. "The owners are the ones who told him to dump cargo if he was ever threatened with boarding. They're the ones to go after."

"With your contacts, we should be able to track them down pretty fast."

"It's not going to be as easy as you think," he cautioned. "A lot of these ships are held by middlemen who are paid to preserve the anonymity of the real owners."

"I don't care how long it takes or what we have to do. Somehow, someway, we're going to get them."

Being forced to admit defeat did not sit well with the silver-haired, authoritative Captain Meredith of the U.S. brig *Stormcrest,* but he met the gaze of the devious Captain Curtis squarely when he faced him the following morning. His men had searched the *Sea Demon* from stem to stern, but had found no solid evidence to prove that he'd been smuggling slaves. Meredith was now forced to set the slaver free, and it infuriated him.

"I'll not forget this incident, Captain," he said.

He knew full well what had happened through the night. Unable to act because of the darkness, he had agonized over the screams of the drowning victims. Now, to his great disappointment, there was not a grain of evidence against the captain. He couldn't prove a thing.

"Incident, Captain Meredith?" Curtis managed to sound puzzled by his insinuation.

"*Incident,* Curtis," Meredith insisted hotly. "You may have eluded us this time, but it will never happen again. From this moment on, I plan to make your life a living hell."

"Are you threatening me, sir?"

"I never make threats . . . only promises. God only knows how many perished at your hands last night, but I swear I'll see you in hell for what you've done."

"I have no idea what you're talking about," Curtis said sharply.

"Take a deep breath, Curtis. Smell the stink of death. How many of them had already died down in your hold before you decided to throw the rest overboard?"

"Perhaps it's time you took your leave of the *Sea Demon.*"

"Your ship is aptly named, Curtis." Then Meredith turned his back on him and without another word left the ship.

When the *Stormcrest* and the other U.S. ship had started to move off, First Officer Jones joined his captain in his quarters.

"You did it, sir. You outsmarted them!" Jones was pleased with their victory.

"I may have outfoxed the authorities, but I'll still have hell to pay when I inform Radcliffe of the

41

loss."

"You saved the *Demon,* sir."

"That I did," he replied slowly as he moved to the window to watch the two vessels moving off in the distance. "That'll be all, Jones."

"There is one other thing, Captain."

"Yes?" he asked impatiently.

"Our two passengers, sir. Shall I let them out now?"

Curtis scowled at the thought of the two interfering fools. "Yes, but I want you personally to keep an eye on them for the rest of the voyage. Don't leave them alone for a minute until it's time to put them ashore."

"Yes, sir. I'll take care of it."

Chapter Three

Nick and Slater parted company in New Orleans, and Nick headed upriver, eager to be home again. Riverwood had never looked so good to him as he rode up the main drive to the big house. The fields were green and the trees were bursting into bloom. He loved this land with his whole being. It seemed almost a living part of him, and he knew he never wanted to leave it.

It seemed an eternity since he'd ridden off to help Slater, and, in truth, Nick felt years older. Before this trip, his biggest concern had been working with his father to make Riverwood a success. Other than that, he'd gone his way, enjoying life as it came, giving little thought to deeper or more meaningful issues. His father thought him a playboy, and Nick knew he was right. Ever since he turned eighteen, he'd been considered one of the most eligible bachelors in the area, and he'd taken full advantage of the dubious honor.

The ordeal with Slater on the *Sea Demon* had changed him, though, and Nick wondered just how he was going to keep it from showing. If he suddenly turned into a political crusader on the slave smuggling issue he'd have a lot of explaining to do, and that was the one thing he couldn't afford to have happen. He couldn't reveal the outrageous incident on the *Sea Demon* to anyone for fear of the questions that would be asked about why he was there in the first place. He was sworn to preserve Slater's secret.

Nick glanced toward the house, silently girding himself for the confrontation to come. In the next few minutes he was going to come face to face with his very angry father, and he knew just what to expect in the way of reprimand. It would not be pretty, but he would not refute his father's accusations that he'd been out living wildly, drinking and gambling, when he should have been home taking care of business. As much as it hurt him, he would let his father go on thinking the worst, for it was easier to allow him believe what he wanted than to try to convince him otherwise without telling the whole truth.

"Mister Nick! You're home!" Ardus, a slave boy who thought the world of Nick, raced down the drive to meet him as he drew nearer.

"Hi, Ardus." Nick was equally fond of the boy, and, since he was in no particular hurry to travel the last hundred yards to the house, he slowed his horse to dismount so he could walk the rest of the way with the youth.

"Mr. Charles, he's been . . ." Ardus started to tell him how his father had been watching and waiting for him, but when he got a close look at his face, he exclaimed without thought, "Lordy, Mr. Nick! What happened to you?"

Nick had known there would be questions, and he gave the boy a wry grin. "I met a few men who

44

weren't too fond of me."

"Looks like they downright hated you."

"Yeah, but you should have seen them after the fight," he joked, wanting to make light of the situation.

"I'll bet you beat 'em all, Mr. Nick. I'll bet they're in a lot worse shape than you are," Ardus said, his eyes shining as he gazed up at the man he idolized.

"I hope so, Ardus. I truly hope so."

"You know, your daddy's been lookin' for you."

"I'll just bet he has," Nick drawled, knowing exactly what was going to happen when he showed up looking like this after such a long and unexplained absence.

"Where you been?" Ardus asked boldly in the innocent way of children.

"Downriver."

It was a vague answer, but the boy took it to mean he'd been in New Orleans and asked nothing more. When they reached the front steps, Nick handed him the reins and tossed him a coin.

"Thanks, Mr. Nick!"

Nick affectionately tousled Ardus's hair as he strode past him and climbed the steps to the gallery. Weddington had seen him coming and was already there, opening the door for him.

"Hello, Weddington," Nick said as he entered the wide, cool foyer with its curving staircase, polished hardwood floor, and lofty ceiling.

"Mr. Nick, it's good to see you!" he greeted him happily, hoping things would be better now that he was back. The old master just hadn't been the same while Nick was away.

"It's good to be back," he declared with heartfelt emotion. He loved his home, the grace and peace of it, and he had honestly missed his father. "Is my father here or is he still out riding the fields?"

"He didn't ride today, sir," Weddington offered in such a way as to hint at what had been happening lately.

"He didn't?" Nick was astounded. His father was a man of rigid routine. For as long as Nick could remember he'd ridden the fields with the overseer every weekday from mid-morning until late afternoon.

"No, sir. In fact, while you've been away, there have been quite a few days when he didn't go out."

"Is something wrong?" He frowned at the thought as he searched the butler's expression for some clue to what was going on.

"I wouldn't know, sir, but he's in the study right now," he replied, keeping his features carefully composed so none of his very real worry was revealed.

Surprised and disturbed by the news, Nick moved quickly down the hall to the study. He knocked sharply once, then opened the door. Steeling himself to play the role of prodigal son, he entered his father's haven to find him sitting at his desk.

Charles's heart had leapt with joy when he'd heard Nick enter the house. He had not rushed forth to greet him, though, forcing himself to stay where he was and wait for his errant son to come to him. He made sure that the happiness and relief he was feeling did not reflect in his expression, and as he glanced up at his tall, handsome son, he kept his face set in a stern mask of disapproval.

"So, you finally remembered where you live . . ." he began, but upon seeing Nick's battered features, he exclaimed, "What the hell did you get yourself into this time?!"

Nick rubbed his bruised chin. "I had an encounter with several gentlemen who, for some reason, didn't take a liking to me."

Though deep inside Charles was thankful that he hadn't been more seriously injured, he didn't allow that emotion to show either. Instead, realizing that Nick might have been killed for whatever his foolishness had been, his resolve to force him to settle down only hardened. "I suppose you're rather proud of yourself?"

Nick's movements were deceptively casual as he dropped into a chair in front of the desk. "No, actually . . . I'm not, but I fully intend to redeem myself, someday," he replied, pushing away thoughts of the losing battle on the *Sea Demon*.

"Someday . . . someday . . ." Charles growled in agitation. It seemed to him that Nick's easygoing actions and glib excuses proved he had no intention of ever getting serious about anything. "Your *someday* may have just arrived, Dominic."

At the use of his given name Nick grew instantly attentive, for it always meant his father was furious with him. He suddenly feared that something very bad had happened while he was gone. "What is it? Was there trouble while I was away?"

"Actually, it was really very quiet around here in your absence." Charles' anger turned his tone to ice. "I think the 'trouble,' as you put it, is just about to begin."

"I don't understand."

"I didn't think you did, son, and that's why I've taken the steps I have."

"Steps? What steps?" Nick was growing increasingly wary. He'd thought his father would rail at him for a while like he usually did, not be so cold.

It put him off-balance. He didn't know what to expect next.

Charles Kane extracted a copy of his last will and testament from his top desk drawer and slid it across the desk toward his son. Nick saw the heading and glanced up at his father, his expression puzzled. Charles met his regard but said nothing. Instead, he waited patiently for him to pick it up and read it.

As Nick read the testament a sense of utter disbelief gripped him. For the first time in his life he knew what it meant to be completely dumbfounded. He went pale, his hands shook slightly, and no coherent thought would form. Only the word *marriage* thundered through his mind, drowning out everything else. He looked up at his father, bewildered.

"Is this some kind of joke? If so, it's not very amusing," was all he could manage.

"It wasn't meant to be amusing, Dominic," his father said sternly.

"You're trying to force me to get married. Why?"

"I need to know that I can trust you."

Nick bristled at that remark. "When have I ever given you reason to doubt me?"

His father snorted in derision. "This is not the first time you've left without a word on one of these little escapades of yours, leaving me to wonder where you were going and when, if ever, you'd be back. This has to stop, and it's got to stop now."

Nick knew a near violent urge to betray Slater and tell his father everything, but he'd given his friend his word. He had to remain silent. "Father, I promise you. I will never leave like that again."

Charles shook his head. "I don't have the time to

waste to see if you can live up to that promise. I want you to marry now and accept your responsibilities here at Riverwood."

"I have accepted my responsibilities. You know how much I love Riverwood."

"Well, if you're serious, if you really do love Riverwood as you say, then you'd better find yourself a suitable bride by September."

Nick was confused and more than a little upset by his urgency. "But why?! Why force me to marry when I don't want to? Why the sudden rush to marry by September?"

"Because, Nick," Charles said in a low, very somber voice as his dark, sad eyes sought his son's. "Dr. Williams says I may only have that long to live."

Nick would never forget that moment for the rest of his life. He had come to his feet, but he had no remembrance of doing it. He found himself standing there, his whole body tense, a stricken look upon his face, staring at his father across the wide desktop.

"What?" he demanded, not believing what he'd just heard.

"I said, I only have a few months left to live, and I want to make sure that Riverwood will continue being run as it has been run in the past."

"Wait . . ." Nick's thoughts were still stumbling over each other as he tried to grasp what he was being told. "What do you mean, you only have a few months to live?"

"Dr. Williams, along with a battery of other specialists, have checked me over and . . ."

"Why didn't you tell me about this before?"

"Because at first I thought it would pass. Things got worse, though, and . . ."

"What got worse?"

"My heart," he answered tightly, keeping a firm hold on his emotions, not wanting to show any weakness before his son. He had always been a pillar of strength, and he would not forfeit that dignity now. He would not give in to the feelings that threatened to tear him apart. He would wait until he was alone and he was sure he wouldn't be interrupted before he gave in to the overwhelming sadness. "Anyway, Michael tells me that I have less than a year."

"I don't believe this . . ." Nick stated slowly, shaking his head in confusion.

"Believe it, and believe, too, that I've made certain this will is legal and binding. I will see you properly married by the fifteenth of September or Riverwood will go to the church—lock, stock, and barrel."

"I see . . ." Nick stood there staring at his father, his misery profound. He didn't understand how this could be happening. A few minutes ago all he'd been worried about was facing his wrath, and now here he was, facing a tragedy of immense proportions. His father was dying. . .

Tension filled the room as they regarded each other without speaking. Nick longed to rush to his father, to throw his arms around him and hug him tightly. He wanted to scream out at how unfair this was. He wanted to cry his sorrow in the comforting safety of his father's arms as he had when his mother had died. But Nick knew he could do none of those things. He was a man now. He was supposed to be strong. He was supposed to be coolly logical and controlled. He wondered, as he faced his father, why he didn't feel any of those things.

"You understand the importance of what I've just told you?" Charles asked as he held himself stiffly erect. With an immense effort of will he kept his features devoid of any emotion. He wanted to do nothing more than take his son in his arms and clasp him to his breast. He wanted to hold him close and tell him how much he loved him. He wanted to explain to him that the marriage ploy was for his own good and that he was sure he would be happy once he'd found the right woman to settle down with. He did none of these things, though. Instead, he held on to what little manly pride he had left. He didn't want anyone else to know of the fears that woke him from a sound sleep in the middle of the night and left him shaking with terror. He had been strong all of his life and he would continue to be strong.

"It would seem that unless I find the woman of my dreams within a mere one hundred eighty two days and convince her to marry me, I'll be forced to consider another means of making my livelihood."

"You're a rich, good-looking young man. You shouldn't have any trouble finding a woman."

"A woman, sure. *The* woman I'm not so sure. Tell me, Father, would you have married just any woman?"

"No. Your mother was special."

"And I'll be satisfied with no less."

"Then I suggest you get busy and start looking, son. Since you took so long getting back here from wherever you were, you've already forfeited almost two weeks of your time."

Again their eyes met, and it seemed that the distance between them had grown.

Forcing down the words he wanted to say, Nick

51

nodded miserably. He turned and left the room, feeling more devastated than he had at any time since his mother's death all those years ago. A sense of profound despair filled him as he again found himself facing a battle that he knew couldn't be won. His father was dying. There would be no preventing it.

Charles watched Nick go and said nothing. Inwardly, he was glad that he'd had the ultimatum to throw at him today, for it was the only thing that had kept him from losing control of his emotions. By concentrating on the will, he'd avoided facing the real issue. When Nick had left the study and the door was safely closed behind him, Charles's rigid rein on his feelings faltered. His stern expression crumpled and his vision blurred as burning tears filled his eyes.

Of all the things he'd done in his life, fathering Nick was by far Charles's proudest accomplishment. It hurt him to have to force his son to act against his will, but he prayed that one day he would understand what had motivated him. True happiness comes only from loving unconditionally and being loved that way in return. Any other life was just an existence. He needed to know that Nick would be happy before it was his time. Leaning forward, Charles braced his elbows on the desktop and buried his face in his hands. Only then did he let the scalding tears fall.

Nick strode from the study, past the waiting, expectant butler and out the front door. His expression was bleak, his mouth tight, his eyes dark with inner pain.

"Mr. Nick?" Weddington called as he hurried after him, wanting to know what had happened to cause such a terrible look on his face.

"I'll speak with you later," came his gruff reply, and then he was gone down the gallery steps and out of sight.

The butler glanced toward the study door and then back in the direction Nick had disappeared. Never in all the years he'd worked for the Kanes had he ever seen the young master so upset. He wondered what awful thing had happened to disturb him so greatly, but knew he'd just have to wait to find out.

Nick didn't have to think about where he was going, he just started walking. The trek to the cemetery was a long one, but he didn't care. He needed the time alone, the time to sort things out.

His stride was long, purposeful, and powerful as he covered the distance to the hilltop that overlooked the Mississippi a mile from the main house. It was here, safe from the spring floods, that his mother was buried. He stopped before the crypt to read the inscription. Andrea Dupont Kane . . . born 1804, died 1834.

Usually when he came to visit the gravesite, Nick was in a mellow mood. He generally just wanted to remember his mother, to recall how gentle and kind she'd been. Today, however, he was filled with anger and deeply troubled.

Fury and desolation raged within Nick. His father was not the kind of man who exaggerated anything, so when he said there was nothing that could be done about his condition, Nick knew he had to believe him. Believing what he said and accepting what he said were two very different things, though, and Nick found himself trying to deny the reality of it, to hide emotionally from the bitter truth.

"This can't be happening . . ." he said out loud. "This just can't be happening . . . not again!"

Memories of the time when he'd lost his mother surged to the surface. Suddenly he was a child again, heartbroken and afraid, lost without the tender loving care of the mother he'd so adored. Once more he felt the pain, the agony, the loneliness, and he couldn't fight back the tears that filled his eyes.

"Mother, this isn't fair. I lost you and now I'm going to lose Father, too . . ." he choked, no longer trying to hide the desolation. "I won't let it happen! I won't!"

Even as Nick said the words, though, he was thinking back over the encounter and realizing for the first time just how tired his father had looked, how very old. Behind his commanding presence had been a very sick man. He was losing him already, and there would be no stopping it.

Nick turned away from the crypt to gaze out across the wide river. The resounding question *why* kept echoing through his thoughts, but as with his mother's death, he knew there were no answers to life's final riddle. There was only the acceptance of that which one could not change.

Nick longed to go to his father, to tell him he loved him, and to spend every last waking minute with him until the end, but he knew that wasn't what his father wanted. If his father had felt strongly enough about the situation to put that clause in his will, then Nick knew he had to abide by it if he wanted to make his last days happy. One way or the other, sometime during the next five and a half months he was going to have to find himself a suitable bride. It wasn't going to be easy, but Nick knew he would do it. He loved his father so much that he would do whatever was necessary to assure him that all he'd so carefully built and loved so dearly would remain intact.

Chapter Four

London, England
Some weeks later
In the offices of Radcliffe + Associates

Luther Radcliffe's blue-eyed regard was impassive as he faced the fair-haired young man standing in panicked outrage before him in his London office.

"You can't be serious!" Philip St. James cried aghast as he searched Luther's face for some sign that it was all a terrible joke. But there was no trace of humor in the handsome, dark-haired businessman's expression.

"I'm afraid it's true," Luther said levelly.

"Everything's lost? It's all gone?" he repeated in stunned disbelief.

"Everything. I'm sorry."

"But you promised me that the money was safely invested! You said it was a sure thing! You said we couldn't lose!"

Luther shrugged his broad shoulders. "It was a rare misfortune, but these things do happen."

"But this is impossible . . ." Philip groaned, practically falling into a straight-backed chair. "Every cent of Jordan's and my inheritance was tied up with you. You said . . ."

"I know what I said, Philip, and I meant it. But sometimes circumstances arise that are beyond my control."

"There's nothing that can be done?"

"Nothing."

"God!" In despair, Philip leaned forward and braced his elbows on his knees to rest his head in his hands. "What am I going to do? How are we going to live? What will I tell my sister?"

"You'll have to tell her the truth, I'm afraid."

"I can't do that! She trusted my judgment in this, and now I've lost everything . . ." Philip was frantic.

Though he kept his emotions well disguised, Luther was almost crowing with delight at the youth's predicament. He'd been waiting for this moment for almost a year! At last, he was going to get what he wanted. . .

Luther's initial reaction to the *Sea Demon*'s lost cargo had been fury, but he'd quickly changed his mind when he realized how he could turn the situation to his advantage. He'd been lusting after Philip's sister, Jordan, ever since he'd first set eyes upon her. She had been only seventeen when their parents had died, and she and Philip had come to him for help in investing their inheritance. Jordan had been entrancing then, a nubile young girl in the bud of womanhood, but now, a year later, he found her absolutely mesmerizing. Her eyes were of the deepest green, her pale blond hair was like spun moonlight, and Luther longed to run his hands through it. Her slender yet very womanly curves had haunted his dreams many a night, and his desire for her had pyramided ever since their initial encounter. He wanted her as he'd never wanted another, and soon he was going to have her!

That Jordan was always coolly distant to him whenever they were together suddenly no longer rankled Luther. Now that she was in terrible financial straits, he was confident that she would see reason. Soon, he thought . . . soon she would be in his power.

Philip was despondent. Their situation was dire. "You're talking about our future. All of our hopes and dreams are in ruins . . . We're destitute . . . We have nothing left . . . nothing . . ."

Seeing how frantic he was, Luther knew it was time to make his suggestion. "There is one idea you might want to consider," he began, his hard blue eyes trained on Philip's face as he prepared to read his reaction to the proposition he was about to offer. "An alternative that just might solve your problem."

The younger man brightened immediately with the advent of some hope. "I'll consider anything at this point. What do you have in mind?"

"Your sister . . ."

"Jordan? What about her?" He was honestly puzzled by Luther's bringing her into the conversation.

As unworldly as the boy was, Luther knew there was no point in being subtle about his goal to have her in his bed. "I will see your every financial need met if she will agree to become my mistress."

Philip was speechless. He stared at Luther. Jordan, Luther's mistress? His light o' love? His whore? Philip stiffened, his pride surging forth. NEVER! He would starve to death before he'd allow his sister to be degraded that way.

With as much dignity as he could muster, he answered, "Never."

"I'm afraid you may not have much to say about it."

There was a certain steel in his voice that Philip had never heard before, and suddenly he saw Luther in a new light. Jordan had cautioned him from the beginning that she mistrusted this man, but he'd ignored her. He'd foolishly forged ahead, and during the past year he'd given this man more and more of their money until everything they had was tied up with his firm.

"What do you mean?" Philip looked Luther straight in the eye and was shocked by the coldness he saw there.

"How do you feel about going to prison?" Luther unlocked the center drawer of his desk and drew out a folder. He sorted through the papers and then pulled out two documents he'd been looking for—one, the ownership paper of the *Sea Demon,* the other, the contract for the slaves.

He had always known it would pay off to have the ownership papers to the *Sea Demon* forged to list Philip and Jordan St. James instead of himself as the owners. This way, were the boat to be caught in the act of slaving, Philip and Jordan would have been the ones to answer to the law. Luther prided himself on never taking unnecessary risks. It pleased him enormously that he could now make even better use of this little bit of intrigue.

"What are you talking about?" Philip challenged.

"I think this will clear everything up for you." He handed him first the document on the *Sea Demon,* then the contract. "Once you peruse those, I believe you'll understand the certain . . . um . . . delicacy of your position."

"You invested our money in slave smuggling?"

59

Philip was shocked. Radcliffe and Associates had come recommended to him as a highly reputable firm. He'd trusted Luther, and now . . .

"Yes, and should the authorities discover that you're the owner of such a vessel . . . Well, needless to say, slave smuggling has been illegal for years. While it is generally a highly profitable venture, there are also major risks involved. Risks like imprisonment for shipowners, and very high fines . . ."

"Dear God . . ."

"I'm afraid God has little to do with this. This is business, Philip, strictly business," Luther said with satisfaction as he closed his trap. He took the papers from Philip and carefully returned them to the folder. "Do you find my offer more acceptable now?"

"I don't know . . . I can't think . . . I have to talk to Jordan . . ."

"Of course. Well, I tell you what. Why don't you do just that? Speak with your beautiful sister about my offer and see what she has to say."

"Yes . . . yes, I will . . ." Philip turned and headed blindly toward the office door.

"Philip?" Luther said his name in such a way that he stopped and looked back. He waited until he was sure he had his full attention before he continued, "I hate to think that I might have to force this issue. It would be much nicer if things were handled in a more amiable way."

He nodded in terrible understanding and started out again.

"Let me hear from you soon. I'll be waiting for your decision."

At the sound of his voice, Philip paused as icicles

of fear raced up and down his spine. Then, straightening his shoulders, he rushed from the room. Luther was smiling triumphantly as he watched him go. He rubbed his hands together as he began to imagine having Jordan St. James all to himself. It was a very pleasant daydream.

Philip strode aimlessly along the streets of London, reviewing his situation over and over again as he walked. He was desperate to find a way out, but he feared they were trapped. Their money was gone, and they were helpless before the power Luther had over them.

Despite the feeling of hopelessness that enveloped Philip, a righteous anger sparked and grew deep within him. Luther's "suggestion" that Jordan become his mistress was nothing more than extortion. There was no way he would give into it. He would go to jail before he would subject his lovely sister to such degradation. She was a St. James, a member of a fine, old family, not some common street slut.

Philip realized now just how right Jordan had always been about Radcliffe. It wasn't the first time her instinctive reaction to someone had been proved correct. He felt shamed that he hadn't had the good sense to listen to her. They'd had several meetings with Luther and some of his associates at the office, and they'd also dined with him privately on occasion. After each of these encounters, Jordan had expressed her disquiet about the man, but he'd been so impressed with him that he'd discounted her opinion. Now he wished he hadn't. Now he knew why she'd disliked him so. As a woman, she'd been able to sense the innate ugliness in him.

Regret filled Philip. He hated the fact that he had to expose Jordan to the depths of Luther's sordid nature, but there was no way he could avoid telling her the complete truth. As much as he wanted to protect her, he had to be forthright with her. They had to decide together what they were going to do next now that their future had been so undeniably changed.

Philip grew determined. Looking up, he was startled to find that he was standing before their townhouse, his troubled walk through the city having brought him home.

Home . . . A moment of sadness overwhelmed him as he thought about how greatly their lives had changed since their parents' deaths the year before. He and Jordan had been raised in a home overflowing with love. Then, suddenly, that life was gone, destroyed by a freak carriage accident that had robbed them of their cherished mother and father. He'd been a shy youth, filled with dreams of books and studies, when he'd suddenly been thrust into the role of protector and provider for his sister. As he mounted the steps to enter the house, he knew that thus far he'd failed miserably, but he vowed to try to figure a way out of it.

Jordan had been in the parlor reading when she heard her brother come in the front door. She adored Philip and hurried forth to meet him, eager to find out how his meeting with the despicable Luther Radcliffe had gone.

"Philip! How did it go?" Jordan got no further and her voice trailed off as she caught sight of his face. There had only been one other time in their lives when she'd seen him look this grim, and that had been when their parents had died. She knew something had to be seriously wrong. "What happened?"

Philip searched to find the right words so he could gently relate the horrible truth, but there was no easy way. He was going to have to be frank, no matter how difficult. There could be no holding back. Jordan was too perceptive for him to even try. "I think we'd better sit down in the parlor while we talk."

"Why?" She nervously gripped his arm as he led her back into the pleasant, airy sitting room.

Philip sat down on the sofa, and she sat next to him. Jordan could feel the tension emanating from him.

"Tell me what happened just now, Philip. What was so important that Radcliffe had to summon you to his office?" Her tone was unyielding, letting him know that she wanted, demanded, the whole story.

"There's some bad news, Jordan," he began, and once he'd started to explain the words just tumbled forth. He quickly told her that their investment had been lost, and that to all intents and purposes, they were penniless.

"But how? I thought . . ."

"I don't know how. It's just gone, that's all." His shoulders slumped in defeat. "It doesn't really matter any more, anyway."

"You can't mean that?! Of course it matters!" Jordan's temper flared. "Surely there must be some mistake. Radcliffe couldn't have lost *all* of our funds!"

"Well, he did, and there's more . . . there's something even worse I have to tell you," he said miserably.

63

"Worse? How can anything be worse than the loss of all our money? You did argue with him, didn't you? He promised us that our investment would be safe with him!"

"I know . . . I know." Philip swallowed nervously, not sure how to broach the subject with any delicacy. "I tried to argue with him, Jordan, but then he showed me the papers . . ."

Seeing his tormented expression, she couldn't imagine what he was talking about. "What papers?"

"Our money was tied up in a slave smuggling operation. Our names are on all the documents."

Jordan whispered, shocked, "But that's against the law . . ."

"Yes."

"Well, we certainly didn't know about it. How can we be guilty of something we didn't know about?"

"It's all legal . . . signed, sealed, and delivered, and Luther's threatened to expose us to the authorities unless . . ."

"Unless what? You're not making any sense. Luther lost all our money in an illegal venture, and now you're telling me that he's going to use that against us when he's the one who set the whole thing up in the first place? Why? What in world would he have to gain? He's already taken our inheritance . . . We've nothing left . . ."

"There's something else he's after, Jordan," her brother told her solemnly.

"What?" Their personal wealth was so limited, their prized possessions so few, that she couldn't imagine what the rich businessman wanted.

"He wants you?"

"*Me?!*"

"I was beside myself when I found out the money was gone. I couldn't believe everything was lost. I didn't know how we were going to live. That's when Luther made his 'suggestion.' He offered to take care of our every financial need—if you'd agree to become his mistress."

Jordan went deathly still. She'd always known there was something disgusting about Luther Radcliffe, and now she knew what it was. The man was an amoral opportunist.

"What did you tell him?" she asked in a hoarse, frightened voice.

Philip was offended that she'd even ask. "I told him no, of course! I would never let anyone take advantage of you that way."

Relief swept through her, but fear soon followed as he continued.

"That's when he threated to turn those papers over to the authorities . . ."

"I have to talk to him," she insisted. Innocent that she was, she thought that once she told him she didn't love him, then he wouldn't want her as his mistress any longer.

"No! I don't want you to go anywhere near that man," Philip said sternly as he grabbed her wrist to stop her from doing anything foolish.

"If he cares for me as you say he does, then he might listen to me. Perhaps if I just go see him . . ."

"Jordan!" her brother cut her off sharply. "I never said he *cared* for you, damn it! I said he wants you as his mistress! If he cared for you at all he wouldn't want to degrade you this way! You stay as far away from him as you can. He's dangerous."

Philip had never spoken to her so forcefully before, and she stared at him in complete surprise.

"Look," he continued, taking her by the shoulders, his eyes boring into hers, "we'll figure a way out of this, just like we always have ever since we were little. It'll just take some time to think it through, that's all."

Jordan wanted to ask him just how much time he thought Luther would give them, but seeing the worry in his expression she quietly acquiesced. "I'm sure you're right."

"Jordan?" Philip said her name earnestly. "I swear to you that I'll willingly go to prison before I'll let anything happen to you."

Her heart swelled with love for him. Philip was so dear to her, so very special in her life. She wondered how she would ever have survived this last year without his constant support and love. She knew in that moment that as long as they had each other, they'd be fine. They would make it.

"Let's just hope it doesn't come to that. I'm sure there's something we can do. We just have to think of what it is." She patted his hand reassuringly.

Philip gave her a crooked smile. "And we will. I know it."

Later that afternoon Jordan pleaded the need for a little rest. She went to her room, but she had absolutely no intention of lying down. Sleep was the last thing on her mind. She had to sort through this whole mess and try to come up with some kind of solution.

"Luther's mistress," Jordan said it out loud to herself, slowly, incredulously, and a shiver of revulsion shook her.

There weren't many fates she considered worse than death, but being Radcliffe's mistress was one of them. Despite the fact that he was a handsome, wealthy man, there was something about him that made her flesh crawl. Still, she knew the only way she would be able to solve this was by facing him down herself.

Jordan knew Philip didn't want her to go anywhere near Luther, and she could understand why. But what they wanted really didn't matter much right now. She was intimately involved in this situation, and she had to do something to help.

Jordan made her decision. She would wait until evening, then tell her brother that she was retiring early. Once he believed her to be in bed asleep, she would sneak out of the house and go see Luther at his home. She figured it would be better to talk with him there, in more private surroundings, than in the middle of his offices where others might overhear them.

Feeling quite good about her plan of action, she finally did stretch out on her bed, but sleep would not come. Instead, her thoughts were flying as she tried to anticipate the events of the evening ahead.

Chapter Five

Jordan bade Philip good night shortly after they finished eating dinner. Retreating to her room, she waited quite a while before she began to dress for her secret outing. She took great care in the selection of the gown she would wear, finally deciding on her dark green walking suit. It bespoke modesty, and that was the exact impression she wanted to give. She didn't want Luther to think she was there because she was accepting his proposition. This was to be a business call, nothing more.

Keeping that idea in mind, Jordan braided her nearly waist-length, pale hair and twisted it into a tight knot at the nape of her neck. She thought the style very severe and hoped it made her look matronly. Little did she know that the actual affect was very much to the contrary. The sleek chignon served to accentuate her perfect bone structure and highlight her flawless complexion. She gave the appearance of being a sophisticated woman of the world, one well aware of the power she could wield over men.

Jordan quietly escaped her room and made her way downstairs. After wrapping her dark cloak about her to ward off the evening chill, she slipped away from the house. She hired a hansom cab at the first opportunity, and after giving him directions to Luther's residence near Belgrave Square, she settled back to nervously wait out the ride through the dark city streets.

They reached their destination far too quickly to suit Jordan. As Luther's imposing mansion came into view, she suddenly found herself wishing that the driver would keep going and never stop. Still, she realized that no matter how she felt about the man, she had to make this attempt to speak with him. Everything depended on it.

When the cab drew to a stop, Jordan descended and found herself staring up at the house. The three story structure was big and intimidating, and bespoke of wealth and power. Though lights blazed brightly in the mullioned windows, she felt no warmth for or attraction to the building. To Jordan, it appeared as cold and as distasteful as its owner.

Worry about the uncertainty of the welcome she would receive assailed Jordan. She wondered if Luther would even take the time to listen to what she had to say. Were he to hear her out, she knew it would be a simple matter for him to call the authorities on the spot and have her arrested here, tonight. The thought filled her with trepidation, and she found her hands were trembling as she paid the driver.

"You all right, miss?" the cab driver asked, noticing how nervous she seemed.

"Yes, yes, I'm fine. Thank you," Jordan answered making a concerted effort to sound confident.

Money in hand, he gave a shrug of indifference, climbed back onto his seat, and drove off. Standing all alone on the walk with the expensive house looming over her, Jordan was tempted for a moment to turn and flee this madness. How could she believe Luther would listen to her? She knew what kind of man he was . . .

Had she not been stranded, her instant panic would have ruled. As it was, she took one last look around the dark, deserted neighborhood and then forced herself to grow calm.

Jordan had never considered herself a particularly adventurous soul, but the memory of everything Philip had told her gave her the nerve to go on. She had to do something. Drawing on an inner strength she'd never known she possessed, Jordan approached Luther's front door and bravely lifted the brass lion's head knocker and let it fall. It made a heavy, hollow, threatening sound in the night.

Luther laughed heartily at some witty remark one of his guests made as he took a deep, satisfying drink of the fine wine he'd chosen to accompany their meal. He'd been so excited about the way things had turned out with Philip St. James that afternoon that he'd been in the mood to celebrate. He'd invited several of his closer acquaintances to dine with him—Marcus Porter, one of his wealthiest investors; his beautiful, yet promiscuous wife, Helen; and James Tilly, a very influential banker in town. They'd just shared a marvelous gourmet meal.

"Luther, it's always a pleasure to dine here," Marcus, a heavyset, balding man in his late fifties, complimented as he saluted him with his crystal wine glass. "You always serve only the finest liquors.

Your chef is beyond compare, and your home is simply magnificent."

"Thank you, Marcus," Luther was pleased with the praise. Egotist that he was, it reaffirmed his already well-entrenched feelings of superiority. He'd always made it a point to surround himself with beauty and luxury. He bought only the best of everything, for he believed he deserved only the best of everything. He was, after all, Luther Radcliffe.

"Luther, darling, when are we going to the opera again? I've missed our little excursions," thirty-year-old, voluptuous, red-haired Helen pouted as she leaned suggestively toward him. The dress Helen was wearing was very low-cut, and her movement deliberately exposed nearly all of her considerable charms to Luther's less than avid gaze.

Marcus was many years his wife's senior and had lost interest in the physical side of their marriage long ago. Sensuous woman that she was, Helen had been left to amuse herself with various diversions, all with her husband's full consent, of course. Luther had been one of those diversions, but she hadn't seen him in nearly a month. She missed their fiery encounters and the expensive trinkets he'd always bestowed on her afterward.

"I've been pretty tied up with business lately," Luther casually put her off, "but perhaps we can arrange something soon."

He'd enjoyed Helen's company, but the woman was so insatiable in bed that he'd found her a trifle boring after a time. And, while he did like her as a person, for she was as caustically witty and as amoral as he was, he had little interest in ever being with her again in that way. There was only one woman on his mind right now. He had no need for

Helen when Jordan would soon be willingly satisfying his every desire.

"That would be lovely . . . we do have such a nice time together." She retreated gracefully, for she knew Luther was not the kind of man who could be pushed. Knowing him as well as she did, she realized that he had to be interested in someone else. The cat in her suddenly wondered who the other woman was.

"So tell me, Luther," James Tilly, a tall, middle-aged man with dark hair and a flowing mustache, spoke up, reducing the tension of the moment, "what do you have planned for your next big venture?" Tilly's bank had backed Radcliffe and Associates numerous times throughout the years, and each investment had yielded a fabulous return.

"Well, I tell you, James . . ." He just started to expound on his next legitimate deal when his butler, Woods, appeared at the dining room doors.

"Sir?"

"Yes, Woods, what is it?" He was slightly annoyed by the interruption.

"There is someone here to see you, sir," the tall, distinguished, white-haired servant informed him.

"I'm entertaining, Woods. Tell whoever it is to see me at the office tomorrow," Luther said dismissively.

"I already told her that, Mr. Radcliffe, but she insisted that you would want to see her now."

"She?" He was instantly alert, his blood suddenly racing through his veins. Was it Jordan? Had she come to him already?

"Yes, sir. She says it's important . . . something about a business offer you made to her brother?"

"Yes . . . yes, of course." Luther tried to keep the

72

eagerness out of his voice, but he was already pushing away from the table in his haste to rush from the room. "Show her into my study and make her comfortable. Tell her that I'll be joining her shortly after I say good night to my other guests."

Helen, Marcus, and James all exchanged surprised looks at his statement. They had expected this to be a late night. Obviously, whoever had shown up was very important to Luther, for it was unheard of for him to behave so badly in a social situation. He was generally the picture of decorum. Helen, in particular, was curious to discover who was there. To her annoyance, though, she was doomed not to find out.

Luther stalled in the dining room just long enough for the butler to usher his visitor from the hall. Only when he was certain she was out of sight did he make his excuses to his dining companions.

"If you will pardon the haste with which I bring this delightful evening to a close," he said, standing and heading toward the doorway, giving them no real choice in the matter.

"Of course," James and Marcus answered agreeably.

Successful dealings with Radcliffe and Associates were important to both their livelihoods. They didn't dare risk upsetting things. Helen, however, had no such compulsion. Her curiosity was driving her wild. When her husband and the banker preceded her from the room, she hung back a bit and then touched Luther intimately on the arm to get his full attention.

"Who is she, darling? Someone I know?" she asked.

"Hardly, Helen."

73

"Oh?" She arched a finely plucked brow at him. "She doesn't move in our circles, hmmm?"

"This is strictly a business negotiation," he provided coldly, trying to discourage her from any more speculation. He knew how vicious her tongue could be.

"So she's charging you, is she?" Helen gave a throaty gurgle of a laugh.

"Good night, Helen," Luther's tone was curt.

"Good night, Luther darling," she tossed casually over her shoulder as she finally followed Marcus from the room.

Luther was pleased to see that Woods had closed the study door behind Jordan. He didn't want anyone else knowing his private affairs. After seeing everyone out, he shut the front door and paused just long enough to straighten his tie and his cuffs. He was surprised when he turned to find Woods standing there waiting for further directions.

"You and the rest of the servants may take your leave now, Woods."

"Sir?" The butler's eyes rounded in amazement at such an unorthodox order.

"You may go, all of you. Take the night off. I won't be needing any of you again until sometime tomorrow morning. The later the better." Luther was firm, leaving no doubt about his wish to be completely alone in the house with Jordan.

"Yes, Mr. Radcliffe." Woods absented himself quickly from the hall and hurried to tell the other servants the good news.

Luther stood there just a moment longer preparing himself for the encounter to come. Jordan . . . ah, Jordan . . . He'd anticipated this for so long, dreamed of this for so many nights, that he could hardly wait to throw wide the study door and sweep her into his arms.

Trouble was, Luther knew he had to stay in complete command of his passions. He couldn't let Jordan know how badly he desired her. He wanted to be in control of her, not the other way around. As he strode forth and opened the door, his smile was cool, his manner that of a man totally at ease with himself and his surroundings.

At the butler's direction, Jordan had taken a seat on the plush sofa in Luther's study. She was nervous, but managing to stay outwardly calm. This wasn't going to be easy, for she knew Luther was not the kind of man who took no for an answer. Her hands were clasped tightly in her lap as she gathered strength for the confrontation to come. The sound of the door opening brought Jordan to her feet, and she turned to confront the man who controlled her destiny.

Jordan appeared a regal, elegant woman of the world, and Luther's eyes were riveted upon her. She was gorgeous. She was everything he'd ever wanted, and now he was going to have her. His chest swelled and heat rushed to his loins. *Soon . . . very soon . .*

"Good evening, Jordan." Luther's deep voice held only a hint of the triumph he was feeling.

"Hello, Mr. Radcliffe," she answered coolly, determined to keep this on a business level only.

"Mr. Radcliffe? I thought we'd gone past that in our relationship, Jordan," he said smoothly. "Please, call me Luther."

"All right . . . Luther." It was difficult for her to get the words out, for he closed the door firmly behind him at just that moment. Something about the sound of the latch clicking shut made her nervous, but she fought it down. She told herself firmly that there was nothing to be afraid of.

"That's much better," he told her turning back to her with a warm, disarming smile.

Jordan watched Luther as he crossed the room. He seemed not at all threatening at the moment, but she knew better than to trust him. As he drew near she met his gaze and a shock of warning screamed through her. There was a look of pure, raw hunger reflected in the depths of his blue eyes. The realization struck her that he was nothing more than a very hungry predator and she was his prey. Her instincts warned her to flee. Necessity commanded she stay.

"Luther," she began, wanting to set things straight between them right from the start. "I came here tonight because . . ."

"I know why you came here tonight," he supplied, the flame in his eyes growing hotter. He had no desire for small talk. He only wanted to have his way with her as quickly as possible. He'd waited long enough.

Reading his avid regard correctly, she stiffened and replied, "No, I don't think you do."

"Come, come, my dear. Of course I know why you're here," he answered with confidence as he advanced even nearer. "Your brother's a sensible man. Obviously, he's explained the situation, and you've made the correct decision."

"I've made the correct decision, all right, but it isn't the one you think," she declared firmly.

Luther wasn't really listening. He was concentrating on how wonderful it was going to be to release her hair from its tight bun and strip away all her clothing. "I promise you, Jordan," he said with fervor. "I'll see that you never regret it." He reached for her.

Jordan sidestepped him evasively, saying with emphasis as she did so, "I don't think you understand, Luther. I only came here to talk, nothing more."

"Talk? We can talk later . . ." The heat in his loins driving him, his need for her was nearly obsessive. He was sure she was playing some kind of game with him.

"I want to talk now, not later," Jordan insisted as she maneuvered herself to put the desk between them.

"What about?"

"About Philip's and my investments . . ."

Luther was not at all amused by being put off, and his expression grew cold and ominous. In a taut move, he rested both hands on the desktop and leaned toward her. "What exactly did you want to know?"

His gesture was not physically threatening in itself, yet Jordan felt the inherent danger in his stance and recognized the growing anger in his eyes. "I wanted to know how we can work things out and come to an understanding . . ."

"There's nothing to come to an understanding about, Jordan. Your money is gone. There's nothing left."

"There's got to be something that can be done . . . something we can do . . ."

His icy regard swept her body with insulting familiarity, lingering on the curve of her breasts and then dropping lower to the juncture of her thighs. "It's a very simple matter, really, just as I told Philip."

Jordan wished there was some way she could shield herself from his hungry gaze, but she knew it would never do to cower before him. Instead, she held herself unflinchingly erect to answer him. "You want me to become your mistress."

"That's right. You can settle this upsetting little matter between us right now, without further delay."

"What you call an upsetting little matter is my brother's and my future! You've lost all our money and now you want me to pay an even bigger price!"

"I'd hardly call being my mistress and having your every wish granted 'paying a bigger price,' Jordan."

"Then you don't know me very well," she retorted, growing angry in the face of his lust-inspired avarice.

"I know you're a beautiful woman and that I desire you. What else is there to know?"

His words were spoken so flippantly that Jordan was taken aback. "There must be other women who would jump at the chance to be your mistress. Why don't you get one of them?"

"I don't want them, Jordan. I want you."

"Why would you want a woman who doesn't love you?" she finally cried in exasperation.

"Love has nothing to do with what I want from you," Luther said coldly. "Now, enough talk. Do you become my mistress, now, here, tonight? Or do you and your brother end up facing prison and possibly the gallows?"

"But I don't want you!"

"I'm going to change all that," he said in a low voice as he advanced toward her. "Before I'm done with you, you're going to be begging for my favors and wanting to please me in every way. I'll make sure of it!" He was upon her before she could escape. Grasping her by her upper arms, he hauled her against him and kissed her hungrily.

Jordan found Luther's embrace vile and disgusting. When he forced her lips apart and thrust his tongue into her mouth, she nearly gagged. The need to fight him rose up within her, and with all the strength she could muster, she shoved hard against his chest. She was thrilled when she managed to break away from him.

"Stay away from me, Luther! I told you! I won't become your mistress!" She felt dirtied by his touch.

Holding her so close and kissing her had sent Luther's desires raging out of control. Jordan was more exciting, more enticing, than he'd ever imagined. Instead of putting him off, her reluctance only excited him all the more, stirring his ardor and goading him to prove himself to her. The thought of changing her protests to purrs of contentment challenged him.

"As I see it, you really have no choice in the matter," he announced with great satisfaction. "Now, you can make this pleasant for both of us or I can take these to the proper authorities." Luther always carried his important papers in a folder with him wherever he went, and he lifted it from the desk to show her. "Philip had obviously told you what this is, hasn't he?"

"Yes." Jordan could feel herself growing pale beneath the onslaught of his cold, calculating viciousness.

"It's very damaging, this information I have on the two of you, and I'm sure the authorities would love to get their hands on it. So as I see it, you really have only two choices, Jordan. You can relax, enjoy my company, and take advantage of all the wonderful things I can give you, or I can turn this over to the proper officials and see you and your brother go to jail for a long, long time," he announced, quite pleased with himself. "Now, Jordan, you decide. Which one will it be?"

She stood rigidly before him, her anger and outrage filling her. Luther was nothing but an animal . . . an animal driven by greed and lust . . .

Luther took her momentary silence for surrender. Feeling he had his long dreamed of ecstasy within reach, he tossed the folder back down on the desk and reached for her.

"No matter how much you deny it, you're going to enjoy being in my bed, Jordan. There are things I can give you, things I can do to you that will leave you crying out for more. I can hardly wait to have you beneath me . . ."

"No! I won't submit to you! Philip and I will fight you every inch of the way! There's got to be someone who will listen to us and believe that we had nothing to do with a slave ship! We'll demand an investigation and . . ."

Her continued refusals infuriated him, and her threat of an investigation sent Luther's temper soaring. He had to stop her foolish protests, and he had to stop her now. What better way than by forcing her to his will?

He grabbed her and yanked her to him, his mouth swooped down to cover hers as his hand ripped at the buttons on her jacket. It took only a second for him to part the cloth, push aside her blouse, and seek out the fullness of her naked breasts. His boldness was such a shock to her that

80

she went rigid for an instant, then she began fighting him with all her might. With ferocious intent, she hit at him, trying to stop him, trying to free herself from the abomination of his touch.

Luther only lifted his head long enough to laugh at her feeble attempts. "You can't escape me, Jordan. You're mine. I will have you tonight!"

He pressed his hips hard against hers as he dragged her back to him for another kiss. His fierce hold almost cut off her breath, and he took advantage, bending her back over the desk, pressing between her thighs and moving against her erotically to let her know exactly what he wanted to do to her.

"Damn you, Luther! Leave me alone! Don't do this!" Jordan was desperate. She could barely breathe or think. This monster was stripping away her clothes, touching her bare flesh, and there seemed nothing she could do to stop him. She tried to twist away, but he held her easily. The edge of the desk was cutting painfully into the backs of her legs as his weight came down more fully upon her.

Luther's passions were ruling him as he prepared to take Jordan by force. The feel of her satiny skin and the sight of her heaving breasts had sent him over the edge. He couldn't deny himself. She was his for the taking! He was reaching for her skirts, ready to claim her.

Jordan could feel the increasing intensity in Luther's actions and her panic became very real. She groped blindly about on the desktop, hoping to find something with which to fend him off. Her hand closed over something round and heavy, and without thought she swung up at his head with all her might.

There was a sickening thud as she struck him on

the temple, and then Luther went limp on top of her. The wound was a gory one, and Jordan knew only fear and desperation as the hot, sticky blood ran from his head onto her bared bosom. Repulsed, she shoved him off her and watched in stunned terror as he crashed to the floor and lay unmoving.

The only thing Jordan heard as she stood there staring down at Luther's limp body was the harsh, raspy sound of her own breathing magnified by her own terror. She waited, frozen, expecting his servants to come running into the room at any moment, but there was only silence and a terrible sense of being completely alone. Blood seemed to be everywhere . . . all over her and the desk and now pooling on the floor by Luther's head.

Jordan could see no sign of life in her tormentor. There was no movement to his chest, no indication that he was alive, and she knew in that moment that she'd killed him. Mortal fear swept through her. She was a murderer!

For a fraction of a second Jordan considered calling for help, but there was enough logic left in her to know that that was no solution to her problem. Who would believe that she'd killed him in self-defense, especially after they found the papers telling of her involvement with the slave trade? There was only one thing she could do, and that was to get away as far and as fast as she could.

Jordan started to flee from the room but then stopped. Once the police started to investigate, they would find the incriminating papers right away. Realizing she could take them now and save both Philip and herself, she snatched up the folder from the desk. They might find out she was the one who'd killed Luther, but she would never let them hurt her brother. As long as she had the papers he would be safe. With one last terrifying look at Luther, she pulled her clothing back together as best she could and raced from the room into the darkness of the London night.

Chapter Six

Philip had stayed up late reading in the parlor. When he heard the front door open he was puzzled, and he hurried out into the hall to investigate.

"Dear God!" Philip exclaimed as he confronted his sister in her terrible state of disarray—her jacket undone and stained with what looked to be blood, her blouse ripped, her face flushed and her breathing ragged from the exertion of her flight. "Are you hurt? What happened? What were you doing out of the house?"

"No . . . no, I'm not hurt . . . Oh, Philip!" she cried, throwing herself in his arms. She was more scared than she'd ever been in her life, and she was completely exhausted from running almost all the way home. "Hold me! Please, just hold me!"

He cradled her protectively, murmuring soothing words to her until she calmed a little. Then, determined to find out what had happened, he led her into parlor and drew her down to sit next to him on the sofa.

"Jordan, I want to know what happened." Noticing that she was clutching something tightly in her hands, he took it from her. "What's this?" He glanced at the crumpled folder and immediately recognized it as Luther's. "You didn't go to Luther's . . . ?"

She nodded, her eyes silently relating the horror of what she'd just been through.

"If he's the one who did this to you, I swear I'll . . ." Philip jumped to his feet and started for the door, but Jordan stopped him.

"No! He didn't hurt me. I'm all right!"

"Thank heaven," he breathed, sitting down beside her again and giving her a reassuring hug. "But what happened? Is that blood? And what about your clothes?"

She couldn't hold it back any longer. Philip was the only one she could trust. She hurriedly explained her reasons for going to Luther and then told him of the outcome of her fateful visit. "I killed him, Philip! He was trying to hurt me, trying to force me to . . ." She couldn't finish the thought, so ugly was it to her. "I had to get away from him, so I managed to grab something heavy off his desk and I hit him with it. I think it was a paperweight . . . I don't know . . ."

"He's dead?" he repeated in disbelief.

Jordan nodded. "It was awful. I didn't mean to kill him. I just wanted him to stop . . . to let me go . . ."

He gathered her close again, "It'll be all right."

"How? How can anything ever be all right again?" she demanded, knowing the price for murder was death. "I've killed a man . . . I'm a murderer!"

"You're no such thing! You were just defending yourself," he told her. "We'll go to the police. We'll tell them what happened. They won't punish you for saving your virtue!" He was ardent in her defense, wanting to reassure her that everything would be fine.

"No! We can't go to the police!"

"We most certainly can. You're not thinking clearly, Jordan. The police will help."

"No they won't, Philip! You're the one who isn't thinking clearly! If we go to them they're going to find out about us! Even if they did believe me about defending myself, they'd still be curious to know why I went unchaperoned to Luther's in the first place!"

"What would it matter? You could make up anything. We've got the papers now," he countered.

"But we don't know that there aren't other copies of those documents, and Luther may have confided in someone else about us. All the authorities would have to do is find that person, make the connection between my visit there and the illegal smuggling, and then they'd be after us."

Philip suddenly realized she was right. They couldn't go to the authorities. Even though they had Luther's papers, they were trapped.

"Did anyone see you at his house?"

"Just the butler when he let me in. There wasn't anyone around later, though, when he attacked me."

"And when you left, did anyone follow you?"

She shook her head. "Not that I know of."

Philip nodded in acknowledgement, lost deep in thought.

"Philip, I have to get away from here right away. When they find Luther, they're going to know I was the one who killed him. They're going to know it was me! I have to escape!"

"If you think I'm going to let you face this all

alone, you're crazy. Whatever happens, we'll handle it together."

"Then we've got to get out of here! They're going to be here any minute!"

Philip stood up and began pacing the room in agitation. He took one last lingering look around at the comfortable furnishings and familiar book-lined walls that were their home, then turned to Jordan. "There's nothing to hold us here any more. We'll go to America."

"But how? We don't have any money . . ."

"We'll go over as indentured servants, it's the only way." He'd read all about how the homeless poor would trade a few years of their lives as laborers for the cost of the overseas fare.

"Indentured servants? Won't the police still be able to find us?"

"We'll sign on using different last names so no one will know we're related."

"All right. Just give me time enough to change and pack a few things."

"Be quick, and only take what you can carry with you in one small bag. I'll do the same."

"I'll be right back," she promised, rushing from the room, eager to strip off the garments that reminded her so vividly of her horrible encounter with Luther.

Philip watched her go, his heart heavy with sorrow. He knew this was going to be difficult for them. It would be foolhardy to think that it wasn't. They were used to a quiet way of life, to an existence surrounded by books and gentleness. He feared what they might come up against, but as much as their decision frightened him, he knew they had no other choice. They would do it, simply because there was nothing else they *could* do. The poor indentured themselves to get a second chance at life, and that was exactly what he and Jordan needed—another chance. They'd lost everything they'd ever owned, but at least they still had each other. Philip believed that with love and a firm, abiding faith they could make it. He would protect Jordan with all his might. He would never let anything or anyone harm her, and somehow he would see that they got through this.

Thoughts of Luther and his criminal dealings rekindled Philip's fury. Luther had been a truly evil man. What he'd almost done to Jordan was unforgivable, and had she not killed him herself, he would have taken great pleasure in doing the deed. Satisfied that the businessman had paid for his wickedness, Philip began to gather his own few precious belongings together in readiness for their flight.

Meanwhile, in New Orleans, Rose Brandford, a petite, gray-haired widow of indeterminate age, sat at the side of the dance floor with her close friend and long-time ally, Elizabeth McKelvey.

"I'm telling you, Liz, there's something strange going on with the Kane boy," Rose declared, keeping an eagle eye on Nick as he danced by with yet another beauty of marriageable age. He'd danced every dance with a different girl tonight, and she couldn't ever remember him acting this way before.

"Oh, pooh, Rosie. You're just jealous, is all. I know you've always had a sweet spot for Dominic. You think I don't know these things, but I do," the white-haired, sixty-five-year-old Liz declared with an authority that came from long familiarity.

"Everyone knows I care about Nick. He's a good boy," Rose replied, knowing Liz was right. She did have a particular fondness for Nick, and she'd felt that way ever since he was little. He'd been a beautiful child, and it had been a real tragedy when he'd lost his mother, her dear friend Andrea. She'd always admired the way Charles Kane had gone on to raise his son to be such a fine young man, and she believed that Andrea would have been very proud of the way he'd turned out, too.

"He's hardly a child anymore," Liz came back, her blue eyes twinkling with devilish delight as she watched the tall, handsome young man dance.

"Compared to my age, he's still a boy." They exchanged looks, then laughed together.

"And isn't it a shame?" Liz mourned, longing for the time when she'd been the belle of the ball with crowds of eager suitors gathered around. Being an elderly matron doomed to a life of overseeing the morals of the young was not her idea of a good time, but she knew it was necessary. Lord knows, she certainly would have been much wilder in *her* younger days had the old women not sat on the sidelines and cast condemning glances her way every so often. It was a terrible cross to bear, this growing more mature.

"I'll tell you, Liz, except for my Everett, there weren't many men who looked as good as Nick when I was young." Her gaze sought him out once more among the crowd.

"What about my Darrell?" Liz countered, insulted that Rose obviously hadn't thought her husband attractive.

"You were already married to him," Rose pointed

out. "And you know darn good and well that if I'd mentioned him you'd have gotten mad. You would have told me that he was a married man and that I'd had no business looking at him then."

Liz primly straightened her skirts, trying to ignore her remarks.

"Well? Am I right?"

"Yes, you're right," she replied, trying not to smile at the friend who knew her so well.

"Thank you."

"Rose . . . why do you think something's going on with Nick?" Liz asked, finally getting back to the original conversation.

"I'm not sure, but I've never seen him so intent on dancing with so many girls. Why, it used to be that he'd arrive late and leave early. You know how those footloose, good-looking bachelors are. He'd meet his friends and then spend most of his time playing cards and drinking with the men in the library."

"You're right about that, and now that I think about it, you're right, too, about him acting different. Why, just last week at the Devol's barbeque, he looked to be flirting with a whole passel of girls."

"I wonder if he's finally decided to get married?"

"Lord knows, it's time. What is he? Twenty-five or twenty-six now? By the time my Darrell was his age, we'd already been settled down for five years and had three babies."

"That was then, darling. This is now. You know how this younger generation is."

"I'm afraid I do," Liz complained, just about ready to launch into the latest gossip she'd heard regarding some scandalous behavior on the part of some of the girls.

"Well, I just hope he doesn't choose that silly Milicent Rogers he's dancing with now. The girl has nothing but fluff between her ears. No, she'd never do. Nick needs a nice girl, someone who's smart enough and pretty enough to keep him on his toes, someone who's his equal in every way."

"Pity I don't have a granddaughter his age."

"I was just thinking the same thing."

While Rose and Liz were discussing the merits of the eligible women they knew who just might be good enough for Nick, the object of their devoted attention was silently praying for the music to end so he could escape from Milicent Rogers. Pretty though she was — in a vapid, blond, fragile sort of way — the vacant look in her brown eyes should have warned him right from the start. As far as he could tell, she didn't possess one spark of intelligence. Her interests ranged widely from herself to herself. She was a simpering, spoiled child in a woman's body, and he couldn't wait to be free of her clinging presence.

"Don't you think so, Nick?" Milicent asked sweetly, honestly believing that he was listening to her every word.

Nick was jerked back to the present by her question. "I'm sorry, I was enjoying the dance so much that I missed what you said."

She gave a pretty little pout as she repeated, "I was saying that I just think big families are wonderful. I'd like to have lots and lots of babies when I get married."

Babies? Marriage? Nick thought in a panic. *How had they gotten on such topics? Why in the hell hadn't he paid more attention to what she was saying?* He knew why, he reflected sardonically. He hadn't been paying attention because he'd found her incessant chatter tedious in the extreme.

Hurrying to discourage any thoughts Milicent might have that he was interested in marrying her, he replied, "I've never really given any thought to marriage or children yet."

Nick saw her expression falter at his last brazen statement, and he was thrilled when the music came to an end right then. With as much grace as he could, he escorted Milicent to the side of the dance floor and deposited her with some of her friends. Then with a deftly offered excuse, he made his getaway.

Nick was feeling not unlike a criminal making a desperate jailbreak as he headed for the sanctuary of the library. After Milicent and her fantasy of living happily ever after with a hundred children, Nick knew he couldn't be held responsible for his actions if he was forced to make conversation with any more marriage-hungry maidens. He needed a stiff drink, quickly, and he didn't breathe any easier until he was safe in the haven of his host's library, where many of the men had gathered to indulge in their favorite masculine pursuits.

Nick mingled easily with the gentlemen gathered there as he made his way to the bar and poured himself a half tumbler of bourbon. Its fiery warmth eased the tenseness that had gripped him, and at last he was able to take a deep breath and smile wryly over his own misadventures. Though he'd balked at his father's command that he marry, Nick had never in his wildest imaginings ever thought it would be so difficult to follow through on it.

The fact of the matter was, up until now, Nick had never really given matrimony much thought.

The few occasions when he had—and that was very seldom—he'd considered it a distant pleasure, something that would happen only after he'd met the woman of his dreams and fallen in love with her. The thought of marriage now invariably reminded him of Slater and Francesca. His friend had been grief-stricken over losing his wife and was only beginning to recover from the trauma of her death. Slater had loved his wife deeply, and Nick wondered if he himself dared to fall in love and marry and risk leaving himself open to the possibility of that kind of pain.

Nick had never, ever thought that he'd be forced to actively pursue connubial bliss. Since true love was not something one could go out and drum up on the spur of the moment, Nick had come to the conclusion that a marriage of convenience was the only answer to his problem.

Still, no matter how simple the idea of a mutually beneficial marriage seemed, the memories of the last long weeks and his fruitless search at each party, barbeque, and ball for a girl who would fit into his plan made him grimace inwardly. He'd expected to be able to find a woman who needed him just as much as he needed her without too much trouble, but each encouraging prospect had eventually proved a false hope. His frustration was growing.

"Nick!"

The sound of Slater's call interrupted his agitated musings, and Nick looked up to see his friend just entering the room.

"So you finally got here, did you?" Nick chided.

"I was following up on a lead I had about the slaver. Rumor had it that one of the owners was from the area."

"And?"

"As far as I can tell, there was nothing to it, but I'm going to keep digging."

"Good."

Slater helped himself to a drink of his own, then cast his friend a mocking glance. He was enjoying his friend's search for the perfect woman. "And how have you been doing?"

Nick turned a thunderous look on him. "Fine, just fine."

"Somehow, judging from your tone, I find I don't believe you," he chuckled. "What's the matter? Won't any of the lovely young ladies have you?"

Nick finished off his boubon before answering. "I wouldn't know. I haven't asked," he replied brusquely.

"Well, why not? You haven't got much time left, you know."

"Thanks for reminding me," he growled.

Slater only laughed again and toasted him with his glass. "You're welcome, but what happened to that tall, pretty, dark-haired girl you were paying particular attention to at the barbeque last week? She was one nice looking woman."

"Then *you* marry her!" Nick retorted sarcastically, and immediately regretted it when he saw the fleeting look of pain in his friend's face.

"I'll never marry again," Slater said solemnly. Then, wanting to regain the lighter mood, he added, "You're getting awfully surly about this."

"I never thought it would be this hard to find a woman who'd be amenable to the kind of marriage I have in mind."

"Which is?"

"Hell, Slater, I'm not in love with anyone, and I don't see the day coming any time soon when I will be. If I have to get married now, I will, but it will be strictly a marriage of convenience, a marriage in name only. Then, after my father . . ." He paused not wanting to say it out loud. "Anyway, when the time comes later, I thought I might be able to work out an annulment of some kind so we could both be free again . . ."

"So what's happened?"

"Well, let's see," Nick began as he refilled his glass and took a deep drink. "First, I considered Lorna McGrath."

"You mean the good-looking redhead you were seeing a month ago?"

"Yes. She's beautiful enough, but all she could talk about was money. How rich her father is and how she has to find someone to marry who'll keep her as well as he did."

"That shouldn't be a problem for you. Your family's got more money than McGrath."

"I know, but if she's after my money, would she be willing to give me the annulment I want when the time comes?"

"I see your point."

Nick nodded. "Then there was Kathleen Ryan . . ."

"What was wrong with her? She's nice looking," Slater remarked, thinking of the petite, raven-haired young woman.

"She loves me! That's what's wrong with her!" he argued. "She has since we were young. I should have known better than to show her any attention. All she did was tell me how much she cares about me and how she wishes we could have a future

95

together."

"You don't care for her?"

"I like her all right, but I don't love her. Just from the few minutes we spent on the balcony together at the Rochester's party a few weeks ago, I can tell you she wouldn't be willing to settle for a marriage in name only."

"I see," Slater agreed, taking great care to keep his expression serious when all he wanted to do was laugh. He'd never known Nick to complain about a woman finding him desirable before, and it struck him as hysterically funny that his friend was suddenly trying to avoid a woman who obviously wanted him.

"And then there's Virginia Marksdale. I really thought she might work, but then I remembered her brothers . . ."

"What about them?"

"Well, Terrence is an expert shot and Mark is quite a swordsman, and they're both very protective of their only sister. I've known them for a long time, and I also know they're not the most upstanding of citizens."

"So? What's that got to do with your marrying Virginia?"

"I may be exaggerating things, but when I heard they'd been losing money on the plantation and were short on cash, I started thinking. What if after the wedding, at her brother's encouragement, she changed her mind about an annulment? With brothers like that, she might end up a rich widow instead of a well-to-do woman with an annuled marriage in her past."

Slater grinned, and without much sympathy said, "You certainly are having a rough time."

"Milicent Rogers, here tonight, was the worst of all, though. One waltz and the woman had us married with babies on the way . . ."

This time Slater did laugh out loud. "Babies?! You're kidding?"

"I wish I was!" In agitation, Nick raked a hand nervously through his hair. "Hell, Slater, I don't want to get married! It's the furthest thing from my mind!"

"Then why don't you just try talking to your father about it? Tell him the truth. Tell him how you feel."

"What I want doesn't matter this time. He's serious about this . . . real serious. I've never seen him act like this before. We've always been able to discuss things, but this time he won't even listen to me."

"Then you've got to do something."

"But what? There's not a woman in that room who would marry me knowing that I don't love her and knowing that I want out of the marriage just as soon as . . ." The terrible thought of his father's death stopped him, and as he looked up, his father walked into the room.

The sight of the older man, his hair silvered, his color pale, his clothing loose on his frame, left Nick's heart aching. A year ago his father had been vibrant and active. Now, he just seemed old.

"Damn it, Slater," he swore in misery. "There has to be a way. There just has to!"

Chapter Seven

The Jordan who stood at the rail of the ship watching as it entered the bay in Mobile, Alabama bore little resemblance to the lovely young woman who'd gone to see Luther all those weeks before. Her face was pale and gaunt, testimony to the terrible food they'd eaten on the voyage and the seasickness she'd had to battle. There had been few chances to bathe during the trip, and the lack of cleanliness left her feeling miserable. As much as she disliked having her hair in a bun, it was so dirty that she'd been forced to tie it back that way so it wouldn't hang down limply around her shoulders. Now, clad in a practical daygown that was wrinkled and soiled, she gazed out across the water wondering what the future held for her. Weary as she was, there was no defeat in her, and it showed in the proud lift of her chin and the gleam of intelligence in her eyes as she got her first look at the new country that was about to become her home.

"I can't believe we're finally here," she murmured to Philip, who was standing staunchly at her side.

"Nor can I," he agreed, pleased that their journey was over.

To say the voyage had been difficult would have been an understatement. The food had been awful, barely fit for human consumption. The accommodations had been horrendous, for all the indentured servants had been jammed together in one area that provided little privacy. There were more men than women, and they were generally a crude, uncivilized lot. Philip had had to pretend to be Jordan's lover in order to protect her from the advances of others. It had been a laughable charade, and one they were sure they'd remember for some time to come.

"I'm a little bit scared about what's going to happen next," Jordan admitted as the ship prepared to dock. "What if we don't get to stay together?"

"Don't worry." Philip tried to sound encouraging, though he was feeling the same trepidation himself. "We've made it this far, haven't we?"

"Yes, but this could have been the easy part," she told him wryly.

"Easy? Jordan, there's been nothing easy about this, and we've done fine," he said, feeling years rather than just weeks older.

"I know, but at least we were together through it all. I hate the thought that we might be separated. It could be at least three years before we see each other again."

Philip wanted to tell her not to worry. He wanted to promise that he would always be there to take care of her, but he knew there was a good chance he wouldn't be. It was very likely that they would be forced to part. "That's true, but think about the alternative."

It took only that simple reminder for Jordan to recall how relieved she'd been when the ship had left London without their being discovered by the authorities. The thought of prison or a possible death sentence confirmed her belief that they'd done the right thing. "You're right. This is the only way."

They fell silent then as they contemplated what would happen next. Since it was almost dusk, they weren't sure if they would spend the night on the ship or be taken into town. It was a terrible thing for them not to know what the future held, and they waited apprehensively to see what was going to happen.

Jordan could sense the tension emanating from Philip, and she cast him a sideways glance, noticing how much older he looked and how much more serious. He'd been boyishly handsome when they'd fled their home, but he was no longer a carefree youth. Now he was a man. Having been unable to shave for the duration, Philip was sporting a beard that had grown in several shades darker than his blond hair. It had changed his appearance drastically, and they'd agreed that he should keep it just in case someone might notice the resemblance between them without it.

Though they'd never talked about it, Jordan knew Philip felt ultimately responsible for their situation. She put a comforting hand on his now as they stood ready to face whatever fate dealt them.

"Hey! Montgomery! You, Douglas! Get over here!" Harrison, the fat, repulsive-looking agent who'd been in charge of the indentured servants on the voyage, directed them to the back of the ship where the rest had gathered.

Philip and Jordan were still always surprised when someone called them by their assumed names. Somehow, they felt the aliases Philip Montgomery and Jordan Douglas didn't suit them very well, but they were the best they'd been able to come up with on such short notice. Sticking close together for fear that they'd be separated, they made their way to join the others.

"Hey, sweet meat!" one of the aggressive indentured men who'd tried to bed Jordan early on during the voyage called out as she walked regally past. "Who's gonna protect you once they sell you away from your boyfriend?"

"Yeah, girl!" another of the men taunted, annoyed by her aloofness and wanting to bring her down. "Maybe you and me will be going to the same place."

Philip was ready to fight, as he'd done on more than one occasion during the trip, but the agent interceded this time, allowing him to usher Jordan a safe distance away. They waited there anxiously to see what would happen next, and as they waited, each prayed silently for a miracle.

"Well, so much for that hot lead," Nick said in aggravation as he faced Slater across a table in a crowded waterfront tavern in Mobile. Having ended up at another dead end tracking the *Sea Demon*'s owner, they'd been sitting there for several hours, drowning their frustrations in some very strong, very bad whiskey. "I'm beginning to understand why the government has such a hard time arresting these people. I mean, if we can't locate the owner acting as interested investors, how can the government find them during an investigation?"

Slater nodded. "Whoever the owners are, they're smart. They've protected themselves from every angle. I'm beginning to think we're going to have to get real lucky to find them."

"I'm going to keep trying until I get lucky," Nick vowed angrily, his fervor for revenge not having dimmed at all since that terrible night.

"We both will," Slater agreed supportively, "but there's nothing more we can do here. We've already let it be known that we want to get involved in the business. It's just a matter of waiting to see if the man's interested in our offer."

"There's no other way? No quicker way?" Patience was not one of Nick's virtues, and as frustrating as his life was right now, he was wishing that just one thing would go easily.

"No. We just have to sit it out."

"Damn . . ."

"I know, I feel the same way you do, but we've got to be careful. You know how dangerous these people are. Curtis let us go once. We might not be so fortunate a second time."

"You're right." Nick was forced to cool his impatience. "I'll wait forever if I have to, just as long as I finally get to see those bastards get what's coming to them."

"We will." Slater said confidently.

"I just wish I could be as certain about the outcome of the rest of my life," Nick grumbled as he took another drink of the potent whiskey.

"Still worrying about your 'wife,' are you?" his friend laughed easily as he downed his own drink.

"I'm worried about my *lack* of a wife. I'd like to see you try to pick out the perfect wife in six months or less."

"No, thanks. I picked out the perfect one once. I don't want another wife. Why settle for less than

102

the best?" Slater told him, wondering after all these months if the endless ache from missing her would ever fade.

"But I don't want one or need one!" Nick declared hotly.

"Well, according to your father, you do."

Nick shook his head as he thought about his situation. "I don't know what else I can do. I've looked at all the possibilities at home, and there was something wrong with each and every one of them."

"Possibilities?" Slater guffawed. "Face it, Nick. There was really nothing terribly wrong with any of them. There's only something wrong with you."

"You're right! I don't want to get married!"

"And that's precisely why you're going about this all wrong. You don't want a marriage. You want a business arrangement, something set up and agreed to ahead of time, right?"

"What's wrong with that?" he asked on the defensive.

"Absolutely nothing, but you're not going to find it where you've been looking. The women you've been seeing want a real marriage. Period. How would they ever be able to hold their heads up in society if they had to admit failure by annulling their marriage to you? What chance would they ever have for another?"

"What do you suggest I do, then? That I go to the market and buy a bride?" As the liquor they had been consuming all evening heated his mood, his sarcasm sharpened.

"Why not? Why didn't we think of this before?" Slater was suddenly cheerful as an idea occurred to him.

"Just where do they make a practice of selling

women, Slater?" Nick drawled. "I'll go order one right now. I know exactly what I want, if I get to choose, that is. I want a beautiful blond with a great figure and a sweet personality. I want her to be a woman who'll stay in the background, not make any trouble for me, and leave just as soon as this ordeal is over." He smiled at the prospect of a made-to-order bride, wishing it were a real possibility instead of a farfetched dream.

"I think you're out of luck. There's not a woman alive who matches that description," Slater joked. "Besides, if she really was that perfect, would you let her go once the time was up?"

Nick only snorted in derision.

"You know, we could pay a visit to Madame La Fleur's House of Exotic Delights. Who knows? For a nominal fee, maybe one of her girls might be interested in making a deal with you."

"I may be desperate, but I'm not *that* desperate. Besides, with my luck, if I tried to pass a lady of the night off as my blushing bride, she'd turn out to know half of my father's acquaintances — intimately," Nick said with a rueful grin, imagining the scene.

"Let's go pay Madame LaFleur a visit anyway," Slater suggested, wanting to be distracted from the memories that haunted him. "The last time I was there, her girls were not only very pretty, they were also very talented. You might not be able to buy a wife there, but you will certainly be able to buy a good time."

Nick definitely felt in need of some relaxation, and he finished off his drink and got to his feet. "Let's go. My father thinks I'm here on a business trip with you, so there's no reason to start back

104

home early."

With Nick in the lead, they made their way slowly through the crowd of rowdy sailors, painted dockside whores, and drunks. Halfway to the door they happened to overhear one sailor talking excitedly to a group of men at the bar.

"They just got here, and they're going to sell 'em tonight."

"How many are there?"

"Fifty or more, I don't know," he dismissed the number drunkenly, "but there's only one I'm interested in."

"Oh, yeah?" came the avid reply.

At first, Nick and Slater paid little attention to the banter. They assumed they were talking about a slave auction.

"I saw her from the dock," the sailor went on, "and though she had a cloak all wrapped around her, she was one nice-lookin' woman. Set my blood to racin', I tell you."

"You say they brought them over from England?" another man asked.

Nick stopped in mid-stride.

The sailor shook his head excitedly. "Yeah, and I'll bet she's one pretty little English rose under all them clothes she's wearin'. I wonder if I got enough left of my pay to buy her?" He started to rummage through his pockets.

"Dream on, you fool. If she's as good a looker as you say, you won't be able to touch her on three months pay, let alone what you got now. Besides, she's an indenture. She's here to work for a living."

"I'll make her work for her livin'!" he snickered as he continued to count out his meager fare of coins.

"Looks like you're going to have to be saving for a long time!" the other man joshed. "Maybe by the time you get enough money, she'll be old and ugly and her price will have dropped so you can afford her."

"Too bad," the sailor mourned, "I would'a enjoyed ownin' her . . . Maybe if I go down by Wilkens's warehouse where they're gonna hold the auction I cån get another look at her."

"Ah, forget it. Stay here and enjoy what you can afford. Don't go dreamin' about what you can't have."

"You're right . . ."

As the conversation drifted off, Nick quickly left the tavern, smiling widely. When he and Slater were outside, he turned to his friend.

"Did you hear that?"

"Where's Wilkens's warehouse?"

"I don't know, but I'm going to find out." Nick's hopes were soaring. "This could be the answer to my prayers . . ."

Jordan was trying her best to maintain her dignity, but as she watched all that was happening around her, she found it almost impossible. Never in her wildest dreams or most vivid nightmares had she thought they would be put on exhibition like farm animals, but they were. Herded together onto the dock then separated according to sexes, they were forced to endure the inspections of whoever came to look. Keeping her cloak wrapped close around her, she made her way to the back of the group of women and tried to make herself inconspicuous, but as lovely as she was she had little

106

success. Several men accompanied by their wives came looking for maids, but the women quickly turned their husbands away from her, branding her "too likely to get into trouble" to work in their households. Though Jordan was sure the women meant to be unkind, their remarks really pleased her. She was thrilled when she wasn't sold right away.

Jordan quietly tried to keep an eye on Philip, watching in misery as he was put through the humiliation of being examined by several men to see if he was strong enough and healthy enough for the jobs they had in mind. To her horror, they even checked his teeth. Though he was in good physical shape, he too was passed over each time, and she was almost joyful about it. There was still hope. But as time passed and more and more of their companions were sold and taken away, her nervousness grew. Their time was coming soon, and she knew there wasn't a thing they could do about it. As much as she could, she kept to the deep shadows, trying not to draw attention to herself.

The fact that Nick was half besotted made considering the unacceptable acceptable. *He would buy a wife!* In his current state, the idea both intrigued and elated him. Despite the cautionary words Slater offered as they strode from the tavern, he had no qualms whatsoever about asking for directions to the warehouse from some workers who were still lingering on the docks. He was pleased to find it was only a short distance away, and he headed off in that direction with Slater in tow.

"I hope you're not disappointed," his friend advised. "That sailor's idea of a pretty woman and your idea of a pretty woman might be quite a different thing. Remember, he's been at sea awhile. Just about anything starts looking good to you when you've been at sea."

"I know," Nick sobered a bit. "But this is just about my last hope. If she's passably fair, it just might work. I mean, if she can speak decently, I can certainly teach her to imitate a lady. With any luck at all, I should be able to pull it off!"

"And you wouldn't have to worry about your father's friends, would you?" Slater quipped.

"No, none of them have been to England lately. We'd be safe on that account," he retorted, feeling lighthearted for the first time in weeks.

They caught sight of the crowd of indentures and potential buyers gathered in a lighted area near the warehouse, and they headed that way.

"Gents! You interested in buying a servant?" Harrison called out as he saw them approaching. He thought they looked very successful and felt certain that their pockets were well lined.

"We might be," Nick responded, but as he eyed the ragged looking, motley group, his hopes began to falter. Not only were they a poor, sickly looking bunch, but they smelled bad, too. He was beginning to see what Slater had meant.

"What exactly are you looking for? Perhaps I can recommend one for you. Are you interested in a field worker or a tradesman? Maybe a maid?" the agent asked, eager to be of service, for he wouldn't be paid for his trouble until all were sold.

"A woman," Slater said, his gaze scanning the females. "A reasonably young one."

Harrison was quick to respond. "I have a few.

108

Take a look and see which one you like."

Nick moved toward the women and Slater stayed with him. They were careful to keep their expressions guarded as they began the search for the one prized beauty who might be the solution to Nick's problem.

Jordan had been watching the two men ever since she'd heard Harrison call out to them. They were different from the other buyers who'd come to look at them. These two were well-groomed and neatly dressed. They appeared respectable from the distance, and they both moved with the confidence and ease of men born to wealth. She heard them mention that they were looking for a woman, and she couldn't help but wonder why. It would seem that if a maid was needed for a household, the wife would have been the one to make the selection.

The taller of the two men looked in her direction just then, and Jordan instinctively froze. He hadn't seen her, she was certain of that, but there was something about him . . . something so elemental and compelling that she couldn't look away. When she could move, her first reaction was to step farther back into the darkness. Only there, obscured by the enveloping gloom, did she feel safe to continue to observe him.

Jordan didn't know what it was she was feeling or why she was feeling it, she just knew that the strange emotion that filled her was very powerful and more than a little frightening . . . Her gaze followed the man as he moved through the group of women, coming ever closer to her. She could see that he was extraordinarily handsome. His hair was darker than his companion's, seeming almost as black as a raven's wing in the lamplight. He was not as heavily built as the man who accompanied him, but his lean, broad-shouldered form spoke of strength and endurance.

Jordan watched with open curiosity as the man made quick work of the other females. It surprised her that he did not touch or otherwise insult the women. Rather, he gave each only a single critical glance before moving on. It seemed as if he was searching for someone special. But who?

Nick was meeting with little success in his quest for a suitable female, and he was beginning to fear that the pretty one had either already been sold or had never existed in the first place. His spirits were just about to plummet when he remembered the sailor saying that the girl had been wearing a cloak. Glancing quickly over the few remaining females, he realized disheartenedly that she was not among them.

Nick was about to give up, admit defeat and go drown his sorrow in more whiskey and some companionship at Madame LaFleur's, when something — a slight movement in the darkness? — an intuitive recognition? — caused him to look up. Peering into the concealing cover of the night shadows just beyond the low glow of the lamps, he spotted her. She seemed a vision, a mere wisp of a woman. She appeared pale and delicate as she stood clothed in darkness. Afraid that she might disappear in the night, he called out to her in a particularly fierce tone.

"You! Come here!"

Chapter Eight

The sound of the man's call was so fierce and commanding that it stunned Jordan. She stood waiting, poised as if for flight. Even on this moonless night, she could feel the intensity of his piercing gaze as it settled upon her, and a shudder of primordial recognition shook her to the very depths of her soul. What did this man want? Why had he called out to her?

Knowing she would have to heed his call, Jordan took a tentative step toward him. She didn't move quickly enough for Harrison, who, at the sound of Nick's call, came rushing forward. He grabbed her by the arm and jerked her out into the dim light to face Nick.

"Was she trying to run away from you?" the agent demanded angrily, ready to reprimand her. She had been a bother to him the whole trip, rousing the men as she had, and he would be glad to see her sold and gone.

"I wasn't trying to run," Jordan spoke up in her own defense, pulling away from his painful grip to stand straight and proud before Nick. Masking any fear she had, she looked up at him and met his gaze straight on.

Harrison didn't believe her, though, and he deferred to Nick. "Sir?"

Nick had been surprised by the well-modulated, cultured sound of the girl's voice and by the spirit she displayed in facing him so boldly. Intrigued, curious to find out how she really looked beneath the voluminous cloak and all the dirt, he was quick to reassure the man. "No, she's fine. I just wanted to get a good look at her, that's all. It's hard to tell anything in the dark."

Nick stared down at her impersonally, his interest in her totally clinical as he tried to see past the dirt and grime. What he thought he saw there satisfied him, but he still couldn't be sure just how pretty she really was.

Jordan had thought this man attractive from a distance, but standing so close to him now she could see that he was more than just attractive. His dark, strong good looks made him about the handsomest man she'd ever seen. She wondered again what he was doing there and why he seemed so interested in her.

"Is there somewhere with more light? Some place where I can get a better look at her?"

His request sent a note of warning through Jordan. She'd heard the terrible rumors about what happened when potential buyers wanted a few minutes alone with the indentured women, and she grew nervous at the prospect.

"We have a room inside the warehouse. You and your friend can have a few minutes alone with her there," he invited.

"Yes, we'd like that." Nick didn't even bother to consult Slater, who was standing off to the side looking on without comment, his expression be-

112

mused.

"Come with me, then. It's much more private," Harrison offered with a lecherous smirk.

The agent's implication had been so crudely obvious that Jordan couldn't prevent the apprehension she was feeling from showing. As nice looking as this stranger might be, she didn't want to go anywhere "private" with him. Luther had been handsome enough in his own way, but inwardly he'd been rotten and mean. Who was to say that this man wasn't just as dangerous?

Nick saw the girl's sudden look of concern and felt sorry for her. He could well imagine how embarrassing it was to be treated in this manner, and he wanted to knock the smug, knowing look right off the agent's face. Somehow he managed to hold himself back. "Just show me where the room is," he said flatly.

Afraid that he might have offended a potential buyer, Harrison was quick to grovel. "Fine, fine, it's right in here . . ."

Jordan thought about refusing to accompany them into the building, but she knew it would be a useless battle. If she didn't go willingly, Harrison would only force her. He tried to take her by the arm, but she evaded his touch. With her head held high and her bearing proud, she walked on ahead of them toward the warehouse.

Philip had been watching what was going on from where he stood with the rest of the men. After hearing Harrison's comment, he'd been hard put not to charge forth and throttle the agent. The obscene remarks coming from the men around him only served to infuriate him further.

"Hey, Montgomery! Hey, loverboy, you know

what's gonna happen to your little girlfriend now, don't you?" one of the other indentures taunted.

"You've been replaced, Montgomery, and it looks like it's going to take two men to do it . . ." another commented with vicious enjoyment.

Philip fought to control his temper, but his concern for Jordan's safety pushed him over the edge. The moment he saw Jordan heading toward the warehouse he erupted. Out of control in his desire to protect her, he lunged forward. He ran toward them, not caring that he was outnumbered or out of line. He only wanted to keep his sister from harm.

"Jordan! Don't! Wait!"

Harrison had been anticipating that Philip might try something, and he turned on him before he could reach them. Yanking out the small, wrapped club he carried with him for just such incidents, he struck Philip in the stomach as hard as he could. The force of the blow sent the young man to his knees, and he doubled over, wretching and gasping for breath.

"Philip!" Jordan cried, and she started to go to him. "No! Don't hit him again! Don't!"

"I don't want any more trouble out of you, Montgomery," the agent snarled as he shoved the injured man to the ground. "If I hear one more word or see you move in the wrong direction, I'll sell you to a chain gang draining swampland in Louisiana, do you understand?"

"Yes," Philip managed to croak as he lay clutching his stomach.

"Good. Keep a hold on him," he directed the other men.

Jordan tried to run past Harrison to get to where

114

Philip lay, but the agent grabbed her and held her back easily. "Now, girl, let's go take care of business. A couple of you men make sure he stays right here while I'm gone."

"Who was that?" Nick and Slater asked when Harrison rejoined them, dragging Jordan along with him.

"His name's Philip Montgomery," Harrison replied tersely.

"What's his connection to the girl?" Nick pressed, thinking that he might be her husband.

"The two of them were thicker than thieves on the ship. I figure he must be her lover to be as hot after her as he is. It'll be good to get them apart. Come on, let's go on inside and get this over with."

Nick gave Slater a troubled look over the news that the girl had had a lover. The idea struck him as strange. He could have sworn there was something very innocent about the way she'd reacted to Harrison's lewd innuendo. Nick found he was disappointed by the discovery that she wasn't as pure as he'd originally thought, and he walked into the warehouse without another word.

Though furious over her helplessness, Jordan elected to remain calm. She went along with the men without further protest, hoping she could keep her wits about her and somehow manage to get out of this. The office inside the building was brightly lighted, but it was a cold, unfriendly room. She shivered in spite of her determination to be brave.

"We'll be all right here. Leave us alone now," Nick ordered coldly.

"If you need any help, I'll be right outside," Harrison replied.

"I don't believe I'll need your help. One young

girl is hardly my match."

"Well, if you do . . ."

Nick cut him off with a look that would have frozen even the boldest of men, and he scurried from the room. In the background, Slater had to turn away so neither man could see the mirth in his expression. Nick watched until the weasel of an agent had disappeared from sight, then locked the door to ensure their privacy.

"Is he gone?" Slater asked, once he'd gotten his merriment under control. He knew his friend wouldn't appreciate him making light of the situation right now.

"Yes, and now we can get down to business," Nick answered, quickly turning to Jordan who was standing as far away from the both of them as she possibly could. Without introduction or further conversation, he abruptly directed her, "Take off the cloak."

Jordan's eyes widened as she stared at him across the width of the room, and he immediately regretted his brusqueness. He knew his command had sounded bad, but he was filled with an urgency to see this done, one way or the other.

Jordan felt chilled by his instruction, and the fact that his face was so impassive left her unsure as to what to expect from him. Had she saved herself from Luther and gone through the torment of fleeing her homeland only to be forced to surrender herself now, here, to this total stranger?

She glanced quickly at the man he'd called Slater, trying to understand what was happening, but he too gave nothing away. Standing casually off to one side, he looked much like a spectator at some sporting engagement, watching the action unfold before him, his arms folded comfortably across his chest.

Jordan looked back at the dark-haired man, searching his expression for some sign of the ugly lust she'd seen on Luther's right as he'd attacked her, but there was nothing. If anything, he seemed quite dispassionate. Sensing no immediate threat of danger, she did as she'd been told.

As Jordan unfastened the tie at her throat, Nick came up behind her to take the voluminous garment from her shoulders. It amazed her that he showed her this courtesy, and what amazed her even more was the reaction she had to the heat of his touch. It was a simple act, the taking of her cloak, but when his fingers accidentally brushed against her arm, she felt a startling jolt of awareness. The sensation was frightening but not altogether unpleasant, and that realization put her even more on guard. Her expression was wary as she stepped away from him, keeping a goodly distance between them.

Nick was pleased to find that she was slender, and he turned to his friend as he laid the cloak aside. "Well? What do you think?"

Both men studied her thoughtfully for a moment as they sized her up. Each man's attitude was the same as it would have been had they been inspecting a prime piece of horseflesh before closing the deal. Nick was studying her more feminine attributes while Slater pondered her hair. Nick thought her figure passable but a little on the skinny side, and Slater agreed.

At their cool-headed exchange, Jordan bristled. She knew she should feel relieved that they weren't subjecting her to a more degrading inspection, but it still left her resentful that they could stand there and size her up like a horse at an auction without

117

giving any consideration to her feelings at all.

After a moment's discussion Slater shrugged, for he was having trouble imagining her all cleaned up. "I'm not sure."

Jordan wondered just how much humiliation one woman was supposed to take. Didn't they realize how embarrassing it was for her to have them see her that way, so dirty and unkempt? How could she maintain the little dignity she had left when they were treating her like she wasn't even a person?

"She's definitely got the potential," Nick said in her defense. He had seen the spark of annoyance in her eyes as she'd suffered their comments, and he couldn't help but feel a little sorry for her. She was as trapped by her situation as he was by his.

"Maybe," Slater hedged.

Solemnly, Nick took one last look at her and decided that with the right clothes and a lot of soap and water she just might work out. Of course, he knew there was probably a lot he would have to teach her before they got back to Riverwood. She was going to have to learn how to walk, talk, and act properly, for without those attributes he didn't have any hope of success at all.

"Her eyes are certainly pretty enough, and the color of the hair might be all right once it's washed."

"It'll take an effort, but I think you might be right. She just might pass," Slater finally agreed.

Pass? Pass for what? Jordan couldn't believe their comments. They were being far crueler in their assessments of her than the couples looking for a maid had been, and her anger and resentment toward them grew. She had no idea what these two men were looking for, but she was certain it was a far cry from a chambermaid.

"When she spoke earlier, she sounded halfway intelligent," Nick went on, listing her merits as he saw them.

Halfway intelligent?! Did they think she was deaf?! If he says one more thing, she thought heatedly, just one more thing, I'm going to tell them exactly what I think about their intelligence.

"You're taking a big chance," said Slater, voicing his doubts.

"I know, but consider the alternative."

Slater rubbed his chin thoughtfully as he pondered the possibility of Nick's bride turning up pregnant with someone else's child. "What about the man outside?"

Nick knew immediately what he was referring to, and he dismissed it without deep consideration. "I don't want to interfere permanently in her life. She can make her own choices later. The only thing that matters to me right now is that she can act the part. Nothing else is important. I can just stall the wedding until . . ."

Wedding!?! What they'd said before was insulting, but this was shocking. They were planning some kind of wedding?

"What wedding? What are you talking about?" Jordan had been quiet and submissive for so long that she shocked both men by her outburst. She stood facing them, a fire in her emerald eyes and resistance in every fiber of her trim body.

In that moment, Nick knew she would be perfect. His father would never have believed it if he'd brought home a mealymouthed, simpering little miss to marry. This one with the nice figure and sparkling eyes would convince him. "What's your

119

name?" he asked, totally ignoring her questions.

Jordan was annoyed and thought he was trying to distract her, but she answered anyway. "My name is Jordan Douglas."

"Well, Jordan Douglas, my name is Dominic Kane, and I have a bargain I'd like to offer you."

Her eyes narrowed as she asked, "What kind of bargain?"

"How would you like to live in a big house, have a beautiful wardrobe, have servants to take care of your every need, and be free of your indenture obligation two years early?"

Jordan blinked in surprise, but caution showed in both her expression and her voice. "What would I have to do?"

"Nothing illegal, I assure you."

"Oh? What then?"

"It just so happens that I find myself in need of a wife, and soon. Since I really didn't want to marry any time in the near future, I decided to find someone who's willing to enter into an arranged marriage, something strictly temporary. When the time comes that the union is no longer necessary, it will be immediately annulled."

"Who's forcing you to get married?"

Nick refused to tell her anything more. "That's a private matter. Should you agree to the bargain, I'll tell you everything you need to know then."

"Let me understand you," Jordan repeated slowly, still a little mystified by what he'd just told her. It seemed the answer to her prayers. She was being rescued by the handsomest man she'd ever seen, and he was going to marry her and take her away from all this. It sounded like a fairy tale, and she was more than certain that it was too good to be true.

"For whatever reason, you have to get married, but you don't want to. So you want to buy my papers and marry me with the understanding that it's only temporary."

"Yes, that's exactly right," he replied, waiting for her answer.

"At the end of whatever time you require, we'd then annul the marriage and my indentured obligation would be fulfilled." Jordan still had trouble believing it.

"Yes, you'd then be free." Nick saw her reluctance to accept what he was saying. Thinking it was because she was concerned about the physical side of the marriage, he quickly hastened to tell her, "In case you're worried about it, this would, of course, be strictly a marriage of convenience . . . a marriage in name only. There would be no intimacy involved. The only demand I would make on you would be that you play the public role of my loving wife whenever necessary."

"I see." Jordan glanced from Nick to Slater and then back again, her mind racing all the while. The idea of marrying this man, this Dominic Kane, was absolutely perfect. If anyone from England did eventually come looking for her, they'd never be able to find her.

Jordan was tempted to say yes immediately, but the thought of Philip waiting outside stopped her. Her own safety and happiness would mean nothing if she couldn't be sure he was going to be all right, too. She knew it was probably the most brazen thing she would ever do in her life, but desperate times called for desperate measures. "All right," she began. "I'll agree to your bargain — on one condition."

121

For just an instant Nick had been relieved, now the fact that she was making a demand of him put him on guard. "Which is . . . ?" he asked cautiously.

Jordan knew Kane's need for a wife had to be urgent, and she only hoped it was urgent enough that she could push him a little and get away with it.

"I'll do exactly what you ask. I'll marry you. I'll play the part of your devoted wife, and I'll even agree to the annulment at the appropriate time, providing you buy not only my papers but Philip Montgomery's papers as well, and give him some position in your household," she offered shrewdly.

An emotion Nick had never felt before and didn't understand gripped him. "This may only be a marriage of convenience, but fidelity will be vital to the charade," he snapped out the words tersely. "My family's name is too important to be linked to a scandal."

Jordan's green-eyed regard turned icy hard as she stared at him. It galled her that he immediately thought the worst of her, but circumstances prevented her from telling him the truth. It was essential that no one find out she and Philip were related, just in case anyone from England did try to track them. Their very lives depended on it.

"You've made all the demands so far," Jordan began, "and I have made only the one . . . Actually, it's not so much a demand as a request. Given the chance, Harrison will find a way to make Philip's life hell. I just want to be sure that he's safe. Is ours to be a bargain or not?"

Nick stared at her, weighing the annoyance he felt against the need he had for a wife. His desire to

122

please his father overruled his other emotions.

"The bargain is sealed," he agreed less than enthusiastically. He didn't like the thought of his "wife's" lover being around, but he figured that would be easy enough to remedy. He'd surely be able to find something for him to do at Riverwood that would keep him very busy—and far away from the girl.

"Thank you, Mr. Kane." Jordan didn't realize how tense and nervous she'd been until Nick spoke the words that saved her and Philip. She nodded and gave him an appreciative smile, but all she really wanted to do was to throw herself into his arms and thank him profusely.

"My name is Nick. Learn to use it or we'll never convince anyone of our intentions."

"All right . . . Nick."

Nick studied her pensively for a moment, then took Slater aside to ask him to stay with her until she'd had time to collect herself. He, meanwhile, would be on the dock concluding the deal with the agent. Slater agreed, and then with one last look at the woman he intended to buy and make his bride, Nick left the room.

When Nick went out to find Harrison, he saw Montgomery again, and his irritation with the situation returned. The fact that it bothered him so much troubled him. Why should he care about this other man? What did it matter if the girl had had a lover as long as she played the role of his wife as he had asked? He had no answers to the questions, and he quickly dismissed them. He had business to conduct.

Jordan was more than happy as she donned her cloak; in fact, she was ecstatic. She couldn't believe that things had turned out so well. Dominic Kane was actually going to buy Philip, too! Kane seemed a godsend. A wide, bright smile lit her face until she looked up to find Slater's eyes upon her.

"You know, Nick is my friend, and this arrangement he's working out with you is very important to him," Slater said slowly. "I'd hate for anything to go wrong—if you know what I mean."

Jordan heard the implied threat in his words and her smile faltered, then failed completely. "You don't have to worry," she managed.

"I hope not," he countered. "I wouldn't want to think that I'd made a mistake in not advising him against this."

"I gave him my word," she told him with firm, unflinching pride. "He won't regret it."

Slater considered himself a pretty good judge of character, and he was beginning to think that Nick might have done the right thing tonight. As far-fetched an idea as it had been to buy a wife, he had an inkling that his friend might have done well for himself. Though they looked nothing alike, something about her reminded him vaguely of Francesca. This Jordan Douglas was obviously well-spoken and reasonably intelligent. She was brave, too, for she'd just stood up to his intimidation better than most men. Slater respected those qualities in her, and he wondered if there was more to this woman than just a pretty face. Certainly, it would prove interesting to watch what developed over the next few months.

Chapter Nine

Nick's stride was purposeful as he crossed the warehouse yard toward the agent, but the closer he got to Harrison the more the doubts he'd tried to ignore began to play in his mind. *Would he be able to do it? Was he a good enough actor that his father would believe he was really in love with this woman?* The thought badgered him.

In love . . . Nick wasn't even sure what that meant. He'd had associations with many women in his life. He'd enjoyed being with them, and he'd enjoyed making love to some of them, but he'd never been "in love" with any of them. He wondered at the difference. *How did a man treat the woman he supposedly loved above all others and planned to make his wife?* The dilemma was still troubling him as he drew near Harrison, who was standing deep in conversation with a short, rather unsavory looking man.

"Sorry, Wilson," Harrison was saying as Nick paused close by.

"Look," the man insisted, "I know she must still be here somewhere. I got the money now, and I'm ready to buy her papers. Bring her out here." He drew out a wad of bills and held them up for the agent to see.

"I'm not sure . . ." the agent hedged. "There's someone else who might be interested in her now."

"I'll give you $500 for her right this minute! You

can pocket the extra $200 yourself and no one would ever know."

"An extra $200, you say?" Harrison wavered, greed beginning to overcome him. He was always open to a little graft.

Nick heard the exchange, realized exactly who they were talking about and quickly broke in. "Sir, I'm ready to settle with you."

"You want to buy her papers?" Harrison was pleased at the prospect of the two men bidding each other higher.

"Yes."

"Well, this other gentleman here, Mr. Wilson, is wanting her too, and he's just offered me $500."

Nick pinned the little man with an assessing glare and understood instantly just what kind of "work" he intended to have Jordan do. Nick turned back to the agent. "I didn't know you were open to bids," he said shortly.

Harrison smiled hungrily. "It's my job to get top dollar, and if this other gent wants to make an offer . . . Well, who am I to refuse?" He tried to look innocent even as he was mentally counting the profit he would make if he could get these two working off each other.

"I'll give you $600," Nick said easily, daring the man to go higher.

"Seven hundred," Wilson insisted. He had scrounged to get the money, and he had no intention of letting the other man have her. She was too valuable a prize. It wasn't often one like her showed up on the docks.

Jordan, once again wrapped protectively in her cloak, emerged from the warehouse accompanied by Slater. They headed to where the three men stood, intending to join Nick. But as they came within hearing range, Jordan was mortified to find that the three were quibbling over her price. She blanched and swallowed tightly, averting her eyes from the spectacle.

Nick was growing very aggravated. He had thought this would be easy when they'd left the tavern. He had thought he would come down here to the warehouse, find the pretty woman he'd heard the sailor talking about, and strike a deal with her. Then he would take her home and pretend to be married. Now, here he was caught up in a damned bidding war over her, and all because of his father's ridiculous deadline. He was almost tempted to forget about the whole thing and let Wilson have her for the $700, but then he glanced up and saw her. Jordan was standing with Slater a short distance away, her face pale, her hands clenched before her, looking embarrassed and disgraced by the scene she was being forced to witness.

"A thousand dollars, take it or leave it," Nick found himself suddenly saying.

"A thousand?" Harrison and the other man repeated in unison, stunned.

"That's what I said," he snapped. "Do we have a deal?"

The agent glanced at Wilson, and seeing the look of frustration on his face he quickly made his decision. "She's yours."

"Fine." He said no more until Wilson had stalked off grumbling. "I also want to work something out with you for the man."

"You want Montgomery, too?" Harrison was even more shocked.

"That's what I said." Nick's tone discouraged any further interest the agent might have had.

They came to terms, and Harrison was positively

127

thrilled over the sale. "I'll get Montgomery for you," he offered, happily rushing off.

Nick stood watching him for a moment, then walked over to join Slater and Jordan.

"Well, it looks like you just bought yourself a wife. How much did it end up costing you? A mere thousand for the girl and three hundred more for Montgomery?" Slater commented with a grin that grated on Nick's nerves.

"If everything works out, it will have been worth it," Nick growled.

"Whatever you say."

Nick shot him a questioning glance, but the look Slater was giving him now was purely innocent.

"As soon as Harrison comes back with Montgomery, we'll go."

Jordan said nothing during the entire exchange, but she was stunned by the amount he'd agreed to pay for her. The fact that he thought she was worth that much, and the relief of knowing that he'd also purchased Philip's papers, buoyed her spirits considerably. She hoped that their luck was finally changing for the better.

The pain of the beating Philip had suffered earlier was nothing compared to the misery he had suffered as he watched and waited for Jordan to emerge from the warehouse. Once he'd regained a little of his strength, he'd tried to go after her again, but the men had done as the agent had ordered and had held him back. With each minute that had passed his torment over her safety had grown, until now it was like a knife in his heart.

When Philip saw only one of the men come back out of the warehouse, his worries deepened. *Where was his sister? What had they done to her?*

Philip breathed a little easier when he saw Jordan, accompanied by the other man, emerge seemingly untouched from the warehouse. He watched the whole scenario between the agent and the two potential buyers. The shorter of the potential buyers stormed off after what looked to be a somewhat heated discussion, and Philip waited nervously to see what would happen next. When the agent headed his way, he tensed. Something had happened, but what?

"Montgomery!" Harrison called out to him.

Philip moved away from the group to confront him. "What do you want?" he asked suspiciously.

"Get your things and come with me. Hurry."

"Why? What's going on? What's happening with Jordan?!" Philip demanded, close to panic. He wanted to know if he'd been sold, and if so, who had bought him. He couldn't just leave without knowing Jordan's fate. What if he went to claim his personal belongings and she was taken away while he was gone?

Harrison glared at him. "Shut up and do as you're told, Montgomery, or I'll follow through with my earlier threat. The Louisiana swamps are something to behold in the summer."

Philip was furious, but he had little choice in the matter. Only when he returned to find Jordan still there with the three men did his fury abate somewhat. Since Harrison was with her, he went directly to his sister, ignoring the others.

"Are you all right?" he asked earnestly, his worry showing clearly in his expression.

"Philip!" she greeted him almost delightedly. "I'm fine. In fact, we're both going to be fine."

"Montgomery!" Shaken by the intimacy of their

129

greeting, Nick said his name sharply, deliberately interrupting the sweet little reunion. He didn't like the way the two of them were looking at each other at all.

Philip glanced up, but said nothing as he guardedly met Nick's hard gaze. Instinctively he knew this was not a man to be trifled with, there was something about him that was commanding and powerful.

"I'm Dominic Kane," Nick informed him, "and I've just bought both your papers."

"I see," was all Philip answered as he glanced quickly over at Jordan.

Nick saw the exchange and worried that he'd been wrong in taking them both. It was obvious that they cared for each other, and he wondered if it was going to be hard to keep them apart during the months ahead.

"About the money . . ." Harrison wanted to be reassured that the balance of his payment would be ready the following day, as they'd agreed. "You'll have the rest tomorrow?"

"Check with me in the afternoon. You have the name of my hotel and the room number, right?"

He nodded. "I'll be there shortly after lunch."

Nick looked over at the two servants whose papers had just set him back more than a nominal sum. It irked him the way Philip stood so protectively beside Jordan.

He was scowling as he grumbled to Slater, "I'd better get my money's worth out of this. Wait here. I'll get a carriage."

As Nick walked away and Harrison moved off to take care of other business, Philip said to his sister, "What's going on, Jordan?"

"Not now. I'll tell you later, when we're alone,"

she told him in a whisper, knowing that Nick was not pleased with Philip's attentiveness.

Philip didn't understand what was going on, but since Jordan was fine and it looked like they were going to be together for the full term of their indenture, he was thankful.

Nick soon returned with a hired carriage and got down to assist Jordan. Giving Montgomery no chance to follow her, he climbed into the vehicle after her and sat down beside her on the hard, narrow seat. Nick intended to make his point right from the start. If she was to play the role of his beloved, she might as well start getting used to him now.

Remembering all too well what he'd said in the warehouse, Jordan was not surprised by Nick's actions. The only thing that did surprise her was her own reaction to his nearness. While earlier his touch had been disturbing to her, the feel of his thigh now pressed tightly to her in the narrow confines of the carriage gave her goosebumps and set her pulse to racing wildly. She tried to shift away from him without drawing his attention, but there was no escape. The vehicle was just too small.

As they waited for Slater and Philip to climb in, Jordan glanced at Nick out of the corner of her eye, wondering why this man, this stranger, could affect her so, and wondering, too, if he was feeling the same thing she was. Nick's expression was inscrutable, though, and she had no clue to what he was thinking.

Needing to distract herself, she turned her attention out the window just as the driver took his seat and the carriage started up. As they turned a corner and the warehouse disappeared from sight, she hoped with all her might that she was leaving her past behind, this time for good.

Nick was very much aware of the softness of Jordan's leg against his. He found it a little disconcerting that a woman he'd just met could affect him that way. He thought her pretty enough, but certainly not a raving beauty. He didn't want to be attracted to her. This was to be strictly business between them, and yet this physical reaction he was having to her puzzled him.

Needing to think of other things, Nick trained his gaze on Montgomery, who was sitting directly across from him. He studied him openly, finding him to be younger than he'd originally thought and certainly better looking, though the beard hid much of his face. The man seemed fit enough and in good health, but on closer inspection Nick could see that he was obviously not a manual laborer, for his hands were neither calloused nor rough. Nick wondered how he'd come to be indentured if he'd led a gentle life, and he wondered too at the depth of his involvement with Jordan.

Philip was studying Nick at the same time and with equal interest. He sensed a veiled hostility in Nick's regard and wondered at it. Philip kept his expression carefully respectful as he tried to find out a little more about their current situation.

"Where are we going?" Philip asked.

"Right now, back to our hotel. Once I've completed the rest of my business here in town we'll be returning to my home in Louisiana."

"Oh," he said tightly, thinking Harrison had followed through on his threat and sold him to a man who would put him to work draining swamps. It was not a happy thought. While he could give a day's labor as well as any man, he'd spent his entire life surrounded by books. He had hoped somehow

132

that it would continue that way.

"What can you do, Montgomery? Have you had any training in a trade?" Nick wanted to know what talents the man had. He couldn't very well go back home and tell his father he'd bought an indentured servant. His father would want to know why, and then he'd be forced to lie about everything. It was going to be difficult enough maintaining his pretense of being madly in love with Jordan. He wanted as few other complications as possible, so he had to come up with a plausible story explaining Montgomery's presence at Riverwood.

"No, I've never learned a trade as such," Philip answered honestly. Seeing the flash of irritation on Kane's face at his revelation, he hurried to add, "But I can read, write, and cipher." Philip said no more than the bare minimum, for he didn't want too many questions asked about his past. The less everyone knew about him, the better.

Nick had to struggle to hide his astonishment and his happiness over the news. "You're an educated man . . . How did you end up indentured?"

Philip felt his sister's eyes upon him and knew she was worried that he might say too much. He was very careful in his choice of words. "My parents were insistent that education was the key to improving one's lot in life, so they made sure I learned as much as possible. But things changed and times got hard. My parents died. The money, what little there was, quickly disappeared." He gave an expressive lift of his shoulders. "I'd heard that a strong mind and back and a willingness to work were all that was needed to make it here. This seemed the best way to make a fresh start."

Though he didn't want to, Nick felt his respect for the young man growing. "We'll see how good

133

you are once we get back to the hotel. I may have the perfect solution to making the best use of your talents."

Philip nodded, not at all afraid of having to prove himself.

"Speaking of the hotel," Slater interrupted, "have you given any thought to accommodations now?" He'd been sitting there quietly, noticing the slight discomfort both Nick and Jordan were showing in each other's company and growing ever more amused by the situation.

"Since our rooms are connected, I was hoping you'd be a gentleman and offer Jordan the use of yours. With all the work that needs to be done, I was thinking it would be better if I have her close by," Nick explained very logically. Not for one minute would he admit to himself that he wanted to keep her near to him so he could make sure she wasn't with Montgomery.

"I see your point," his friend agreed, his eyes sparkling even as he tried to hide a smile.

"Good. Then you'll agree to do it." Nick didn't appreciate Slater's sense of humor one bit.

"Have I ever let you down?"

"No, and don't start now."

Philip didn't like the thought of Jordan being in a room adjoining Kane's, and his phrase "with all the work that needs to be done" worried him. He let his gaze swing over to Jordan, but was surprised by how calm she looked. He wished he knew what was going on, but he realized that there was no way he was going to find anything out right now. Resigned to playing a guessing game for the time being, Philip settled back to wait out the ride.

When Jordan heard Nick tell Slater about the "work" that had to be done, it took a great deal of

134

willpower for her not to speak up, for it hurt her to find that they thought she needed so much improvement. She longed for the days at home, when she was always clean and well-groomed. She hated to think that she looked so bad that these two couldn't picture her beauty.

As much as it upset Jordan, though, she didn't blame them. She reminded herself that it was because of Nick that she was here with Philip and not still standing on the dock or being sold to someone who wanted a maid to scrub floors and clean. Soon she would get her first real bath in weeks—and then she would show them!

Thoughts of impressing Nick and Slater faded as she imagined herself in a tub of hot water, scrubbing herself clean with a scented cake of gentle soap. It would be heaven after the harsh conditions on the ship. For the first time in weeks, Jordan felt almost contented. Things seemed to be looking up.

That contentment instantly dimmed, though, when the reason for her being here in the first place crept insidiously back into her thoughts. Dominic Kane seemed pleased enough so far with the way things had turned out, but she wondered dismally how he would feel if he knew the truth about her . . . if he knew she was a murderer. She forced the thought away, refusing to dwell on it. She and Philip were safe now, and she had to make sure they stayed that way.

The carriage rolled to a stop before the hotel, and Jordan was impressed by her first sight of its grandeur. Obviously, Nick hadn't been exaggerating when he'd told her she'd be living a very comfortable life with him. He certainly had to have money if he could afford to stay here . . .

Carrying her single bag for her, Nick ushered her

quickly through the sumptuously appointed lobby, leaving Slater to see about getting the additional rooms that would be needed. She didn't say anything as he escorted her down the wide, carpeted hallway and unlocked the door to his room.

"This is where we'll be staying for now," Nick announced as he pushed the door wide to allow Jordan to enter before him.

It was a big, well-appointed room with a dresser, washstand, and massive four-poster bed. Jordan struggled to keep her eyes averted from the bed, for it seemed too personal, somehow.

"Your room is right through here." He led her to the connecting doorway and in gentlemanly fashion opened that for her, too.

The room beyond was as nice as Nick's, and she was surprised. "Are you sure your friend doesn't mind letting me take his room?"

"My friend's name is Slater MacKenzie, by the way, and no, I'm sure he doesn't mind," Nick answered easily, adding to himself, *He owes me.*

"Well, thank you," Jordan told him over her shoulder as she moved farther into her room and started to take off her cloak.

Suddenly Nick was there behind her, and his voice was a deep drawl that sent shivers down Jordan's spine as he helped her shed the garment.

"I'm sure Slater will be here shortly to get his things. Until then, make yourself comfortable. I'll be right next door. If you need anything just let me know." Nick found himself staring down at the slender slope of her shoulders and the nape of her neck, where a few stray strands of pale hair had escaped their strict confinement. For a second he longed to press a kiss to that delicate spot, but he managed to hold himself back, giving himself a

136

mental shake as he moved quickly away from her.

"I would like to take a bath." Jordan requested, turning to look up at him. It was important to her that he see her looking her best as soon as possible.

"I'll see that one is sent up." He found he couldn't deny her anything, and a vision of her bathing crystallized in his thoughts. Slater's knock at his door saved Nick, and he was glad when his friend walked right in with Philip following.

"We've got our rooms. They're the last two at the end of the hall on the opposite side," Slater announced as they came to stand in the doorway between the rooms. "And you can rest assured that Philip here can read and write. He took care of his own registration."

Nick was about to make an approving comment to his indentured servant when he noticed that Philip's gaze was locked with Jordan's. He scowled blackly.

"Good," Nick said sharply. "Now let's see how good he is at figuring. Jordan, we'll leave you to your privacy for the night, now. I'll see to ordering that bath you wanted."

"Thank you."

"Plan on breakfasting early. We have a lot to do tomorrow." With that he closed the door between the rooms and went to quiz Philip on his mathematical prowess.

Jordan stared at the closed door for a moment after they'd gone, wondering how in the world she was going to get the chance to talk to Philip and explain everything. She had seen the concern in his eyes, but there was no way she could tell him anything with Nick and that too-observant friend of his, Slater, there. She hoped that later on she might be able to sneak out of her room and find Philip. It

137

would only take a few minutes to clear everything up, and she hoped he had no quarrel with what she'd decided to do. They really hadn't had much choice in the matter, but at least this way they were still together.

Jordan sat down on the edge of the bed to think over all that had happened since they'd arrived in Mobile earlier that day. The bed's softness delighted her, immediately distracting her from her troubled thoughts. A sigh of ecstasy escaped her at the prospect of finally getting a good night's sleep again after all those weeks on the miserably crowded ship. Knowing she had a few minutes before her bath arrived, she took the time to pull the pins out of her hair and run her fingers through the silken length. That done, she couldn't resist lying back for a moment. With great relish, she stretched out and closed her eyes, intending only to rest for a minute. She could hear the sound of the men's voices through the closed door, and though she couldn't make out what they were saying, she was lulled into a sense of security by their deep mellow tones. She slept.

Nick studied the column of figures Philip had just added and was impressed by his ability. "This is good," he told him. "You've done well."

"Thank you."

"There's no need to thank me. You're going to be earning your keep."

"That's what I intend to do."

"Good." Nick eyed him up and down, noticing the poor condition of his clothes. "I take it you don't have much in the way of clothing?"

"No. There wasn't much I could bring," he managed not to lie.

"Then we'll take care of that tomorrow. For now,

go on back to your room. I'll see you in the morning . . . early."

"Yes, sir." Philip left the room after bidding them both good night.

"Well, well, well," Slater spoke up from where he sat on Nick's bed, his back against the headboard, his long legs crossed casually at the ankle. "This has been quite an eventful evening for you."

Nick's smile was satisfied. "Yes, it has, hasn't it?"

"Do you really think this is going to work?" He gestured toward the adjoining room.

His smile faded. "It better work considering all the money I've got invested."

"Well, what do you say we go out and celebrate your good luck? Madame LaFleur's is still waiting."

"I don't know . . ." He hedged, hesitant to leave Jordan there alone.

"You're soon going to be a married man, Nick."

Nick glowered at him for reminding him of that part of it.

"Think about it. Once we get back home your bachelor days will be over."

He grimaced distastefully.

"Trust me, you need this one last fling. The girls at Madame LaFleur's are very special."

"All right, all right. Let's go."

They were heading for the door when someone knocked. Nick answered it to find that it was the maids with Jordan's bath.

"You can come through here if you like. Let me tell her that you're here." Nick knocked on the connecting door. "Jordan?"

Jordan had been so exhausted that she'd fallen into a very sound sleep. At Nick's call, she came awake, only vaguely aware of her surroundings. She called out sleepily as she sat up, "Yes? What is it?"

Nick opened the door. "Jordan, the—" He stopped in mid-sentence at the sight of her sitting there with her hair down around her shoulders and her cheeks flushed from sleep. Even in her disheveled state she looked absolutely beautiful, and it left him floundering for words. "Jordan, ah . . . I didn't know you were asleep . . . ah . . . The maids are here with your bath."

"Oh . . ." She stared at the tall, handsome man standing in her bedroom and blinked in confusion. She paused briefly to orient herself and then swung her legs off the bed and stood up, "Oh, good, I can hardly wait. Please, have them come in."

"Ladies," Nick invited as he stepped aside to allow the women passage. He watched Jordan as she greeted them with open warmth and genuine delight. He found it difficult to believe that she could really be so thrilled over a bath, but for some odd reason, the thought that he'd provided it for her filled him with pleasure.

"Nick? Are you ready?" Slater's reminder brought him back to reality.

"Yes . . ." he answered over his shoulder, and then spoke to Jordan again. "Jordan, I'll be going out for a while, so I'll bid you good night now. If you need anything more, I'm sure one of the maids will be able to help you."

Jordan looked up intending to answer, but Nick was already closing the door. She wondered what had caused him to hurry so.

Chapter Ten

Nick's expression was a bit pensive as he sat down across from Slater in the carriage they'd hired to take them to Madame LaFleur's.

"You look worried," Slater remarked as he leaned back against the side of the carriage and folded his arms across his chest.

"I'm not," he denied. "It's just hard to believe everything's worked out so well."

"Do you really think Jordan's going to be a good enough actress to fool your father?"

"What's so difficult about pretending to be in love with me?" Nick demanded, offended by his friend's suggestion that it would be a hard thing to do.

Slater erupted into laughter at Nick's reaction. "Nothing, I'm sure. It's just that you don't know much about Jordan yet. I mean, how can you be certain that she'll be convincing?"

Nick grew thoughtful. "Once she's cleaned up and I've bought her some new clothes, she'll look the part. She's got a lot of spirit and she's quick enough. Whatever she doesn't know, I think I can teach her before we get back."

"What about her past? How are you going to

avoid that?"

"Her real background doesn't matter. I'll make something up that's believable but can't be verified."

"You sound like you've pretty much got it all figured out."

"I think so. The hardest thing, though, is going to be convincing my father that I'm really in love with her."

"You don't think he'll believe you when you bring her home?"

"I think he'll have his doubts after all the trouble I've been having."

"Well, you're just going to have to pretend, that's all. Draw on some of your past experiences."

Nick shook his head. "I've liked a lot of women, but I've never been in love with one."

"It's easy," he advised.

"If it's so easy, why haven't I fallen in love before?"

"How should I know?" Slater exclaimed in exasperation. "Besides, that's not what we're talking about. We're talking about now . . . about you and Jordan."

Nick only grunted.

"This is what you wanted, remember, Nick?"

"Yes."

"Now, listen, there are some important things to remember if you want people to think you're in love."

"Like what?" Nick was suddenly very interested. He needed all the advice he could get on this subject.

"Well, when you're in love with a woman you can't stand to be away from her. You want to be with her every minute of every day. When you're with her, all you can think about is holding her and kissing her and hopefully, some time in the not-too-distant future, making love to her." A glimmer of the abiding pain he lived with glistened in his eyes for a moment as he remembered his life with Francesca.

"I've felt that way about quite a few women in my time, but it's never lasted much beyond a few weeks," Nick observed, thinking back over his past love affairs.

Slater gave him a strained look. "Pretend this time, Nick."

"I know, I know. What else?"

"If you're really going to make your father believe you love her, you've got to act like her happiness is more important to you than your own. You have to put her first in all things."

"All right."

"And there's one other thing."

"Which is?"

"The most important thing to remember if you're going to satisfy your father is that when you're in love, there's not another woman alive who can tempt you—not even if she took all her clothes off and danced in front of you naked."

Nick laughed out loud as he imagined the scene, and he wondered if there was any woman alive who could wield that kind of power over his emotions. "The real thing is that powerful?"

"It is, and I'm telling you now, you're going to have to be *very* careful."

"Why? About what?"

"You know how charming you can be when you set your mind to it, just remember Jordan is a female and just as susceptible as the next woman."

"You think she might really fall in love with me?"

143

The idea had never entered his mind. He'd been too busy concentrating on the business end of their arrangement.

Slater nodded. "It's definitely a possibility, and there's something else . . ."

"What?"

"Watch out, or you might find yourself falling in love with her."

"Never." Nick was quick to deny that it might happen. "This is strictly a marriage of convenience. I hope I come to like her during the next few months. It would certainly make our time together more palatable. But fall in love with her? Impossible."

"You're sure about that?"

"Positive. The only thing I'm interested in is keeping my father happy and claiming Riverwood."

"Well, I hope this 'marriage' works out the way you've got it planned."

"It will."

Nick sounded far too confident for Slater's peace of mind, and he knew he had to warn him about the one thing that might disrupt all of his carefully laid plans.

"Now, there's one last thing you need to realize about this marriage if you're going to prove anything to your father," Slater began.

"What now?"

"Fidelity. It means everything in marriage . . ."

His final observation conjured up immediate thoughts of Jordan and Philip, and Nick wondered if she would be able to stay away from her shipboard lover while they were carrying out this charade. He certainly hoped so. He knew he could hold up his end of the bargain, and he was counting on her to do the same.

"There should be an overriding desire to be faithful to each other no matter what," Slater finished.

"I won't have any trouble."

"What about Montgomery?"

"I've been thinking about him, and I think the best course is to tell my father that he's an accountant I've hired. There would be no reason for my father to question me on it as long as things go according to plan."

"Are you going to let him stay in the main house?"

"No. He'll be staying out in the old overseer's cabin," he answered quickly as their carriage drew to a stop before the infamous house of ill-repute.

They descended, their mood jovial. They were ready for a little relaxation and a little celebrating, and this seemed the perfect place. Their knock at the door was answered by Madame LaFleur herself, a tall, buxom, hard-looking blond of indiscriminate age, who was wearing a skin-tight, low-cut red velvet gown.

"Good evening, gentlemen," she greeted in her throaty voice as she studied them both. "Come on in."

She held the door wide and sized them up as they entered. She found she couldn't decide which one was the more attractive—the taller one who was darkly handsome with an electrifying presence or the one who had sun-bronzed hair, a more rugged physique, and a smile that could charm the pants off an old maid. As she eyed them, she decided it was a draw. They were both delicious and promised to liven things up considerably. Her girls were going to enjoy this.

"Ladies! We have visitors," Madame LaFleur announced.

At her direction, Nick and Slater strode from the dimly lighted, red-papered foyer with its curving staircase into the parlor, where two seductively clad young women were lounging on two overstuffed, red velvet sofas. As they caught sight of Nick and Slater, they came to their feet and rushed forth to meet them.

"Hello . . ." the dark-haired, curvaceous woman called Delilah drawled as she approached Nick. She slipped an arm through his to rub her full breasts against him. "My name's Delilah. What's yours?"

"Nick," he responded with a smile.

Delilah appeared to be the kind of woman who instinctively knew exactly what a man wanted and never hesitated to give it to him. The thought appealed to Nick. He was looking forward to a night of pure abandon and sexual release. As Slater had said, this would be his last chance for a long time to come, and he might as well take advantage of it. Yet even as he contemplated the heated hours to come, Nick found himself thinking about Jordan and the way she'd looked when he'd awakened her.

"Well, Nick," she said running a hand up his chest, "would you like to have a drink down here . . . or go upstairs and enjoy one there?"

"Why don't we just go on upstairs now?" he agreed quickly, trying to put thoughts of his future "bride" from his mind.

"Oooh, you sound like my kind of man."

"What kind of man is that?" he asked.

"One who likes action instead of small talk. I've never been big on chitchat."

"Believe me, Delilah, talking is the last thing I feel like doing tonight."

The tall redhead named Charice came to join Slater, and he was delighted. He was standing with his

146

arm around her talking in low tones when Nick and Delilah started from the room.

"Take good care of him, Delilah," Slater called out. He earned a black scowl from Nick when he added, "He deserves a little extra attention tonight."

"Oh? Why is that? Has he done something really special?"

"He's getting married soon."

Her amber eyes lit up at the news. The predatory female in her was pleased that she would be taking another woman's man, even if only for a little while. "Well then, I'm just going to have to show you an extra good time so you'll remember it, and me, for a long, long while." Delilah's smile was hot and avid.

"Enjoy yourself, Nick," Slater chuckled as they disappeared from the room.

Now that they were gone, Charice took the opportunity to draw Slater over to one of the sofas. "Would you like a drink, Slater? We have some wonderful brandy and some very potent bourbon."

"Bourbon sounds fine."

Slater watched in appreciation as the voluptuous beauty moved sinuously to the small bar and poured him a liberal amount. When she came back to hand it to him, she leaned forward just enough so he could get a revealing look at her cleavage. Then she sat down closely beside him and rubbed provocatively against him.

"Are you in a hurry tonight?"

"No, I've got all the time in the world," he told her and then wondered at the tinge of regret that he felt.

"Good," Charice responded huskily. She kissed him hungrily, and he returned the embrace with equal fervor. When the kiss ended, she breathlessly cooed in Slater's ear, describing all of her very special talents to him. It was all the encouragement Slater needed. Keeping an arm around her, he stood up, holding her firmly against him with one arm and keeping the tumbler of bourbon safely balanced in the other hand.

As they made their way from the room, Slater found he was a little tense. He had come here tonight because he wanted to relax and enjoy himself. To his distress, though, thoughts of the conversation he'd had with Nick in the carriage kept haunting him, and with those thoughts came vivid memories of a woman with hair the color of midnight and skin as soft as silk.

In that moment, Slater was glad Charice was a redhead, for he needed to forget, not to be reminded. He dragged Charice against him and kissed her wildly. His embrace was passionate, almost too much so, but Charice didn't notice. She reveled in it.

Despite the desperation of his kiss, Slater found that the woman in his memories was still there, alive, deep inside of him, and he wondered if he would ever find peace without her. Francesca had been the one woman whose touch had left him burning with an unquenchable flame and whose kiss had given him the only sheer bliss he'd ever known. She had been his heaven. Her death had condemned him to hell. This beauty in his arms might satisfy the aching physical needs of his body, but there was no other woman alive who could heal the ache in his heart.

"Are you all right?" Charice asked, drawing back to see the sudden bleakness in his expression.

Slater finished off the bourbon in one swallow, then gave her a big, deceptive smile. "I'm fine," he lied, and he started up the stairs, pulling her along with him.

Nick pulled on his pants and shirt before he turned to look at Delilah. Even though he'd started out wanting to enjoy himself to the fullest, something had changed. Somewhere in the midst of the unadulterated lust he'd just shared with the willing Delilah he'd discovered a great emptiness.

Oh, Nick knew he'd performed admirably, and they had both been satisfied by the encounter. But while she wanted to continue all night long, he could only think of escaping her clinging nearness. He'd found no peace or relief in her embrace. Nick was puzzled by his reaction, and he could make little sense of it. He only knew that he felt trapped, almost stifled, and he wanted to leave.

"She must be very special," Delilah said with a bittersweet smile as she rolled to her side, posing artfully as she watched him.

"Who?" Nick asked distracted from his disturbing thoughts.

She gave a soft, derisive laugh. "Your fiancée of course."

"Oh . . ." At the mention of Jordan he suddenly felt even worse.

"You must really love her."

"Why do you say that?"

Delilah gave him a knowing look. "What we just shared was wonderful, but let's face it, your heart wasn't in it. Your thoughts were somewhere else . . . *with* someone else."

Nick had sense enough not to argue. Try as he might, he'd been unable to completely wipe Jordan's image from his thoughts.

"She's a very lucky girl to have a man like you. I hope she realizes it."

Inwardly, Nick grimaced. Instead of pleasing him, her compliments left him feeling jaded. He finished dressing quickly, tossed her money on the nightstand and headed for the door. "Good-bye, Delilah."

After the maids had gone, Jordan lost herself in the absolute glory of her first hot bath since leaving England. It was pure heaven. The water felt like liquid silk upon her body, and the perfumed soap the hotel provided was luxurious. She scrubbed every inch of her skin until it glowed and then shampooed her hair until it was squeaky clean. Jordan lay back and soaked in the tub until the water got too chilly for her to remain comfortably. Regretting that she had to get out, she vowed never again to do without a daily bath.

Jordan wrapped a fluffy towel around her slim body and then dried her hair as best she could with the extra towel they'd given her. That done, she sat on the side of the bed where she could see herself in the mirror over the washstand and worked at combing out the tangles. She had just finished when there came a soft knock at the hallway door.

"Yes? Who is it?"

"It's me, Jordan, Philip."

Jordan hurried to the door, but only opened it wide enough so she could talk to him. "I'm not dressed. Give me a few minutes to get some clothes on and I'll come down to your room."

"Why don't you just let me in?"

"Harrison told Nick that we were lovers, and he believed it, just like everyone else did on the ship. I

150

don't want to risk him coming back early and finding you here."

Philip groaned, but did not argue the necessity of lying to Nick. "My room number is 224, the last door on the right."

"I won't be long."

Jordan tied her hair back with a single ribbon, then pulled on her clothes. With one last glance to make sure she look presentable, she hurried down the hall to join her brother.

"Come in," Philip called out when she knocked on his door.

"I made it." She was a trifle breathless as she hurried inside after taking a quick look down the vacant hall. She'd been afraid that she might come face to face with Nick on her way to see Philip. Feeling safe knowing that he wasn't back, she closed the door firmly behind her.

Philip didn't understand what was going on, and he wanted an immediate explanation. His voice was stern as he demanded, "All right, Jordan, what's going on? I don't like your staying in a room that's connected to Kane's."

"It's nothing like what you think," she offered quickly, wanting to soothe him with the truth.

"It's not what I think, it's what *is*. You're practically living with the man!"

"You mean my fiancé, don't you?" she ventured and then waited nervously for his reaction.

"Your *what?*" He stared at her aghast.

"Nick wants me to marry him, and I've agreed."

"Marry him? Are you out of your mind? You don't even know him!" Philip was staggered by the idea.

"I'm hardly out of my mind," she responded evenly.

151

Philip couldn't imagine how she'd gotten herself into this. She had no idea what kind of man Nick was! Why on God's earth would she consent to marry him? "I won't allow you to do this."

"You can't stop me, Philip, and you won't want to once you know everything. Now, hush a minute, and give me a chance to explain."

"This had better be good," he growled, dropping down on the bed while she sat in the only chair.

"I know it sounds crazy, but this really is a godsend."

"You're so innocent, Jordan . . . You don't know what you're letting yourself in for!"

"Oh, yes I do."

"How can you say that when you're planning to marry a man you don't even know?"

"I am going to marry Nick, but we've already agreed that it will be a marriage in name only."

"What? What's going on?"

"I don't know all the facts yet. He's promised he'd tell me everything tomorrow. I only know that for some reason he needs to get married right away, and since he doesn't really want to get married, he has decided to buy a wife. That's why we're here." She went on to explain to him about their conversation in the warehouse. "I told him I'd do it, but only if he bought your papers, too."

"I'm sure he was pleased with that idea, especially if he thought we were lovers."

Jordan shrugged. "I don't care. All that mattered was that we be together."

Philip thought the whole thing sounded strange, but the fact that they weren't going to be parted tempered his reaction. He got up from the bed and went to kneel on one knee before her. He knew what a true innocent she was, and he wanted to make sure that she wouldn't be hurt by this arrange-ment of Kane's. He took her hands in his as he looked deep into her eyes. "You're sure that it's go-ing to be a marriage in name only?"

"Quite," she assured him, going on happily, "and then, when he doesn't need to be married any longer, we're going to annul the whole thing. Then you and I will both be free."

"This is wonderful . . . It sounds almost too good to be true." Philip was thrilled, and he took her in his arms to give her a big hug. "It's just so good to know that we're not going to be separated."

Suddenly, without warning, the unlocked bed-room door flew open and in stalked Nick, his face a mask of disapproval.

Chapter Eleven

Nick stood in the doorway, staring at Philip and Jordan. He couldn't believe what he was seeing or what he'd just overheard.

After leaving Madame LaFleurs', Nick had returned to his room at the hotel. Seeing the glow of lamplight from beneath the connecting door, he'd thought Jordan was still awake, and he decided to ask if she had everything she needed to spend a comfortable night. He knocked and waited for a response, but when none was forthcoming, he became both concerned and suspicious. Nick opened the door only to have his worst fears confirmed. Jordan was gone. He'd known immediately where he would find her.

Nick had been furious as he'd started down the hall to Montgomery's room. He'd told Jordan that he wouldn't tolerate such behavior; and yet here she was, the moment his back was turned, running off to her lover. If she couldn't respect his wishes in this matter, if she couldn't be trusted to keep her word, then there would be no point in going through with the bargain.

As Nick stared at the intimate little scene before him, he was stunned at the depth of affection and caring that was mirrored on their faces. Jordan looked almost radiantly happy in Philip's arms.

At the sight of Nick glowering at her, she quickly pushed away from Philip. Feeling guilty about being found in what looked like a compromising position, a telltale blush stained her cheeks. "Nick . . ." she gasped in surprise.

"I thought we had an understanding, Jordan," he said in clipped tones, his accusing gaze upon her.

"We do . . . it's just that . . ." Jordan was still in shock from his unexpected appearance, and she wasn't thinking clearly enough to make up a good lie quickly.

"I told you that this dalliance of yours could not continue. I instructed you at the start about how things were to be. Did you forget your promises to me the moment I left the hotel room?"

Philip was infuriated by Nick's insults. He surged to his feet, his hands clinched at his sides. He wanted to throttle Nick for his insolence, and only barely restrained himself.

Nick understood the threat in his action and also realized that Philip had managed to restrain himself. He turned a deadly glare on the indentured servant. "Wise decision," he said coldly.

"Please . . ." Sensing her brother's temper was about to explode, Jordan moved between them, wanting to diffuse the situation. She couldn't believe the terrible timing of Nick's arrival. "I'll go on back to my room. Good night, Philip." She shot him a pleading look.

He saw her look, and the belligerence went out of his stance. "Good night, Jordan."

Nick stood back to allow Jordan to pass, then gave Philip one last ominous glance before following her from the room. He shut the door firmly behind him.

155

"Jordan," he said her name with sharp emphasis and stopped her rapid flight down the hall.

Jordan drew a deep breath, then turned toward him, her emerald eyes wary and questioning. "Yes?"

"Join me in my room, please. I believe there are a few things we need to discuss."

Jordan gave a slight nod of her head, then continued on her way. Nick was surprised by the quiet dignity she commanded, and his initial anger at having found her with Montgomery faded.

The white-hot haze of his fury slowly easing, Nick found himself quietly observing her as she walked away. He realized for the first time that she was wearing a different gown, and though it was plain and serviceable in style, it fit her quite nicely. His gaze followed the rhythmic sway of her hips as she moved, and an unwelcome heat began to build within him. His warm regard lifted to her pale hair, and he visually caressed the silken tresses. Her hair shone like moonglow in the softly lighted hallway, and he wondered vaguely what it would feel like to run his hands through it.

When Jordan reached the door to his room and paused to look back at him questioningly, Nick gave himself a hard mental shake and hurried after her. He told himself sternly that he wasn't attracted to her and that it didn't matter to him personally what she did with Montgomery just as long as she waited until after the annulment. This was a business deal between them—nothing more.

"What was it you wanted to talk about?" Jordan asked once they were inside the room. She seemed coolly composed, while in truth, she was trembling inside for fear of matching wits with him. He held their futures in his hands. She couldn't afford to upset him.

"If our bargain is to work, you must hold to what we agreed upon. I thought you understood that your liaison with Montgomery could not continue. You must put an end to it now, before anything goes any further."

"Philip and I were merely having a conversation," she returned. "There was no harm in that."

Nick gave a harsh laugh. "A conversation is one thing. What I saw was something else. But even if I hadn't walked in on you, consider how it would look if someone else discovered that my fiancée was spending time alone with another man in a hotel room."

"I'm not your fiancée yet!"

"As far as I'm concerned, we sealed the deal in the warehouse earlier this evening. Or have you forgotten?"

"I haven't forgotten anything!" Jordan was torn between the frustration of wanting to defend herself and the misery of knowing she couldn't. She wanted to tell Nick the truth, but she feared the consequences. She couldn't let him find out about her past. Tears threatened, and she fought against them. Afraid that he might see her distress, she turned away, meaning to escape to her room.

Nick interpreted her action as an arrogant dismissal, and he erupted in anger. Grabbing her by the arm, he swung her back around to face him and took her by both shoulders.

"Jordan . . ." he began threateningly, having every intention of lecturing her further on her behavior. He stopped abruptly, though, when he saw the sheen of tears in her eyes. He immediately assumed she was crying for the loss of her lover, and annoyance filled him. His gaze dropped to her mouth. Though her expression was proud, her lips were trembling.

Some driving hunger, some compelling need, filled Nick. He wanted to force all thoughts of Montgomery right out of her head. His eyes darkened, and he was like a man possessed as his mouth claimed hers. Jordan knew it was going to happen but was unable to prevent it.

"No!" she cried, but it was too late.

With unerring precision, Nick's lips found Jordan's and began to plunder their softness. It was a fiery kiss, an explosion of wonder that rocked them both. Without thought, his grip on her changed from a firm hold to a caress. He urged her closer gently, and in that moment they molded together, full breasts to hard-muscled chest.

For one long sweet moment, she let herself enjoy the embrace. Nick was, after all, the handsomest man she'd ever seen, and in a way, he had rescued her from what could have been a terrible life. But just as she was about to loop her arms around his neck to melt closer to him, her sanity returned. She couldn't allow this to happen! She couldn't allow herself to feel anything for this man!

"No!" Jordan panicked, backing away from him. She was afraid of what he was making her feel, and she had to fight it. It would be far too easy to surrender to this unexpected desire. She wasn't about to let that happen.

"Jordan?" Nick frowned, startled by her reaction and by his own. Even after his time with Delilah, Jordan's one simple kiss left his body throbbing with excitement.

"How can you have the nerve to lecture me on keeping my word where our bargain's concerned?! What about *your* word? You told me this arrangement would be in name only."

Nick's mouth thinned and his gaze hardened. "You

needn't worry, Jordan. I'm a man of honor."

"It's not your honor that's worrying me!"

"Jordan," he drawled, affecting a look of pure boredom while he fought down the desire to take her back in his arms and kiss her again, "I've been with many women who were far prettier than you. You needn't be concerned that I'm so overcome by your . . . er . . . 'charms' that I won't be able to control myself."

His words, so casually flung at her, stung, and she was strangely hurt by the thought that he'd been unaffected by the embrace. She refused to allow it to show, though, reminding herself that all that mattered was that she and Philip not be separated. "Then why did you kiss me just now?"

"Let's face it, if we're going to convince anyone we're madly in love, we're going to have to learn to act the part."

"In public only! That was our agreement!" Jordan came back at him.

Nick was growing more and more aggravated by her attitude. No other woman had ever acted this way when he'd kissed her. "Slater seemed to have some doubts about your ability to carry off the charade, and frankly, though I defended you at the time, I'm beginning to think he might have been right."

The thought that Nick might change his mind and decide not to go through with their deal left Jordan suddenly nervous and a little uncertain. "You don't have to worry. When the time comes, I'll be the most adoring fiancée you can imagine."

"I hope so. This is too important a matter to take any risks."

"Why is this so important? Why are you being forced to find a wife so quickly?"

Nick had meant to explain things to her tomorrow,

but he figured tonight was just as good a time as any to set things straight between them once and for all. Taking off his coat, he threw it casually on the bed, then started to untie his cravat. As he began to speak, he tried hard not to let any of his emotions show.

"My father is a very strong-willed, very successful man. Ever since I reached my majority, he's wanted me to settle down and start a family. I knew he felt that way, but until lately he hadn't pressed the issue. A few months ago, though, the doctors discovered that he has a serious health problem. They believe that he doesn't have long to live."

"Oh . . . I'm sorry," she murmured, her eyes meeting his in a look of compassionate understanding. She had lost her parents not too long before, and she remembered all too well how awful it had been.

Nick looked down into Jordan's sympathetic gaze and for a moment found himself wanting to tell her everything . . . how he'd been devastated over the news of his father's illness and how he'd felt completely helpless in the face of it. With an exercise of will, he managed not to blurt out his life's story. He frowned as he wondered what there was about her that encouraged such revelations from him when he'd only known her for a matter of a few hours. The thought was unsettling.

"There's nothing that can be done," he said in a brusque tone to cover his discomfort, "and he knows it. That's why he did what he did."

"What did he do?"

"He added a clause to his will stating that unless I married by September 15 of this year, I would be disinherited."

"What about your mother? Couldn't she do anything about it?"

"My mother's dead. She died when I was young.

160

There's just the two of us . . . my father and me."

"So you've got to find a wife or lose everything . . ."

"Yes. If I don't find a bride soon, my father's estate will be given over to the church upon his death, and I can't let that happen . . ."

Nick said it so fiercely that Jordan got the wrong impression. She didn't understand that he loved his father deeply and that he loved Riverwood, too. She didn't understand that he'd labored beside his father for years to make the plantation into the showplace it was now. To her, it sounded like the money was all he cared about. He came across as a greedy, conniving, self-serving bastard, and the sympathy she'd felt toward him cooled.

"I see," she replied. "So, in essence, what we have to do is fool your dying father into thinking we're a love match so you can claim your inheritance. Right?"

. The way she phrased it, his plan sounded terribly calculating, but Nick suddenly felt too downhearted to try to convince her otherwise. "That's right. You're future, as well as mine, rides on the ultimate success of our bargain."

"I'll do my part," she agreed, knowing it was her only way out.

"That's all I expect," he replied, turning away to unbutton his shirt. "I'll see you in the morning. After breakfast, we'll see about getting you some suitable clothes."

Summarily dismissed, Jordan took the opportunity to retreat to her room. She quickly changed into her nightgown before lying down, but as weary as she was, sleep proved elusive.

The discovery of Nick's true motivation added to her growing disillusionment. For a little while she'd

161

almost thought he was wonderful . . . a knight in shining armor, so to speak. Now she realized just how wrong her judgment could be. He was nothing like what she'd imagined. Attractive though he was, he was a man without a conscience. He was a man who would do whatever he had to in order to achieve his objective. It saddened her, and when she finally fell asleep, it was with a heavy heart.

Nick shed everything except his pants and stretched out on his bed, his arms folded behind his head. He wanted to sleep, but his mind refused to let him rest. In the silence of his thoughts he debated the wisdom of all that he'd done. He hated deceiving his father, yet he could think of no other solution that would make his last days happy. He wanted him to believe that he'd found the woman of his dreams and that he was going to be happily married.

Though it sounded simple when he thought of it that way, somehow it was far more complicated. Finding Jordan in Montgomery's arms had sent a flash of fury through him the likes of which he'd never known before, and he still couldn't figure out the strange sense of lacking that had possessed him while he was with Delilah. The thought of Jordan's kiss and his reaction to it left him frowning into the darkness, and he quickly told himself that he was worrying needlessly. None of it was important. All that mattered was making sure his father's remaining months were contented ones.

Nick settled down then, his sense of purpose firmly restored. But as he closed his eyes against the blackness of the night an ethereal vision of Jordan crept into his thoughts. It was quite a while before he slept soundly.

* * *

Philip's emotions were running hot and high, and he, too, could not sleep. He'd been stalking about his room like a caged beast ever since Jordan had left with Kane. It had been ugly listening to Kane insult his sister, and he realized now that it was a good thing she'd come between them.

Philip hated that fact Kane thought so little of Jordan as to believe that she could be his mistress, but for their continued safety he could do nothing to change his mind. They were caught up in a set of circumstances that they could not alter. He was going to have to do whatever Kane wanted—whether he liked it or not. He would support and help Jordan all that he could, but he knew he would have to be very careful. It wouldn't be smart to make Kane angry. He didn't look like a forgiving sort of man.

Swallowing what was left of his battered pride, Philip finally went to bed. He turned out the light and lay there staring into the darkness as the hours crept slowly by.

As Slater dressed in Charice's room at Madame LaFleur's, he pondered his quixotic mood. He didn't understand why he felt as if he'd betrayed Francesca when all he had done was to bed a willing wench. Francesca was dead, he told himself. A man couldn't be faithful to a memory forever. Still, the aching in his heart didn't ease. She had a hold on him even now, and he wondered if he would ever be able to get on with the rest of his life.

"Slater . . . don't leave," Charice begged in a husky voice. "It's not light yet . . ."

"Sorry, little darling, but I have to go," he answered. She had been more than accommodating in the heat of their couplings, but enough was enough.

He needed to breathe some fresh air instead of stale perfume, to look up at the clear night sky and see the twinkling stars.

"You'll come back again?" She was hopeful. There were very few men around like Slater MacKenzie.

"Next time I'm in town."

"I'll be waiting," she promised, and she meant it.

Slater half expected to find Nick waiting for him. He was surprised to discover that he'd left long ago, and he couldn't help but smile.

Slater's smile stayed with him all the way back to the hotel. Nick was probably going to use the excuse that he had to check on Jordan as his reason for not staying at Madame LaFleur's longer, but Slater knew that the truth of it went much deeper than that. His friend probably wasn't even aware of it yet, but time was going to tell. Slater grinned—he was going to enjoy this . . .

Chapter Twelve

It was morning, and after finally getting a few hours of sound sleep, Nick was feeling much better. His confidence in what he was doing had returned, and for the first time in months he faced a day without the oppressive weight of his father's commandment hanging over him. He believed he had everything well in hand.

Nick reviewed his plans for the day as he stood before the mirror to finish tying his tie. First, there was breakfast. He needed to see how Jordan conducted herself at a meal so he could gauge how much she knew about manners. He did not relish the thought of tutoring her in the social graces, but he would do whatever he had to to make sure this worked out. Jordan seemed quick enough, so he hoped he wouldn't have too much trouble.

Following breakfast, Nick intended to take Jordan to the best *couturière* in town. Since she was going to have to impress his father, he wanted her outward appearance to be perfect. He would see that she got the very best of everything. From her shoes to her hats, no part of her appearance would be open to criticism. Once he knew her manners were passable and her wardrobe correct, then he would be able to relax and concentrate on playing his role.

Nick was just turning away from the mirror when Slater knocked at his door. "Come in," he said.

Slater entered without delay, eyeing him with interest as he crossed the room. "You look rather bright this morning. Had an early night, did you?"

Nick had known he would hear about leaving LaFleur's early. "I managed to get a little sleep. What about you?"

"Sleep wasn't what I had on my mind last night."

"So, Charice was quite entertaining, was she?" Nick grinned at his friend.

"Delilah wasn't?"

"She was a woman of rare qualities."

"Weren't they both?" They chuckled in easy male camaraderie. "So why did you leave early? I thought you'd be waiting for me downstairs."

"I had too much on my mind last night," Nick answered evasively.

"Like Montgomery?"

"Among other things."

"It couldn't have been the girl, could it?"

"Jordan? No . . ." he said disparagingly. "Why would I come back here because of her?"

Slater gave him an enigmatic smile as he goaded, "I thought maybe you were more pleased with your bargain than you let on."

"No, Jordan doesn't mean anything to me. Oh, she'll be pretty enough once I get her the right clothes to wear and teach her how to behave in public. But there'll never be any more to it than just a friendly business arrangement. We're both in this for our own convenience, that's all."

"Whatever you say."

Slater's tone sounded suspiciously mocking, but when Nick glanced at him sharply, there was no emotion on his face. He looked merely interested, leaving

Nick to wonder if he was overreacting.

Changing the subject, Nick asked, "Could you do me a favor and keep an eye on Montgomery for me today? I'm going to be busy with Jordan and won't have the time."

"Sure. Shall I get the man some new clothes? If you're really going to tell your father that he's an accountant, then he's going to have to look the part."

"I suppose you're right. Get whatever he needs and let me know the cost." Nick was interrupted as Jordan knocked softly on the connecting door and then came in.

Jordan was in a much better mood this morning. Through the long hours of the night she had made a fierce determination to try to put the memory of Nick's kiss firmly from her and to remember that, as much as she didn't like his reasons for doing what he was doing, it was still to her benefit.

Jordan had hoped that by accepting the things she couldn't change she would have some peace of mind, and so she had until Nick had knocked on her door earlier that morning to let her know how soon they'd be leaving for breakfast. He hadn't shaved yet, and the dark beginnings of his beard had lent him a rakish, almost dangerous look that had left her nearly breathless. She'd been tongue-tied, and was only able to answer him in monosyllables. She felt utterly stupid when he disappeared back into his own room again.

Knowing they were going to be seen in public together, Jordan had made certain she looked her best, fixing her hair in a soft style that drew it away from her face and then let it fall around her shoulders in a cascade of loose curls. Pleased with the effect, she donned her dress and, after smoothing the wrinkles from it, went to let Nick know she was ready.

"Nick . . . I'm ready now," she announced before

167

she saw that Slater was with him. "Oh . . . Mr. Mac-
Kenzie . . . I'm sorry . . . I didn't mean to interrupt."

"Slater, please," he invited quickly. "And you're not
interrupting."

His gallantry was rewarded with a blinding smile,
and for a moment Slater was nearly struck speechless
by her unaffected beauty. The night before on the
dock, he'd thought she had reasonable potential, but
nothing in his imagination had prepared him for the
sight of her this morning. She was lovely — not in the
flashy way of some women, but beautiful in her own
right. She had an elegant presence about her, to say
nothing of her natural good looks. Her hair was a
tawny mane of tumbling curls, her peaches-and-cream
complexion was flawless, and her figure, while not
voluptuous, was perfectly proportioned. He knew that
if she could do such wondrous things for the plain,
ordinary dress she was now wearing, she was going to
look fantastic once she was outfitted properly.

"Slater, then. Good morning," she was saying, a
little more at ease in his company.

"You look lovely this morning," he complimented.

"Why, thank you," she replied, beaming. It thrilled
her that he'd noticed the change in her appearance.

In that moment, Slater knew for sure that Nick was
being less than honest with himself about his real reason for rushing back to the hotel the night before.
Slater knew that had Jordan been waiting for him, he
would have rushed back right away, too. *Hell,* he
thought wryly, *I would never have left in the first
place!* Whether his friend would admit it or not, he'd
gotten lucky this time, and he hoped Nick realized it
before it was too late.

"Well, we've got to get going. We've got a lot to do
this morning," Nick said as he opened the door and
held it for Jordan. "If you'll take care of that one thing

for me, we can meet back here around noon."

"I'll see you then," Slater quickly agreed, and he watched with interest as Nick ushered Jordan from the room. There was a definite male possessiveness in the way his friend stayed right with her, and Slater was forced to stifle a grin.

"Good bye, Slater." Jordan was completely oblivious to the undercurrents of the situation as she stepped out into the hall ahead of Nick. She thought Slater much less threatening in the daylight, and she was pleased that he'd asked her to call him by his first name.

Jordan was very much aware of Nick beside her as they walked down the hall to the stairs. When she'd seen him earlier that morning, he'd left her stammering over her own words. Now, dressed in a dark, fashionably tailored suit with a snowy white shirt, high collar, and a narrow tie, he was even more handsome. He was dressed as well as any of the young men she'd encountered in London, and he cut quite a dashing figure. Obviously he was a man who knew what looked good on him and wore it with style.

Before Jordan let herself get too carried away, she reminded herself firmly of Luther. He too had given the appearance of being quite the man about town, when in fact he was nothing more than a lecherous scoundrel. She couldn't let herself be fooled by Nick's good looks. She knew what he was really like.

"We'll dine here at the hotel," Nick told her as they started down the steps. "The chef is renowned for his cuisine."

"Oh, good," Jordan replied, "I'm famished."

It occurred to Nick then that she hadn't eaten a thing since he'd bought her. "You must be," he agreed. "You should have said something sooner."

"I really haven't been thinking too much about food

169

lately," she confessed. "It was a rough voyage and I was very seasick. Once I began to feel better and wanted to eat something, the meals were barely edible."

"You can make up for it this morning. Order whatever you like from the menu," Nick invited. He was heartfelt in his wish that she enjoy herself, but he also knew he could take this opportunity to judge her tastes.

When they reached the bottom of the staircase, Nick casually put a hand at the small of her back to guide her across the lobby to the dining room. He'd meant the touch to be an impersonal courtesy, but he found himself marveling at how tiny her waist was and how sweetly the curve of her hip fit against his palm.

Jordan was shocked that his simple touch sent waves of awareness through her. The sensation left her bewildered, and she quickened her step a bit just to escape the heated intensity of it.

The dining room was as luxurious as the rest of the hotel; Jordan was impressed. They were seated almost immediately at a table for two covered with a pristine white linen tablecloth and set with service of the finest china. The silverware was polished to a high gleam, and in the center of the table a crystal vase held a small bouquet of brightly colored fragrant flowers. Martin, the tall, dignified, well-dressed black waiter who had served Nick and Slater since their arrival in Mobile, appeared almost magically beside them.

"May I bring you some coffee this morning, Mr. Kane?"

"Jordan?" Nick, not knowing her tastes, looked to her.

"Yes, please," she accepted.

"Two, Martin, thank you," he ordered. He was a bit surprised by Jordan's wanting coffee, and he remarked in a teasing way, "I thought you English girls drank

170

only tea."

"Oh, I enjoy tea, too, but my father introduced me to coffee as a child and I loved it instantly. My mother was scandalized, but she got over it." The happy childhood memory lit up Jordan's face and lent a sparkle to her eyes.

Nick had never seen her looking so radiant, and he was almost mesmerized. "You really haven't told me much about yourself."

"There really isn't a lot to tell," she said evasively. Her happiness faded at having to confront the issue of her past.

"Tell me what there is," he encouraged. He told himself he wanted to know only because he had to make up something to tell his father, but actually he was curious about her. She was turning out to be so much more than he'd ever hoped to find.

"Well, my family's from London," she began, taking great care not to lie, but then not to tell the whole truth, either. She had to make sure he didn't make any connection between her and Philip. "My father made a fair living, but we were far from rich. Both my parents died not too long ago, and I was left without funds."

"You didn't have any relatives to take you in? There was no one to help you?" It outraged Nick to think of her all alone and unprotected.

"No . . ." She thought of Luther's betrayal and where she would have been right now had they not escaped. "There was no one who could help. That's when I heard about indenturing. It seemed an honest way to start a new life for myself. If I'd stayed in London, God only knows how I would have ended up." She shivered in spite of herself as she fought against the terrifying image of an executioner's rope around her neck.

Nick noticed how the light in her eyes had dimmed,

to be replaced by something he didn't quite understand . . . something that almost looked like sadness. Her vulnerability sent a surge of protectiveness through him, and he instinctively reached across the table to take her hand in a reassuring gesture.

"You don't have to worry any more. You're under my protection now," he told her ardently. "Nothing bad is going to happen to you ever again. I'll see to it."

Jordan looked up, her eyes meeting his. She was torn between what she saw reflected there and what she believed was the real Nick. There was a rock-solid confidence mirrored in the warm brown depths of his gaze that was not arrogance but a firm belief in his own abilities. She wanted to believe him, to trust that he was right, that nothing would ever happen to her again, but she knew he would have little power to help her should the truth of her terrible secret ever come to light.

"Here you are, Mr. Kane," Martin announced with a flourish as he returned with their coffee.

His presence broke the spell that had held them for that fraction of a moment. They were both a little taken back by the intensity of what they'd been feeling and were glad for the distraction.

As the waiter served the coffee he asked, "And here are your menus. Would you like a few minutes to decide?"

"Yes, thank you." Nick watched while Jordan took the proffered menu and quickly scanned its contents. "You read?"

"Yes. My mother taught me."

"So, your mother was an educated woman?"

"Very much so. My father was educated too. Both my parents had a profound love of literature. I know Father planned to write a novel someday, but he never got to it." There was a melancholy note to her voice.

"Did they also teach you how to write?"

"Yes," she answered simply.

His respect for her was growing by leaps and bounds. "I'm impressed and, to be honest with you, I'm relieved."

"Why?"

"There would have been enough time for me to teach you basic etiquette and manners before we got back, but there would never have been enough time for me to teach you to read and write."

"Your father cares about such things?"

"Let's put it this way. Had you not been so well educated, he most certainly would have questioned my choice of a bride."

"Mr. Kane, are you ready to order now?" Martin had again quietly approached, and now stood ready to serve as needed.

"I believe we are. Jordan?" he deferred.

She was thrilled by the selection of food. After the fare on the ship, the items listed sounded like manna to her. "I'd like an omelet with ham and a beignet with strawberries."

"Yes, ma'am."

Nick quickly followed with his own order, and then, when the waiter had gone, he turned his attention back to Jordan. She was an enigma, and as such she was becoming more and more intriguing to him with each passing moment. Not only could she read and write, but her manners were impeccable and she was familiar with French cuisine.

Jordan saw the questioning look in his eyes and wished she'd been smart enough to allow him to order for her. It was too late to worry about it now, but she knew she had to put his interest in her past to rest. "Though he was only a bookkeeper, my father always had a taste for the finer things in life," she said quickly.

"French cuisine was one of them. My mother and I used to spend hours in the kitchen trying out new dishes we thought he might like."

"So you're a good cook, too?"

"I like to think so, but I won't make any claims until I've had the chance to fix a meal for you."

Though her remark was made in the course of general conversation, there was something intimate about it,

"I'll be looking forward to it," Nick replied, his gaze darkening.

Jordan felt a little uncomfortable under his steady regard, and she wanted to direct the conversation away from herself. "Well, now that you know all about me, tell me about Louisiana and your home."

"Louisiana is beautiful and so is Riverwood."

"Riverwood?"

"My home. It's a plantation on the Mississippi River."

"It sounds grand."

"It is big," he stated without bragging. "The main house has twenty-five rooms, and we own quite a bit of land, too. We grow mostly sugar and cotton, and we've invested quite a lot in our stables."

Jordan heard the pride in his voice and realized just how important his home was to him. "You obviously love your home . . ."

"Very much so."

"And your father . . . What do you intend to tell him about me?"

"As little as possible," he responded. "I need to come up with a story my father will accept. I can't very well tell him I bought you on the docks in Mobile."

"What do you suggest?"

"I came here on business. It's probably safest to let my father think I met you at a social gathering through a mutual acquaintance. We'll say a Mr. Harrison, he'll believe that . . ."

Though Jordan knew that what Nick proposed was ultimately for her own good too, her disappointment in him deepened. He was lucky enough to have his father still with him, and yet here he was concentrating only on winning his inheritance, instead of doting on him and loving him while there was still time. She would have given anything to have her father back. She'd loved him dearly, and she missed him terribly even after all this time.

"What if he questions me about my past?"

"Tell him the truth when you can. Just say that after your parents died, Harrison offered you the opportunity to come here, and you decided to accept since there was nothing left to hold you in England. Once you got to Mobile, it was by a pure stroke of luck that we met . . ." Nick paused to give her a considering look. "It was truly a matter of good fortune. I usually only travel to Mobile once or twice a year at the most."

"It was lucky for the both of us," she agreed, "and I'll do my best to convince your father that we fell in love at first sight."

"He won't believe anything else, given the time involved. I can delay our return for another week, but no more than that."

Martin arrived with their food just as Nick finished speaking and carefully set the steaming delicacies before them. "Will there be anything else?"

"Not now, Martin. Thanks."

As Nick ate of his own more manly fare of steak, eggs, and sweet potato biscuits, he surreptitiously watched Jordan take a small ladylike taste of her beignet. Her expression seemed to turn almost rapturous, and she ran the tip of her tongue over her bottom lip to make sure she hadn't missed a crumb. When she glanced up to find his eyes upon her, she blushed a bit.

"I hope I'm not making a spectacle of myself, it's just that it's delicious," she confided with an innocent glee that struck him as almost childlike.

"I'm glad you're enjoying it."

"Would you like a taste?"

"Yes . . ." he answered, feeling enthralled as her shining eyes held him captive.

Jordan broke off a bit and offered it to him on her fork. Her gaze never left his as she gently fed him the morsel. There was something about his reaction that sent a slow burning heat throbbing through her, and she watched, entranced, as he slowly chewed the delectable bite.

"You're right . . . It *is* very special . . ." Nick murmured, not quite sure whether he was talking about her or the food.

The strange sensations that were filling Jordan left her suddenly very nervous. She looked away and tried to concentrate solely on her food.

Nick, too, devoted his full attention to his meal, but he couldn't help but steal an occasional look at Jordan. For some reason, he felt as if she weren't quite real, as if she were a figment of his imagination. Everything about her was feminine and ladylike. She displayed none of the coarseness he'd originally feared when he first saw her. He meant it sincerely when he told her it had been a matter of good fortune that he'd found her. She was the answer to his prayers . . .

Noticing that she'd cleaned her plate, he smiled. "I see you enjoyed the food."

"The chef was as wonderful as you said he was," she said, giving him a contrite smile. "I'm afraid I made quite a pig of myself, but it was so delicious that I couldn't bear to let any of it go to waste."

Her grin was so infectious that he was completely

charmed. He smiled back at her.

"I'm just glad you enjoyed it, and if you want anything else, you have only to ask."

"Oh, no," she laughed lightly, putting a hand on her stomach. "I doubt that I'll eat again for days."

"I'll bet you're hungry again by dinner."

"You're probably right," she laughed again.

"Well, it will be more than my pleasure to satisfy your appetite at any time of day or night . . ." Nick didn't realize how his statement sounded until after he'd said it.

Being the innocent she was, Jordan completely missed his double-entendre. "You may be leaving yourself open for trouble."

"I'll take my chances."

"My parents often teased that I probably could have eaten my weight at every meal if they hadn't stopped me."

"You're hardly bigger than a mite. I'm not worried," he commented, his gaze upon her slender form. Then realizing the direction his thoughts were taking, he quickly changed the subject. "We'd better get going, if you're sure you're done."

"Yes."

After signaling Martin for the check and signing for it, Nick rose from the table and assisted Jordan from her chair. "The dressmaker is expecting us."

Chapter Thirteen

Eleanor Marsh was a cheerful, rotund, silver-haired woman with a great sense of fashion and the uncanny ability to determine instantly what would look good on a woman. Years before, when her husband had passed away leaving her with three small children to raise and no income to speak of, she'd set about making her living with a needle and thread. It had been difficult in the beginning, but somehow she'd managed.

Eleanor's philosophy of her work was simple. She believed that each and every woman had her strong points, and all that had to be done was to identify and highlight them through color and style. As word of her expertise had spread, she'd turned her gift into a very successful business. Women from miles around came to her shop, clamoring for her services, and she'd always been happy to oblige. One of her greatest joys in life was to see a dowdy, poorly dressed woman transformed into a social delight merely by altering her wardrobe. It was her calling, and she did it with great joy.

Eleanor had just finished a final fitting and was bidding her customer good-bye when Nick and Jordan entered her shop. Her first impression was that they were a most striking couple. The man was tall and undeniably attractive, and he moved with the easy grace of a man most sure of himself. He was the kind of male who could stir the heart of many a woman, and Eleanor was impressed. It wasn't often that someone as good-looking as he was came into her shop. Her gaze swept over Jordan next, and she couldn't help but despair. As lovely as the young woman was, the dress she was wearing was hideous. Eleanor wondered what addled creature had selected her clothes for her.

"Good morning," she said in welcome. "I'm Mrs. Marsh. Can I help you with anything today?"

"I'm Dominic Kane and this is my fiancée, Jordan Douglas."

"How do you do?"

"Jordan's just arrived from England, and unfortunately, most of her clothing was ruined during the voyage. She's in dire need of a complete new wardrobe," he told her.

That explains it, Eleanor thought, relieved to know that the young woman's current state was not her normal one.

"What exactly did you have in mind?" She allowed Nick to lead the conversation, for although he looked the prosperous businessman, there was no way of knowing for sure just how well-lined his pockets were.

"I want only the best of everything for Jordan. We heard you were the most talented *couturière* in town, and so we came here."

"Thank you," Eleanor responded with pride and pleasure. "I enjoy my work. It's more a labor of love than drudgery. There is no greater thrill than seeing a woman looking her best."

"I agree," Nick said, his eyes warm upon Jordan.

"Please, come this way. I have a sitting area here, where you can relax while you go through the latest

179

sketches from Godey's. Once you've chosen the ones you like best we'll work from there."

At Eleanor's direction, Jordan and Nick sat on a small overstuffed loveseat and began sorting through the pictures spread out on the low table before them.

Nick was a man on a mission. He wanted Jordan to be dressed to perfection. He cared little for the cost. The only trouble was, having had no women in his life since his mother died, he wasn't quite sure what the task entailed.

The sketches of the dresses and gowns, Nick found, were no problem. As they quickly went through the drawings, he instinctively recognized what would look good on Jordan and ordered them without hesitation. He selected daygowns, traveling suits, and several different ballgowns, all in a variety of colors and fabrics that he knew would grace her beauty. One fancy gown in particular caught Nick's eye, and he knew he had to have it for her. It was a full-skirted, off-the-shoulder creation with puff sleeves and low-cut bodice. Done in emerald satin to match her eyes, it would be simply stunning on her.

"You're absolutely right. It will look beautiful," Eleanor agreed with real enthusiasm.

Jordan was hesitant to say anything as she listened to all that was going on. The more Nick ordered, the more amazed she became. Her wardrobe had been adequate when her parents were alive. She'd had one rather ordinary ballgown and enough daydresses to meet her needs. She had expected Nick to select about the same amount. His generosity was proving startling, and she wondered if she would ever have occasion to wear so many different styles and colors.

"Nick . . . are you sure I'll use all this?" Jordan interrupted.

Nick was surprised by her comment. Through the

years he'd purchased gifts for other women, but they'd always wanted more from him, not less.

"Trust me in this. Once our engagement is announced, there will be more social invitations than you can imagine. Since I can afford it, allow me this pleasure."

Nick's tone was deep and mellow and sent a small shiver up Jordan's spine. For just a moment she allowed herself to believe he really meant it, that he was enjoying this, but his next statement shattered that illusion.

"You know how important it is that you look your very best," he finished.

The feeling of intimacy his first words had evoked vanished, and Jordan was forced to remind herself that this was all only an act. He had simply phrased everything that way for the seamstress's benefit. She was playing the part of his fiancée, and it was essential that she dressed the part. That was all.

"Mr. Kane's taste is flawless," Eleanor complimented. "Every garment he's chosen will be delightful on you. Shall we consider your more delicate accessories now?"

Now came the hard part, Nick thought as he sat back. The two women discussed the intimate underthings Jordan would need and the material to be used. He attempted only to half listen to their conversation, but as they went over the merits of soft muslin, sheer batiste, and clinging silk, an unbidden image of Jordan clad only in a delicately revealing shift drifted through his thoughts. Against his will his blood stirred. He let his gaze drift around the shop as he tried to distract himself. But even as he did so, the scent of her perfumed soap and the feel of her sitting so close beside him taunted him. He felt trapped, and his discomfort grew.

"Would that be all right with you, Nick?" Jordan was asking as she glanced at him for approval of her final selections.

"Whatever," he replied abruptly, not quite sure what she was asking and not about to let her know that he hadn't been paying attention.

Jordan gave him a puzzled look at his curtness, but she had no time to question him. The seamstress stood up.

"Good. It's all settled then," Eleanor added. "Shall we see about taking your measurements now? Then we'll be done for today."

Relief showed plainly on Nick's handsome features. "Good."

"Obviously, you haven't done this very often," Eleanor observed.

"Actually, this is my first time."

"Well, your fiancée is most fortunate to have you along. Don't you agree, miss?"

"Absolutely. Without Nick, none of this would have been possible."

They both knew what she was talking about, but to Eleanor they just seemed like a couple madly in love.

Nick was glad for the reprieve when the two women disappeared into the curtained-off fitting room. He drew a deep breath and told himself that it would all be over soon. When he looked up again, Nick was surprised to find that the curtain had not been fully drawn across the fitting area and that he could see Jordan's reflection in the mirror inside.

Nick knew the proper thing to do. He knew he should either adjust the curtain himself or at least warn the women that it had not been properly drawn. And he fully intended to do so, but when Jordan slipped out of her daydress and stepped up on the small platform in the middle of the room clad only in her chemise, he froze. His gaze raked boldly over her mirrored image, lingering on the soft swell of her breasts beneath the worn cotton of her shift. His body reacted fiercely to the sight of her. Nick moved uneasily in his seat, but he could not tear his eyes away.

"Your fiancé certainly has a natural talent for knowing what looks good on you," Eleanor commented to Jordan as she took out her tape and began to measure her.

"He certainly does. I had no idea he was so observant." As Jordan spoke, she happened to cast a quick look at her own reflection only to find herself staring at Nick.

The sight of Jordan so scantily clad set a flame burning fiercely within Nick, and he made no effort to pretend he wasn't watching her. In fact, his appraising regard remained boldly upon her, savoring the view.

Time stood still as their eyes met and locked in the mirror. Jordan's breath caught in her throat, and her heart suddenly began to hammer in her breast. She wanted to look away, but there was something so magnetic . . . so compelling about him that she found she couldn't. She was held a willing captive of his gaze, and she was only freed from it when the seamstress shifted her position and inadvertently brushed the curtain the rest of the way closed.

Nick couldn't believe the near violent reaction he had when the curtain was suddenly shut. He longed to throw wide the offending drape and take Jordan in his arms. Only his firmly established common sense held him back. She was attractive, but so what? So were a lot of other women. Besides, Jordan had made it perfectly clear last night that she was completely happy with their arrangement, and he was going to keep it that way. Just because she was going to pretend to be his wife didn't make her one.

He stood up and began to pace the shop in agitation, wishing this foolishness was over and done with so they could leave. When, at long last, Jordan and Eleanor reappeared, he was more than ready to depart.

"We're finished for now," the *couterière* announced. "How soon do you need these things?"

"As quickly as possible," Nick told her. "There will be a substantial bonus for you if you can have the entire wardrobe completed within the week."

Eleanor knew it would mean a lot of hard work and long hours, but she didn't hesitate to agree. It was far too large an order to risk losing it. "That will be fine."

"By the way, do you have anything here today that Jordan could wear now?" He was already tired of seeing her in the plain gown. "Something nicer than this everyday one?"

"Nick . . . another gown?" Jordan interrupted, honestly taken aback.

"I think I may have just the thing," Eleanor said with enthusiasm, pleased at the prospect of getting Jordan out of that dreadful dress. "I made a daygown for a lady some time ago, and she never came back to pick it up. Let me get it for you so you can see what you think."

Alone in the outer room, Jordan turned to Nick, her eyes wide and questioning. "Are you sure you want to do this? I mean, you've already spent a small fortune on me. I could just wear this dress until the others are ready."

Nick found her willingness to make do with what she had endearing. "It will probably take the full week to get your other things, and I have a feeling you might be ready for a change long before then."

"Actually, I'm ready for a change now, but you've been so generous already. I don't want to take advantage of you," she confessed, hating the gown but knowing it had served its purpose well.

"You're not taking advantage of me, Jordan, but if it will make you feel better, think of this as an investment in both of our futures."

Put that way, it reminded her of their true purpose and tempered her happiness. "I'm grateful for your generosity."

"Gratitude is not what I want from you, Jordan." For some reason, her statement irritated him.

"Here we are," Eleanor announced excitedly as she came bustling back into the room with a blue gown thrown over her arm. "I can't believe our luck. It's nothing very fancy, but I do think it will do until all your others are ready. It might even fit without any major alterations. Shall we go try it on?"

"I'll be right back." Jordan disappeared back into the dressing room following the seamstress.

The thought of Jordan standing in her chemise just beyond the curtain again left Nick feeling very restless. He stared at the closed drape for a long minute, as if debating something within, and then contented himself with walking around the store to distract his thoughts.

Nick was trying to rationalize what he was feeling for Jordan. He told himself that she was just a woman like any other. He'd known many in his time, and none of them had made a very lasting impression on him. He'd shared good times with them, and he'd shared more than a few of their beds, when they'd been willing, but when the affairs ended he'd gone on his way to his next encounter without so much as a backward thought. Surely, he reasoned, Jordan was just like all the others. Surely this unexpected magnetism that existed between them would pass and he'd be able to forget all about her when the time came.

"Nick? What do you think?"

At the sound of Jordan's voice, Nick turned to face her. Though he gave the appearance of being unaffected by the change in her, actually he was very much aware of the difference. The gown fit her to perfection, nipping in at the slim waist and flaring out fully over the new petticoats Eleanor had provided. Its vibrant blue color brought out the loveliness of Jordan's complexion and the tawny beauty of her hair.

"It's fine. We'll take it."

"Wonderful. I'll just put your other dress in a box for you and then you can be on your way."

Jordan waited as Nick gave the *couturière* their room number at the hotel and then paid a substantial deposit on the order.

"I'll send word to you just as soon as the gowns are ready for a final fitting, Mr. Kane," Eleanor promised.

"We'll be expecting to hear from you soon."

Nick gathered up the box containing the hated dress and then escorted Jordan outside. The visit to the seamstress had taken the better of the morning, and it was time they returned to the hotel to be there when Harrison arrived to pick up his final payment. Nick flagged down a coach, helped Jordan in, and then climbed in beside her after giving the driver directions to their hotel.

"Since your gowns won't be ready for quite a while, we're going to have some time on our hands. Is there anything in particular you'd like to do or see while we're here in Mobile?" Nick asked.

"I don't really know anything about Mobile. But if we're anywhere close to the seashore, I'd love to go there," Jordan replied without hesitation as she watched the passing city out the carriage window.

"I'll see if we can arrange an outing for us later this afternoon. I'm not sure how far it is, but we should be able to make it."

"I haven't been to the shore since I went with my parents when I was young." She turned back to him, smiling.

Staring at Jordan now, looking so relaxed and happy, Nick thought she barely seemed old enough to be on her own, let alone to have had a lover already. Nick scowled at the unwanted thought.

"How old are you, Jordan? I don't believe you ever told me your birthdate."

"I just turned eighteen in February, on the twentieth, actually," she answered, a bit bewildered by the sudden fierceness of his expression. "What about you?"

"I'll be twenty-seven on the twenty-fourth of August," he answered, his frown fading a little.

"You're old," she teased, hoping to lighten the mood of the conversation.

"I prefer to think of myself as mature," Nick countered, his frown disappearing completely as he gave her a lopsided grin. "Although there are a few people who would disagree with my assessment, my father among them."

"Tell me more about your father. He sounded rather intimidating when you spoke of him last night. What if he doesn't like me?"

"I don't think you have a thing to worry about," Nick replied reassuringly. The more time he spent with her, the more convinced he became that he'd made the perfect choice. He felt reasonably certain that his father was going to take to her right away. She was pretty and intelligent, she could read and write; and she was good company. All he had to do was make sure there was no hint of a scandal where her involvement with Montgomery was concerned, and everything would go well.

"I hope you're right."

"I am. You'll see. Women generally like my father a great deal, and he feels the same way about them. Although he never remarried after my mother's death, he's never been without women friends."

"He sounds nice."

"He is," Nick said in a slightly strangled voice. It hurt to talk about his father. He loved him and he didn't want to lose him.

Nick's comment caused Jordan to glance over at him. There was no trace of any telltale emotion in his expression, so she decided she'd just imagined that he'd sounded upset. After all, she knew the truth — Nick was only after his inheritance.

They both fell silent as the carriage wound its way back to the hotel. Lost in thought, they stared out the windows at the passing scenery of Mobile, with its charming, iron-lace bedecked houses, tall oaks, and lush gardens filled with flowering azaleas and oleanders.

When they reached their destination, Nick descended first and then aided Jordan. His hands at her waist, he swung her down. The contact turned electric when she accidently brushed full-length against him as he set her down. Time hung suspended as they paused there before the hotel entrance, staring spellbound at each other. Only the driver's crude clearing of his throat dragged them both back to reality. Jordan quickly moved off, leaving Nick to settle the fare.

Slater and Philip had already returned to the hotel and had stopped in the lobby for a minute so Slater could speak with the man at the desk. Philip saw Jordan the moment she entered, and since Nick was nowhere to be seen, he felt bold enough to greet her.

"Jordan!" he called out happily as he crossed the room to join her.

The familiar sound of Philip's voice drew Jordan's attention, and her face lit up at this first sight of him since the terrible interlude the night before.

"Philip! It's so good to see you . . ." He'd obviously just been to the barber shop, for he was clean-shaven once more, and Slater had treated him to a suit of new clothes, too, for he looked very much like his old self again in a white shirt and dark pants. Jordan thought he looked most handsome. She touched his arm in an innocent gesture. "You look wonderful."

"So do you," her brother told her as he took in the new gown she was wearing. She looked happy enough, and it pleased him to find that Kane was treating her well. He'd been worrying about her all day, but it looked as if things were going all right.

"Thank you. Nick's being very good to me."

"You're sure?"

"There's nothing to worry about," she promised. "He's basically a good man, and I trust him."

Philip heard something in her voice that troubled him. "Don't trust him too much."

"Why?"

"Because we have no friends, Jordan. Don't ever forget what we're running from," he warned, knowing the dangers they faced were far from over.

Reminded of the ugliness of what had happened in London, Jordan paled. "You're right, I know."

"I just don't want you to be hurt, that's all. You can't let yourself come to care about anyone or anything. At least, not until our indentureship is over and we're far away from here. All right?"

She nodded tightly, smiling once more to convince him she could do it. "All right."

Nick came into the lobby just then, and he stopped dead at the sight of Jordan deep in conversation with Montgomery. Anger rushed through him, and it was

189

all he could do not to yank her away from the indenture. Hadn't he told her to stay away from him? Hadn't he warned her about continuing her association with him?

Tempting as it was for Nick to consider calling the whole thing off, logic won out. He'd already invested far too much money in the scheme to back out now. No, he decided, he was going to go through with it and so was she. All he had to do was find a way to make sure Jordan and Montgomery were kept apart, every minute of every day, and he knew exactly how to do it . . .

His expression was stony as he crossed the lobby to join Slater at the desk. He waited patiently until his friend had completed his business and then took him aside to tell him what he wanted done that afternoon.

Chapter Fourteen

Slater was feeling quite smug as he settled into the seat of the hired carriage opposite his companion.

"Are you comfortable, Miss Layton?"

"Yes, thank you, Mr. MacKenzie," replied Audrey Layton, the prim, sixty-year-old, silver-haired spinster he'd just hired to act as Jordan's chaperone. She folded her gloved hands in her lap.

"Since we're going to be spending a lot of time together over the next several weeks, I'd be honored if you'd call me Slater," he offered.

"Oh, no, sir, that would never do. I'll call you Mr. MacKenzie, as is proper." She stiffened a little, shocked that he'd even suggest such a thing. To her way of thinking, it would be scandalous to be so familiar with him.

Slater half smiled. He'd been right in his assessment. Audrey was perfect. She was just what Nick wanted. She might not prove to be what he needed, but she certainly fit the bill as a strict guardian to protect Jordan's reputation.

"I'll abide by your wishes, but know that the invitation is always there should you change your mind."

"Yes, sir. Now, tell me more about this young lady I'm to accompany to Riverwood plantation in Louisiana. You say she's English and her fiancé is Dominic Kane of the Riverwood Kanes?"

"That's right. Jordan Douglas just arrived from London late last night."

"So she's already spent one night alone without proper supervision?" She was alarmed, fearful that the young lady's reputation might already be damaged.

"We weren't certain when she would arrive, and, as it happened, it was very late when we finally did meet her at the docks." Slater told himself firmly that he was not lying to her. "There was no time to arrange for a chaperone then, but it was one of our main concerns today. We know that the future wife of Dominic Kane must be above reproach."

"As I recall, I had the pleasure of meeting Charles Kane and his wife once years ago when I was visiting with relatives in New Orleans. They were a wonderful couple, and I was quite saddened when I heard later that she'd passed on."

"It was a terrible tragedy for them, but Charles, with Nick's help, went on to build Riverwood into one of the best plantations on the Mississippi."

"Dominic Kane . . ." Audrey pursed her lips and her expression turned thoughtful. "I'm afraid I've heard nothing about the young man, but coming from the wonderful family background that he does, I'm sure he's quite an upstanding young man."

"Oh, yes." Slater agreed as seriously as he could.

"Then I foresee no problems at all with our arrangement."

"Well, I appreciate your taking the job on such short notice," he said. He was thankful that Rodney Louis, a business acquaintance of his here in town, had known of Audrey and had been able to make the necessary introductions for them. It had all worked out well.

"Well, I've known our mutual friend, Mr. Louis, for

192

many years, and I trust his judgment implicitly."

"I do, too," Slater acknowledged, and they both settled back to enjoy the rest of the ride to the hotel.

After meeting with Slater in the lobby, Nick had escorted Jordan upstairs to their rooms and waited for Harrison to arrive. When the money-hungry agent appeared precisely at the noon hour to collect his funds, Nick was happy to conclude his business with him. That done, he and Jordan were free to do as they pleased the rest of the day, so he commissioned Martin to pack them a picnic lunch and then hired a carriage to make the trip to the Gulf coast.

In a way, Nick had been looking forward to the outing, for it had been a long time since he'd been able to just sit back and relax. Thinking about it, he figured that between rescuing Slater and his desperate search for a bride, it had been the better part of five months since he'd been able to simply enjoy himself. Now, his quest completed, he was ready to take it easy for a while.

Nick had expected that this trip to the shore would be the perfect opportunity to learn more about Jordan and her likes and dislikes. According to Slater's advice, if he was to appear to be in love with her, he was going to have to put her wants and needs before his own. Nick figured he couldn't do that very well if he didn't know what her wants and needs were, and this would be the right time to find out.

After the first half hour in the close confines of the carriage, though, Nick began to wonder if he hadn't made a big mistake in agreeing to the trip. Jordan was sitting next to him, and because of the small size of the vehicle, her leg was pressed almost full length against his. Not only that, but the heady scent of the perfumed soap she'd used kept taunting him. It was impossible for Nick not to be aware of her as a woman. He kept the conversation going, discussing her tastes in books and food, but despite his best efforts, the image of her at the dressmaker's clad only in her shift kept drifting through his mind.

"Oh, Nick, look!" Jordan exclaimed as the carriage made a turn and the beauty of the Gulf coast became suddenly visible through the window on Nick's side. She was so excited over the first glimpse of glorious white sand and turquoise blue water that she impetuously leaned across his lap to get a better view.

Jordan's delight at nature's spectacular panorama was real, and her move was made in all innocence, but there was absolutely nothing innocent about the feelings that jolted Nick. His breath caught, trapped in his throat, and he felt himself go pale at the soft crush of her sweet young body against his.

"Isn't it beautiful?" she asked, completely oblivious to his state of torment.

"Yes . . . yes, very," Nick answered tightly, his jaw clenched against the heat that was pounding away at him and threatening to erode his rigid control.

"I'm so glad we came," she said more softly, truly appreciating his thoughtfulness in bringing her here. "Thank you."

Jordan was slanted across him, and she turned her head to look at him, making no move to shift her position. One hand was resting on Nick's arm with easy familiarity, while her right breast was pressed against his chest. She didn't notice, however. She was too caught up in seeing the seashore to be concerned about sensuality. She didn't notice that he was having trouble breathing or that he'd gone terribly still. When her eyes met his, she saw something reflected in their warm brown depths that puzzled her, but before she could remark on it, it was gone. It almost seemed to her that he was in some kind of pain, but it had passed so quickly that Jordan guessed she'd probably just imagined it.

"You're welcome," Nick managed to sound normal, but for the life of him, he didn't know how. He felt as if his vitals were on fire. He felt as if he might explode if he didn't take her in his arms right then and there, kiss her passionately, and strip away the offending dress that hid those wondrous, silken orbs from his view. He wanted to . . . he wanted to . . . "Driver!" Nick found he was practically shouting. "Driver! Stop here!"

It was the desperate measure of a desperate man. He had to get away from her before he disgraced himself. He had to get out of the carriage right now!

"Oh, Nick! Are you going to take me for a walk on the beach?" Naive as she was, Jordan had no idea of his discomfort. She thought he was just being considerate.

"Yes . . . of course," he replied, grasping for anything that would ease his pounding need.

"Oh, good!" She sat back, smiling so brightly that he almost felt guilty.

When the driver reined in at the side of the road, Nick climbed out immediately. He stood there in the warm sunshine and drew a deep strangled breath before turning back to help Jordan down. It was a mistake to touch her. He'd known it would be. When his hands circled her small waist as he set her to her feet before him he felt as if he'd been burned. Nick couldn't let go of her quickly enough.

On the pretense of giving the driver his instructions, Nick moved away from her. In reality, though, he just needed some time to pull himself together. He told the driver to wait for them at the grove of trees they could see about half a mile away. Still he stalled, taking the time to shed his coat and tie and toss them inside the carriage. Nick waited until the man had driven off before turning back to Jordan.

Nick had thought he was fine. He'd thought he was under control, but the sight of Jordan, standing there gazing out at the sea once again filled him with the realization of just how naturally beautiful she was. Beneath the sun's caress, her hair looked to be of the finest spun gold; and unbound as it was, the gilded curls tumbled casually down her back. He longed to caress it, to run his fingers through it to see if it was as soft as it looked, but he told himself no.

Just then, Jordan glanced his way, her eyes alight with the happiness she was feeling and her smile artless and real. There was a genuineness to her that put to shame all the calculating women he'd ever known, women who'd only used their wiles and their smiles to manipulate him. Nick could only stare at her, wanting to take her in his arms and kiss her senseless, wanting to have his way with her, wanting to . . .

Somehow, through some miracle of forbearance no doubt inherited from some long dead ancestor, Nick managed not to do anything he wanted to do. He kept his hands, and his thoughts, to himself. It wasn't easy, and his thoughts were not pretty.

The memories of the many times she'd spent frolicking on the beach as a child were among Jordan's fondest, and she longed to be carefree like that again today. She turned to see what was taking Nick so long and found him standing there watching her. Without the jacket and tie he looked very casual and very handsome, and Jordan couldn't help but smile.

"Ready?" she asked, barely able to contain her exhilaration any longer.

"If you are," he replied. "I told the driver we'd meet him at that copse of trees down there."

"Wonderful!" With all the enthusiasm of a little girl, she slipped her small hand in his big one and tugged him along with her. "Come on!"

She ran ahead, dragging Nick with her down the slight, grassy incline to the edge of the sand.

"Hurry!"

"I don't think the water's going anywhere," he told her bemusedly.

"I know that," she said with teasing indignation. "It's just that we have so little time. I want to enjoy every minute of it."

With nary a thought to propriety, Jordan dropped to the ground and quickly stripped off her shoes and stockings. Leaving them in a haphazard pile, she got to her feet. The sand was warm beneath her toes, and she loved it.

"What are you waiting for, Nick? You can't very well walk in the sand with your shoes on!" She was laughing at him with such good humor that he was unable to resist her.

Sitting down, Nick quickly pulled off his boots and socks and left them with hers. "All right, I'm ready, let's go . . ."

Again Jordan took his hand, and they walked slowly down to the water's edge, feeling no need to rush or hurry any longer. They didn't say much as they wandered along, they just took the time to enjoy the sun and the breeze and the roar of the waves as they swept in to shore. Occasionally, Jordan paused to pick up seashells, exclaiming over their polished beauty. She saved the prettiest ones for souvenirs, tucking them safely away in her pockets and drawing a charmed chuckle from Nick.

Nick was amazed at how right everything felt being here with Jordan. He felt younger and freer, somehow, as he watched her move along the beach. Her cheeks were flushed with excitement, and she seemed to be the very essence of innocence. His gaze remained fixed upon her as she playfully skirted the edge of the water, dancing out of the way of each wave's advance with the joy of a small child. Suddenly, the age-old need to protect filled Nick, and he knew a deep-seated desire to keep her safe from harm.

Jordan was unaware of his thoughts. She was just having fun. Unable to hold back any longer, she gathered up her skirts in a devilishly daring display and raced toward the next oncoming wave.

"Nick! Don't just stand there! Come on!" she called over her shoulder, and then squealed in delight as the rushing cold water splashed her bare legs with its icy chill.

Nick was enthralled by the glimpse of her shapely calves. He found himself studying her trim legs and ankles with open admiration. He could almost envision her thighs, so creamy and firm, and he thought about running his hand over that satiny flesh and . . .

"Nick? Aren't you going to come wading too?"

Much to his chagrin, Jordan's invitation forced his thoughts away from his deliciously erotic musings. Though she looked like she was having a good time, Nick had never been much on wading.

"You go ahead, I'll just stay here and enjoy the view," he replied, still not looking away from her.

"Coward!" she teased, but she still felt disappointed that he wouldn't join her.

Jordan didn't let his reluctance bother her for long. The day was too glorious, the sun too bright, the gulf too beautiful. Accustomed to the water's temperature now, she enjoyed the feel of it swirling around her ankles and calves and moving the sand beneath her feet. She loved every minute of it.

Jordan cast a glance back at Nick to find him staring

out to sea. Her heart beat a little faster as she studied him. He was a magnificent specimen of a man, and it troubled her that she felt drawn to him this way. She didn't want to be attracted to him. It was pointless to even think about it. What they had between them now was too good to ruin by becoming emotionally involved with him. He'd made it clear this was no lasting match, and she too wanted it that way.

Jordan'didn't wish to get caught up in thoughts of the past. She wanted to stay lighthearted and carefree. Eager to break her mood, she knew immediately what she had to do. Her eyes were filled with merriment as she bent down and began to splash water wildly at Nick.

Nick had forced himself to look away from Jordan, and when she attacked she caught him completely unawares. She managed to do a good job of soaking him before he could even think of retaliating. Knowing time was of the essence, Jordan called a hasty but intelligent retreat. Hiking her skirts up as high as she could without being totally brazen, she took flight down the beach.

Nick's ego was bruised at having been caught so unprepared, and he charged after Jordan, intent on making her pay. Like a predator running down its slower prey, he caught up with her in the blink of an eye and snared her by the waist. Jordan cried out in mock terror as he lifted her high in his arms and swung her around to face him.

"Thought you could soak me and get away with it, did you?" He growled. His tone was threatening, but he was smiling.

"Let me go!" Jordan laughed as she tried to wiggle free.

She almost broke away, and Nick had to tighten his grip so as not to lose her. He made the mistake of pinning her against his chest. The resulting shock was like a bolt of lightning striking them both. They stood stock still, breathlessly staring at each other in awe-struck wonder.

What Nick had felt in the carriage had been child's play compared to this. Every fiber of his being vibrated with an intensity he'd never experienced before. It was a sensual recognition, an instinctive, glorious knowledge of what would be theirs if they only gave in to it. He wanted her. God, how he desired her!

The roar of the surf and the heat of the sun faded from Nick's consciousness. He wasn't aware of anything except the softness of Jordan in his arms. He bent to her, his lips seeking hers in a tentative exploration. At first it was sweet, gentle, perfect . . . and it wasn't enough! That first taste of paradise only whetted his appetite for more. Unable to help himself, his mouth slanted across hers in passionate possession, his lips urging hers apart so he could draw her very breath from her.

Jordan gasped at the strange sensations sweeping through her. Heat was radiating from somewhere deep in the womanly recesses of her body. She felt lightheaded and clutched at his shoulders for support. When his hand sought the fullness of her breast, a small moan escaped her.

Neither of them spoke. They kissed, then kissed again. It was the beginning of something rapturous . . . a moment of ecstasy that defied all reason.

Jordan knew she shouldn't be doing this, yet where Luther's touch had repulsed her, Nick's filled her with a fiery yearning she didn't understand. His kiss was so intoxicating that her head was spinning. She found herself clinging to him, loving his strength and trying to get closer and closer . . .

It was the raucous cry of a gull as it soared overhead,

along with the distant sound of the carriage horses whinnying, that finally intruded on their sunlit bliss. Nick looked around, disoriented. For the first time since he'd taken Jordan in his arms, he became aware of the fact that they were standing out in the open in knee-deep water. His pants legs were soaked to the knees and her dress was sodden as well. The realization that he could have been rendered so completely unaware of his surroundings stunned and troubled him.

Needing time to think, Nick ended the embrace abruptly and moved slightly away from Jordan. He told himself that what had happened between them was perfectly normal. She was a pretty woman and he was a full-blooded man. It hadn't been important. It meant nothing.

"Not bad for practice. No doubt we convinced the carriage driver we're madly in love with each other," he remarked with an arrogance that grated on her.

Jordan opened her eyes and blinked in disbelief, unable to believe the expression on Nick's face. He was grinning down at her mockingly.

"And," he went on, "if you perform this well for my father, we should have no problems at all."

Perform!! Jordan was mortified. This was all a game to Nick, a charade he was playing! No matter how affected she might have been by his kiss, it was just play acting to him. He had bought and paid for her, and he expected her to live out her end of the deal. Emotions had no part in this at all. He had a plan for his life, and she was not a lasting part of that plan.

"I told you I'd act the role the way you wanted it done. I didn't disappoint you, did I?" she responded with a calm she did not feel. Jordan gave the impression of being unconcerned as she trudged up the beach and busied herself wringing out her skirts.

"Not a bit," Nick answered as he too waded out of

the water. He thought about trying to wring out his pants legs, but knew it was too late. The damage had been done. He could only hope to dry out before they got back to town. When Jordan finally gave up her efforts to fix her skirts, he asked, "Shall we go eat?"

"Sounds wonderful." She went along easily, giving him no clue to her inner turmoil.

It was dark before they returned to the hotel. Their clothing had dried, but that was about all that could be said for it. Wrinkled and sandy, they entered the lobby to come face to face with Slater and Miss Layton.

"Here they are now," Slater announced with quick relief, for the elderly woman had been growing more and more concerned about the time and the damage that might result to Jordan's reputation if she didn't show up soon.

Audrey turned to meet her new ward, and at the sight of Jordan and Nick her expression turned from pleasant to a scowl of definite disapproval.

"My dear, where have you been?" she asked in an urgent but hushed voice as she went straight to her newly appointed ward's side and took her hand.

"Excuse me?" Jordan had no idea who she was, and she automatically drew back.

"Jordan, Nick, this is Miss Audrey Layton. She's to serve as your chaperone for the journey to New Orleans. Miss Layton, this is Jordan Douglas."

"Miss Layton . . ." Jordan managed, surprised. It hadn't occurred to her that Nick would think of the propriety of their situation, but now after what had happened at the beach, she was glad.

"I'm fine, Jordan, dear, but it's you we have to be concerned about. Let's get you right on upstairs before anyone takes note of the scandalous condition of your

202

clothing. Heaven knows what tongues would be wagging in the morning if someone got a good look at you." She turned a frosty glare on Nick. "I'll speak with you later." With that, Audrey took Jordan under her protective wing and hustled her up the staircase and out of sight.

Nick had been ready to speak up when the elderly lady had nailed him with her deadly look. Seeing the serious glint in her pale blue eyes, he'd had sense enough to back down. He had always prided himself on being a quick study of people, and he already could tell that Miss Audrey Layton would prove to be a formidable opponent. He certainly wasn't going to be foolish enough to cross her. Judging from the look she'd just given him, he wasn't about to challenge her authority over Jordan, either.

Nick was having mixed emotions as he watched them walk away, Jordan, so young and graceful, and Miss Layton at her side, so old and protective. Ever since he'd had the sense to end their amorous embrace at the shore he'd been certain that his idea to hire a chaperone for Jordan would be the answer to all his problems. Not only would a guardian assure that Montgomery stayed away from Jordan, but she would also keep *him* away from her, too. He'd thought it was a great idea all the way back to the hotel. But now, watching the straight-backed, silver-haired woman with a will of iron escort Jordan upstairs and out of sight, he was beginning to think he might have made the biggest mistake of his life.

Chapter Fifteen

Charles Kane stood on the gallery of his home gazing out across the lush green fields of Riverwood with pride and sadness. There wasn't much time left. He knew it without anyone having to tell him. During the last week he had been filled with a great weariness that even his love for his home couldn't ease. Usually when he spent time outside he felt uplifted and invigorated, but no more. He only felt tired now, and he missed Nick desperately.

"Mr. Charles?" The butler emerged from the house.

"Yes, Weddington, what is it?" Charles didn't glance back from where he stood at the railing.

The ever-observant Weddington knew the truth of his condition, and he had noticed a change in Charles in recent days. Concerned, he had grown more vigilant in his efforts to serve him.

"I was just wondering, sir, if I could get you anything? A cool drink? Some lemonade, perhaps?"

"No . . . no, thanks. There's only one thing that could make me feel better right now, and it's not food."

"What is it then, sir? Tell me, and I'll get it for you," he offered earnestly. He cared deeply for this man who had saved him from almost certain death as a boy when he was being forced to work in the swamps.

Charles Kane had bought him on the spot and had taken him into his own household. During all the years since, Weddington had always tried to do his best for him. He considered him to be more than just his owner.

"I was just wishing Nick was here," Charles answered, turning to give him an almost wistful smile. "I miss him."

"It is awful quiet around here without him, that's for sure. Well, if you need anything, you just let me know."

"I will, don't worry."

When the servant had gone and Charles was alone with his thoughts again, he found himself sighing in deep regret. Regret was one emotion he'd never dealt with very often, for he always took the time to think his decisions through carefully. Once he made up his mind, he never looked back. This time, however, he was afraid he'd been wrong.

Charles had thought Nick hadn't married because he was having too much fun. He had thought he would settle down quickly once the line had been drawn. Instead, he'd had to sit back and watch his son's frantic search for a wife. It hadn't been easy.

Charles certainly hadn't meant to force Nick into choosing someone he didn't love. He'd wanted him to find someone like he'd found Andrea, all those years ago. There had been nothing frantic or desperate about their courtship and marriage. It had been the best, most wonderful time of his life. He had thought his ultimatum would make Nick realize that he could love one of the girls from the area and that it was time to marry. How wrong he'd been.

If Nick had ridden up the drive at that moment, Charles knew he would have welcomed him with open arms. He would have told him he'd changed his mind and that he didn't have to get married by September.

He would have told him that he loved him, and then he would have hugged him, as he had longed to do for so many days now.

Charles's eyes were suddenly burning and his throat felt tight. He turned away from the view of his beloved property, hoping that the business Nick had to take care of in Mobile would be quickly dispatched and that he'd be coming home soon. His left arm was aching dully again, an occurrence that was growing more and more common, and he massaged it distractedly as he went back indoors.

"Weddington!" he called loudly for the butler as he closed the main door behind him.

"Yes, sir?" He came rushing from the back of the house.

"Send word into town. I want to see Aaron O'Neill right away."

"I'll send someone right now," Weddington promised.

Feeling a little better, Charles wandered into his study and sat down at his desk. He could hear Weddington's footsteps echo through the massive house as he went in search of an errand boy, and he knew he had to agree with him: *It was far too quiet around here when Nick wasn't home.*

Jordan's nerves were stretched taut as she sat at the small dressing table in the hotel room, wearing only her shift and brushing out her hair. The day had finally come, and she wasn't sure whether she was more frightened or excited. In just a few scant hours they would be going onboard the ship that would take them to New Orleans, and within three days she would be at Nick's home meeting his father for the very first time.

The prospect of finally coming face to face with

Charles Kane frightened her. From the things Nick had said about him, he sounded like a very powerful, very intimidating man. She wondered if he'd like her, and she feared that he wouldn't.

"You look pensive, my dear. Is there something bothering you?" Audrey asked as she observed her young ward from across the room. Her sense of decorum had been outraged when she'd discovered that Jordan and Nick had connecting rooms, and she'd immediately directed that a trundle bed be installed in Jordan's chamber for her. She had been at her side ever since.

"I was just worrying a little about meeting Nick's father."

"Ah," Audrey clucked knowingly, "your first encounter with your future father-in-law." She paused thoughtfully. "Well, as I told Mr. MacKenzie, I did have the occasion to meet Charles Kane socially many years ago. He was a very nice man . . . so handsome and completely devoted to his wife. With your Nick having had a good example to follow, you're going to have a wonderful marriage. It's easy to see that he's very much in love with you," she told her with a happy little sigh. "Why just look at all the fine, wonderful clothes he bought you! That was so kind of him after your things were ruined on the trip."

Audrey gestured toward the big traveling trunk that was now filled with the fashionable garments Eleanor Marsh had taken such great pains to see finished in time for their departure.

Jordan smiled softly at the little woman who had come to mean so much to her in such a short period of time. She was glad Miss Layton thought they were very much in love. It meant their little performance was believable. Since she'd arrived to guard her reputation, Nick had played the perfect fiancé. He'd been atten-

207

tive, courteous, and always thoughtful. Thanks to Miss Layton's vigilant presence, he'd had no occasion to press his more amorous affections, and Jordan had been relieved. Jordan wondered what Miss Layton would think if she ever found out the whole truth — that he didn't really care about her and that all those wonderful clothes were just stage props necessary for his deception.

"Nick is special."

"That he is. He's a good-looking young man, and according to what Mr. MacKenzie told me, he's very hard working, too. The Kane family owns one of the richest plantations on the Mississippi. They're quite prominent, you know. Your future is assured."

"I'm probably just worrying needlessly."

"That's right," Audrey sympathized as she came to give her a reassuring hug. "Just the wedding jitters, I'm sure. It's difficult enough to make plans to marry while you're living in the bosom of your family, but here you are, practically alone, in a strange new country, without even your mother to guide you through all this."

"There are moments when I miss her a lot. I loved her very much."

"I'm sure you did. No one can ever take the place of your mother, and I shall not even endeavor to try. I shall, however, try to help you in every way I can, so you can enjoy your big day to the fullest. How soon after you arrive at Riverwood do you plan for the ceremony to take place? Are you having a big wedding or just a small private one?"

"I'm not really certain. Nick and I haven't really discussed the details yet. I think he's waiting until I meet his father first before we set the actual day, but I'm sure it will be soon, sometime before the middle of September."

Audrey gave her another impetuous hug. "Weddings

are so exciting. This will be fun, you'll see. Now, I don't want to see another worried frown from you. You've the looks and disposition of an angel. There's no way Charles Kane won't love you."

At that precise moment the connecting door flew open and Nick came striding into the room without thinking. "Jordan, I . . ."

"Mr. Kane!" Audrey quickly moved to block his view of the scantily clad Jordan and turned a icy gaze on him.

Nick realized immediately that he'd made a mistake. He had only wanted to tell Jordan that they would be leaving for the docks within the hour, and he found himself flushing hotly under Miss Layton's aggrieved glare.

"Sorry . . . ah . . . I just needed . . ." He was backing into his own room and stammering like a green, callow youth.

"Whatever it is you needed, you should have taken the time to knock first. As a gentleman, surely you know it's not proper for you to come in here unannounced," she lectured. "Now, please . . . go. Go on . . ." She waved him out and did not move from her protective position until the door was safely shut.

Nick closed the door and stood there staring at it, scowling blackly.

"Damn . . ." he muttered, feeling like a fool and knowing that he'd just acted like one. The unexpected glimpse he'd gotten of Jordan sitting at the dressing table in such a delectable state of undress had rendered him simple-minded. The lovely sight of her bared shoulders and the hint of cleavage had stricken the very reason he'd gone into her room in the first place from his mind.

Nick didn't like making an ass out of himself, and he slammed around his room getting the last of his belongings together. Ever since Miss Layton's arrival on the scene a little over a week ago, Nick had taken to playing the ardent suitor. It had been easy for him, for Jordan had played her part with equal dramatic ability. Still, knowing that it was all a charade, Nick didn't understand why just the sight of Jordan half dressed could affect him so. He was no bumbling virgin unfamiliar with the female form. He was a man, tried and true. Why was it then that Jordan, a woman he couldn't possibly want, could stir him up so? He didn't know, and it was aggravating him.

A knock at the door dragged his thoughts away from his frustration, and he was glad when he discovered it was Slater. He would let *him* be the one to inform Miss Layton of their plans to leave.

The main emotion Philip was feeling was relief as he stood on the deck of the ship and watched as the vessel manuevered its way out of Mobile Bay heading now for New Orleans. Every additional mile they put between themselves and their port of entry only helped to insure his and Jordan's safety that much more.

Philip would never be pleased with their situation, but he was as content as he could be. Though he hadn't been able to speak with his sister since that day in the hotel lobby, he rested much better now knowing that the imposing Miss Layton was protecting her honor. No doubt Kane had hired her to keep the two of them apart, but in doing so, he'd helped Philip's own cause. Philip knew if he couldn't get near enough to Jordan to speak to her privately, then neither could her "fiancé." Jordan's virtue was assured.

"These arrangements will be fine," Audrey announced as she surveyed the small stateroom she and Jordan would be sharing for the short voyage. "Although, I must warn you that there are times when I do not travel by sea very well."

"You get seasick?" Jordan asked, sitting down on the side of one bunk and testing its softness.

"It happens occasionally. I'll be fine until we leave the bay, then we'll just have to wait and see. How was your trip over? Was the sea rough?"

"Very much so," she told her. "Our accommodations were not nearly this nice, and there were days on end when I was so sick the thought of food nearly laid me low. It was not a pleasant experience."

"Well, hopefully we'll both make it to New Orleans just fine," Audrey declared with optimism.

It was less than an hour later, as they were still settling into their cabin, that Audrey's dire predictions came true. As the vessel entered the Gulf waters and headed on its westerly course, the terrible sickness struck. Her coloring paled dramatically until she was as white as a sheet, and the nausea and weakness forced her to take to her bed.

When Nick knocked on the door, having come to accompany both ladies to the midday meal, he found that Jordan was busy tending the prostrate chaperone. She had rolled up the sleeves of her new turquoise daygown and had unbuttoned several of the buttons at the bodice of the high-necked gown to keep from getting too warm.

"Miss Layton's not feeling well?" he asked, his eyes darkening in concern as he saw Jordan. Earlier, when he'd first seen her wearing the new gown, he'd meant to tell her that she looked pretty. Somehow there hadn't been time then. Now, seeing her with the bodice partially undone, he thought she looked even more beautiful. His gaze lingered on the V created by the

211

parted fabric, and he wondered what it would be like to press a kiss to her throat there.

Jordan was unaware of the direction of his thoughts as she gave him an apologetic smile. She stepped out into the companionway, pulling the stateroom door almost closed behind her to afford Miss Layton her privacy. "Yes, I'm afraid she's quite seasick. We won't be able to join you."

"Are you hungry? Shall I have something brought over?" Nick offered, knowing that while Miss Layton might not want to eat, Jordan was probably starving. It had been a while since they'd breakfasted.

"Thanks, but no."

"You're not getting sick, too?"

"No, I'm fine, really," she hastened to reassure him, wondering why he was even bothering to act concerned since there was no one around to hear. Surely, he didn't truly care. "I just thought that as miserable as she's feeling right now, she shouldn't be left alone. Perhaps by dinner things will be better."

"I hope so. I'll check with you then." Nick started to go, then changed his mind and turned back to her just before she shut the door. "Oh, and Jordan?"

She stuck her head back out to see what it was he wanted. "Yes?"

"I meant to tell you earlier . . . That dress is lovely on you. I knew the color would be good when we picked it."

With that he strode off to join Slater, leaving Jordan staring after him with something akin to amazement.

Jordan passed the afternoon tending to the other woman's needs. She bathed her face with cool water and tried to keep her distracted with light conversation, punctuated by trips to empty the slop jar. Audrey appreciated her efforts, but the queasiness grew so bad that it was impossible for her to talk much. She lay

212

quietly upon the bed, longing for either *terra firma* or a quick, painless death—neither of which she was afforded. When a particularly bad wave of nausea wracked her, she gave an abject groan of misery.

"Do you feel worse?" Jordan was instantly at her side.

"It's impossible for me to feel worse, my dear," Audrey tried to make a joke of it, but somehow at that moment, it wasn't really funny. Maybe later . . . "If I felt any worse, I'd be dead, and then I'd feel better."

Shock registered on Jordan's features when she noticed that her guardian's color had turned a particularly sickly shade of green. "Is there anything I can do?"

"No, no. I've lived through this several times before, and while it's never pleasant, it's also never fatal. I think if I could just manage to fall asleep for a little while, it might pass," she told her weakly.

Jordan could hear the exhaustion in her voice, so she sat down on her own bunk to keep the vigil. She was hungry and her stomach grumbled in protest, but she ignored it. Maybe later when Nick came she'd have him bring her something.

The soft knock at the door made Jordan realize that she must have dozed off herself. She glanced over at her companion to find her sound asleep. Pleased that she was finally getting some rest, she hurried to answer the door before whoever it was knocked again. Jordan opened the portal a crack, and seeing Nick, slipped silently from the room. She put a finger to her lips to stop any questions he might have until she was safely out in the hall.

"She's asleep, and I didn't want to wake her."

"It's time for dinner. Can you get away?"

"I am hungry, but I wonder if I should leave her . . ." Jordan looked back guiltily.

"You have to eat, Jordan. There's no reason for you to starve to death just because Miss Layton's under the weather. I promise we won't be gone long," he coaxed, wanting to spend some time alone with her without the eagle-eyed Miss Layton hovering nearby.

"I suppose not," she agreed. She liked his logic, but she had a feeling her guardian wouldn't. "I'll need a little time to freshen up a bit."

"Shall I meet you on deck?"

"Fine."

For some reason, Jordan was feeling decidedly wicked when she reentered the stateroom. She used her hunger as justification for her going with Nick, but she still couldn't help but feel a rush of forbidden excitement over the idea of being with him without Miss Layton.

Jordan carefully selected a demure, rose-colored gown that set off the beauty of her complexion. Once she'd dressed, she turned her attention to her hair and wound it into an attractive chignon. She took the time to study her reflection in the small mirror over the washstand. Jordan wanted to make sure she looked her best, and as she smoothed back an errant curl, she wondered why she was suddenly so concerned with her appearance. She wasn't going to impress anyone tonight. She was merely going to the ship's dining room, enjoy her dinner, and then return to her cabin. That was all. Even so, as she crept quietly from the stateroom, her heart was racing.

Nick was waiting alone at the rail when Jordan came up on deck. She spotted him immediately, for he stood out among the others, a man among men, and her heart beat a little faster. There was a certain male power that emanated from him. Nick was the kind of man any woman would have been proud to call her own, and for the time being, at least, she could pretend she really did hold his love. Her head held high, a small smile curving her lips, she walked regally toward him.

Nick did not know why he felt the need to look around at that particular moment, but he did. As he glanced over his shoulder and saw her coming toward him looking like an angel straight from heaven, something flared within him. He straightened slowly, never taking his eyes off her, then strode forth to meet her.

Chapter Sixteen

As Slater folded his napkin and placed it back on the table, he reflected on when, if ever, he'd passed a more amusing evening. From beneath lowered lids, he glanced at his dining companions and was hard put not to smile. Nick was glowering, Montgomery was glowering, and Jordan was trying her best not to notice either man's discomfort.

Slater had been truly entertained watching Nick tonight. His friend was not one for jealousy, but Slater knew enough to recognize the green-eyed monster even when Nick didn't. No matter how much Nick might try to deny it, he was coming to feel something for this girl, and he resented the relationship she'd had with Philip. Why else would he have sat there through the meal so tense and on edge? Why else would he have shot the other man such deadly looks every time he tried to make conversation with Jordan? He was jealous all right.

When Nick had told him of Miss Layton's condition at the midday meal, Slater had seen the spark of delight in his eyes. Not that his friend wished ill-health on the older woman. But it had been obvious that his friend was looking forward to spending some time alone with Jordan, something he hadn't been able to manage since their outing to the beach over a week ago. It was even more obvious now, as Nick, anxious to get her away from the attentive Montgomery, pushed his chair back and made to stand up from the table.

"Shall we go for a walk on the deck, Jordan?" Nick invited.

"Yes, I'd like that. I'm sure I need the exercise after the meal I just ate," Jordan responded, getting to her feet as Nick helped her with her chair. A walk in the fresh air sounded heavenly after the afternoon she'd just spent in the airless sickroom.

"A walk sounds good. I'll . . ." Philip was about to say, casually of course, that he would join them for the stroll, but Slater inobtrusively clamped a restraining hand on his arm, effectively halting him.

Philip tensed as he watched them leave the dining room. Nick's hand was resting with possessive familiarity at the small of her back, and Jordan was looking happy and relaxed as she gazed up at him.

Philip was worried and it showed on his face. His brow was furrowed and his eyes were hard with suspicion. He didn't like the idea of Jordan being on deck at night alone with Kane while her chaperone was asleep in the stateroom. He'd seen the way Kane had been looking at her during dinner. There was a gleam of something in his eyes now that hadn't been there before, and it troubled him.

Slater waited until Jordan and Nick were completely out of sight before he eased his viselike grip on the impetuous young man's arm. "That wasn't smart."

"She shouldn't . . ." he began, then cut himself off. It was not his place . . .

"She's not your concern any longer," Slater warned him, and then bluntly added. "She does not need or want your protection."

Philip felt frustrated. He knew what Slater was saying was right, but Jordan was still his sister. Philip sat back

217

in his chair, hoping she could handle herself with the worldly Dominic Kane and wishing Miss Layton a very speedy recovery.

The sky was a black velvet canopy spangled with a myriad of twinkling stars as Nick and Jordan emerged on deck. The normal bustle of the day was over, and all was quiet. They strode slowly toward the rail, her arm linked through his, to gaze out over the moonlit sea.

Nick was relieved to get away from the dining room. Between Montgomery's annoying presence and Slater's subtle, knowing smirk, he'd barely managed to tolerate sitting through the meal. If he hadn't known Jordan was so hungry, he might have made his excuses and left even earlier.

Nick wasn't sure exactly what it was that Slater found so amusing. He certainly didn't think there was anything funny about their situation. He'd hired Jordan to play the part of his adoring future bride, and yet he was being forced to sit across the table from her and make polite conversation with her ex-lover. It had not been an easy or comfortable thing to do, and it had been for that reason and that reason alone, Nick told himself, that he'd wanted out of there as quickly as possible.

As he walked the deck now with Jordan by his side, Nick was finally beginning to relax a little. There was a faint cooling breeze blowing and it felt refreshing to them as they paused by the rail.

"Is anything wrong, Nick?" Jordan asked. She'd noticed that he'd had very little to say during dinner and that his expression had been rather forbidding all evening.

"No. Not at all. We finally managed to escape the ever-vigilant Miss Layton, how could anything be wrong? We should be celebrating, you know."

218

"We are celebrating. We're taking a walk all by ourselves." Jordan laughed easily, then asked in a mock serious tone, "You don't think my reputation will be besmirched if I'm seen out here this late at night all alone with you, do you?"

Nick's gaze darkened as he looked down at her. She looked so young and beautiful and happy that he was hard put not to sweep her into his arms right then and there. Holding himself back, he lifted one hand and touched the softness of her cheek with a single finger. "Should anyone dare make a derogatory remark about your character, my love, I'll call them out for you."

His touch sent shivers of delight coursing down Jordan's spine. But just as she was about to let herself believe his words, she realized that an older married couple she'd seen in the dining room earlier had emerged on deck. His actions had all been for display. She turned away from his touch to gaze out across the sea.

"Your gallantry is appreciated, kind sir," she replied, keeping her voice light.

Nick was slightly insulted at her flippant remark and the way she'd turned away from him. "I've never said that to a woman before," he murmured.

Jordan felt a thrill at his statement, but denied it. "You've never been engaged before," she explained with a shrug.

"That's true enough. If I had, I wouldn't be in this predicament now. I'd be at home all settled down . . . an old married man with four children and another on the way."

The thought of Nick having children filled Jordan with a real warmth. She was certain he'd make beautiful babies, for he was such a handsome man, himself. "Do you like children?"

"Yes, in fact, I've always wanted to have quite a few. I grew up without sisters and brothers and I've always felt like I'd missed something. What about you? You're an only child, aren't you?"

"No," she answered, before she realized she shouldn't say anything.

"No?"

"I have a brother."

Nick frowned at her revelation. "Why didn't you mention him before? Where was he when you were forced to indenture yourself? Why didn't he help you when you needed it?"

Thinking quickly, she used Philip's middle name. "John couldn't help me. He's at sea."

"Does he know what's happened to you?"

"I hope so. I wouldn't want him to worry."

"And?"

"And what? There's nothing more he can do for me. There was no money. I had to start a new life, so I did." Jordan suddenly felt very cornered. She didn't want to talk about these things. She didn't want to have to watch every word that came out of her mouth.

Jordan started to look away from Nick, but he took her by the shoulders and made her face him. He lifted her chin with one hand so their eyes met.

"Just when I think I know you, I discover something new." How much more was there about her that he didn't know? The thought both intrigued and troubled him.

As he spoke, Jordan prayed desperately for the strength not to reveal any more to this man. She wanted to slide her gaze away from his, but his power over her was too great.

"There are so many secrets in your eyes, Jordan . . ." Nick was saying. "Will I ever learn them all?"

Every time he thought he had her figured out, she changed. When he first saw her on the docks, he thought her passably attractive—and an illiterate. He'd discovered later that she was lovely to look at and well-mannered, well-read, and well-educated. At the dress-maker's, she'd shown him her knowledge of fashion and good taste. On the beach, she'd seemed the sun-kissed gamin out to charm him with her innocence, even though he knew better. Tonight, in the lovely gown she wore, she appeared the sophisticate. Nick wasn't sure of anything anymore, but he felt determined to find out who Jordan really was.

Aware that the other couple had disappeared from sight, Nick was unable to resist any longer. Slowly, al-most cautiously, he drew Jordan to him and bent to kiss her. The kiss was gentle, and he paused, pulling slightly away to gaze down at her in the moonlight.

Jordan's eyes had drifted shut as she'd lost herself in the wonder of his embrace, and when Nick saw her dreamy expression, all thoughts of remembering their bargain fled. Her lips were moist and parted and beg-ging for his kiss, and he took them in an exchange that was devastating in its intensity.

There was no fighting for Jordan. She wanted this . . . she wanted him. She knew it was right from the moment Nick's lips met hers. That there could be no future for them didn't matter now. All that mattered was that she was in his arms.

Of their own volition, Jordan's arms wound around his neck, drawing him even closer to her. When his hand sought the swell of her breast, she arched against him, wanting to get as near to him as she could.

Audrey stirred in her bed and came slowly awake. At the feel of the boat's roll beneath her, a wave of nausea wracked her, and she managed to grab for the slop jar just in time. When her trauma had passed, she lay back weakly staring into the darkness and trying to compose her thoughts. Where was Jordan?

221

"Jordan?" she croaked her name hoarsely, but there came no reply. "Oh, my God," Audrey muttered, struggling to sit upright.

It was so dark, it had to be late. But if the hour was so advanced, then where was her ward? Jordan might have gone out for dinner, but she should have been back by now, safely tucked away in her bed.

Audrey became concerned, and that worry gave her strength. She had been hired to do a job. She had been hired to protect Jordan, and she'd let her illness interfere. She'd failed.

Determined to set things to rights, she swung her legs over the side of her bunk. Audrey sat there for a long minute waiting for the dizziness to pass before making her first attempt to stand. She had some difficulty, but by bracing one arm against the wall, she could move about. Fighting down the queasiness that threatened to force her to return to her bed, she lit the lamp, then reached for her clothing.

Nick's breathing was hot and heavy as he crushed Jordan to his chest. Kiss after drugging kiss had sent his desire soaring. He wanted her as he had never wanted another. The scent of her, the way she trembled at his touch, the honeyed taste of her passionate kisses, all threatened to drive him out of his mind. These few stolen moments weren't enough. His body commanded that he take her.

"Jordan . . ." he said her name in a deep and husky voice.

He held her a little away from him to look down at her, and what he saw in her open, unguarded expression electrified him. She wanted him just as much as he wanted her. He was sure of it. Her eyes were heavy-lidded and her cheeks were flushed. Nick knew he had to get them belowdecks to his stateroom before he lost his control and took her right there on deck. He kissed her once more, his lips parting hers in a soul-stirring exchange that left her knees weak.

"Nick . . ." she breathed, bewildered by the tumultuous emotions that were surging through her.

"Come with me . . ." he told her, taking her hand.

Jordan was lost in a haze of sensuality unlike anything she'd ever experienced before. Their kisses on the beach had been arousing, but tonight, here in the moonlight, something more was happening. She'd discovered the meaning of true passion, and she wanted Nick now as only a grown woman could want a man. When he drew her with him, she didn't protest but went willingly. This was what she wanted, what it seemed she'd waited her whole life for.

Nick didn't want to waste a minute of their precious time alone explaining. Slipping an arm around Jordan's shoulders, he started straight for the companionway and his cabin. He kept her close to his side, loving the feel of her near to him. He could hardly wait to have her in his bed, naked beneath him. He wanted to lose himself in her velvet softness. He wanted to kiss every inch of her satiny flesh and hear her moan with excitement as he pleasured her. He wanted . . .

"Thank heaven I found you two!" Miss Layton exclaimed as they came face to face abruptly at the top of the companionway. "I was so worried! I've been looking everywhere thinking something terrible might have happened to you!"

Jerked back to reality from the sensual oblivion that had enveloped them, the would-be lovers stood perfectly still, frozen in their heated tracks. Their hands fell quickly away from each other, and they were both grateful for the covering of darkness that hid their expressions from the conscientious guardian.

"Miss Layton . . . You're feeling better?" To Nick's profound relief, Jordan found her voice first.

"A little, my dear, a very little. But I knew I couldn't just lie there and not do my duty by you."

"Well, there was really nothing for you to worry about. Nick has been taking very good care of me. We just had dinner, took a short stroll around the deck, and were just heading back to the cabin now." Jordan didn't lie, she just didn't say which cabin.

"You're as much a gentleman as your father," Audrey complimented the still-silent Nick. "I'm sure Jordan must have been tired of being cooped up in our stateroom. I'm glad you enjoyed yourselves, but don't you think it's getting a little late now? We'd better go . . . oh . . . !"

She swayed, suddenly feeling terribly lightheaded and woozy. She put one arm out to brace herself against the wall, but Nick was quickly there at her side, supporting her.

"It looks like we'd better get you back to bed," he said sympathetically as Jordan hurried to take her other arm.

"Yes, let's get you back to our stateroom where you belong," Jordan agreed. Her eyes met Nick's over the top of Audrey's head, but there was nothing to say.

They helped her back down the steps. It was no short walk to the cabin, and by the time they reached the door, the guardian was leaning heavily on Nick.

"I'm sorry about this, Mr. Kane. I promise you, I'll be fine once we dock tomorrow."

"We should reach New Orleans by mid-afternoon."

"You can't imagine how I'm looking forward to it," Audrey replied with dying humor as Nick opened the door and helped her inside. "Thank you for all your kindness."

"You just take care of yourself. Jordan, I'll be waiting in the hall." He retreated from the room as she got ready to lie down. He closed the door, but waited just outside to say good night to Jordan.

Jordan helped her undress, then drew a blanket over her, stalling for a moment before she went to speak to Nick. As her passion had cooled her common sense had returned. The realization of what she'd been about to do sent a shudder through her. She had to make sure that she was never alone with Nick again. He was far too attractive. All he had to do was touch her and she melted. She almost feared that she . . . but no! That couldn't be. It just couldn't. Finally, no longer able to delay it, Jordan went out to see Nick.

While he was waiting for Jordan, Nick, too, had had time to think. His mood turned black as he realized what he'd almost done. He had almost broken his word to Jordan. Theirs was to be a relationship in name only. How could he have forgotten that? What was the matter with him? Why did a single kiss from her render him senseless?

It was ridiculous, Nick told himself. She was just a woman, like all the others he'd ever known. She was nothing special. Oh, yes, she had a pretty face and a nice body, but so had the other women he'd been with. What he was feeling was lust, pure and simple, and he would just have to learn to control it for the next several months, that was all. There was no way he was going to let himself get personally involved with her.

When Jordan emerged from the room, Nick's expression was guarded.

"Is she resting comfortably now?"

"As well as she can, I guess. Nick, I . . ." Jordan didn't get the chance to finish what she was going to say.

"You realize that it's a good thing we ran into her when we did, don't you?" He wanted to make sure this sort of thing didn't happen again, and he made sure his tone was serious.

"Of course," she said with a proud lift of her chin. Though his words struck pain directly to her heart, she would never let him know. He'd always told her that he wanted nothing to do with her in that way, and she should have remembered it.

They bid a rather quick, cool good night to each other and parted. Later, when Jordan lay alone in her bed across the cabin from the sleeping Miss Layton, she tried to imagine what would have happened had the chaperone not come to her "rescue." She envisioned herself in Nick's arms, losing herself to his strength and power. As she dwelled on the memory of his potent kisses, she could feel the flame of her need rekindle deep inside her.

With a smothered groan, Jordan rolled over and buried her face in her pillow. She shouldn't feel these things for Nick! But even as she tried to fight it, her body betrayed her. Her body acknowledged what she was trying to deny—she was falling in love with Nick.

Was she in love with Nick? At the thought, Jordan went still. Could it be? Was that what was troubling her so deeply? Was that why she couldn't get him out of her mind? Was that why his kiss and touch drove her to distraction? Slowly she came to realize it was true. No matter how hard she'd tried not to, she had fallen in love with him.

Jordan fought down another groan as she accepted the fact of her heart's wayward yearnings. She did love Nick. Yet even as she admitted it to herself, she also accepted the painful truth that she couldn't let it come to anything, for she could never really be the wife he needed. She was living a lie. She would only ruin him if the truth came out about her past. Jordan drew a ragged breath and curled on her side. Perhaps with sleep the ache in her soul would ease.

Chapter Seventeen

Peri Kane Davidson, a vivacious, dark-haired nineteen-year-old, sat with her Uncle Charles Kane in the parlor at Riverwood, enjoying a cool glass of lemonade. A pretty girl with a lively sense of humor and open personality, she was a favorite of her uncle. Having heard that he wasn't feeling well, she'd come to spend some time with him, arriving only that very morning by steamer from New Orleans, where she lived with her parents, Marjorie and Randall.

"So tell me, Uncle Charles, where is my handsome cousin today?" Peri asked in a teasing tone as she sipped of her refreshing drink. She always heard a lot of gossip about Nick and knew quite a bit about his amorous escapades. She wondered where he'd gone and what he was up to this time.

"Hopefully on his way home from Mobile," the older man responded. "He went there on business several weeks ago and should be back soon."

"Good. I've missed him. It'll be good to see him again."

"I've missed him too."

Peri had always been perceptive as a child. She had the uncanny ability to pick up on others' feelings. When Charles had met her at Riverwood's dock, she'd been surprised by how much he'd aged in the few short months since she'd last seen him, and right now she sensed a terrible loneliness within him. She set her glass down on the table and leaned forward to ask him in earnest, "Uncle Charles, Mother told me you haven't been feeling very well lately. Are you all right?"

"I'm fine, child," he assured her, "as fine as I can be, and once Nick gets back I'll be even better."

Peri accepted his explanation, but harbored some doubts. "Well, that's good. I wouldn't want to think that my very favorite relative wasn't well."

Charles gave her a warm smile. "You don't have a thing to worry about with me, but what about you?" His expression turned mischievous.

"Me? What did I do?"

"Here you are already nineteen and no husband," he baited her. "It's a good thing you're not my daughter . . ."

"Uncle Charles!" Peri cried in mock anger. "It's not my fault I haven't found my prince yet."

"Prince! You've been reading too many fairy tales and dime novels," he said in disparaging good humor. "There are no princes out there, Peri, there are only men."

"That's where you're wrong," she retorted, her eyes twinkling as she matched wits with him. "You're a prince. I'd marry you in a minute if I could. You're tall and handsome and a gentleman through and through, and those are exactly the qualities I'm looking for in my future husband."

"You flatter me, child." His heart warmed as he gazed on the lovely young woman.

"It's not flattery, it's the truth," she said staunchly. "But as far as my finding another one like you, I don't know if I can . . . I'm beginning to wonder if there are any more."

"We'll just have to keep looking for you, I guess. If you

need any help picking someone out, I'd be glad to . . ."

"No, Uncle Charles!" Peri declared in laughing protest. "I don't need any help, thank you just the same. I'll find him. It's just a matter of time."

"All right. I bow to your judgment. I just hope you find him soon. I'd like to meet the man who could win your heart." Charles said the words lightly, but they were poignant to him. He wanted to see all those he loved settled and happy before . . .

"You will, you'll see. He's out there somewhere."

The distant sound of a riverboat's whistle signaling a stop at the dock interrupted their conversation.

Charles's face lit up as he quickly got to his feet. "Since you're already here, I can only hope this is Nick."

"Let's go see," Peri urged.

The two of them headed for the front hall, their tall glasses of fresh lemonade and talk of missing princes forgotten in their anticipation of Nick's return. Peri had always adored her older cousin. Nick was the closest thing she'd had to a brother, and she thought the world of him. She could hardly wait to see him again.

"We need to go down to the dock, Weddington," Charles told the butler as he found him waiting at the door.

"Yes, sir, I know. I've already told one of the boys to run and get the carriage for you just in case it is Mr. Nick and he has a trunk with him. They'll be round in a minute."

"You're a wonder, Weddington," Peri declared affectionately.

"Thank you, Miss Peri." Even the servant was not untouched by her gentle happy spirit, and he smiled broadly at her compliment.

Within minutes, the open carriage was brought to the front door and they were on their way to the Riverwood dock, Charles at the reins. It was not far, less than a mile actually, but Charles was secretly glad he hadn't had to walk it. The steamer was already at the landing when they rode up, and they could see Nick coming down the gangplank with a very fashionably attired young woman on one arm. An elderly matron and a young, blond man followed a few steps behind them. Peri found herself watching the strange man with interest.

"Who do you think he's got with him, Uncle Charles?"

"I have no idea, but I think we're going to find out."

Charles tied the reins and jumped down, then turned to help Peri. Together they went forth to greet them. Charles felt good. He was eager to see Nick and talk to him, to tell him that he wanted him home, that the marriage clause had been a folly of a desperate old man, and that he'd finally come to his senses and had it stricken from the will. He had so much he wanted to say to him, but he knew most of it would have to wait until later, when they were alone.

Jordan was nervous as she watched the tall, silver-haired man and beautiful young woman walking down to the landing from the carriage. Her entire future rested on the next few minutes, and she was afraid. What if Charles Kane didn't like her, or, worse yet, what if he saw through their charade? Nick had mentioned many times how brilliant his father was. What if he wasn't fooled for a moment by their ploy? What if he took one look at her and knew . . .

At that thought, Jordan laughed inwardly at herself. If Charles Kane looked at her and believed she didn't love his son, then he was not the astute judge of character Nick had made him out to be. Despite her convictions to the contrary, the days since she'd discovered her true feelings had not given her any reprieve from them. No matter how she fought against it, there was no escape. No matter how she tried to tell herself that Nick

230

didn't love her, it didn't seem to matter to her rebellious heart. In spite of the futility, in spite of the heartbreak she knew would be hers one day, in spite of the deceit on both sides, she loved Nick.

Because of that love, Jordan regarded the other woman suspiciously. Who was this lovely creature with the perfect figure and beautiful dark hair? Was she one of Nick's past loves? The way she looked at Nick with love in her eyes stirred ugly jealousy within Jordan. She'd never been jealous before, and it made her decidedly uncomfortable. Jordan clung a little more tightly to his arm, wanting him for herself, not wanting to share him with anyone.

Nick thought Jordan was clinging to him because she was worried. He put one of his big hands over her much smaller one where it rested on his sleeve.

"Don't worry. It'll work, you'll see," he encouraged her, his gaze sweeping over her face in a loving caress.

"Nick!" Peri and Charles both called out to him at once as they lifted hands in greeting.

Nick had not realized how much he'd missed his father until he saw him again. A pang of bittersweet emotion rushed through him, and he hurried his pace.

Peri and Jordan both stood back as the two men came together. Father and son first clasped hands then embraced warmly as the others looked on. Peri watched the scene through loving eyes, for these two wonderful men meant the world to her. When their embrace finally ended and Nick turned to her, his arms spread wide in invitation, she flew into his embrace with a laugh of pure delight. He swung her around and around as he'd done ever since they were children and then set her to her feet before him, still holding her hands in his.

"Peri! I'm so glad you're here!"

"It's about time you came home, Nicky!" Peri scolded, her face glowing with the love she felt for him.

"Have you been here long, Peri?" he asked.

"No, as a matter of fact, I only arrived this morning. Your timing is perfect. But tell me, Nicky, we're dying to know." She took his arm and pulled him close. "Who are your friends?"

The way she drew him to her looked like the possessive gesture of a lover, and Jordan felt an unbidden white heat growing within her. Her jaw was clenched, and her hands were balled into fists. She hadn't known she'd be subjected to any of his past loves. She felt humiliated and embarrassed. She wondered how he could subject her to such a display and then expect to introduce her as his fiancée. Jordan fought to keep her expression a bit haughty and aloof.

Nick straightened and looked to his father. "Father . . . Peri . . . I have a surprise for you." He let go of Peri and held out one arm to Jordan inviting her back to his side.

"You do?" Charles studied with interest the beautiful, young woman who moved to his son's side.

"Yes . . . Father, this is Jordan Douglas, my fiancée. Jordan, this is my father, Charles Kane, and my cousin, Peri Davidson."

At the introduction of the other woman as his cousin, Jordan felt all the jealousy drain away. She was greatly relieved, for the girl was so pretty she would have been strong competition for Nick's love had she been an adversary. When she saw the warm, welcoming expression on the other woman's face, she returned her smile with ease.

"Your fiancée? How wonderful!" Peri exclaimed happily as she gave her a quick hug. She thought Jordan absolutely beautiful, far more gorgeous than any of the girls from the area, and she believed Nick had chosen well.

"Your fiancée?" Charles repeated, not sure whether

232

to be pleased or upset. Here he had been ready to admit his mistake and make amends, and now there was no need. He could tell just by the way they were looking at each other that everything he'd hoped for had happened. Nick had found the woman of his dreams. His ultimatum had been foolish, true, but it had accomplished what he'd wanted. It hadn't been a failure if Nick had truly fallen in love.

"How do you do, sir?" Jordan asked, turning her emerald gaze from Nick to her future father-in-law. Their eyes met for the very first time, and in that moment Jordan knew she was going to love Charles. She saw no suspicion or meanness in his expression, only open loving kindness and immediate acceptance.

"How do you do, Jordan? What a wonderful name. You're obviously English. Wherever did you meet my son?" he inquired politely as he took her hand in his.

Charles's voice sounded so young and full of life that Nick suddenly felt much better about his deception. If his bringing home a bride could make his father happy, it was worth every cent it had cost him and every minute of the aggravation.

"We met through a mutual acquaintance in Mobile," Jordan supplied, just as she and Nick had agreed.

"Well, you must tell me all about it, Jordan," he told her as he took her arm and drew her along with him away from Nick toward the carriage.

"Father, you haven't met Miss Layton or the new accountant I've hired, Philip Montgomery," Nick pointed out in exasperation as his father took command of Jordan.

"Bring them along up to the house, son. You can make the rest of the introductions there. Right now, I want to escort my future daughter-in-law up to Riverwood."

"But . . ."

"Peri? Aren't you coming with us?"

Peri had been watching the new accountant from beneath lowered lashes. At her uncle's call she dashed after him, wanting to find out all she could about Nick's love.

Nick had no time to protest further as Charles handed both women into the carriage and climbed in with them.

"I'll send the carriage back for you and the others."

Swept away by Charles's charming insistence, Jordan could only glance back helplessly at Nick. Her expression was a mixture of doubt and pleasure until she saw him smiling widely as he watched them go.

"I'll see you at the house in a few minutes."

Charles slapped the reins to the back of the horse and they moved off.

Jordan's first sight of the Riverwood plantation house nearly took her breath away. Majestic in its white-pillared Grecian design, it sat on a low hill, glistening brilliantly in the afternoon sun amidst the perfectly manicured lawns and bright flowering gardens. Jordan knew she was gaping, but she didn't care. She'd had no idea Nick's home would look like this. When he'd said the house was big, she'd never dreamed it was a mansion, especially not one this beautiful.

"It's lovely," Jordan whispered.

"Thank you," Charles swelled with pride, pleased that she was impressed.

"Do you live here, too?" she asked Peri.

"Me? Oh, no. My family's from New Orleans. I just came upriver to visit with Uncle Charles for a few weeks."

"I can understand why you'd want to. It's . . . so peaceful."

"Uncle Charles and Nicky have . . ."

"Nicky?" Jordan repeated, and she couldn't help but chuckle at the nickname.

"I'm sorry." Peri laughed, too. "I should stop calling

234

him that now that we're both grown, but he's been Nicky to me ever since I was little and used to follow him around the plantation. Anyway, Uncle Charles and Nicky have worked for years to make Riverwood the showplace it is."

"It's been a labor of love, Peri," Charles corrected.

"Riverwood is heavenly, Mr. Kane. I never imagined it would be this wonderful."

"Please, call me Charles."

Jordan favored him with a bright smile, liking him more with every passing minute and regretting his ill-health. "Charles."

"But tell us about you, Jordan," he asked as he drew the carriage to a stop before the house. "How did all this come about?"

She had just begun to give them the version she and Nick had concocted when a tall black man came out of the house.

"Mr. Nick . . . I'm . ." Weddington stopped abruptly when he realized that Nick wasn't there. "Mr. Charles, I'm sorry. I thought it was Mr. Nick coming home."

"He's here, all right, Weddington, but I left him down at the landing. I wanted to bring his surprise home myself."

"Surprise, sir?"

"Jordan meet Weddington. He's the mainstay of my household. Weddington, this is Miss Jordan Douglas, soon to be Mrs. Dominic Kane."

Weddington's eyes widened as he glanced from the young woman to Charles. "Mr. Nick's finally gone and done it? Mr. Nick's found himself a bride?"

"He most certainly has, and she was well worth the wait, don't you agree?" he asked as he climbed out and helped her and Peri down.

"Yes, sir. Absolutely." He grinned as he held the door

235

wide to allow them entrance to the house.

"Have one of the other servants take the carriage back down to the landing to pick Nick up. There are two other guests with him."

"I'll see to it right away, and I'll have light refreshments brought to you in the parlor and tell the cook that there will be guests for dinner."

"That'll be fine," he answered as he led the two young women into the sitting room.

Jordan was in awe from the moment she stepped through the front door. The house had been magnificent from the outside, but nothing had prepared her for the interior. The high-ceilinged foyer was breathtaking with its impressive staircase, cool white walls, and highly polished wood floors. If it were possible, the parlor was even better. Nothing was overdone. Everything was elegant and understated — from the pooling, deep green velvet drapes to the imported French wallcovering to the marble fireplace and sumptuous overstuffed furniture.

Jordan found it hard to believe that she was going to be living amidst all this splendor. When her parents had been alive, they'd lived comfortably, but it had never come close to this. She fretted for a moment that Charles might be the kind of man who was enamored of his things, but this fear was soon put to rest as he waved her and Peri into the chairs and then dropped down easily on the sofa nearby.

"This will be your home from now on, Jordan. I want you to be happy here," he said expansively. "I'll let Peri and Nick give you the guided tour later. For now, let's just get acquainted, shall we?"

"I'd like that."

By the time Nick arrived with Miss Layton, Philip, and their trunks, Jordan, Peri, and Charles were chatting like old friends. Nick paused in the hall briefly to listen to their conversation, and the sound of his father's easy laughter struck pain in his heart. He was thrilled that things were going so well, but his worry about the state of his father's health gnawed at him. As he entered the parlor with Philip and the chaperone, he had to force a smile.

"So, I can see you're well on your way to getting to know each other."

"Oh, yes, Nick," Jordan replied, turning a loving gaze to him. "Your father and Peri are wonderful and so is your home. I never realized it would be this beautiful."

"I'm glad you like it," Nick said as he moved to stand beside her. "Father, and Peri, this is Miss Audrey Layton, Jordan's companion for the trip. Miss Layton met you once before, years ago when Mother was alive."

"Audrey Layton, of course I remember, but it has been years." Charles rose to greet her. "I appreciate your diligence in safeguarding my future daughter-in-law's reputation. Knowing what a rake my son is, I'm sure she needed every bit of your expertise."

Nick tried to laugh off his father's remark, and Jordan blushed a bit, remembering Miss Layton's perfectly-timed "rescue."

"Except for the seasickness on the ship, everything went very well. Miss Douglas is a lovely young lady, and your son was the perfect gentleman."

Charles glanced at Nick, a glimmer of newfound respect in his eyes.

"And this is Philip Montgomery." Nick had already cautioned Philip to say nothing about his indentured status. "I met Philip here at the same social occasion where Jordan and I were introduced. He's an accountant just over from England, and he was looking for work. We needed someone to help out with the books, so I offered him the job."

Charles went forward to shake hands with Philip. He'd already judged him to be an honest young man, for he was most forthright in meeting his gaze. "Welcome to Riverwood."

"Thank you, Mr. Kane."

"I thought he might be able to use the old overseer's house."

"That sounds like a good idea. Join us for some refreshments now, and then you can show him to his quarters before dinner. Miss Layton, I hope you'll be staying with us until after the wedding?"

"That would be fine," she readily agreed, looking forward to spending some time at Riverwood.

"Good, then everything's settled." He smiled happily. "Welcome home, son."

Chapter Eighteen

"So how are you feeling, really?" Nick asked as he sat with his father in the study later that night after the others had retired. Dinner had been a cordial affair, and everyone had seemed to enjoy themselves, especially Charles.

"Much better," Charles answered, and he wasn't lying. With Peri there to cheer him and now the pleasant surprise of Jordan, he was feeling better than he had in ages . . . younger and more alive.

"I'm glad. I worried about you while I was gone."

"There was no need. I've been taking it slow and easy and doing only what had to be done."

"Good." He got up and went to the small bar to pour himself a tumbler of his father's best bourbon. "Well, tell me. I'm waiting to hear. What do you think of Jordan?" He had his back to his father as he spoke, and when there was no immediate answer he glanced at him over his shoulder, concerned about his silence.

"Son," Charles began in a very serious tone that matched his expression, "I think Jordan is just about the best thing that's ever happened to you."

"You do?" Nick was pleased. He'd felt they'd gotten along well, but he wanted to be sure.

"Yes. I'm so proud of you and the choice you've made. Jordan is a wonderful girl. She's warm and bright and intelligent, not to mention the best looking woman in the parish, with the exception of your cousin, of course. I'm glad you waited and took your time about this, and I can tell you right now that I'm going to be very glad to have her as my daughter-in-law."

Charles' endorsement was wholehearted. He held nothing back in his praise. He'd originally planned to tell Nick not to worry about the clause, to reveal that he'd had it eliminated from the will, but now it didn't matter. Nick was obviously very happy with Jordan, and he was very happy for Nick.

With each compliment his father paid him, Nick grew more and more uncomfortable. He was riding the double-edged blade of a desperate lie, and it was a cutting experience. On one hand, he felt good that he'd made his father happy. He loved his father. There was nothing in the world he wouldn't do for him. It was that love that had driven him to buy Jordan, but now that the deed was done and the charade set in motion, his conscience was bothering him.

"And," Charles was still saying, "since I approve so completely of your fiancée, I have something for you."

Nick looked puzzled. "What?"

His father unlocked and opened his center desk drawer. He took out a simple jewelry box and held it out for him to take.

"It was your mother's," was all he said as he waited for Nick to open it.

Nick stared down at the beautiful white gold ring with its large solitaire diamond set in a filigree design and remembered clearly that his mother had worn it often. "But Mother's ring . . . I know it means so much to you . . ."

"It does, and that's precisely why I want Jordan to have it. She's special, Nick. Your mother would have approved of your choice, and she would have loved her, too. You'd honor us both if you gave it to her."

There was a terrible knot in Nick's throat that he couldn't seem to swallow, and when he looked up at his father, his eyes were misty. "I hadn't even thought about a ring yet . . ." He paused to swallow tightly. "But there's no other ring I'd rather give her than this one. Thank you."

It was a tender moment. They faced each other across the room, each nearly bursting with emotions that they fought to contain.

"You're more than welcome, my son, and congratulations."

Jordan lay awake in the middle of the wide four-poster bed in the spacious, beautifully furnished room the Kanes had given her. Though it was late, sleep would not come. Her thoughts were confused as she struggled with all the lies she was being forced to live.

Jordan had not intended to care for Nick's father. From Nick's description, she'd expected him to be a domineering old man. What she'd found had been just the opposite. In the space of just a few hours, Charles Kane had won her completely. He was one of the most intelligent men she'd ever met. He had a good sense of humor and a profound sense of family. She liked him.

She could tell that Nick's bringing her here had made Charles very happy, and so she was not about to let anything ruin their carefully laid plans. The wedding would take place, and she would, at least for a short time, really be the daughter-in-law Charles so wanted.

Letting her thoughts drift a bit, Jordan wondered how Philip was faring. He'd been seated as far away from her as possible at the formal dining room table, so she'd had no opportunity to speak with him at all outside of general conversation. She hoped he was comfortable wherever he was, and she vowed to try to find the chance to talk with him soon.

Jordan had noticed that Philip and Peri seemed to have a lot to say to each other. She smiled a bit sadly at the thought. Peri was a very nice young woman. She had taken a liking to her right away, just as Philip obviously had, but it was essential that he guard his heart just as protectively as she had to guard hers. With a deep, weary sigh, she rolled over and closed her eyes, and eventually, sleep did claim her.

Peri had tried to fall asleep, but found she was just too excited to rest. Slipping from bed, she wrapped her robe around her and hurried from the room. She guessed that her uncle would still be in his study talking to Nick, and she was pleased to find she was right. She knocked once softly on the door, and Nick bid her to come in.

"How did you know it was me?" she asked as she entered.

"Who else would be so inquisitive that they'd come down here in the middle of the night to see what was going on?" Nick teased as he watched his favorite cousin cross the room, her feet bare, her ebony hair tumbling around her shoulders in disarray. Though she was nineteen, right now she barely looked old enough to be up this late. He'd always loved Peri, but there had been moments during his adolescent years when he'd been greatly tempted to run every time he'd seen her coming. She'd meant nothing but trouble to him in those days, always asking him questions a girl shouldn't ask and constantly following him around. As much as he'd railed against her attentions at the time, he'd secretly enjoyed her interest.

"I couldn't sleep, and I thought it would be nice just to talk with you and Uncle Charles for a while. You know, I only arrived a short time before you did," she said very primly, with the dignity of a woman full grown.

"Please, just ignore my uncouth son and join us," Charles welcomed her.

Peri longed to stick her tongue out at her cousin as she'd done often in the past, but she managed to control the impish urge. "Thank you." She curled up on the sofa, tucking her bare feet under her. "So, what are you talking about?"

"Actually, we were just getting ready to retire," Nick teased with a fake yawn.

"Oh, you . . . !"

"Dominic, be kind to Peri," his father scolded with a smile.

The banter between the two of them was practically a ritual, and it could go on for hours if not nipped in the bud. Nick fell obediently silent, but he cast her a wicked look.

"As I was about to tell you," Charles went on, "I just gave Nick your Aunt Andrea's engagement ring. I thought it would be perfect for Jordan."

"That's wonderful," Peri's eyes filled with tears, for she knew what the ring meant to her uncle. "When are you going to give it to her?"

"Oh, no," Nick balked at revealing any of his plans. "I'm not telling you a thing or you'll be hiding in the bushes behind us or sitting on a tree limb over our heads just to watch."

"I'm grown up now, in case you hadn't noticed, Dominic Kane," Peri said haughtily. "I was just thinking like a woman, that's all. I knew she'd be excited, so I thought you might want to give it to her as soon as possible."

"I will, don't worry."

"Have you talked about the wedding yet? How soon are you getting married?"

Nick didn't look at his father as he answered, "The sooner, the better. I feel like I've waited an eternity for her already."

Charles was thrilled at Nick's remark, for it wiped away any lingering doubts he might have had about the marriage. It was plain to him that his son was in love. "You'll need three weeks for the banns," he pointed out.

"Does she have a wedding dress?" Peri inquired. "If not, you'll have to get a seamstress out here right away. And what about a honeymoon?"

"This isn't going to be simple, is it?" Nick almost groaned.

"No, but just leave everything to me. I'll handle it," she offered. She'd planned her own fairy-tale wedding in her daydreams so many times that she knew exactly what had to be done.

"I don't know if that's such a good idea," he hesitated, fearing what his cousin might do to him.

"Please, Uncle Charles," Peri appealed to the higher authority. "Let me help. It'll be fun, and Jordan and I will be able to get to know each other then. Please? I know all the right shops and all the right people . . ."

"Peri's quite capable of helping you with this, Nick. I think you should accept her generous offer and be grateful for it."

He gave in gracefully, as he'd known he would from the beginning. "All right," he agreed. "What do we have to do first?"

"Set the date, of course," she announced.

"I'll talk it over with Jordan, but I'm sure she'll agree that the earliest day possible is fine with her."

"Since this is Thursday, we can start your banns this Sunday. Shall we plan for the Saturday following the last bann?"

"Fine."

"Good, that gives us just a little over four weeks to get

244

everything set up. There are invitations to write, a reception to plan . . ."

"Slow down for just a minute," Charles spoke up, then turned his attention to Nick. "Do you want a large ceremony or would you prefer a small, more intimate wedding?"

Though Charles seemed much like his old self, Nick could still see the effects of his illness on him. He might act as if he were feeling fine, but Nick knew better. He knew a private wedding would be much easier on him.

"Since Jordan won't have the opportunity to meet very many people before the wedding day, I think we ought to confine our guest list to family and our most intimate friends. What do you think?"

"That sounds sensible to me," Charles added.

"Good. I'll check with Jordan first thing in the morning, but I'm sure there will be no problem."

"Then everything's set. All I have to do tomorrow is send a message to New Orleans to my dressmaker. You do want Mademoiselle Marilynn, don't you? She is the absolute best."

"Yes, spare no expense," Charles directed before Nick could answer. "Order whatever she needs. I want nothing but the very best for our Jordan."

"Wonderful, Uncle Charles. You won't regret it. Jordan will be the most gorgeous bride, you'll see."

"I'm looking forward to it," he told them both. Then realizing how tired he actually was, he got slowly to his feet. "Now, if you two youngsters will excuse me, I think I'm going to call it a night."

They said their good nights, and he headed upstairs to the master bedroom. The stairs seemed terribly steep tonight, but he struggled on anyway. He was short of breath when he made it to the top, and his movements were slow and painful as he walked down the wide hall to his room.

As was her habit, the maid had already turned down his bed and left a lamp burning low on his dresser. Charles thought the bed looked particularly inviting tonight, and feeling suddenly too tired to undress, he stretched out across it fully clothed. His mood was mellow as he stared at the oil portrait of his long-dead wife where it hung opposite the foot of the bed.

"He's finally done it, my love," Charles whispered to Andrea's picture. "Your son has fallen in love."

He paused and sighed deeply. Contentment filled him. It was almost as if he could feel her presence there with him.

"Her name's Jordan, and she's a pretty girl. There's nothing spoiled or coy about her. She seems very straightforward, and that's not something you find very often in the girls of this younger generation."

His eyes closed as he sighed again and finally felt himself start to relax. He was so tired . . . so very tired.

"I like her, Andrea, and you would too."

Too exhausted to say any more, he slept, and for the first time in ages his dreams were sweet.

Jordan was up early the next morning. The maid had showed her where the bedpull was, and so shortly after dawn she summoned the servant to request a bath. She was amazed at the speed and efficiency of the servants here at Riverwood, and she intended to compliment Charles as soon as she saw him again.

"Can I get you anything else, ma'am?" the maid named Claire asked.

"No, this is perfect," Jordan replied.

"Then I'll come back in a little while to help you dress."

"That'll be fine. Is there a certain time for breakfast?"

"Yes, ma'am. Mr. Charles usually comes down to eat

246

about 7:30."

"And Nick?"

"Whenever he's home, he joins him."

"Thank you, Claire. I'll plan on breakfasting with them this morning."

"I'll tell the cook."

When the servant had gone, Jordan shed her wrapper and stepped into the tub of hot water. It was a rapturous experience and she loved every minute of it. She knew she couldn't dally too long, though, for she still had to do her hair and pick out a dress. If she was going to breakfast with Nick and his father she wanted to look her best.

By the time the maid returned, Jordan had already donned her chemise and was brushing out her hair before the large mirror at the dressing table. Because of the heat and humidity of the Louisiana summer, Claire suggested that they pin her hair up, and Jordan quickly agreed to the cool style. She chose a simple yet pretty yellow daygown, and when she started downstairs she felt fresh and well-rested. The nervousness she'd experienced the day before was gone. She had settled into her role with relative ease. Now, if she could just make it through the wedding, she'd be all right.

The dining room was deserted when Jordan entered, but the French doors that led to the gallery were open. It was still early enough that the temperature was cool, so she wandered outside to enjoy the breeze and to view the flowering garden that bordered the house on that side. Peri had pointed it out to her the day before when she'd taken her on a whirlwind tour of the house, but they hadn't paused to look for more than a minute then. Now, Jordan just wanted to enjoy the fragrant serenity.

As she left the gallery and strolled the narrow garden path, Jordan understood completely why Nick was so determined to keep his home. She had fallen in love with

247

the house the day before, and now she was finding herself enchanted by the grounds, too. The heady scent of the flowers and the profusion of colorful blossoms made Riverwood seem like heaven on earth. She realized then that if their places had been reversed and it had been her home, she too would have done everything necessary to keep it . . . even marry someone she didn't love.

Nick had slept reasonably well. It felt good to be home, and the fact that things had gone so smoothly between Jordan and his father left him encouraged. He bathed, shaved, and dressed, then headed downstairs for his usual early morning breakfast with his father. He entered the dining room to find that his father hadn't come down yet and that an extra place had been set at the table.

"Is Peri joining us this morning?" Nick asked Weddington as he came into the room carrying a silver coffee service.

"No, sir. Miss Jordan is the one who's up, and she's already come down stairs. I expect she's out on the gallery somewhere."

Nick was pleased with the news. "Thanks. I'll go find her. Call us when my father comes down."

"Yes, sir."

Nick touched his pants pocket to make sure he had his mother's ring with him as he started for the French doors. He had hoped to find a moment alone with her sometime today so he could give the ring to her privately, and this looked to be the perfect time. As he stepped outside on the wide, shaded veranda, he caught sight of Jordan in the garden. Rather than call out to her and risk disturbing the still-sleeping Peri, whose room was directly above the dining room, he merely went into the garden after her.

Jordan was daydreaming as she wandered through the lush foliage. In her fantasy, she imagined that her trouble with Luther had never happened and that she wasn't wanted for murder. She pretended that Nick had fallen in love with her just as she had with him and that their marriage was really going to be a love match. She envisioned herself living here at Riverwood, loving Nick, and raising his children. She sighed dreamily at the thought and sat down on a small wrought iron bench near the splashing fountain she'd found near the center of the garden.

Nick found her sitting there, looking absolutely lovely as she gazed into the splashing waters. "Jordan?"

"Nick?" She was surprised to find that he'd come for her, and she had to fight down the urge to believe that her dream was coming true. "I didn't know you were up yet."

"Weddington told me you'd gone outside, so I thought I'd come look for you."

"I was just taking a walk through the garden. It's beautiful."

"Thank you. My mother started it years ago right after they'd completed the house, and my father's worked very hard to keep it up. It's his living tribute to her, I think."

"He's done a remarkable job."

"Tell him. I'm sure he'd be pleased to know that you like it."

"I will."

Nick paused to study the way the sun glinted off her pale, golden hair and the way her eyes held such a dreamy, faraway look this morning. He was tempted to touch her, but he didn't. "He's very taken with you, you know. You're doing a great job of winning him over."

Jordan stiffened, a bit offended by his words. "I like your father. He's a very nice man."

"Yes, well, that's good. I'm glad you like him. It

249

makes it that much easier for you," Nick answered, a little uncomfortable with the subject.

"It's not very difficult pretending I'm happy here. Who wouldn't be? Riverwood is the most magnificent estate I've ever seen, and your father and cousin are two of the friendliest, most honest people I've ever met. They accepted me immediately and did everything they could to make me feel right at home."

"I'm glad it's going so well . . ." Nick wanted to change the subject. "I've got something here for you . . ." He dug into his pocket and pulled out the ring.

"A ring?" Jordan was startled. She didn't know why, but she hadn't really been expecting one.

"Yes, my father wanted you to have this. It belonged to my mother."

Nick took her hand and slowly slid the ring on her finger. Jordan's hand was trembling as she stared down at the delicate keepsake.

"It's lovely . . ." She lifted her gaze to his, and doubt was reflected in the sparkling emerald depths. "Nick . . . are you sure about this?"

"Yes . . . yes, I'm sure," Nick said slowly, unable to look away from her. She was sitting there gazing up at him, looking so absolutely desirable that it was all he could do to keep from embracing her. He wanted to hold her and touch her and possess her completely.

It was then, while he was waging war within himself whether or not he should give in to his passion and touch her, that Peri's intrusive voice rang out from her second-floor bedroom window high above the garden.

"Go on, Nicky! Kiss her! It's not every day you give your fiancée her engagement ring!"

250

Chapter Nineteen

"We have an audience," Nick murmured, needing no further encouragement to draw Jordan to him.

They both went perfectly still, shocked by the current that passed between them as they stood so close together. There was nothing gentle or sweet about what they were feeling. It was elemental and near violent in its intensity. Nick's lips found Jordan's with unerring accuracy, and his mouth claimed hers with passionate dominance. His kisses were hungry, devouring all she could give him and demanding more.

Jordan found herself rising up on her toes and looping her arms around his neck to fit herself more tightly to him. His arms couldn't seem to hold her close enough, and she was aching to get nearer.

At her unspoken invitation, Nick boldly deepened the kiss. Thrusting his tongue between her parted lips, he sought her own in a sensual, rhythmic imitation of love's most intimate dance. Jordan shivered with delicious delight as she returned his fervid embrace.

When they finally broke apart, unable to stand the nearly unbearable tension of their desire, she whispered his name in a helpless plea. "Oh, Nick . . ."

"Congratulations, you two!" came Peri's teasing call, convinced by their performance that their love for one another was very real. "Imagine! You've got over three

251

whole weeks to wait!"

"Three weeks?" Jordan looked up at Nick, uncertain what Peri was talking about.

"Our wedding, my love. If it's agreeable to you, the banns will be published starting this Sunday, and we'll be married the Saturday after the third set."

Jordan was certain that he was mocking her, that his interest in her opinion was only for Peri's benefit. Though she'd been momentarily caught up in the power of her attraction for him, the truth of Nick's game returned with a vengeance. She kept her voice cool as she replied, "Yes. Yes, of course. You know whatever you decide is fine with me."

The wildfire of desire that had possessed Nick flared and died at her composed answer. He realized that her response to his kiss had simply been for show. Montgomery was the man she loved . . . the man she wanted. Stepping away from her, he offered her his arm.

"Shall we go in for breakfast?"

Jordan nodded.

"Wait for me in the dining room! As soon as I finish getting dressed, I'll be down!" Peri announced happily. "Then Jordan and I can start making all the plans!"

Peri wasted no time in throwing on her clothes, and she hurried downstairs. She found the two of them settled at the table, enjoying the bountiful meal of fluffy scrambled eggs, thick slices of ham, and hot biscuits and honey that the cook had prepared.

"It looks and smells delicious," Peri said as she slid into the chair across from Jordan and began to help herself. Weddington appeared, bringing her a glass of cool, sweet milk, and she thanked him profusely for remembering her favorite beverage. After he'd gone, she asked innocently enough, "Where's Uncle Charles?"

"I guess he must be a little extra tired this morning. There was a lot of excitement yesterday," Nick offered, though he, too, wondered at his absence. Nick knew his father was no longer keeping to his rigid work schedule, but before he'd left for Mobile he'd still been getting up early every day. Nick decided that he'd finish his breakfast and then go check on him before relaxing with a cup of coffee.

"That's true enough. My showing up was a big enough surprise for him, but then when you came home with Jordan, he was really excited. Have you told Jordan what we talked about last night, Nicky?"

"Yes, we've already discussed the wedding date?"

"And I'm in complete agreement," Jordan put in, giving Nick a look that could only be interpreted as loving. "It's just too bad it couldn't be sooner."

"Don't worry, Jordan. We've got so much to do, you'll soon be wishing we had more time instead of less." Peri pointed out, mentally drawing up a list of the multitude of tasks they faced. "First, we have to arrange for the banns to be posted and engage the priest."

"I'll take care of that today," Nick volunteered.

"Good. That's one less thing we'll have to worry about. What about a gown?"

"I don't have anything suitable," Jordan replied, glancing at Nick.

"Then we're going to have to order one for you right away. I'll make all the arrangements there. You don't mind if Jordan and I travel into New Orleans for a few days, do you?" Peri asked.

"Not at all. Get whatever you need and charge it to our accounts."

"Fine. Now, Jordan, what do you think about styles?"

As the two women began to discuss fashion, Nick excused himself to go check on his father.

Peri watched out of the corner of her eye until Nick had gone from the room, then asked her newfound friend, "Jordan, tell me . . . What do you know about

Philip Montgomery?"

"Philip?" She was caught off-guard by the question. "Not a whole lot, why?"

"I don't know . . ." she hedged, then confessed all. "Actually, I thought he was very nice and very handsome. You've been around him for a few days now, what's he like?"

Jordan quickly recovered from her mistake as she realized the direction of Peri's thoughts. "Yes, well, I've been around him for more than just a few days. We traveled all the way from England together."

"And?"

"He's very much a gentleman and quite well-educated. I enjoyed his company."

"I'm glad you think so too. I really enjoyed talking to him at dinner last night."

Jordan liked Peri a lot, but she wondered at the wisdom of encouraging her to think about Philip in a romantic way. "Do you think your family would approve of your being interested in the hired help?"

Her question took Peri by surprise. She had never suspected that Jordan would be the type to be concerned with someone's social status. "You sound just like my parents. They're always trying to pick out the perfect man for me."

"Did you ever think that maybe they might be right?"

"I know what I want in a man. They don't have to tell me. I haven't married yet because I haven't found him yet."

"Tell me about your ideal man."

Feeling a growing kinship with the other young woman, Peri opened up to her. "He'll be tall and handsome and very gentle. He'll have to like children and animals. He'll be smart and he'll be honest."

Jordan felt her heart sink. A few months ago, before all their trouble started, her description fit Philip perfectly, but now . . . "He sounds wonderful . . . almost too good to be true."

"He sounds just like Nick and Uncle Charles," Peri said ruefully. "I swear, if I wasn't a relative, I'd be madly in love with both of them. You're a very lucky girl to have caught Nicky. A lot of the eligible women around here have been trying to get him to the altar for years, and not one of them even came close before you."

"I'm glad," Jordan responded, meaning it.

"So am I." She gave her a friendly smile. "And like you found Nick, I'm going to find my dream man. I know he's out there somewhere."

"I'm sure he is. I'd almost given up completely on the idea of falling in love and getting married when Nick came into my life. He was a godsend, I'm sure of it."

"I just want you to be very happy together. Uncle Charles loved my Aunt Andrea so much . . . It was a terrible thing when she died. I really don't think he's ever gotten over losing her. A love like theirs doesn't happen often. I hope you and Nick have that kind of devotion. It's a beautiful thing to see."

"I know I do," Jordan said softly, admitting out loud for the first time the depth of her caring for him.

"You can be sure Nick does, too. He's never been one to be halfhearted about anything. If he loved you enough to propose, then I'm sure he's wild about you, and that's why we have to make sure this wedding goes perfectly. Nick's only going to marry once, and I want it to be special for him."

While Jordan and Peri discussed all that needed to be done, Nick was in the upstairs hall, knocking lightly on his father's bedroom door.

"Are you up yet?"

Until that moment, Nick had only been mildly con-

255

cerned about his father's failure to appear for breakfast, but when there was no answer to his knock, he knew a sinking feeling in the pit of his stomach. He remembered how tired his father had looked when he'd retired the night before, and he grew terribly worried. He tried the door and was glad to find it unlocked. Nick let himself in to find his father fully clothed, lying very still in his bed. He rushed to his side, thinking the worst.

"Dad! Are you all right?"

"Nick?" Charles awoke slowly, blinking in confusion to find his son bending over him with a terrible expression on his face. "What's the matter? Is something wrong?"

There were no words to describe the feeling of relief that washed over Nick as his father came awake. "You were just sleeping . . ."

"Of course I was sleeping . . . What made you think . . . What time is it, anyway?" Charles fussed, feeling at a distinct disadvantage as he realized he was still dressed and lying on top of the covers.

"It's going on nine."

"Is it really?" He was surprised by the news, for though he'd gotten a lot of sleep, he did not feel rested. "I guess I was more tired than I thought."

"Do you want to rest some more?"

Charles felt so weary that he elected to stay in bed. "I think I'd better. I'll just lie here for a while. You go ahead and take care of business. I'll be down some time before noon."

"All right."

"How are the girls this morning?"

"They're fine. They're planning a trip into town for a few days to get what Jordan needs for the wedding."

Charles nodded. "You just make sure that there's someone with them . . . someone watching over them."

"Don't worry. I'll send Miss Layton along. Nobody

gets past Miss Layton. Nobody."

"So you tried, did you?" His father picked up on what he didn't say.

Nick grinned. "With a woman like Jordan, what man wouldn't?"

"She is a beauty, but you behave yourself," Charles scolded lovingly. "Your mother and I waited for our wedding night. It was difficult, but definitely worth the wait."

Nick's expression didn't change. "Three more weeks is a long time."

"You'll manage. Jordan is a lady; treat her like one."

"I will."

"I know. I felt the same way about your mother. There's nothing I wouldn't have done for her. I would even have died for her — if I could have." He let his gaze drift to Andrea's portrait for a moment, then he looked back at the man who was his son. "Now, go on and get out of here. I need some rest if I'm going to keep up with the three of you for the next couple of weeks."

"All right, I'm going. I'll see you later on."

Nick acted as if nothing was wrong as he left the room, but as soon as he'd closed the door, he slumped against it. His father had looked terrible. His coloring was gray and there had been little spirit in him. It was almost as if his very life was draining away, and there was nothing that could be done to stop it. Nick ran a hand over his eyes as he tried to pull himself together. The unfairness of it all weighed on him again, and he once more affirmed his determination to do everything he could to see that his father's last months . . . or weeks . . . were happy ones.

Nick pushed away from the wall and made a conscious effort to straighten his shoulders. He strode off toward the staircase, clearing his throat as he went, for he didn't trust his voice right now.

* * *

The next three weeks passed in a blur of activity for Jordan. Between the trip to the city, the sending of the invitations, the fittings for the wedding gown, and a myriad of other wedding-related tasks, she had little time to think about anything else.

It seemed to Jordan that she only saw Nick to speak to him at breakfast and dinner. He was always on the move, riding the fields, dealing with the overseer, or meeting with agents from New Orleans regarding the sale of the crops. She missed him, and she found herself watching for him, hoping to see him. Whenever she was able to catch a glimpse of Nick riding off on his sleek black stallion to take care of plantation business her heart beat a little faster.

What free time Jordan did have, she spent with Charles. She had loved the older man from the moment they'd met, and that affection had only grown deeper. Sometimes they took short walks in the garden together, and other times they would just sit and talk. He often entertained her with tales of Nick as a boy, and she loved hearing them.

It pained Jordan to admit it, but she couldn't deny any longer that his health was failing. She had the terrible feeling that Charles was only fighting to stay alive because he wanted to be there for their wedding. She'd hoped she was wrong, but when she'd accidentally overheard a conversation between Nick and Dr. Williams the week before the wedding, her horrible suspicions had been confirmed. The physician had been on his way out when Nick had stopped him in the hall. Jordan had been in the parlor with Peri and they'd heard every word.

"How is he? Is he showing any improvement?" Nick asked the physician.

"Nick, I'll tell you honestly," the physician said, "I don't know what's keeping him going any more."

"Then . . ."

258

"It's just a matter of time now."

"But how long does he have?" Nick pressed for an answer.

"I don't know, Nick. I wish I could be encouraging, but I can't. The only thing positive I can tell you is that his spirits have lifted since you came home with your lovely fiancée."

At this news, Peri had taken Jordan's hand and held it tightly. Their eyes met, and they shared the agonizing sorrow of knowing someone they loved was going to die.

"I had hoped meeting Jordan would help," Nick was saying, distractedly.

"It has. He's very happy now that he knows you're going to settle down with a wonderful girl, but while his spirit may be willing, his body is growing weaker by the day."

"Thank you . . ." Nick accompanied the doctor outside to bid him good-bye.

Jordan and Peri said nothing as they sat, hands clasped in the sudden silence that followed the men's departure from the house. Their expressions were raw with emotion as they were both lost deep in thought.

Nick's voice had been choked with grief, and Jordan realized then just how much he really did love his father. The truth struck her a painful blow. All this time she'd harbored distrust toward Nick because she believed he'd only become engaged to her for his inheritance. Now she knew that he'd gone to all the trouble to buy her papers and transform her into his "fiancée" not to get the money but to please his father. The love Jordan harbored for Nick grew even stronger as she faced the truth about him. They might be deceiving Charles, but it was a loving deception. Jordan was suddenly glad that she'd agreed to go along with his plan, even though she knew it would mean heartache for her in the end.

"Uncle Charles is dying . . ." Peri said numbly as tears

fell unheeded down her pale cheeks. She'd known he was ill, that he hadn't really been himself lately, but she'd had no idea before now that he wasn't going to recover. "But how? Why?" She looked to Jordan, her distress very real.

"It's his heart," Jordan offered.

"Why didn't they tell me?"

"I don't think Charles wanted anyone to know." ˑ

"But I could have done something . . ."

"What could you have done? The doctor said there's nothing any of us can do," Jordan told her gently.

"Oh, poor Nick . . . This must be so hard for him. He loves Uncle Charles so much. They've always been so close . . ."

"I know," she sympathized in full understanding now.

"Jordan . . . you'll have to excuse me now. I've got to be by myself for a little while. Don't worry, though, I won't let on that I know . . ."

"I wasn't worried, Peri. You love him just as Nick does . . . and as I do."

Peri gave a tight nod as she hurried from the room. She fled the house through the French doors and didn't allow herself to lose control until she was deep in the gardens, far out of earshot. Miserable, she sank down on the stone border of a flower bed and gave vent to her heartbreaking sorrow.

Philip was working on the books in the office allotted to him in the small outbuilding that housed the overseer's office and quarters when he heard the sounds of someone crying. He didn't pay much attention at first, but when it continued unabated he grew slightly annoyed. After a few more minutes of trying to ignore the woman's misery, Philip cast his pencil aside and went to see if he could help.

The weeks here at Riverwood had been lonely for him. Kane had seen to it that he'd been given quarters far away from the main house, and so in all the days since their

260

arrival, he'd been able to speak with his sister only once. She had been with Peri, so there had been no chance to say anything personal. Jordan had looked fine at the time, and he could only hope that she was doing all right.

Philip thought of Peri then, and of how beautiful she was. From the moment he'd seen her that first day here at Riverwood he'd been smitten. She was like an elusive butterfly, lovely to look upon but difficult to catch. Every time he'd seen her she'd been laughing and happy and full of energy. Where he was quiet and reserved, Peri was open and eager for life. He had never met anyone like her before, and he doubted he ever would again. She was one of a kind.

Philip followed the sound of the crying toward the garden that bordered the big house. He knew Nick didn't want him anywhere around, but the abject misery of the woman's weeping drew him on. He entered a narrow, shell-lined path that led into the thick greenery, and had only gone a short distance when he saw her.

"Peri?" Philip couldn't believe it was her. He couldn't imagine what she would have to cry about. "Peri, what is it?"

Peri heard him and quickly tried to pull herself together. She wiped the tears from her cheeks, but it was useless. "Oh . . . Philip . . ."

"Are you all right? Are you hurt?" Philip went straight to her, not caring that she might want to be alone. He could only think that she was hurting in some way and he wanted to help.

"No . . . no, I'm all right," she snuffled, trying to regain her composure.

"But I heard you crying and I thought you might need something . . ." he tried to explain what had drawn him to her.

Peri lifted tear-filled eyes to his. "That was sweet of you, Philip. I appreciate your caring . . ."

Without thought, Philip reached for her. He was no ladies' man, having no great experience with women, but he felt a need to hold her and soothe her.

Peri didn't resist. She stood and went willingly as he took her in his arms and held her close. It felt so good to be there in the protective circle of his embrace that she sighed brokenly and went slightly limp against him.

"Can you tell me about it? Can I help?" he offered in a low, caring voice as he unconsciously began to stroke her hair.

"No . . . there's nothing you or anyone else can do," she answered miserably, making no move away from him. "It's something I can't talk about. It's something I just have to deal with on my own." She shifted slightly away so she could look up at him. "But thank you for caring enough to ask."

Philip gazed down at her, seeing the sweetness of her trembling lips and the sadness in her eyes, and he couldn't help himself. Without conscious thought, he kissed her. His lips met hers in a tender exchange that was only meant to comfort, but what they felt was much more than comfort. Instinctively, his arms tightened around her, bringing her closer to him. The soft curve of her body seemed to fit perfectly against him, and Philip discovered that he never wanted to let her go. Peri was like a part of him that had been missing all his life.

Peri was completely immersed in the wonder of his kiss when it dawned on her just what she was doing. Confused, she broke it off and took a stumbling step backward out of his embrace.

"I'm sorry, Philip . . . I've got to go . . ."

"Peri, I . . ."

But before he could finish, she had turned and fled, leaving him standing there staring after her.

Chapter Twenty

The night before the wedding Charles planned a celebration dinner for just the closest of family and friends. Peri's parents traveled from New Orleans to attend, as did Aaron O'Neil and his wife, Caroline, and Slater.

As Slater rode up the main drive, he was in a curious mood. He and Nick had seen each other only twice in the last few weeks, and both encounters had been at parties where they'd had no time to talk. Slater was eager to find out how things were going between Nick and Jordan . . . and with his father.

Though Slater didn't put much faith in gossip and loose talk, rumors about Nick's engagement had been flying hot and heavy in their social circle. Jordan had won the approval of just about all who'd met her. The few who weren't singing her praises were the rejected maidens who'd hoped to snare Nick for themselves. The general consensus was that the rich, elusive bachelor had finally met his match and had fallen in love.

Knowing how uncomfortable Nick had been with the idea of playing the lovestruck fiancé, Slater wasn't sure how his friend had managed to be so convincing. It wasn't an easy thing to fool the matrons, but he had. Slater hoped when they got the chance to talk today he would find out it wasn't an act. He hoped they had fallen in love. He reined in before the main house to find Jordan sitting on the gallery with Peri and Charles.

"Slater!" Peri had known Slater for years and adored him much as she did Nick. She charged from the porch to greet him with an enthusiastic hug and a warm kiss on the cheek. "I'm so glad you came early!"

"I am too," he replied easily, returning her kiss with almost brotherly affection. He glanced up to see Jordan standing with Charles at the top of the steps. He wondered how it was that she seemed to grow more beautiful each time he saw her. "Good afternoon, Jordan, Charles."

"Good to see you again," the older Kane welcomed him, and they shook hands as Slater mounted the stairs to join them on the porch.

"Hello, Slater," Jordan said softly. She had come to like him, but the fact that he knew the truth about her always left her feeling at a disadvantage around him.

Ever the gallant where beautiful women were concerned, Slater bent over Jordan's hand. "How is it that you seem more lovely every time I see you?"

She flushed with pleasure, but answered lightly, "How is it you always know the right thing to say?"

"Practice," he told her with a wicked grin, and everyone laughed. "Is Nick around?"

"He's in the study going over some figures with Montgomery," Charles explained. "Why don't you join us for a few minutes and have a drink? He'll be out soon."

They all settled into the comfortable chairs in the shade as Slater inquired, "How's the new man working out?"

"I don't see much of him. His work keeps him away from the house most of the time, but he seems to be doing a fine job."

Slater cast a quick look at Jordan, trying to read her response to this mention of Philip, but he could discern no outward sign of interest. He was glad. "Then it looks like Nick made a good choice."

Peri was listening attentively to all the talk about Philip. No matter how she tried to deny it, ever since that day in the garden she'd known he was the man for her. She had no doubt that her parents would object to her interest in him, for he was not of their social class, but she didn't care. Just because he had to work for someone else to make a living didn't mean he was a bad person. Somehow she was determined to find a way for them to be together.

The only trouble with Peri's discovery that he was the man she wanted was that Philip appeared to have no interest in her. She'd deliberately taken to riding past his quarters and office on her early morning excursions on horseback, but other than to wave a friendly greeting whenever he happened to be out, he made no effort to speak privately with her again. It was maddening.

Peri had never chased a man before, and she wasn't sure exactly how to go about it. Everything she'd ever done in her life had been straightforward and honest. She wasn't used to resorting to subterfuge, she was the type of person who, if she saw something she wanted, went after it. Peri thought her bulldoggedness was one of her more redeeming personality traits. However, there were others, like her parents, who thought this quality undesirable and less than feminine. Luckily, Peri was self-confident enough that she usually didn't give a hoot what other people thought.

The sound of the front door opening drew her thoughts back to the present, and she found herself staring up at Philip as he left the house with Nick. She practically devoured the sight of him, and she had to take care not to let her heart shine in her eyes. She didn't want to be too obvious.

"Your figures were very accurate, and you're absolutely correct about that billing problem with the agent. I'll take care of it next week," Nick was saying.

"Good. Once that's cleared up, everything should straighten out."

"Well, Philip, it looks like things are working out for you," Slater remarked, coming to his feet to greet him.

"Hello, Mr. MacKenzie, it's good to see you again," Philip replied, glancing briefly in Jordan's direction. They rarely saw each other any more, and it was good to know that she looked to be doing fine. "Yes, everything's going very well, thank you."

"Good."

Nick saw the direction of his gaze and he tensed. He didn't want Montgomery looking at her or talking to her or anywhere near her. He was hard pressed to stay calm.

"Hello, Philip," Peri spoke up, unintimidated by the presence of the others.

"Peri." He nodded slightly, struggling not to show what he was feeling for her. It was difficult for him, though, for the memory of their intimate moment in the garden was scorched upon his heart. "I'd better be getting back to my work." He looked again to his sister. "Just in case I don't get to speak with you again, congratulations on your wedding." His daring earned even more of Nick's unspoken wrath.

"Thank you," Jordan replied with a smile to let her brother know everything was going all right.

Nick's jaw tightened as he watched her smile at the other indentured servant. He didn't like it at all, but he couldn't do a damn thing about it without making a scene and raising questions he didn't want to answer. By sheer force of will he managed to smile at Slater.

"Come join me in the study, I've still got a few things I have to finish before I can relax and enjoy the rest of the evening."

They made their excuses to Charles, Peri, and Jordan

266

and disappeared inside.

"So," Slater began as he relaxed in the chair opposite the desk where Nick sat, "tomorrow is the big day. Are you ready?"

"I guess I'm as ready as I'll ever be," Nick replied casually, then gestured his friend toward the liquor cabinet. "Fix me a bourbon while I double check these figures, will you?"

Slater was more than willing to enjoy some of their fine liquor, and he poured himself one as well. Setting Nick's glass before him on the desk, he sat back down in his chair to wait and watch.

Nick felt Slater's eyes upon him and finally looked up questioningly. "All right, let's have it. What's on your mind?"

"Not much. It's just that we haven't talked much lately and I was wondering how everything was going for you and Jordan."

Nick gave an expressive lift of his shoulders. "Everything's going as well as it can."

"Montgomery's doing a good job?"

"Yes. In fact, he's working out much better than I'd thought he would." His comment was terse.

"So why do you sound so annoyed?" he probed. "Has he given you any trouble."

"No."

"I see."

"What's all this interest in Montgomery about?"

"Oh, nothing. It's just that there have been a lot of rumors going around town . . ."

"Rumors?" Nick glanced up at him sharply, fearfully.

"About you and Jordan. You should have known that you were going to be the talk of the town when you brought her home. As gorgeous as she is, the men all want her for their own and the girls you courted before are all jealous. Even the old women are convinced that you've found the love of your life. Evidently you've been very convincing. Hell, you even convinced me." He let the idea hang, hoping Nick would pick up on it. He was disappointed when he didn't.

"So?"

"Damn it, Nick, I've never known you to be so obtuse! Are you really that good of an actor or are you in love with her? Seems to me only a month ago you were telling me you didn't know how to act, and now . . ." Slater leaned forward, glowering at his simpleminded friend.

Nick scowled back at him. "I learned quick, and no, I'm not in love with her." His denial was harsh, and he downed the rest of his bourbon in one fiery swallow, the glass clenched tightly in his hand.

Nick couldn't admit that Jordan's kisses and caresses affected him as no other. He couldn't face up to the fact that he continually watched for her around the plantation and that he missed her when their paths didn't cross during the course of the day. He liked Jordan, he told himself, that was all. They got along well and they were making his father happy, that was all. If he allowed himself to care more than that, he'd just end up the fool. Jordan loved Montgomery, not him.

"If you don't love her then why are you glaring at me now for asking, and why did you look like you could kill when Montgomery accidentally ran into Jordan on the porch?"

Nick cast an even blacker look in his direction, but said nothing.

"Face it. Jordan's beautiful, intelligent, and everything any man could want in a woman."

"So why does that mean I have to be in love with her? That romantic spirit of yours always has you thinking that everything's going to work out right, but you, most of all, should know life isn't like that. This isn't a fairy tale I'm living. Jordan and I have both known from the very beginning that this was only a temporary arrangement. It'll pass."

Nick's words hit a painful nerve with Slater, and he slowly got to his feet. He set his glass quietly aside and walked toward the door, his carriage stiff and erect. "I hope you're wrong, Nick. I really hope you're wrong."

Nick sat staring at the door long after Slater had gone.

The elegant dinner party was a huge success. Nick looked debonair in the dark suit he wore, and Jordan looked positively radiant in her emerald gown. She'd known it was his favorite and so had worn it just to please him. Her effort had been rewarded, for he hadn't left her side all evening. Everyone thought them a most loving couple. Only Slater had doubts, but he hid them well as he looked on with jaded interest, watching as Nick couldn't seem to take his eyes off his future bride. The meal was a gourmet's delight, each course proving more delectable than the last, and everyone ate their fill. As the evening came to an end, Charles rose from his place at the head of the table.

"If I may have your attention please?" he announced in a robust tone, feeling proud and contented as he stood there surveying his guests. Everyone he loved, everyone he truly cared about, was here at his home tonight. Nick and Jordan were sitting to his right. Peri and her parents were on his left, with Aaron, his wife, Audrey Layton, and Slater at the far end. He had waited a long time for this moment, and it was important to him that he let everyone know just how happy he was and how much it meant to him that Nick was going to marry.

"Weddington . . ." he called for the servant.

The butler entered the room with a newly opened bottle of the finest champagne in his wine cellar. He deftly poured a glass for each of the guests, then filled

Charles's, too.

"Thank you. Now, as you all know, we're here tonight to celebrate the upcoming union between my son and his beautiful Jordan. I want to tell Nick now just how proud I am of him and of his choice of a bride. Jordan is a wonderful woman, and probably much too good for him."

There was general laughter at his remark.

"I propose a toast to them—and to their future." Charles lifted his glass in salute. "Dominic, may your love for Jordan grow stronger with each passing day. May your heart always guide your decisions, and may you live a long, happy life together. And Jordan," Charles continued, "may your every dream come true. May you grow in beauty, wisdom, and faith, and may your love for Nick be everlasting."

Nick turned to Jordan to touch glasses with her in honor of his father's loving toast. Their gazes locked, and he found he couldn't look away from her. The emerald color of the gown was perfect on her, bringing out the sparkle in her eyes. The style was stunning, its low-cut décolletage hinting at but not revealing the pale beauty of her breasts. He was mesmerized . . . enthralled . . . His dark-eyed regard took on a peculiar gleam as he and Jordan sipped the wine without breaking eye contact.

Jordan longed with all her heart for this moment to be real, but her mind argued that it was a dream that was going to end all too soon. Even if by some twist of fate Nick did come to love her, it could never be, for any association with her could only hurt him in the long run. She managed to smile softly at him as her eyes grew bright with unshed tears.

"You're sad?" Nick asked in a soft voice, puzzled.

"No . . ." she whispered back.

Nick's expression turned tender. It was almost as if he

was seeing her for the very first time and realizing just what a delicate woman she really was. Much to the delight of the onlookers, he leaned forward ever so slightly to kiss her with infinite gentleness. When he drew back, he saw a look of wonder in her eyes. He smiled, touching the rim of his champagne glass to hers once more, and then offered her his to sip from.

It was an erotic ploy that sent a frisson of excitement shivering through Jordan. She was entranced as she took a small drink and then returned the gesture. Nick's hand covered hers as she held her glass out to him, and he helped bring it to his lips, never taking his gaze from hers.

Jordan felt a tingle of desire rocket through her. Her breasts grew taut with wanting and a coiling heat grew low in her body. In that moment, her love for Nick was more powerful than any emotion she'd ever known, and she wondered how she was ever going to be able to leave him. Desperate to hold onto the moment forever, Jordan vowed to herself then and there that she would take whatever bits of happiness life had to give and savor them while she could. She would live each day as if it were their last together and cherish the joy of her love for him for as long as fate allowed.

"Isn't it wonderful?" Peri sighed out loud as she watched the two lovebirds. "It's almost as if they were made for each other."

"Yes, isn't it, though?" Slater added with a small grin that he quickly squelched when Nick finally happened to glance his way.

When the meal ended the ladies went to the parlor to visit while the men retreated to Charles's study to enjoy a few drinks and talk. The mix of champagne and bourbon quickly took its toll on Charles, though, and he was the first to excuse himself and go on up to bed. Slater and Randall Davidson soon followed. Nick, however, was too tense to even think about going to sleep, so he remained downstairs talking with Aaron. The atmosphere between the two men was comfortable, for they had known each other for years and liked and respected one another.

"You know, Nick," Aaron began from where he relaxed in one of the wing chairs, "I've always envied you and your father. You have such a wonderful relationship."

"We do, Aaron. I love him very much. I guess we're just about as close as a father and son can be."

"I know, and that's why I challenged Charles on that ridiculous clause he put in the will earlier this year."

"You did?"

Aaron nodded in confirmation. "I did. I knew you'd come around and settle down when you found the right girl. I mean, Jordan's living proof of that. I tried to convince your father of that at the time, but you know how your father is. When he gets his mind set on something, he rarely backs down."

Nick knew exactly what he was talking about. "I know what you mean."

Aaron stood and walked easily over to the liquor cabinet to refill his tumbler. "And that's precisely why I was so shocked when he rescinded it last month. I don't know what happened to make him change his mind, but I was glad."

Nick was sitting there in shock staring at the attorney's back, wondering if he'd heard him correctly. *His father had removed the clause last month?!*

"No man should be forced to marry against his will. I guess for some reason Charles finally saw the light. As luck would have it, though, you found Jordan anyway." Aaron turned back to him, smiling happily. "So every-

272

thing worked out for the best after all."

Nick kept his expression relaxed, but there was nothing relaxed about the way he was feeling. "Yes, it did, didn't it?"

"He's so pleased for you, Nick. I know we're laboring under unhappy circumstances here, but I'm glad things have turned out so well."

"Thank you, Aaron." Nick swallowed the remnants of his bourbon in one big, bolstering gulp then stood up. "Well, I think I'll walk in the garden for a while and get a breath of fresh air before I go on up to bed. I'll see you in the morning."

"Good night, Nick. And Nick? Congratulations. You've made a wise choice in Jordan."

Nick nodded and quickly escaped onto the veranda. His pace was driven as he left the porch and strode off into the gardens. His thoughts were racing, his head spinning as he considered the information the lawyer had just given him. His father had retracted the marriage clause. He didn't have to get married tomorrow! It would be embarrassing, but he could stop the wedding if he wanted to. He could go back to his old lifestyle and be happy. He could give Jordan her papers and set her and Montgomery free tonight and be done with them both. He could . . .

Nick stopped as reality descended upon him. Jordan . . . As he thought of her, he suddenly realized with painful clarity that he didn't want to be done with her. He didn't want to send her away. He remembered how beautiful she'd looked tonight and how that one small kiss had stirred him, and he knew he didn't want to let her go . . . ever. Slater's comments earlier that day echoed through his thoughts as he acknowledged finally that he wanted Jordan for himself.

The recognition of his true feelings struck him like a thunderbolt, and he knew there was only one thing he could do. He would go through with the wedding. He was no longer doing it to please his father, though his father would be happy about it. He was marrying Jordan because he wanted to. It was his choice.

The spectre of what would happen later loomed in the back of his thoughts, but Nick ignored it. He didn't want to think about that now. He would deal with it when the time came.

Nick started back to the house, and as he passed beneath the open parlor windows he could hear the lilting sound of Jordan's laughter coming from inside. It sounded so wonderful that it touched a chord deep within him, and he found himself hoping that he could make her this happy always.

Chapter Twenty-one

As the sun sank lower in the west, Philip grew deeply troubled. He paced his small office in agitation, hoping for time to pass quickly and all the while knowing that it wouldn't. This was it. Tonight was the night. Guests had been arriving at Riverwood since early morning. Within a few short hours Jordan would be married to Kane, and his frustration came from the fact that there wasn't a damn thing he could do about it.

Logically, Philip reminded himself of their situation. He told himself over and over that this was all for the best. Still, he couldn't help but have some doubts about this marriage "in name only." He knew Jordan cared for Nick, and several times lately he'd caught Nick staring at Jordan when he didn't think he was being observed, and his expression had been one of almost pained desire. Philip knew that if Nick decided to press his attentions on her, Jordan would not be able to resist, and that was the one thing he didn't want to happen. If Jordan gave in to Nick she would only end up being more hurt when the time came for them to leave.

Gritting his teeth against his helplessness and frustration, Philip accepted what he could not change. But he knew if he got the chance, he would caution his sister again against the danger of losing her heart to a man she could never really have or hold. Miserably, Philip dropped back into his chair and tried to concentrate on the ledgers before him. It was a long time later, as the shadows of the day began to lengthen, that the faint sounds of music came to him and he realized the ceremony was about to begin. He braced his elbows on the desk and rested his head in his hands as he said a silent prayer that his sister would be safe and everything would turn out all right.

"Oh, Jordan, I envy you so!" Peri exclaimed in delight as she watched the maid finish arranging Jordan's full skirts over the hoop. "You look absolutely breathtaking."

Jordan was nervous. There was no doubt about it. In just a few short minutes she was going to become Mrs. Dominic Kane. "Do you think Nick will think so?"

"How could he not? You look like an angel! I only hope I look this good when my big day finally comes."

"You will."

Peri gave her a quick hug then stepped back once more to take a last look. "I honestly think the seamstress outdid herself this time. I've never seen such a beautiful creation."

The full-skirted gown was of white satin and tulle and was indeed a sight to behold. Off-the-shoulder in style, it was fitted to the waist, and the skirt was a series of eight flounces, each trimmed in gold embroidery and exquisite lace. Small white satin rosettes adorned the sleeves, and her veil and headpiece were trimmed in white seed pearls.

"It's all because of you," Jordan told her with heartfelt appreciation. "If I hadn't had you to help me through this, I don't know what I would have done."

"You would have done just fine, and you know it.

You won Nick's heart all by yourself, didn't you? I'm sure that was no easy task."

Jordan laughed, but only because she was feeling quite hysterical. She wanted more than anything to be Nick's wife, but she had to hang on to the reality of what was happening.

"You're right . . . It wasn't easy . . ."

The sound of the music drifted upstairs to them, and they knew it was just about time. Miss Layton came bustling into the room.

"Everyone's here and waiting," she related happily, then she confided with all the excitement of a small child. "Mr. Kane looks so handsome. Are you ready?"

"I think so . . ." Jordan answered breathlessly.

Peri carefully arranged Jordan's veil and then pressed a bouquet of fragrant blossoms cut from Charles's garden into her hand. She could feel how badly she was trembling, and she gave her hand a reassuring squeeze.

"Don't worry. It'll all be over before you know it."

Her words held such a double meaning that Jordan had to force a small smile. "I know," she managed to whisper. "I guess I'd just better go and get it over with."

"Nick's a good man, Jordan, and I know he loves you."

"And I love him . . ." Jordan confessed.

"Then what are you afraid of?"

This time Jordan managed a real smile at Peri as she wondered if the girl had ever had a negative thought in her life. "Absolutely nothing. I think I'd be a severe disappointment to you if I were."

"You're right. Now, let's go see how Nick's holding up. If you're this upset, I can just imagine how nervous *he* is."

Father Evans, a tall, heavyset, dignified man of fifty, was a longtime friend of the Kane family. When

Charles had requested that the wedding be held at Riverwood, he'd been more than gracious about making the trip. He was waiting in the crowded parlor now with the family and other guests for the bride and her attendant to enter.

Nick stood next to Father Evans with Slater, who was serving as his best man, at his side. The furniture in the parlor had been pushed back, and chairs had been set up in such a way as to create an aisle straight from the door to where they waited. His attention was focused solely on the door as he anticipated Jordan's appearance.

Peri came into the room first, carrying a small bouquet. She smiled brightly at the friends and family she recognized as she walked slowly up the aisle. When she reached the men at the front of the room, she stepped to the left, leaving the way clear for Jordan. Strains of the wedding march announced the bride's imminent arrival, and everyone turned to watch.

Since there was no way Jordan could have asked Philip to give her away, she'd asked Charles to be her escort. The elder Kane had assumed the duty with pride and love, and he accompanied her now, standing tall and straight at her side in his formal dress. Oohs and aahs and whispers of how beautiful Jordan was filled the room as they made their way forward to join Nick.

Jordan was a vision to behold in the stunning white gown. Nick's chest felt tight and his mouth went dry at the sight of her approaching on his father's arm. He'd never dreamed he could feel this way about any woman . . . both hot and cold at the same time. Distractedly, he realized his hands were shaking, and he clenched them into fists to regain his control. When his father stopped before him and handed her over to his loving trust, Nick appeared completely at ease, a man totally in command and completely confident.

The waiting was over. The time had come. Father Evans intoned the greeting and welcome, and the ceremony that would irrevocably join them in the eyes of God began.

Neither Nick nor Jordan would ever remember much about the wedding. They were only conscious of each other. Jordan thought Nick had never looked more attractive. His formal clothing was dark, but his shirt and cravat were snowy white, emphasizing his bronze tan and dark good looks. She loved him with all her heart, and though they might annul the marriage later, Jordan knew in her soul as she repeated her vows, that she would consider herself Nick's wife forever.

"Do you, Jordan Douglas, take Dominic Kane to be your lawful wedded husband, to have and to hold, in sickness and in health, for richer or poorer, from this day onward?"

"I do," she replied without hesitation.

"And do you, Dominic Kane, take Jordan Douglas to be your lawful wedded wife, to have and to hold, in sickness and in health, for richer or poorer, from this day onward?"

"I do," came Nick's firm response.

"Do you have the ring?"

Nick turned to Slater, who produced the simple gold band engraved with Jordan's and his own initials.

"May the circle of this ring be a symbol of your unending love and devotion to one another." The priest blessed it.

Nick took Jordan's icy left hand in his and slipped the ring on her finger, branding her as his.

"By the power invested in me by God and man," Father Evans continued, "I now pronounce you man and wife. What God has joined together let no man put asunder," he concluded. "You may kiss your bride."

Nick carefully lifted Jordan's veil and drew her to

him. He studied her seriously for a moment, commiting to memory the perfection of her loveliness . . . her flawless complexion, her wide, innocent eyes, her slightly parted, trembling lips, and then he kissed her. It took will power on his part, but because of the audience of onlookers he managed to keep the embrace chaste.

There was no describing the disappointment that wracked them both when he released her and moved slightly away. But there was little time to think about it, for they were immediately surrounded by a crowd of well-wishers. Nick was kissed and hugged and congratulated by everyone from his father to Miss Layton. Jordan, too, was engulfed in a sea of love as all the guests offered their best wishes.

Then the reception began. The Riverwood ballroom ran the entire length of the house on the opposite side of the main hall from the parlor and study, and Weddington had done a masterful job in seeing to its preparation. The three sets of French doors that led onto the gallery were open to allow for a refreshing breeze. The small orchestra Charles had hired for the occasion was set up at the far end of the ballroom, and a multitude of chairs lined the walls for those who chose to visit rather than dance. The light from the two huge crystal chandeliers sparkled brilliantly off the glossy white walls and the highly polished hardwood floor. Yards and yards of ribbon and mounds of fragrant, fresh-cut flowers bedecked the refreshment table, where endless glasses of freshly poured champagne and a huge punch bowl filled with a sweet, intoxicating concoction awaited the arrival of the guests.

Laughter abounded as everyone entered the ballroom for the beginning of the real celebration. The music started and so did the dancing.

Nick stayed attentively at Jordan's side, his arm familiarly around her waist. As they casually made their way around the room, greeting and visiting with their company, he anticipated her every need and made certain that her champagne glass was never empty.

Jordan was swept along on a tide of rapturous emotion. She loved Nick, and for this one night she was going to pretend that everything happening between them was real. The touch of his hand, the heat of his body so close to hers, the way he catered to her and saw that she was never wanting for anything filled her heart with joy. She knew it was a game, but for now that was enough.

Peri was delighted as she watched the two of them together. She took a glass of champagne from a passing waiter's tray and sipped of the dry, bubbling wine with great appreciation. While her happiness for Nick and Jordan was unmatched, she couldn't help but feel the sting of her own loneliness. She wished Philip was there so he could see her looking her best in the new dress, but because he was hired help, he had not been included on the guest list. Peri was about to mourn his absence when Rod Acklund, a thirty-year-old moneyed bachelor with a rakish reputation, suddenly appeared before her.

"Peri, I just had to tell you how very lovely you look tonight," Rod said, his brown eyes alight with appreciation.

"Why, thank you, Rod. You look rather handsome yourself," she replied with a warm, open smile. She had known him for years and liked him, in spite of his roguish ways.

"Shall we dance?"

"I'd love to."

Peri went into his arms and followed his expert lead with ease. She enjoyed their dance, but her thoughts were elsewhere. She found herself picturing Philip in formal dress clothing and wondering if he could dance as well as Rod.

When the music ended, the announcement was made that it was time for the bridal couple's waltz. Peri and Rod joined the rest of the guests on the sidelines to watch Nick and Jordan.

"Shall we?" Nick murmured in Jordan's ear. He had been longing to take her in his arms ever since he'd seen her come through the parlor door, and he could hardly wait to hold her close.

There was nothing Jordan wanted more than to be in Nick's embrace, and she nodded readily at his invitation. When he guided her out onto the dance floor, she moved gracefully into his waiting arms.

The waltz began. It was a haunting melody that neither of the lovers would ever forget. Jordan let herself be swept away by the wonder of it all. Nick was holding her and they were moving about the floor in perfect unison. She lifted her starry eyes to his, making no effort to disguise the truth of her feelings for him.

Nick had never imagined that dancing with a woman could be such a sensual experience. Just having Jordan this close to him as they swirled about the dance floor set his blood racing. He was hot with desire for her.

Nick knew he would have to control this burning need. After all, he had given her his word that he wouldn't touch her, and he was a man of honor. But just because he knew he shouldn't want her didn't mean he could stop that easily.

Nick had never dealt with feelings like this before, and he was troubled by them. When Jordan looked up at him with what seemed to be love shining in her eyes, all thoughts of resisting his desire vanished. A part of his mind told him this was all a charade, and one he'd orchestrated, at that. But his heart overruled his head, telling him something else, something much more profound. He loved her. She was his wife. They were married. It was a heart-stopping revelation for Nick as he waltzed around the floor with Jordan in his arms. He had known that he'd wanted her, but until this moment he had not realized that he had fallen completely under her spell. He was no longer playing the role of ardent lover, he was living it.

The melody came to an end, but not the magic that had enveloped them. They stopped dancing but remained standing in the middle of the ballroom, gazing at each other with lovestruck expressions. The applause of the onlookers was the only thing that broke the enchantment, and it was a good thing, for in another minute Nick would have swept Jordan up in his arms and disappeared upstairs with her. They both looked a bit embarrassed, and Nick quickly signaled for the musicians to start another waltz.

"My dear daughter, may I have the honor of this dance?" Charles asked as he appeared at Jordan's side.

"I'd love to dance with you, Charles," Jordan answered honestly, giving Nick a sweet smile as she took his father's arm and allowed him to draw her out onto the floor.

Nick watched them dance away to the gentle rhythm, and he felt a great sense of rightness about it.

"You two looked good together out there," came Slater's droll comment from behind him. "Jordan's a gorgeous woman."

"Yes, she is," Nick replied, taking a glass of champagne from one of the circulating servants and drinking deeply from it.

"You're a better man than I am," his friend remarked, taking a drink of his own champagne.

"I've always known that, but why are you finally admitting it now?" he countered.

"I confess it freely now, because I think you deserve a lot of credit." Slater glanced around to make sure there was no one within earshot.

283

"Credit for what?"

"If I had just taken Jordan as my wife, there's no way I'd be able to keep my hands off her. Think about it, Nick. Every man for four parishes around is panting over her, and you're the one who's going to be sharing her bed tonight."

Nick's expression turned thunderous, but he said nothing, which gave Slater the clue he needed.

"So, that's how it is. You're not sharing her bed tonight . . ." he paused. "Nick, don't you realize what you've got here? Open your eyes and see how lucky you really are! Take your happiness while you can and savor every minute of it. Don't let it slip away from you . . ."

Nick turned back to watch his father and bride. When he spoke, his voice was cool. "Slater, as far as Jordan is concerned, this is a bargain. We made a deal. She's fulfilled her part of it, and now I have to live up to my end."

"I'm sorry." Slater could almost feel his friend's frustration and pain. "I thought . . ."

Before he could say any more, Charles danced Jordan over to join them.

"I'm afraid that's all the dancing I can handle for tonight," he told them, breathing a little heavily. "Jordan, my dear, I thank you for the delightful turn around the floor. Nick, I leave your lovely wife in your safekeeping."

Nick saw the true happiness in his father's face and knew that no matter how it would hurt him when he finally had to give Jordan up, it would have been worth it. "Good, I missed her," he replied.

"If you'll excuse me, I'm going to go find a quiet place to rest for a while." Charles pressed a quick kiss on Jordan's cheek and then left.

Nick started to draw Jordan to his side again when Slater effectively cut in between them.

"Wait just a minute. I think the rest of this dance is mine," Slater announced. "We'll see you later, Nick."

Jordan could do little more than wave to Nick as Slater whisked her off. Nick watched them blend in with the crowd of dancers, and he felt a pang of loss. It was almost as if he were anticipating the time when he really would have to say good-bye to her. It hurt Nick to think that that moment would come, but he knew there was no question about it. Jordan was in love with Philip Montgomery. Though the man was dirt-poor and had nothing to offer her, he was the man she wanted. Loving Jordan as he did, Nick knew he could do no less than let her go.

Had he been alone, Nick would have thrown his champagne glass against the wall and watched with perverse satisfaction as it shattered. Trapped as he was in the crowded room, he merely turned and set the empty glass on the table nearby. The need for something stronger to drink was powerful within him, and he strode from the room to get himself a tumbler full of bourbon in the study.

Philip was restless. He had finished his work and returned to his quarters, miserably aware that the wedding was over and the reception in full swing. Though he knew he had no business going, he couldn't resist the temptation to try to catch a glimpse of his sister. He doubted he would get the opportunity to speak to her, but right now seeing her would be enough.

It was a night of celebrating all over the plantation, and so Philip passed unnoticed on his way up to the big house. He cut through the garden and tried to stay out of sight. Circling the house, he waited just off the gallery outside the ballroom in hopes of seeing her.

Peri had had quite a few glasses of champagne as the

evening progressed, and she was feeling decidedly giddy as she wandered out on the veranda to cool off.

She had not lacked for male attention that night, but none of the men there had excited her. In a businesslike manner, she analyzed all the men who had danced and flirted with her. Rod had been nice, but not her type. Michael had been sweet, but far too easy to control. Stephen had been masculine and domineering, but much too obnoxious. And Warren had been only interested in her inheritance. Oh, she'd had her fair share of suitors, all right, and not a one of them could hold a candle to Philip.

Peri gave a hopeless shake of her head as she sipped from the glass of the bubbly. Lightheaded, she pondered her alternatives where Philip was concerned. She could play coy and hope against hope he would notice her. Or she could continue to make herself available as she had lately during her morning horseback rides and continue to suffer his lack of interest with good spirits and high hopes. Or she could chase him down, declare her love for him, and demand that he return her affections. That possibility brought a half-stifled giggle from her as she imagined throwing herself at him bodily in her quest to win his devotion.

Peri took another sip of wine as she moved to the railing to stare out into the darkness of the Louisiana night. There was a moon tonight, but it was only a narrow silver wedge in the black velvet sky. The sounds of the orchestra added a romantic touch, but alone as she was, she wasn't feeling very romantic.

Peri didn't know what it was that caused her to look up at that particular moment, but when she did, she saw him. Philip was standing just beyond the line of light that shone from the ballroom's French doors watching the festivities. Had she been sober, she would have had second thoughts about being so blithely brazen, but tipsy as she was, she only knew she wanted to talk to him.

"Philip!" she called his name in an urgent whisper. She took a quick look behind her to make sure no one was around, then hurried down the steps to go to him.

Chapter Twenty-two

The sight of Peri standing all alone on the gallery mesmerized Philip. He'd come to the main house looking for his sister. He'd ended up finding the one woman he'd been secretly longing to see but knew he had to avoid.

"Hello, Peri," Philip began lamely, unable to stop staring at her. He thought she was the prettiest girl in the world, and he remembered in detail everything about the kiss they'd shared in the garden.

"Why are you here?" Peri asked, hoping in her innocence that he'd come to find her.

His first reaction was to take her question as an insult. He knew his position, and he knew he wasn't supposed to be there. He answered, defensively, "I went for a walk, that's all. When I heard the music, I thought I'd come by and see how the reception was going."

Her disappointment was real, but she refused to let him know it. "It's going marvelously. Everyone's having a wonderful time. Nick and Jordan make the perfect couple, and she looks so beautiful tonight . . ."

"I'm sure she does. She's a very lovely woman. He's

lucky to have her."

"And she's lucky to have him. I know Nick thought long and hard before he finally settled on Jordan as his choice for his bride."

"I'm sure he did," Philip replied.

Peri was oblivious to the double meaning of his words. Her liquor-induced bravery urged her to ask, "Have you ever thought about getting married, Philip?"

"No, not seriously." He kept his answer terse to discourage her questions.

Peri missed his innuendo completely. She was too busy remembering how it had felt to be held in his embrace and how exciting his kiss had been. "Why not? You're handsome and intelligent. Surely, there must have been any number of women in England who would have loved to marry you."

"Actually, I was so busy with my studies that I didn't have much time for courtship or affairs of the heart."

The news thrilled Peri. There was no one in his past, no one to reappear and stake a claim on his heart. All she had to do was win him.

Champagne-inspired bravado gave her the boldness to ask, "What about now?" She looked up at him questioningly in the semidarkness.

Philip stared down at her and saw the deep longing in the depths of her gaze. It frightened him to find that she was feeling the same thing he was. "Now?" he repeated in a husky tone.

"Yes, now . . . Do you have time for an affair of the heart now?" Peri knew she was behaving outrageously, saying things to him a lady should never say, but she didn't care. She figured the worst thing that could happen would be she would find out he really wasn't interested. Peri was convinced that knowing the truth, no matter how painful, would be far superior to be left hanging in limbo as she had been for the past weeks.

The sound of the music drifted from the ballroom and, carried on the night wind, caressed them with its sweet melody. In their diamondlike brilliance, the myriad stars overhead twinkled in seductive splendor. A single shooting star marked a shining path across the heavens, and Peri saw it, exclaiming at its beauty.

"Philip . . . look!" She had rarely seen such a heavenly display.

"I am looking," he replied. It wasn't the meteor that held him fascinated, however. It was Peri. She was unlike any woman he'd ever known. She was guileless and completely honest. She always said what she thought. Yet, at the same time she was smart enough to listen to others when the occasion called for it. She was a total optimist in her thinking, always expecting the best of people and situations and never giving in to the blackness of despair.

God knows, Philip wanted her. He longed to be a part of her unwavering happiness, to cling to her gentle spirit and live as she lived, but his life was in ruins. He was a bond slave, not a hired accountant, and his sister was on the run for murder. How could he even hope to have any kind of relationship with some like Peri under these circumstances? At that moment, though, when she turned back to him, he cast all reasons not to love her aside forever.

"You're so special, Peri . . . I've never known another woman like you," he murmured, and without another word he reached for her.

Peri needed no encouragement. She made a throaty sound of surrender as she went to him, her champagne glass dropping unheeded from her fingers to lie in the grass. Her arms looped around his neck, and she kissed him with the flaming passion of a woman who knew exactly what she wanted.

Her excitement fueled Philip's, and he crushed her to him, his mouth demanding upon hers. He parted her lips, tasting of her, loving her. She was beauty and innocence and all the things he wanted and needed in his life. He never wanted to let her go.

The sounds of guests making their way out onto the gallery intruded on their bliss, and Philip broke off the kiss. When she started to protest, gazing up at him in puzzlement, he lifted a finger to his lips to hush her. He then took her hand and led her into the privacy of the darkness among the trees. Once he was sure they were out of sight, he pulled her back to him and kissed her again, this time holding nothing back.

"Oh, Philip . . ." Peri whispered when his lips left hers to press hot kisses to her throat. She shivered at the power of the emotions surging through her, and she held him close. "I was so afraid you didn't want me . . ."

"Want you? I can't get you out of my mind," he growled, his desire for her at a fever pitch. "You haunt me day and night. You're like a fire in my blood."

His mouth took hers again and she melted against the broad width of his chest. His hand sought the fullness of her breast, and she gave a low moan of ecstasy at his touch. This was love, it had to be. Nothing else had ever felt this perfect . . .

"Love me, Philip . . . please."

There was nothing Philip wanted more than to take her to his bed and make love to her, and he knew there was nothing more forbidden to him than her love. Desire her as he did . . . want her as he did . . . love her as he did, he knew if he took her he would ruin her. She was too wonderful, too precious to him.

291

To make sure she was safe, he had to protect her most of all from himself.

"Peri . . . no . . ." He took her gently by the shoulders and held her slightly away from him.

She blinked up at him, trying to understand why he was stopping, when she knew instinctively that he wanted her as much as she wanted him. "No?"

"This won't work, love," he tried to explain.

"I love you, Philip. Of course, it will work," she stated, confident that everything would work out fine.

"You don't understand. It's impossible. You're Peri Kane Davidson. Your parents are rich. Just look at what your uncle owns . . ."

"So?"

"So, I'm just plain Philip Montgomery. I work for my living. I have nothing to give you . . . nothing."

"I only want your love, Philip. I never asked for anything else."

"I'm a man, Peri. If I love a woman, I have to be able to provide for her."

"But money doesn't matter to me. It's not important. I have money, more than enough for both of us. All I want is you," she insisted.

"It's no good, Peri." He released her and stepped away. Her bewildered expression was like a knife in his heart, but he knew he had to stop this madness now. Even when the time came and he was freed from his indenture, there was still Jordan and her danger. "Go on back to your party. Find yourself a rich man who can give you all the things you should have. Forget about me."

"But Philip, I love you."

"I'm sorry."

Before she could say another word, he turned and vanished into the concealing darkness. Peri stood frozen where he'd left her, staring off after him, her cheeks wet with tears of frustration and regret. It was a long time before she felt composed enough to return to the reception. When she did, she sought out another glass of champagne. An hour later, she was already beginning to plot.

Nick thought the celebration was passing far too quickly. It was nearing midnight, and the time was coming when it would be expected that he and Jordan would retire for the night. If they stayed longer to avoid the trip upstairs, questions would be asked. There was no way out of it. They had to give the appearance that they were going up to bed to share their first night of connubial bliss.

Nick downed his bourbon as he listened with little interest to the conversations going on around him. Aaron had claimed Jordan for a dance about half an hour before, and she'd been gone from him ever since as man after man followed his suit and sought her out for a dance. He realized Slater had been right in his assessment. Every man in four parishes *was* wanting her, and it looked like they were all standing in line waiting their turn to get their hands on her.

Nick watched Jordan dance by now, doing a schottische with a young bachelor from a neighboring plantation, and he acknowledged the truth of his jealousy for the first time. If he felt this way over just a few harmless dances with friends, he wondered how he was going to feel when the time came for him to let her go to Montgomery. He stared down at his glass and was amazed to find it empty. He contemplated getting a refill, but decided against it. Tonight of all nights he needed a clear head. He needed to keep his wits about him. It was not going to be easy to share a

293

bedroom with Jordan and not touch her. It would take all his considerable self-restraint to follow through with the bargain, but he had given his word.

"Here she is, Nick," Ralph Murphy said as he returned Jordan to her waiting husband. "She's as graceful a dancer as she is beautiful."

"Why, thank you, Ralph," Jordan was pleased by his comment.

"You're one lucky man."

"I know," Nick answered without hesitation. When the other man had gone, he turned to Jordan and asked, "Would you like to dance again?"

"Actually, I was hoping to find a quiet place to rest," she told him honestly.

"Do you want to go upstairs now? It's nearly midnight."

"I hadn't realized it was that late . . ." Jordan was surprised and a little nervous. "I guess maybe we'd better. We don't want to raise any suspicions."

"Why don't you go on up, and I'll meet you there shortly."

"All right." A shiver of anticipation shot through her. This was her wedding night. She wasn't quite sure what to say, so she said nothing. Instead, she raised up on tiptoes to give Nick a soft, unexpected kiss on the lips, then hurried from the room.

Slater appeared magically at his side. "Are you sure about this bargain of yours?"

"I'm sure." Nick sounded bitter. He knew her seemingly impulsive kiss had been for show, but it had unnerved him.

"Jordan's turned out to be one hell of a better actress than I gave her credit for, then," he commented. "Want to join me in the study for one last drink?"

"I think that sounds like an excellent idea." Common sense warned Nick that he shouldn't do it, but he rationalized the warning away, telling himself that the drink would help fortify him for the hours to come.

Rose Brandford and Liz McKelvey were sitting at the side of the ballroom, watching the newlyweds. Rose elbowed her companion in the ribs as discreetly as she could when Jordan left the ballroom and headed upstairs.

"I told you they wouldn't be able to wait past midnight. Heaven knows, if that had been me, I would have dragged the boy upstairs hours ago."

"Rosie!" Liz scolded in a shocked whisper, giving her a scandalized look.

"Oh, Liz, don't you remember what your wedding night was like? I know I certainly do," she confided with a sly grin. "Why, my Everett was one fantastic lover, and I can just imagine how the Kane boy . . ."

"Rosie!" Her friend began to blush as she opened her fan and began to fan herself nervously. "You mustn't say such things out loud!"

"Why not? I'll bet you there isn't a woman in this room who isn't thinking about it."

"I most certainly am not thinking about 'it,' "

"Well, you should be, especially since your Darrell is still alive," Rosie chided.

"You have a dirty mind."

Incensed, she puffed up in her indignity. *"I do not!"* she snapped, then added calmly, "I'm a romantic. I'm wishing the same love for Jordan and Nick that I had with Everett."

"He did make the perfect choice, didn't he? She's so pretty — and such a lady."

"Indeed, he did choose well. I know Andrea would be proud of him tonight. You can certainly see how happy Charles is."

"He's pleased as punch. You should have heard

him bragging about Jordan. You'd have thought he handpicked her." The two women exchanged contented smiles, but then Liz's expression grew serious. "But, Rosie, did you notice that he's not looking particularly well?"

"I did notice that he looked tired. You don't suppose he's ill, do you?"

Jordan had no idea she'd won the seal of approval of every matron in attendance, she was just glad to be able to escape the revelry. She needed time to think before Nick came up to the room. To be honest with herself, she wasn't quite sure *what* to do.

Jordan knew that though she loved Nick with all her heart, he did not love her. He had no intention of making this a lasting marriage. He'd made it clear from the start that he wanted out as soon as it could be arranged, and she had to live with that knowledge. The only thing that made the whole thing bearable was that he seemed to be coming to like her. Certainly all of his attentiveness couldn't have been merely for show. And then there were his kisses . . .

A heady determination filled her. This was her wedding night. She would forget about tomorrow and grasp her happiness now, while she could. A small smile curved her lips as she entered the bedroom they would share that night. When Nick came up to join her, he wasn't going to find a bought-and-paid-for servant, he was going to find a loving, devoted bride.

"Good evening, ma'am. What can I do for you?" Claire, the maid, asked as Jordan came in the room.

"Help me unfasten the back of my dress and then lay out my white negligée, please. I don't have much time. He'll be here any minute," Jordan told her excitedly.

"Don't worry. I'll hurry. This is your night. Everything will be perfect for you."

"Thank you." Jordan turned her back so the girl could loosen the gown.

Between the two of them it only took a few minutes for her to shed the wedding dress. When Claire produced the nearly transparent, lace-trimmed nightgown from Nick's armoire, Jordan was surprised.

"My things have been moved in here?" She had not known that Nick planned for them to share his bedroom. The idea was not at all unpleasant to her.

"Yes, ma'am. According to his instructions, we moved everything earlier this evening."

Jordan said nothing more as she donned the nightdress. The delicate gown felt luxurious against her skin, and she couldn't resist running a hand over its frothy softness. She went to sit at the dressing table to brush out her hair while Claire turned back the covers on the big four-poster bed.

"Will there be anything else, ma'am?"

"No, that'll be all for the night."

The servant started for the door, then turned back. "I just wanted to tell you best wishes on your wedding, Miss Jordan. I hope you and Mr. Nick will be very happy."

"Thank you, Claire." Jordan stopped brushing her hair and turned to look at the girl. "I hope we will be too."

Claire left the room then, thinking that Mr. Nick was the stuff dreams were made of and that Miss Jordan was one lucky girl.

Nick lingered over the bourbon as long as he could. He and Slater had sought peace and quiet out on the gallery, and they took the opportunity to privately discuss the latest news on the *Sea Demon*'s owners. It seemed there were a few solid leads that needed to be followed up on, but nothing concrete yet. Though it wasn't too encouraging, they resolved never to give up.

When at last the time came for Nick to follow Jordan upstairs, his mood was dark. The thought of being so close to her and being unable to touch her had him twisted up in knots inside. He wanted to hold her and love her. He wanted to give her his world, but he was bound by his honor.

Nick bid a sympathetic Slater good night and mounted the steps with dragging feet. He knew any other bridegroom would be practically vaulting up the stairs, but not him. There was no joy awaiting him in the wedding chamber. There was only frustration, deception, and the loneliness of unrequited love.

As he reached the top of the staircase and started down the hall, the noise of the celebration below faded. Nick felt almost as if he was entering another world, and he seemed to be moving in slow motion. His actions were tired and almost defeated as he loosened his cravat. He stopped before his closed bedroom door to draw a deep, reinforcing breath, then he opened it and went in.

Nick was expecting to find Jordan waiting there to debate the issue of where they were going to sleep. He'd expected she would still be either fully dressed or else have donned something suitably demure that would do nothing to encourage him or arouse his passions. He stepped into the room thinking he was in control of his wild desire for her. He entered the would-be torture chamber intending to abide by his pledge to a marriage in name only. He went forth, firm in his belief that he could hold to it, but the sight that greeted Nick when he came through the door rocked him to the very heart and rendered him speechless.

Chapter Twenty-three

A single lamp was burning low in the bedroom, its light muted and soft. Jordan had just finished brushing out her hair when Nick entered the room, and she rose from the dressing table to greet him. She was nervous. Her heart was in her throat, but she didn't let it show. He was her husband and she wanted him. Nick was transfixed. He closed the door but had no memory of doing it. He could only stand there and gaze at Jordan, enthralled by her beauty.

Jordan's tawny mane, tumbling about her shoulders, looked like molten gold in the soft glow of the lamplight. The gossamer gown, a confection of ruffles and lace, had slipped off one shoulder in a sensuous display that revealed the beginning swell of her breasts. Sheer as it was, it veiled her slender form in a cloud of maddening mystery, allowing Nick only hints of the luscious beauty it concealed. The negligée was daringly short, draping only about her hips and leaving her long legs tantalizingly bared to his heated regard.

Desire thundered through Nick. He was totally captivated. When she raised one hand toward him and whispered his name, his breath caught in his throat, for he saw there reflected in her eyes both desire and acceptance. He moved slowly toward her and took her hand in his. Standing but inches from her, the seductive scent of her perfume twined its tendrils around him. His voice was hoarse when he spoke.

"Are you sure, Jordan?"

"Yes," she answered softly, "very sure."

He put his hands on her waist to draw her closer, and, for a moment, he simply held her. Her warmth against him was one of the deepest pleasures he'd ever known. When he could bear no more of this quiet ecstasy, he kissed her gently, his lips barely brushing hers, as if he were tasting the deep sweet nectar of her.

Jordan was in his arms then, her head resting on his chest, her body against his. She could hear the strong beat of his heart as he held her; it matched the excited, pulsing rhythm of her own. She drew back to look up at him, and their eyes met in unspoken understanding.

Nick bent to her, claiming her lips again. He moved slowly, not wanting to spoil the perfection of the moment. The kiss was soft and gentle, and they both trembled with the force of their need.

Jordan wanted to feel the heat of his body on hers. She ached to know him only as a woman could know him. She slipped one hand behind his head to bring him nearer, and Nick could wait no longer. He deeped the kiss. She was unprepared for the wild flood of heat that swept through her, and she melted against him.

To Jordan, it seemed this was something that had been predestined. She belonged to this man, this place, this time. Her breath came in short gasps as he began to caress her. Her passion and desire for Nick were building to a fever pitch. The world as she knew it faded to nothingness. There was only Nick and the wonder of his touch and kiss.

With a soft sound from deep in his throat, Nick lifted her in his arms and carried her to the bed. He lay her gently against the pillows. Slowly, with the utmost care, he untied the ribbons that held her gown and then slipped the filmy garment from her. His eyes were hot upon her flesh as they raked over her, and she flushed with shy excitement.

Nick moved away from the bed only long enough to shed his own clothing. He came to her then in all his male splendor. Jordan's gaze roamed over the glory of him, visually caressing his wide, muscular shoulders and strong arms. Dark hair furred his chest. His waist was trim, his hips and flanks lean, his legs straight and powerful. When Nick joined her on the bed, her hands traced the path her gaze had forged, burning his flesh like a hot iron, branding him hers.

Nick sought out the sweetness of her breasts, bending lower to kiss the crests. Jordan had never known such intimate caresses, and she arched wildly against him as his mouth closed over one aching peak. Ecstasy throbbed through her as he tormented her with his sensual expertise. Consumed by an unquenchable demanding flame of pleasure, she gave a soft moaning sob. Her body instinctively sought his, knowing that he alone could release her from the exquisite agony.

Nick raised up to kiss her, his mouth taking hers in a hot, hungry exchange, and passion exploded between them. There was no pretense, no deception. There was no thought of bargains or deals. There was only man and woman and love's quest for fulfillment.

Nick tangled his hands in her hair as he deepened his kiss. He could feel the crush of her breasts against his chest. The scent of her, the softness of her, drove him wild with need. His mouth left hers to seek out the sensitive chords of her throat. She shivered beneath him, and he could feel the tips of her breasts harden at his erotic play. When he moved even lower to trail heated kisses across the slope of her bared shoulder, she gasped and called out his name.

"Oh . . . Nick . . ."

Her desire-drugged cry filled him with a depth of emotion he'd never known before. He lifted his head, his dark eyes searching hers for any last sign of reluctance, but he read only ecstasy in her sparkling emerald gaze. Her cheeks were flushed with passion, and her lips were red and swollen from his kisses. He shifted over her, his body fitting itself to her curves with breathtaking intimacy.

The melding of hot male flesh with cooler female flesh was intensely erotic, and Jordan gasped at the fiery heat of him. Her arms wrapped around him, holding him close as they kissed, then kissed again. She felt the alien hardness of his manhood against her thigh, and in a bold, daring move, reached down to touch him. Nick was jolted by her caress, and he went rigid momentarily.

"Did I hurt you?" she whispered fearfully, drawing her hand away.

"Oh, no, love . . ." he groaned, covering her hand with his own and guiding it back. "You could never hurt me . . ."

It pleased Jordan to know that her touch could affect him so, and she was filled with a sense of great feminine pride and an awakening knowledge of secret feminine power.

Nick was almost out of control. Her intimate caress was driving him nearly out of his mind. In an act of self-preservation, he shifted away from her. Setting the tempo for their lovemaking himself, he took over. He began a sensual assault on Jordan with practiced caresses and potent kisses. He wanted to give her joy

303

to the fullest. He wanted her to know passion's promise.

His hands explored every inch of her, tracing patterns of delight over her bosom and thighs. He continued to press kisses to her lips and throat, moving lower to the succulent mounds of her breasts when he felt her begin to stir beneath him. He laved attention on that sensitive flesh until she was clutching at him in the throes of her desire. Nick slipped a hand between their straining bodies to seek out the heat of her womanhood. Jordan bucked nervously, trying to evade his touch when he tried to caress the core of her femininity, but he'd soon soothed her with gentling words.

"Easy, darling, easy now. I won't do anything you don't want me to do . . ."

"Nick . . ." The tension eased from her body and she gave herself over to his ministrations, trusting him completely, wanting to take all he would give. "I want this . . . I want you . . . Please . . ."

That was all he needed to hear. His lips mets hers as he positioned himself between her thighs. Ever so slowly he eased himself forward until he was resting against the portal of her love. He could feel the heat of her body and the wetness of her welcome. Without ending the kiss, he slid his hands down to her hips to lift her to him. In a smooth, masterful stroke, he entered her. He hesitated for only a heartbeat at the barrier of her virginity. Shocked though he was by this proof of her innocence, there was no thought of drawing back. He couldn't stop. He had to have her. With a single determined thrust, he sheathed himself in her velvet sweetness.

Her murmer of pain was drowned in his kiss. He moved deeply within her. The pain seemed to melt away and suddenly she was engulfed in an urgency, a wanting, that blinded her to every other thought. She clung to him, whispering his name over and over as his rhythm of love drove her to the frantic edge. There was no beginning, no end, just this one moment in time when two became one. They were man and woman . . . complementing each other, giving to each other, taking from each other, in an unending cycle of life and love. It was eternal and perfect.

They blended in perfect harmony, slowly scaling the heights of ecstasy. Theirs was a melody of love, a mating of souls. He played her body like a finely tuned instrument, his every touch and caress striking a new chord of excitement within her until she felt as if she would die from wanting him so much.

Nick quickened his pace as his own body demanded fulfillment. She was holding him so tightly within her that each thrust was exquisite agony for him. He didn't want to hurry, but being buried in her this way was so heavenly he couldn't hold back any longer. He drove onward, his rhythm building, carrying them both to a frenzied, throbbing, heart-stopping crescendo that transported them both to rapture—and beyond . . .

Jordan's breathing was ragged, matching the harshness of Nick's as they lay wrapped in each other's arms. The explosive climax left them both in awe of the powerful force that claimed them. Silently, they each explored the wonder of their feelings so vividly revealed to them now. They loved, but neither could admit it.

Only when the tension of their ecstasy had calmed completely did Nick move. He turned to his side, bringing Jordan close against him, her back to his chest, her thighs cupped against his. He rose on one elbow to press a soft kiss to her temple, then lay back keeping one arm possessively around her just beneath her breasts. Brushing her hair aside, he kissed the nape of her neck and was pleased when she quivered in his arms.

"Nick . . . I . . ." She was worried. She'd wanted this . . . oh, how she'd wanted this! She loved him more than she'd ever thought it possible to love anyone. But now that she'd tasted of his love, she wondered how she would ever be able to leave him.

"Hush, Jordan. Rest now," was all Nick said. He didn't want to talk. He was too confused by everything that had happened. Her wanting him . . . his response to her kisses and the ecstasy of loving her . . . the startling proof of her virginity. Obviously she hadn't been Montgomery's mistress, but Nick knew she loved the man. How could it be that she hadn't given herself to him? His thoughts and emotions were in turmoil.

Pleasure's aftermath finally claimed them both, momentarily washing away their concerns, bathing them in soothing sleep. They rested.

Jordan slept deeply and peacefully at first. Then for some unknown reason, images of Luther suddenly appeared in her dreams, turning them from blissful visions of Nick to nightmares of hellish proportions. In her mind's enslaved eye, Luther was chasing her . . . his hands were ripping at her clothes, his lips and hands were touching her, making her flesh crawl. She was frightened, desperate to get away. She tried to fight, but it seemed useless. She tried to cry out to Philip for help, but she had no voice. She was trapped and there was no way out! She saw Nick standing in a beam of light at the end of a long, dark tunnel. She ran toward him, but the harder she tried to reach him, the longer the tunnel seemed to get. Suddenly there was a gallows before her with a laughing, hideous, be-wigged judge sitting on the high bench, who declared her guilty . . . *guilty* . . . *GUILTY!*

"Jordan . . . Jordan . . . wake up. It's all right . . . I'm here . . . I'll take care of you . . . You're safe . . ."

Her unconscious struggles had wakened Nick from his sleep. He was trying to hold her close now and reassure her against whatever secret monster seemed to be chasing her.

Jordan's eyes flew open at the sound of his voice, and she found herself gazing up at him. His expression was concerned and his brow was furrowed with worry over the unknown demons that tormented her.

"Nick . . . oh, thank God . . ." She threw her arms around his neck and hugged him close.

When he tried to pull back to look at her, she wouldn't let go.

"Jordan?" Finally he reached up and loosened her arms from his neck. He studied her face and was troubled by the frantic, hunted look in her eyes. "What is it? What's wrong?"

"Nothing . . ." she quickly denied, knowing she could never tell him the truth. "Nothing . . . Please, just hold me . . ."

There was such desperation in her voice he could do nothing less. Cradling her against him, he held her safely in the haven of his arms. But having her lithe form that close to him, stirred another desire besides the need to protect her. His mind told him she needed comfort, his body demanded he taste of her passion once again.

Nick's hands began a tender assault, caressing her back and shoulders with long, lingering strokes as his lips sought hers. Jordan felt so safe and so secure that she willingly gave herself over to his keeping. Their joining began slowly. There was no frantic passion, no frenzied need as they came together this time.

307

There was only gentleness and joy, a celebration of discovery.

The haunting traces of Jordan's nightmare were swept from her mind by the force of the emotions he aroused within her. They came together in a miracle of breathless wonder, their bodies fusing into one. Nick kept his pace slow and steady, bringing her to the peak of ecstasy first before allowing himself the same thrilling release. They clung together, fulfilled in each other.

Long minutes later, Nick raised himself up on his elbows to gaze down at her. With a gentle touch, he brushed back an errant curl from her cheek and then kissed her softly.

"Tradition dictates that a groom should always give his bride a gift on their wedding day," he murmured. "But I'm afraid I didn't have time to go into New Orleans and buy you anything."

"It's all right, Nick. You've already given me so much . . ."

"But I insist," he said, refusing to let the matter drop. He was so in love with her in that moment that he would have promised her the moon had she asked for it. "Tell me what you want . . . money is no object."

"Let me think about it for a while . . . There's something else on my mind right now." Jordan caressed his lean cheek as she stared into the brown velvet depths of his eyes. Then, ever so slowly, she drew him down to her for a kiss. As he began to move within her again, she wondered vaguely if there could be anything more wonderful than loving Nick. All conscious thought fled as their passions flamed to life once more.

* * *

308

Nick came awake slowly. His sleep had been deep, almost drugged, for the potent bourbon had finally taken its toll. His first thought was of Jordan, and he reached for her in the darkness, wanting her warm, soft curves against him. When his hand encountered nothing but cool sheets, Nick was puzzled. He couldn't imagine where she'd gone, and he got up from the bed to look for her.

For some reason, Nick was drawn to the window. As he gazed out over the gardens below, he was stunned to see Jordan hurrying down the path that led through the flowering shrubs. He knew exactly where she was going, and stark pain was suddenly etched on his handsome features.

The knowledge that she could leave his bed and go to the indentured servant struck Nick like a vicious physical blow. Pain and humiliation pounded through him as he realized what a fool he'd been. He might have taken her virginity, but that didn't mean it ended anything she was feeling for the other man. Why had he allowed himself to think otherwise?

Fury filled Nick. He wanted to scream his anger, he wanted to hit out at something or someone, but he was helplessly caught in a web of lies, and they were all of his own making.

Control, Nick told himself firmly. Self-control was his only hope if he was going to get through this. He'd always been proud of the firm rein he had on his emotions, and he drew upon that strength now as he went back to lie down on the bed and await her return. The sheets were icy beneath him, and he knew if he tried hard enough, his heart would soon be the same.

It was very late, almost near dawn, when Philip heard the sound of a very soft knock at his door. He lay still, thinking at first that he'd imagined it, then, when it came again, he flew from the bed to see who was there. There were no words to describe the shock he felt when he threw wide the portal and came face to face with his sister. She was barefoot and looked to be wearing only her gown and wrapper.

"Jordan?" he whispered in disbelief. Without another word he quickly ushered her inside and closed the door. "You shouldn't be here." He closed the shutters to his one window to insure their privacy, then lit a lamp. When he turned to her, he saw her tear-stained face and thought something tragic had happened. "Jordan . . . what is it? What happened?"

"Oh, Philip . . ." she cried heartbrokenly as she went into his arms. "What am I going to do?"

"What's the matter? What has Kane done to you? I swear if he's hurt you, I'll kill him . . ."

"No . . . no . . ." Jordan protested quickly.

"Then, what?"

"Philip, I was afraid this would happen and now it has . . ."

"What?"

"I've fallen in love with Nick . . . I can't deny it any longer."

Philip's hands tightened on her upper arms as he forced her to look up at him. "Jordan, you know the danger . . ."

"I know," she admitted, "but I want him so. I keep thinking that there must be a way I can make this work. Philip . . ." She paused, her tears fading as her eyes took on a glow that reflected the glory of her love. "We're so perfect together. He's everything I've ever wanted . . . everything I've ever needed."

Her brother held her close. "I know. I feel the same way about Peri."

"You do?"

310

"Yes," he confessed with a heavy heart. "I love her, but it can never be."

"Why not? There's no reason for you two not to be happy."

"I'm an indentured servant, Jordan. I've lost everything. I have nothing to offer her, not even my good name."

"But, Philip, what if we're really safe here? What if all our worries are needless? We're in a new country. Our names are different. Who would come after us? Even if they did, how would they ever find us?"

He looked a little more hopeful, but he still had his doubts. "But what if they did manage to track us down?"

"Listen to me, big brother, this may be our one and only chance for happiness. Shouldn't we take it?"

"I want you to be happy, Jordan. It's just that I'm afraid for you, that's all."

She managed to give him a small smile. "I know, and I thank you for caring. But I think this time we have to risk it. What kind of life will we have if we cut ourselves off from the very people we love? Would it even be worth living?"

"Whatever you decide, you know I'll support you, but you haven't said how Kane feels about you."

"I'm not sure yet, but I think he loves me too."

"For your sake, I hope he does, Jordan." He kissed her cheek. "Now, you'd better go back to the big house right now before someone sees you. God only knows what would happen if you got caught down here with me."

"You're right." She kissed him quickly, then fled back into the night to return to her marriage bed.

Jordan's spirits were high as she hurried through the garden. Talking things out with Philip always made her feel better, and she knew now what she was going to do. She was going to take the chance. She was going to do everything in her power to make Nick fall in love with her. His lovemaking tonight couldn't have been a lie, and physical desire, while not in and of itself love, was still a good place to start in building a permanent relationship between them. As she slipped back into the house, she only hoped that Nick had not awakened while she was gone.

Nick was lying in bed, his hands clenched into fists of fury at his sides, staring sightlessly into the darkness, when he heard the bedroom door open. He heard Jordan enter and cross the room. He felt the bed dip under her slight weight as she lay down beside him again, but through it all, he did not stir. In silent testimony to his fury and pain, he pretended to be asleep. He knew this was definitely not the time for a confrontation. He couldn't talk to her right now. Morning would be soon enough. Only then would he feel in control enough to deal with the terrible mistake he'd made tonight.

Chapter Twenty-four

Jordan had slept soundly after she'd crept back into bed with Nick. She'd given thanks that he hadn't awakened to find her gone, and she vowed from that moment on that she was going to make him the best wife in the world.

It was very late when she awoke the next morning, the bright morning sun streaming in the bedroom window. Knowing what an early riser Nick was, she wasn't at all surprised to find that he was already up and gone, but she was a bit disappointed. The wonder of the night before was still warm within her. Jordan smiled a satisfied, catlike smile as she stretched languidly. Nick was a marvelous lover, and could hardly wait to see him again. She shivered deliciously at the thought.

Jordan believed she had everything figured out. Her life would be simple from now on. She loved Nick, and she was going to make him fall in love with her. Philip was her only problem, but since Nick had promised her a wedding present, she knew what she should ask for . . . she would ask for Philip to be released from his indenture now. That way he would be free to marry Peri and everything would work out perfectly. With Philip married, Nick would have absolutely no reason to be suspicious of him any more. She hoped one day to be able to tell him the truth about her brother, but for now, as much as it pained her, there were some things she had to leave as they were. Jordan bounded from the bed to get ready so she could hurry downstairs to find her husband.

Slater knocked once on the study door and stuck his head inside to speak to Nick. "Weddington said you were in here. You busy?"

"No, come on in."

Nick voice was terse, and Slater wasn't really surprised. He could just imagine the kind of night his friend had just passed.

"Bad night?"

Nick shot him a black look that silenced any further questions Slater might have had.

"What's on your mind?" Nick asked, turning their thoughts away from the obvious.

"Late last night, after you'd gone upstairs, I got a message from one of my contacts in New Orleans."

"And?" Nick's interest was immediate.

"It seems Kirkwood, our prime suspect with the English connections, has put out feelers, letting it be known to a privileged few that he's looking for new investors in a very private yet very profitable shipping enterprise. He's in New Orleans now."

"Is there any chance that we can get in to see him?"

"I was going to go into town today and see what I could arrange."

"I'll come with you," Nick announced with no hesitation.

"But Nick . . ." Slater protested. "You just got married. Don't you think it will look a little suspicious if you rush out of here the morning after your

314

wedding?"

"Not if I tell my father there's a pressing business problem I have to deal with personally."

"What about Jordan?"

"What about her?" His voice was flat and emotionless.

Slater knew not to press when he heard that tone. "Never mind. Look, this is the way I thought we'd handle this thing with Kirkwood . . ." He began to explain his strategy.

Jordan descended the staircase, her mood happy and lighthearted as she was met by the butler at the foot of the steps.

"Good morning, Weddington," she greeted, her gaze scanning the hall in hopes of seeing Nick.

"Good morning, ma'am," he replied, his deep voice holding just a touch of puzzlement. When Nick had come downstairs several hours before his mood had been poisonous. He'd been so close-mouthed and grim that he'd been barely able to get a word out of him during breakfast. The butler had been wondering what could have caused Nick to be so sullen and angry, and he'd waited for Miss Jordan to come down, hoping she would provide a clue. He could tell there was no answer to be found with Jordan, though, for she looked positively glowing this morning in her turquoise daygown.

"Have you seen my husband anywhere around?" Jordan asked, cheerfully.

"Yes, ma'am. He's in the study."

"Is he alone?" She didn't want to interrupt him if he was talking business with anyone.

"Mr. Slater's with him, Miss Jordan," he replied.

"Thank you, Weddington." She practically danced

315

down the hall, her whole being vibrant and alive at the thought of seeing Nick. She wanted to kiss him good morning. She wanted to tell him he was the most wonderful man alive. She wanted to hug him and never let him go. Jordan knocked lightly on the study door, and when she heard Nick respond, she opened it and went in. "Nick, Slater, good morning."

Nick had known the moment was going to come when he was going to have to face Jordan. He just hadn't expected that seeing her again would hurt him so badly, but the sight of her looking innocent and completely happy wrenched at his vitals.

"Good morning, Jordan," Slater said, truly perplexed by the couple's mood. He sensed Nick was tense and angry, while Jordan was obviously very pleased with herself.

Jordan was feeling so good she didn't even notice that her husband hadn't greeted her. Singleminded of purpose, she went straight to him, lovingly linked her arms about his neck, and pulled him down for a kiss. "Good morning, Nick," she said in a low, husky voice when the kiss ended.

Slater watched the whole scene with something akin to amazement. There was no need for Jordan to play the loving wife for him. He wondered at her motive, then pondered the possibility that she had no motive . . . that things really had worked out between them and she did feel that way about Nick. But if that were true, why in the world would Nick be in such a frame of mind? It didn't make sense to Slater, and since something was obviously amiss, he decided to get out of there and give them time to talk.

"I think I'll leave you two lovebirds alone for now. I'll be in my room packing." He left quickly.

Jordan stepped back, smiling brightly, thrilled that they were finally by themselves. "Remember last

316

night, when you asked me what I wanted for a wedding present?"

"Yes," Nick replied cautiously.

"Well, I've finally decided what it is I want."

"Oh? What is it?"

"I want you to release Philip from his indenture now instead of later."

Nick paled and stood absolutely still. Anger surged through him, and he knew a sudden desire to hurt her as she was hurting him. He didn't doubt for a moment that Philip's freedom was her heart's desire, he just wondered why she'd bother to wait until this morning to request it of him. Why hadn't she asked him last night when she came back from Montgomery's bed?

"I see," he said brusquely, through tight lips. His eyes were hard and his face a mask of stone. "I'll take care of it right away."

"Thank you, Nick." She threw her arms around him, unaware of his volatile mood.

"Spare me your gratitude, Jordan."

She was surprised when he extricated himself from her embrace and moved coolly away from her. "Nick?" She found herself speaking to his back.

"I'm leaving for New Orleans with Slater," he informed her as he walked toward the study door.

"Now? Today?" Her heart lurched as she stared at him. She was suddenly aware of the terrible coldness in him.

"Yes. There's some business I have to attend to." He paused at the door to look back.

"But what about our marriage? What about last night?"

"Jordan, please, I don't need all this play-acting. It's just you and me here."

"I don't understand . . ." She suddenly had a horri-

317

ble sinking feeling in the pit of her stomach.

"I deeply regret last night. I should never have touched you, but . . ." Nick gave a casual, expressive lift of his broad shoulders. "I'd had too much bourbon, and, well, things just got out of hand. I apologize for not sticking to our original bargain. I assure you what happened didn't change anything, and I'll make sure it doesn't happen again."

Jordan's spirits crashed from the heights of happiness to the depths of despair in that one brief minute. All of her hopes and dreams were dashed upon the craggy rocks of the reality Nick had just revealed to her. Later, she would never know how she managed to stay in control of her emotions.

"You're right, last night was a terrible mistake," she stated with a calm composure that surprised even her. "In the future we'll have to be more careful."

Her cool manner and indifferent words sounded a death knell to Nick. "I have to pack. My father's still resting. Please tell him when he gets up that I couldn't delay the trip, but that I should be back in a couple of days." He opened the door, and with one last look at her he was gone.

Jordan stayed where she was, staring blankly after him. Then, ever so slowly, she sank down in one of the wing-backed chairs, her strength suddenly drained from her. She tried to make sense of the past twelve hours, but her thoughts were despondent. Her dreams had been only fantasies, and stupid ones at that. She should have remembered that Nick had never wanted to marry. She should have remembered the bargain . . .

Peri had gotten very little sleep. Mostly she'd tossed and turned all night, trying to think of a way to convince Philip that they could be together. When no bright idea came to her through the long dark hours of the night, she decided there was only one thing she could do. She would ask Nick for his advice. He'd been her confidant since she was small, and she knew he would help her.

Peri came downstairs that morning eager to seek Nick out, but he was already closeted with Slater in the study. She lingered over breakfast then took a walk in the garden to pass the time while waiting for him to emerge. When she came back inside, she caught sight of him at the top of the staircase.

"Nicky! Wait!" she called out, hurrying up the steps after him.

Nick glanced back, wondering what was so important she had to chase him upstairs. "What do you want?"

"I need to talk with you. It's important."

"Peri, I really don't have a lot of time . . ." he hedged, in no mood to talk to anyone right now.

"This won't take long, I promise." Peri refused to be put off, and she dogged his steps as he headed down the hallway.

Nick grimaced, but held back any caustic comments. This was his Peri. He always had time for her. "Come on with me, then, but you're going to have to talk while I pack."

"Pack?" She stopped short.

"Yes, pack."

"You're leaving? But why?"

"There's a problem in town . . ." he replied evasively as he entered his bedroom.

"Couldn't somebody else take care of it?"

"There is no one else, Peri."

"But you just got married. It doesn't seem fair that you have to leave already . . ."

"I know, but it's something I have to do," he bit out tersely.

Peri heard the aggravation in his voice and figured it was because he was upset over leaving his bride of less than twenty-four hours. "I'm sorry."

"So am I. Anyway, what is it that's so important, you've got to pester me now?"

Peri was glad to hear the teasing tone back in his voice. "It is important, Nick. Honest."

"Well?" he asked as he started taking clothes out of his armoire and laying them out on the bed.

"I need your advice."

"About what?"

"I'm in love and I don't know what to do about it."

Nick arched a brow at her in disbelief. "I find it hard to fathom that you're at a loss to handle a man."

"Nick! Be serious! I am."

She sounded so upset that he dropped his joking manner. "All right, darling, what is it? Tell me everything."

"He's so wonderful, Nick. He's tender and kind and handsome . . ." She sighed. "I love him. I really do, but he doesn't want me."

"How could any man not want you? You're one of the most lovely women I know."

"Obviously, looks aren't enough . . ."

"Does he knew how you feel?"

"Oh, yes."

"And he doesn't feel the same way about you?"

"Well . . . that's where the trouble comes in. He does care about me, but he says he can't marry me because he doesn't think he's good enough for me."

"Who is this paragon you've fallen for?"

"It's Philip . . . Philip Montgomery, and you've got to help me think of some way to convince him that he's wrong!"

320

The name roared through Nick with brutal intensity, and he couldn't quite believe she'd said it. "Montgomery?"

She nodded.

"For God's sake, Peri! He's hired help!" Nick wanted to yell the truth at her and tell her that Montgomery wouldn't marry her because he was already in love with Jordan, but he couldn't. Nick silently cursed the roiling tangle of deception he'd created.

"Nick . . . I'm disappointed in you. I never thought you'd be one to hold a man's fortunes against him. Philip can't help it if his parents were poor. It's not his fault he didn't inherit a fortune. He's willing to do an honest day's work for his pay, and that's more than I can say for a lot of men."

"Peri, you're such an innocent. Be serious for a moment," he countered, fighting to appear calm and stay in control of his temper. "Montgomery is an honest man, true, but he's never going to amount to anything. He's not for you. He's even told you so himself. Why don't you listen to him?"

"Nick!"

"Listen to me, Peri, this is probably just an infatuation. You don't really love him, you just think you do."

"I know what I feel for Phillp, Nick, and I know he loves me, too. It's just that he refuses to do anything about it."

"Then I give the man credit for some sense. A man like Montgomery will only ruin you, Peri. How can you even consider sacrificing everything for a man you barely know?"

"I know him well enough. I love him . . ." she argued.

"You have to forget him," Nick commanded, his patience wearing thin. "He'll mean nothing but trouble for you. Stay away from him."

"But . . ."

Nick held up a hand to silence her. "Give yourself some time, and pretty soon I'll bet you'll find you're in love with someone else."

Peri was devastated by Nick's callousness, and she felt betrayed. Still, the Kane in her blood refused to allow her to show anything but strength. She stood erect and proud before her cousin as her eyes met his.

"I can see that we have a significant difference of opinion here, and there's really no point in discussing anything any further." Peri started for the door.

"Peri . . . what are you going to do?"

"Don't worry about it, Nick. My mistakes will be my own." With that, she was gone.

Nick stared after her, wondering if his life could possibly get any more miserable. Jordan loved Montgomery, and now Peri did, too. With bewildered anger, he wondered what the hell the other man's attraction was for women.

Nick grabbed a small valise and furiously began to stuff his clothing into it. He would follow through on his "gift" to Jordan and sign Philip's papers back to him as soon as he returned from New Orleans. He longed to throw the man off the plantation as soon as the ink was dry, but he knew his father would question his actions, and he couldn't risk that. Resigned to being tormented by the other man's presence, he snatched up his case and quit the room. Nick had never been a man to run from his problems, but the way he felt right then, he couldn't get away from Riverwood soon enough.

It was long past noon when Weddington finally decided it was time to check on Charles. His knock was firm, yet not alarming. "Mr. Charles, sir? You stirring yet today?"

Charles had awakened some time before, but hadn't had the energy to get out of bed. He'd been lying there half awake, half asleep, lost in sweet reverie of his beloved Andrea and the happy, seemingly carefree days before her death. The butler's call dragged him back from his imagined delights of the past, and he knew he had to respond.

"Yes, Weddington, you can come on in," he called, his voice sounding ever so weary.

The servant entered to find Charles looking terribly pale and drawn. "Good morning, Mr. Charles . . . or should I say, good afternoon?" He tried to keep it light, but he was concerned.

"It's that late, is it?"

"Yes, sir. Would you like some breakfast? Or should I bring you lunch?"

The old man waved a hand as if dismissing the thought of food. "I'm not hungry, I'm just tired. I guess all the excitement of the wedding wore me out."

Weddington turned away from him and busied himself with straightening the room so Charles wouldn't see his worried expression. He knew he was ill, but he hadn't expected him to deteriorate so quickly. Yesterday he'd been up and around, greeting his guests and even dancing with Miss Jordan, and now today . . .

"Is there anything I can do for you?"

"No, I don't think so. I think I'll just sleep for a while longer."

"All right, sir. Oh, Mr. Nick said to tell you that he had to travel into New Orleans to handle some kind of business problem and that he should be back in a day or two."

Charles scowled. "But what about Jordan?"

"Mr. Nick said it was very important. He and Mr.

323

Slater left about an hour ago."

"I see. Well then, if my son is too busy running Riverwood to pay attention to his bride, I'll just have to be the one to keep her company. Have Jordan come see me whenever she has a few minutes."

"Yes, sir."

Charles was dozing when Jordan knocked on his door a little later that afternoon. He called out groggily for her to come in, and though he was tired and looking terrible, his eyes lit up at the sight of his beautiful new daughter-in-law.

"My dear, I'm so glad you came to see me."

"You're my favorite father-in-law," she teased, trying to be light-hearted and not show him either her heartbreak over Nick's rejection or her very real concern over his condition.

"I would certainly hope so." He gave a shaky grin, then made an attempt to sit up against the headboard.

"Let me help you." Jordan went quickly to his aid, plumping his pillows for him and making him comfortable. When Charles was settled, she drew a chair to the bedside so she could sit with him.

"Thank you," Charles sighed, reaching out to take her hand and patting it affectionately. "I'm so glad you came up. I enjoy your company."

"I like being with you, too," she said, a deep, abiding ache growing within her as she realized just how weak he was. It hurt her to think that only the day before they'd been dancing together . . . it was almost as if the doctor's words had been prophetic. He'd been hanging on for the wedding.

"Now, tell me, what's my errant son up to? I just can't imagine him leaving anyone as beautiful as you after only one day of marriage." Charles was trying to make easy conversation. He had had no idea that he was going to strike a nerve with Jordan, but he saw the fleeting flicker of pain in her eyes and knew something was wrong.

"He didn't tell me too much. He just said it was business only he could take care of and that he'd be back as soon as he could." Deep within her a great anger began to blossom and grow against Nick. His personal feelings for her aside, there could be no justification for his running off to New Orleans this way when his father was so seriously sick.

"I'm sorry he had to leave, but it must have been important."

"I'm sure."

"So, are you happy?"

"Of course," she answered quickly. Then realizing that, as perceptive as he was, he had sensed some of her distress, she added, "I'm just disappointed."

"Nick can be hard to handle sometimes, but basically he's a good man," Charles told her with sympathetic understanding. "He has his faults. I know he's far too proud and occasionally he can be very pigheaded, but he's also strong and honest and always honorable."

His defense of Nick tore at Jordan. She had to fight to keep herself on an even keel. "I know. Those are some of the reasons why I married him," she responded.

He gave her hand a loving squeeze. "Jordan, you and I both know I'm not going to be around much longer."

His gaze sought hers, and though she didn't want to acknowledge the truth of his words, she could see his serene acceptance of his own mortality mirrored there in his eyes.

"Nick's told me you were very ill."

"It's my heart. I know it, he knows it, and I expect Peri has guessed by now."

Jordan nodded to verify that his niece was aware of his condition.

"The doctor told me some time ago that I didn't have long to live, and I've accepted it." He paused to draw a ragged breath, his grip on her hand tightening a bit. "It does hurt, though, to know that I won't be around to see my grandchildren."

"Don't say that," she insisted, trying not to think about his dying.

"Jordan," Charles spoke firmly but with tenderness, "there's no point in trying to deny reality. It's much easier for me now. I just want you to know how much you've come to mean to me and how happy I am that Nick chose you to be his wife."

Jordan's breath caught in her throat and tears suddenly welled up in her eyes. She loved this old man. She adored him. It was crushing her to know there was nothing she could do to stop his death. "Oh, Charles," she said brokenly, "I wish you could be with me forever."

"So do I, but sometimes we don't always get what we want in life. But you have my Dominic. He'll be there for you always, for I know he loves you as I loved my Andrea." Charles nodded toward her portrait.

"She was a very beautiful woman," Jordan commented, seeing the resemblance between Nick and his mother.

"Indeed she was, and I loved her more than life itself. The thought of being with her again is the only thing that makes dying tolerable," he confessed with a wry smile. Giving her hand one last squeeze, he sighed heavily. "I think I'd better sleep again now. Will you come back later?"

"You know I will. You just let me know when you want me and I'll come running."

326

"I'll do that." He closed his eyes, and suddenly, lying there so quietly, he looked very old and very near the end of his life.

Anguish filled Jordan, but she fought to keep it carefully camouflaged until she was out of the room. Only when she'd made it safely back to her bedroom did she give vent to her tears.

Chapter Twenty-five

"He sent word through channels that he'd like to meet with us to discuss the various investment opportunities he has to offer. He said he could meet us at noon a week from tomorrow in Mitchell's Tavern on the River Road," Slater informed Nick when he returned to their room at the St. Louis Hotel in New Orleans.

"Damn!" Nick swore, aggravated that they were being put off. He wondered if his life could get any more miserable. "Why couldn't he see us today, while we're here in town?"

"If he's the one we're after, I'm sure he wants to check our backgrounds before he tells us anything."

Slater's explanation didn't temper Nick's mood. In fact, nothing he'd said to him during the course of the two days since they'd left Riverwood had helped, and Slater had had about enough. He knew it would probably help Nick if he'd open up and talk about whatever it was that was bothering him, so he tried to think of a way to make him relax.

"Do you want to go home tonight, or would you rather go downstairs and have a few drinks and head back tomorrow?"

"Tomorrow's soon enough," he answered brusquely. "Let's go." He stalked to the door, tension in every line of his body.

They settled in at a quiet table in the hotel's bar, taking a full bottle of bourbon and two glasses with them. Slater watched as Nick slugged down two quick drinks, not even bothering to savor the fine stock, and he finally decided he could wait no longer to say something. With the undaunted courage and daring that had made him one of the government's more successful agents, Slater tackled the problem head on.

"You know, that's mighty fine bourbon you're drinking there. Have you bothered to taste it yet?"

Nick glowered at his friend. "It's potent. That's all that matters."

"Nick . . ." Slater said his name with emphasis, so he'd know he was serious. "The other night you were upset, but nothing like this. You haven't been yourself for days now. What is it? What's wrong?"

"Nothing's wrong," he growled.

"Talk to me. What happened that night?"

Having barely kept himself under control since leaving home, the last thing Nick needed was to start talking about Jordan. He didn't want to think about her, let alone talk about her. At Slater's well-intended chiding he erupted, taking his frustrated fury out on his friend. "It's none of your damned business, so stay the hell out of my affairs!" He slammed down another slug of bourbon without glancing up.

In all the years he'd known him, Slater had never seen Nick like this. "If you need any help, you know I'm here," he offered.

"I don't need your help or anybody else's."

"Nick, I . . ."

"There are some things a man has to handle on his

329

own."

Rebuffed in his attempt to help. Slater let it drop. He only hoped that whatever the problem was, Nick would be able to solve it. He hated to think that he might go the rest of his life feeling this embittered and angry.

The days passed in a haze of worry for Jordan as Charles's condition gradually worsened. While he did manage to get up and move around the house a little bit every day, even that slight physical activity wore him out. He was deteriorating right before her very eyes, and it was breaking her heart. Each moment of Charles's life was precious, and it hurt and angered her deeply that Nick was nowhere around to share these times.

"Missing my son?" Charles asked Jordan as she sat with him on the gallery late in the afternoon of the fourth day of his absence.

"Yes," she replied honestly, wishing Nick was there for his father.

"You know, six months or a year ago, I'd have worried about Nick being away, but not now."

"Why?"

"Because of you, my dear. Since you came into his life he's a changed man. I'm sure whatever it was that forced him to go to New Orleans the other day was very important, and I know he'll be back just as soon as he can."

"I hope so."

"It's good that you miss him. Andrea and I were always close that way too. We could barely stand being separated . . ."

"Do you miss her still?" Jordan ventured.

"Every minute of every hour," Charles answered

passionately. "She was my whole life. After she died . . ." He paused, a faraway look in his eyes. After a moment, he went on rather shakily. "Well, if it hadn't been for Nick, I don't suppose I would have wanted to go on. He's been such a blessing in my life. Watching him grow to manhood was wonderful, and now he's brought me you."

Jordan flushed with pleasure over his compliment. "I'm glad he married me. I wouldn't have missed knowing you for the world."

The whistle of an approaching steamer sounded, interrupting their conversation. Charles could tell by its signal that it would be docking at Riverwood, and he flashed Jordan a warm smile.

"That should be Nick coming home. Go on . . . go on down and meet him. I'm sure after all this time away there's no one else he'd rather see right now than you."

A feeling of tense anticipation gripped Jordan at the thought of seeing Nick again. Their parting had been so cold that she wasn't sure exactly what to expect from him. She did know, however, that she couldn't let her doubts show here in front of Charles. He believed they were madly in love. She had to continue the charade no matter how much it hurt her.

"I'll be right back!" she promised.

"Don't you want a carriage?" he asked.

"No! That would take too long!" She heard Charles chuckling as she hurried down the path. As she focused her gaze on the steamer that was gliding smoothly into the landing some distance away, she wondered why her heart was pounding so fiercely and why her hands had suddenly gotten so cold.

As the steamer took the wide bend in the river,

Nick was on deck watching for the first sight of his home. Usually when he returned to Riverwood he felt a deep, abiding sense of peace. Today, however, knowing Jordan was there and that he would be seeing her shortly, he felt only frustrated anger. The thing that made it even worse for him was that he knew he had only himself to blame for the state of their relationship. He had known how it was for her from the very beginning. He thought it wouldn't matter as long as he kept them apart, but then he hadn't counted on falling in love with Jordan . . .

Visions of their night of love crept into his thoughts, and Nick scowled, looking almost as if he were in physical pain as he tried to push her from his mind. He didn't want to think about loving Jordan. He didn't want to remember how perfectly their bodies had fit together and how responsive she was to his touch. He didn't want to dwell on the fact that he had taken her innocence.

The fact of Jordan's virginity still left him bewildered. It was a mystery Nick couldn't solve. He had assumed from the start that she was Montgomery's lover. Certainly she'd never done anything to indicate otherwise. Why, the little scene he'd witnessed in Philip's hotel room should have been enough to convince even the most ardent of skeptics, but he'd been wrong, and that troubled him.

Nick considered himself an excellent judge of character, but he was discovering he was completely mystified where his bride was concerned. Jordan was like a kaleidoscope. Every time he thought he understood who she was he found out something new. She was an enigma, and he was intrigued. It was almost as if she were hiding something from him, but he was never quite sure what.

As the boat pulled in Nick gathered his bag, and

when the gangplank was dropped into place he started down it. He heard Jordan call his name as soon as he'd stepped on solid ground. He looked up to see her waving to him from the top of the slight incline that led to the landing. Gritting his teeth, he assumed his role and returned her greeting. He acted the lovesick newlywed, knowing to do any less would lead to questions. Hurrying up the hill, he dropped his valise, swept Jordan into his arms, and kissed her.

Jordan had been expecting just about anything from Nick except that. As he enfolded her in his embrace she was held spellbound, and when his lips found hers the breathless shock immediately gave way to demanding desire. Her reaction to him startled and frightened her. She had hoped to control her feelings for him, but with just this one kiss everything she'd experienced the other night returned fresh and vibrant within her. When Nick released her, Jordan stared up at him, trying to read his eyes, but his expression was coldly remote.

"Well done, my dear," he drawled, noticing her flushed cheeks.

His sarcasm froze the warmth within her, and she stiffened imperceptibly as she prepared to do verbal battle with him. "Welcome back, my husband. Might I say that you were missed?" Her words were cutting as she linked her arm through his in a display that, to the onlooker, seemed perfectly casual, perfectly affectionate . . .

"Really? Somehow, I find that hard to believe." He picked up his bag and they started up the path.

"Your father has missed you sorely," she told him, deliberately making her tone icy so he would think she hadn't missed him at all. "Nick . . . he hasn't been well."

At this news Nick stopped to look down at her.

333

"What are you talking about? He was fine the night of the wedding . . ."

"The excitement of the celebration exhausted him, and he hasn't recovered much of his strength."

"Did you send for the doctor?"

"Charles didn't want to see him. He said he knew what was wrong and that there was no point in Dr. Williams making the trip just to tell him something he already knew."

Nick's jaw tightened as he realized how foolish he'd been in taking off for New Orleans. At the time he'd been desperate. Getting away had been all that mattered to him, but now he was ashamed of the fact that he'd gone. "How is he now?"

"He's up now and waiting for you on the gallery, but he's very weak. He can only be out of bed for a few hours at a time."

Jordan could feel the tension radiating from him, and without another word they picked up their pace. Though Nick knew he should be acting the happy, loving husband, he couldn't help but look concerned as they mounted the front steps to the gallery and he got his first glance at his father. If it hadn't been for Jordan, tugging lightly at his arm, chatting happily about nonsensical things that had happened while he was away, he would have stopped dead in his tracks. Though he resented her distraction, he realized it was a good thing, for it kept him from revealing too much of what he was thinking and feeling.

"Nick! I'm so glad you're back . . ." Charles called out, smiling at the sight of his handsome son and his lovely wife coming up the steps arm in arm.

"I'm glad to be back." Nick commented as he set his bag aside and went to him. He had to take great care not to show the worry he was feeling, for his father looked terrible, very pale and gaunt.

334

"How did the business go?" he asked, eager to know how his son had fared.

"All right, I guess, but I've got to meet with the agent one more time next week to firm up the deal."

"What was the problem?"

"It had to do with some shipping arrangements I'd made, but that's not what's important. What's important is that Jordan tells me you haven't been feeling yourself since I left." Nick pulled up another chair and sat down beside him as Jordan hovered protectively nearby.

"I haven't been able to get my strength back. I suppose I'm just tired . . ."

"And you don't want to see the doctor?"

"What can he tell me that I don't already know?"

"You're a stubborn old man," Nick said in a hoarse voice.

"And I imagine you're going to end up just like me. Now, enough of this. Let's go inside and see what Weddington can fix up in the way of a meal."

Nick and Jordan got on either side of him and helped him from the chair. They looked the loving family as they went indoors. Peri heard the commotion and quickly hurried downstairs to join the happy group.

Despite his stated interest in eating, Charles only nibbled at the dishes the cook created for them. By the time the main course was served, the little sparkle he'd felt at seeing his son again had drained from him. It took both Nick and Weddington to help him upstairs, while Jordan and Peri watched from below, their hearts heavy with sadness.

Weddington helped him undress and get into bed, then quickly left father and son alone together. Nick was standing at one of the windows staring sightlessly out at the green fields, one hand braced against the casement, the other stuffed into his pants pocket. He revealed no outward emotion, his face remaining impassive, but inwardly he felt like screaming in outrage over his father's fate.

"Nick . . ." Charles called to him. "Come sit with me for a while. We need to talk."

Nick drew a strangled breath, then turned to face him, trying to keep in control. "Are you sure you feel up to talking?"

"Of course. It was much too quiet around here without you . . . not that Jordan isn't delightful company, she is, but I like having you home, too."

Nick didn't say anything as he sat down on the side of the bed close to his father. Guilt filled him.

"I'm so proud of you, Nick," Charles began, surprising his son more than a little.

"You are? Why? I should have been here. If I had known you were sick . . ."

"Nonsense! You love Riverwood as much as I do. You must if you were willing to sacrifice your honeymoon to take care of plantation business," he praised his dedication.

Nick groaned to himself at the tangle of lies he'd created.

"Jordan's coming to love the place, too. We spent a lot of time talking these last few days, and my first opinion of her holds. She's a wonderful woman. You're going to make beautiful babies together. Don't wait too long, son. Children are the one real joy in life," Charles counseled, his voice growing ever softer as weariness overcame him. "I know you have been to mine."

"I'm just sorry I caused you all that worry before . . ." Nick was miserable. There was nothing he would have liked more than to spend the rest of his life with Jordan at Riverwood, raising a brood of strong, healthy children. It was a bitter dream for him, though, for it could never be. She wanted only Philip.

"You only needed to mature some more. I remember how it was when I was young, but your mother was good for me, just as Jordan will be good for you. You're very fortunate, son, for she loves you very much."

"I know," was all Nick could manage for the moment, but he knew he would have to compliment Jordan on her thespian skills. She really had his father convinced that she was in love with him.

"Nick . . ." Charles was suddenly somber.

Nick looked attentive and worried. "What?"

"I may not have much time left."

"Don't say that . . ."

"Be quiet and don't argue with me. There are things I want to tell you . . ."

"Dad . . . you're going to be fine. Just rest up and then . . ."

"Dominic Kane, I did not raise a coward. I raised you to be strong, now show me that I haven't failed!" Charles snapped at him, the fire of the disciplining father flaring for a moment in his dull eyes.

Memories from his childhood flooded through him, and Nick straightened. Lifting his eyes to his father's, he swallowed with some difficulty before answering, "Yes, sir."

"Listen to me! I am *not* going to be fine. We've both known it for months now. I've accepted it. Now, it's time for you to come to terms with it."

"But I don't want you to die . . ." he confessed. He had thought himself grown up, but he was feeling very much like he had when his mother had been taken from him.

"We all have to die someday, Nick. That's what I'm

337

trying to tell you. Live every minute to the fullest. Hold onto your happiness and make it last for as long as you can. That's what life is about. That's what love is about . . ." Charles reached out, grabbed his hand, and held it tight as his father's gaze burned into his. "Make your life here with Jordan as special as mine was with your mother. Give her everything you have and more. I've found that with love, whatever is freely given is returned a hundredfold."

"I'll do my best to give her everything she wants."

Charles's fierce, piercing gaze faded, and he lay back against the pillows, exhausted. "Good . . . good. That's all I've ever asked of you . . . to do your best . . ." He closed his eyes.

The intense emotional moment was over. The room was silent except for the sound of their breathing. It took Nick a minute to realize that his father had fallen asleep almost instantly. He stared down at him for a while, committing to memory the intimacy of this moment they'd shared, knowing he would treasure it forever in his heart. Quietly Nick leaned over his father and pressed a tender kiss on his sunken cheek, then without a word he got up from the bed as carefully as he could and left the room.

As Nick strode down the upstairs hall he knew what he had to do. It had been on his mind incessantly since he'd walked out the front door with Slater on their way to New Orleans, and he knew now the time had come. He met Weddington coming up the stairs.

"Your father, Mr. Nick?"

"He's resting comfortably right now."

"Good." The servant looked relieved. "I'm sure glad you're back, sir. Things haven't been too good around here. Mr. Charles, well, he just hasn't been

338

himself, no matter what Miss Jordan and I try to do . . ."

"I know, but I'm back now. We'll handle this together." Their eyes met in silent understanding.

"Yes, sir. Can I do anything for you now?"

"Weddington, there's one thing I need. Could you send someone to find Philip Montgomery for me and have him meet me in the study?"

"Right away."

Nick went downstairs and locked himself in the study. He was glad that he hadn't seen Peri or Jordan. He was in no mood to speak to either woman. Walking straight to the liquor cabinet, he poured himself a stiff drink and downed it in one swallow. It occurred to him vaguely, that he'd been drinking too much lately, but he dismissed the thought. He needed solace from somewhere, and if bourbon provided the release, then why not?

At the sound of a knock on the door a few minutes later, Nick set the glass aside and went to open it. He found himself face to face with Philip Montgomery, and he was hard put to keep his features set in a benign expression.

"Come in."

"I got word you wanted to see me?"

"Yes. Please take a seat." He waved him toward one of the chairs facing the desk, then went to sit down himself. He didn't say another word, but unlocked the desk drawer that held his private papers and took out the packet that held the bond servant's indenture. In silence, he picked up his pen and signed the release at the bottom of the contract. "Here." With no preamble, he shoved the papers that freed Philip of his obligation across the desk to him.

"I don't understand . . ." Philip gave him a confused look as he picked up the paper. His eyes wid-

339

ened in surprise as he read that he'd been freed, then they narrowed suspiciously. "Why are you doing this?"

"I have my reasons," he answered coldly.

"What about Jordan?"

"What about her?" Nick tensed. He was glad that he'd cautioned Peri away from him. It was obvious that Jordan was the only woman he was interested in.

"Is she free to go too?"

"Jordan has not yet fulfilled her obligation to me. When the time comes, she'll be free to leave at her discretion. Until then, things will remain as they are. I would appreciate it, however, if you would continue to work here at Riverwood for the next several months. If you were to leave abruptly there would be questions asked, and I don't think either one of us wants that to happen. You'll be paid a fair wage for your work."

Philip studied him openly, trying to read his thoughts, but Nick wasn't about to let him know how he felt about Jordan. Philip concluded that Nick was a terribly cold bastard, and he wondered how his sister had ever managed to fall in love with him. He wished there was some way he could talk to her so he could find out exactly what had happened, but their paths never crossed and he knew better than to come up to the big house on his own.

"Is there anything else?" Nick demanded rigidly, wanting this moment over with as quickly as possible.

"No . . . no, nothing. Thank you." Philip hurried from the room. He was elated at having his freedom but troubled by the unexpectedness of it all. As he was walking out of the house he heard Peri's voice drifting down from upstairs, where she was talking to one of the servants. His heart gave a heavy lurch, telling him he was a free man now. He could go back in, find her, run away with her, and marry her. His common sense stopped him, telling him to walk out that door and never look back, that she wasn't for him, that he could never give her the kind of life she was used to. His strength of will overpowered his emotions, and he left the house. As he strode back toward his office, though, the ache that hearing her voice had created within him remained.

Chapter Twenty-six

The evening meal that Jordan, Peri, and Nick shared later that night was a strained affair. They had to struggle just to make pleasant conversation. After dinner Nick was in desperate need of some time alone, and it was a great relief to him when the women finally announced they were going to bed. He missed Peri's puzzled look when he declined to retire with his new bride, choosing instead to give Jordan a brotherly kiss on the forehead before disappearing into the study alone.

"Is something wrong, Jordan?" Peri asked as they mounted the staircase. She knew it was really none of her business, but it seemed strange that Nick wouldn't want to go to bed at the same time as his new wife after having been away from her for so long. Peri knew if she was married to Philip she would never want him to leave their bedroom.

"No, no, nothing's wrong. I think Nick is just really upset over Charles's condition and needs some time to be by himself."

"Sometimes, though, being alone is the worst thing for a person," she remarked.

"I'm sure if Nick wanted me with him, he would have asked me to stay. For now, I have to respect his privacy." She took care to keep from revealing her pain.

Jordan sounded so convincing that Peri believed for the moment that that was all there was to it. She went on to bed, not knowing that Jordan would pace her lonely room for hours before finally falling asleep, and that it would be nearly two in the morning before Nick made his way upstairs.

Nick's steps were unsteady as he entered his bedroom. He'd been drinking steadily since dinner and was convinced that he'd fortified himself strongly enough with the potent liquor that he would be able to share the bed with Jordan and still get some sleep. He closed the door soundlessly behind him and silently crossed the room, coming to stand beside the bed.

Moonlight streamed through the open window, bathing Jordan's sleeping form in its pale glow. She was wearing a more demure nightgown tonight, and it covered her from neck to wrist to ankle. But though it wasn't as revealing as the negligée she'd worn on their wedding night, it was still a very feminine garment. Nick stood there, staring down at her, his heart pounding in his chest.

Jordan lay on her side, her hair unbound, tumbling gloriously about her. Nick ached to run his hands through the silken tresses, but he restrained himself. His gaze caressed her features, and he felt a familiar ache grow deep within him. He wanted her; he loved her; and he desired her as he'd never desired another woman. She was forbidden to him, though, and he had to live with that.

Nick turned away from the bed and the alluring sight of his wife. It would have taken very little en-

343

couragement for him to cast his honor aside and take her like an animal right then and there, and it distressed him that he felt that way. With firm self-control he stripped off his shirt and made his way to the small sofa. Miserable as it was, he would seek his comfort there.

Jordan awoke first the following morning, and for a moment she feared that Nick hadn't come up to their room at all. It was only when she started to rise that she saw him. She longed to go to him and tell him to come to their bed, but she knew that after what he'd said to her the morning after their wedding he didn't want anything to do with her. It hurt, but she had no alternative but to accept the way he felt. That she had fallen in love so hopelessly with him was her own misfortune.

As quietly as possible, Jordan quickly dressed. She didn't want to call a servant to help her and risk anyone finding out that he hadn't slept with her. She tried to act happy as she left the room to go down to breakfast, but her heart was breaking. With a force of will she turned her thoughts from her love for her husband, concentrating instead on her father-in-law and what she could do to keep him entertained today.

Several days passed. Charles's condition grew ever weaker. Nick sent for the physician, but after seeing the now bedridden man, Dr. Williams advised Nick that the end was near and that there was nothing more that could be done. They could only make him comfortable and pray.

The strain of Charles's illness took its toll on each of them. By day, Nick and Jordan stayed with him whenever he was awake. They pretended to be happy, but their conversations grew more and more superficial. By night, Nick stayed up late, going upstairs to try to rest on the sofa only after he was sure Jordan was asleep. His heavy drinking and lack of sleep were telling on him. His nerves were stretched taut. Dark hollows underlined his eyes, and he lost his appetite almost altogether.

Peri thought her cousin looked awful, and she commented on it one afternoon when he came in from a short ride inspecting the fields.

"Nick, are you all right? I mean, I know we're all worried about Uncle Charles, but you look terrible."

"I'll be all right. I'm just not sleeping very well. It'll pass." He dismissed her remarks and walked into the study without looking back.

Peri was irked by the way he was closing himself off from her. She sensed that there was far more wrong here than just Charles's illness. Surely, if he and Jordan were truly happy they would cleave together in a situation like this. Refusing to be put off by his coldness, Peri grew determined to get him to talk to her. She knew he was hurting, and she followed him into the study and shut the door behind her. Nick stood with his back to her as he poured a tumbler of bourbon.

"Don't you think it's a little early to start drinking?"

"No."

"Nick, we have to talk."

"About what?"

"About what's going on here."

"What's going on here is that my father's dying!" he snapped, turning on her as he took a deep drink.

"I know that's a big part of it, but Nick, there's something else troubling you. Something else is wrong."

"I don't know what you're talking about."

"I'm talking about you and Jordan," Peri said brazenly.

"Really?" He sounded very sarcastic.

"Yes, really. You both look so unhappy. I can see it in your eyes and in the way you talk to each other. What happened? What did you do?"

"Me?" Nick was outraged that she would question him. *"I* didn't do anything, dear cousin."

"Then Jordan did? What did she do to ruin things between you? You were so ecstatic at your wedding . . ."

Pushed to the brink by the memory of Jordan's betrayal on that fateful night, the fragile hold he had on his emotions cracked. "My precious wife is in love with someone else, sweet cousin. She's never loved me, only him."

"Jordan loves someone else?" Peri repeated, stunned. "Who?"

"Think about it Peri. They've been close from the very beginning . . ."

The image of Philip's face flashed before her, and she felt a blinding pain in her heart. "Philip . . ." she whispered fearfully.

"The same," he confirmed. "Why do you think I told you to stay away from him? Why do you think I warned you that he was no good for you?"

"You're wrong!" She jumped blindly to his defense.

"I wish to hell I was!" he blurted out. "Now, get out of here and leave me alone. I've got things to take care of—things to do . . ." He gestured at the paper-strewn desk. He didn't move again until he heard the door slam behind her on her way out. Then he sank down in the desk chair and drained the contents of his glass.

Peri's heart was in her throat as she fled the main house. For days she'd been trying to think of a way to convince Philip that he was the man for her. Now she was filled with the deep, abiding fear that it was really impossible, that he could never love her because he was already in love with someone else— Jordan . . .

Peri allowed herself to consider the unthinkable. Was it possible? Could Jordan and Philip really be lovers? She tried to reason it out, but her emotions were too involved. Her fear gave way to anger, and she knew she had to find out the whole truth. Without hesitation, she ran down the path that led to Philip's office. There would be no waiting and endless worrying. She was going to find out the truth right now, one way or the other.

Philip was busily working at his desk when he heard someone approaching. He glanced up to see Peri storming through the door.

"Peri? What are you doing here?" He came to his feet, surprised and more than a little pleased by her presence.

"I came to talk to you, Philip Montgomery. I want some answers from you, and I want them now," she declared fiercely, drawing a stunned look from him.

"What kind of answers?" he asked, suddenly wary as the fear that Jordan's and his real identities had been somehow discovered overcame him.

"The truth. I want the truth from you."

"What truth?"

"I love you, Philip. You know that."

He breathed a little easier. "Yes, I know how you feel, Peri, but I also know that a relationship is impossible between us."

"I want to know why you think that, Philip," she

347

demanded, her hands on her hips as she confronted him.

He stared at her, taking in her flushed cheeks and flashing eyes, and knew at that moment that he loved her deeply and would never stop loving her. He also realized that despite the fact that he was now a free man, he was still dirt poor and completely involved in Jordan's dilemma. He couldn't marry her and drag her down with him. He cared too much about her to do that to her.

"I'm a nobody, Peri. I'm without funds or family. I have nothing to give you."

"You don't know me very well, Philip. If you did, you'd know that money's not that important to me. You would have realized, too, that all I ever wanted from you was your love. Can you give me your love?"

"Peri, I . . ." He hedged. He wanted to blurt out that he loved her more than he'd ever dreamed it was possible to love someone. Instead he said nothing.

"I asked you a question, Philip. I'm tired of your evasive answers. I want the truth from you. Do you love me or is there someone else you care for?"

"Someone else?" He was dumbfounded by the suggestion. "What are you talking about? Where would you even get such a crazy idea?"

Peri straightened her shoulders as she looked him directly in the eye. "I got the idea from Nick. He told me that you and Jordan were in love. Is it true?"

Philip was as close to panic as he'd ever been. So, Nick still thought they were lovers . . . He hadn't talked to Jordan since her wedding night, but he'd thought things had worked out for them then. Obviously something had gone seriously wrong.

He began cautiously. "What Jordan and I share . . ."

"Then you admit it!?" Her eyes flared with pain and disillusionment.

"I admit that Jordan and I are close, but we are not lovers!" he denied hotly. "We never have been, and believe me, we never will be."

"Then where would Nick get such an idea?"

"I don't know. What Jordan and I have is a very special relationship that's been forged over a long period of time. She trusts me and I trust her. I love her, but not in the way you're thinking."

"I don't understand . . ."

"I know you don't. But right now there's nothing more I can say or do to convince you otherwise. Someday, maybe the truth will be known, but that will be Jordan's decision, not mine. For now, I'm asking you to trust me and believe in me."

"Philip . . ." She gave him a pleading, desperate look. This was all too confusing.

Philip knew defeat when he faced it. He stepped around the desk quickly to take her in his arms. "Peri, there's only one woman I love as a man should love a woman."

She lifted her brilliant gaze to his and leaned toward him ever so slightly. He needed no further invitation, and his mouth moved over hers with possessive force.

"I love you, Peri . . . God knows, I do . . ." he told her when he'd broken off the kiss.

"I love you, too, Philip."

They embraced again, this kiss even more desperate than the last. The dams of Philip's resistance were swept aside by the tidal wave of their passionate devotion. He clasped her to his chest, kissing her over and over again, wanting her to know that he loved her, no matter what. Worries about the past and his lack of funds dissolved in the surging rush of emotion that set him free.

"Peri, will you do me the honor of becoming my wife? Will you marry me?"

Peri's eyes were filled with tears of joy as she hugged him. "Oh, Philip! Yes, I'll marry you!"

He kissed her once more, then held her slightly away from him. "You know it won't be easy, living on my salary . . ." he ventured seriously, wanting to discourage her now before things went any farther.

"It doesn't matter. I'll be content as long as I have you," she vowed passionately. "I just can't wait to tell everyone."

"Do you think that's such a good idea? I mean, with your uncle as sick as he is, don't you think we'd be better off to wait."

Peri knew he was right, and she felt ashamed to have forgotten the seriousness of her uncle's illness in her happiness. "You're right, Philip. I wasn't thinking. It would be better if we waited."

"Is he improving any?"

"No, he's not, and there's nothing more we can do for him except be there for him and love him."

"I'm sorry."

"So am I. I love him very much."

"Peri, you know if you ever need me I'll always be here for you. Knowing how Nick feels about me, I think it's best if I stay away from the big house."

"I understand. I'll come to you . . ." There was a twinkle of mischief in her eyes.

"Whenever you can . . ." he invited. He loved her, and he knew that somehow they would find a way to make it together.

They kissed again in tender recognition of the depth of their caring, and then they moved apart, stung by embarrassment, for they hadn't even considered that someone might walk right in while they were embracing. They both realized that in the future they would have to be more careful.

"I'd better get back . . ." Peri said breathlessly.

"I'll be waiting to see you later."

She nodded, gave him one more quick kiss, and then hurried from the office. Her heart was singing as she made her way back to the house. She loved him and she trusted him. She believed him completely when he'd said that he wasn't Jordan's lover, and she wanted to tell Nick the good news right away. Maybe if Nick knew Philip's side, then things would smooth out between him and Jordan. Peri entered the house and found him at his desk, deeply immersed in paperwork.

"Nicky! I need to talk to you." The excitement was obvious in her voice as she stood in the doorway waiting for him to invite her into the room.

Nick looked up. "What about? I'm busy."

"I can see that, but this is important." When he waved her forward, she quickly came to stand before him. "I just had a long talk with Philip, and I . . ."

"You what?!"

"After we talked I went to see Philip. I had to ask him about what you'd said. I had to know the truth," she rushed on. "He vehemently denies that there's anything between him and Jordan."

Nick came to his feet as he snarled, "What the hell did you expect him to say?! Did you expect him to confess to adultery?!" Then, his fury vented, his expression changed and he looked disconsolate. "I know what I know, Peri," he said in a flat, dull voice. "Now, get out of here and let me get back to work. This is something I don't ever want to talk about again."

She stared at him, unable to believe his anger. She understood then just how much Nick was hurting and how much he must truly love Jordan. As she turned and quietly left the room, her thoughts were confused. Philip had admitted that there was something between him and Jordan, but he'd sworn to her that it was innocent. Because she loved him she trusted him, and she hoped with all her heart that whatever the trouble was between Nick and Jordan, they'd be able to work it out.

Nick watched her go, then slumped back down in his chair. He leaned forward, resting his elbows on the desktop and his head in his hands. His mind was racing, his thoughts in turmoil. A part of him wanted to believe what Peri had told him, but he knew the truth. The memory of her leaving his bed to run to Montgomery in the middle of their wedding night stabbed at him like a deadly blade. At the same time, the fact of her innocence remained to torment him.

The more Nick tried to make sense out of everything that had happened the more confused he became. In the end, he drew upon his substantial willpower to put the whole tangled web of deceit and lies from him. After all, Jordan was the one who had come to him that following morning to ask for Philip's papers. It was she who had agreed that things had gone too far between them and that they would have to be more careful in the future. Since that time, Jordan had made no overture to him, just as he'd made no overture to her. It was obvious that that night had been a mistake for the both of them, for Nick was certain that, had he not made love to her, he would have been free of this demon that haunted his heart and thoughts night and day.

When Weddington knocked at the door a few minutes later to tell him that his father had awakened again and wanted to see him, he was more then glad for the interruption.

Chapter Twenty-seven

Nick was torn. The day of the big meeting with Kirkwood had come, and the fierceness of his determination to catch the owners of the *Sea Demon* was warring with his need to stay close to home for his father. When Slater showed up that morning, he still hadn't made a decision whether or not he should leave.

"Are you ready to go?" Slater asked as he followed him into the parlor.

"Do you think you can handle it without me?"

"You can't go?" Slater was dismayed by his request. "What's happened? Is your father worse?"

"He's getting weaker every day. The doctor said it could happen at any time now . . ."

Both men were pensive as they considered what Kirkwood's reaction might be if one of them didn't show up.

"I'd like to think that he wouldn't balk, but as cautious as Kirkwood is, I can't be sure," Slater told him slowly. "The whole deal might fall through if he has the slightest doubt about our sincerity."

"That's what I was afraid you were going to say." Nick gave a resigned shake of his head. "I'll leave word where we're going to be, that way if there's any change they'll be able to find me."

"Mitchell's Tavern is only about a half an hour's ride. If he's on time and we get straight down to business, you could be back by mid-afternoon."

Encouraged by the knowledge that he'd be back so soon, Nick sought out Jordan to tell her that he was leaving and to give her directions to where the meeting was taking place. He was surprised when he found her on her hands and knees working in the garden.

"What are you doing out here?" he asked incredulously. "We have servants who can do that."

"I know," she replied, sitting back on her heels to look up at him. An ache grew in the emptiness of her heart as she thought of how handsome he was. "But I enjoy it." She looked away, wiping her brow with the back of her hand, leaving a smudge of dirt on her face.

Nick continued to stare at her, unable to believe how desirable she looked to him. Her hair was pulled back straight away from her face and plaited in a long single braid. She had obviously borrowed an old dress from someone who was bigger than she was, for it hung on her very loosely, giving her the appearance of an unruly child at play. Dirt stained her skirts where she'd been kneeling, and she'd unbuttoned several buttons at the bodice to help keep cool. There was nothing remotely childish about the glimpse of pale, smooth flesh he had seen while she'd been bent over working.

Nick's expression was so strange that when he didn't speak right away she immediately assumed something had happened with Charles. She got to her feet and wiped her hands negligently on her skirts. "Nick . . . Your father, is he all right?"

He realized then that he'd been staring at her, and

355

he quickly cleared his throat and tried to be business-like. "No, no, he's the same. I just came out to tell you that I'm leaving with Slater now for my meeting." He paused, his gaze settling on the dirt on her face. He wanted to wipe away the dirt and kiss the spot where it had been, he wanted to finish unbuttoning that gaping bodice and caress the satiny orbs he knew were concealed there. Jarred by the direction his thoughts were taking, he brought them up short. "I wanted to tell you where I'm going to be, just in case you might need me for anything."

He quickly gave her the directions to the tavern.

"I hope there won't be any need to disturb you," Jordan said. "I checked on him before I came outside, and he was resting comfortably."

"Well, regardless, I should be back by three at the very latest."

"Fine."

He stood there a moment longer, then turned and headed back into the house to get ready to leave.

It was over an hour later that Jordan went back into the house to get cleaned up. She washed and changed into one of her pretty new dresses, then started down the hall to Charles's room. Peri had volunteered to sit with Charles that morning, and she was just coming out as Jordan approached.

"How is he?" Jordan asked, hoping for good news.

Peri's downcast expression gave her the answer. "It's just awful, Jordan," she confided, pulling the door closed so they could talk in the hall without disturbing Charles. "He rarely wakes up, but when he does, he's not coherent. He didn't even know me the last time. He called me . . . Andrea." She bit back a small sob, and Jordan gave her a reassuring hug.

"I know . . . It's so sad, but we have to be strong," she encouraged. "Why don't you go get something to eat or maybe just go outside for a while? It's a beautiful day, and it might lift your spirits."

"All right," Peri agreed, drawing a shaky breath. "You'll call me if you need me?"

"Of course, I will," Jordan promised. "I'll stay with him now until Nick comes back from his meeting. He said he'd be home in a few hours."

Jordan entered the bedroom to begin her vigil while Peri left, feeling confident that her uncle was in good hands. Food held no appeal for her, but Jordan's idea of a walk outside sounded wonderful. She knew exactly where she wanted to go and who she wanted to see. She hadn't really spoken to Philip since the day before, when he'd proposed, and the thought of being with him again lightened the burden of her despair over her uncle.

Peri made the trek to his office on winged feet, but to her disappointment she found it deserted. There was no one around to ask where Philip might have gone, so she took a bold chance and went to his quarters to check.

Philip had thought of nothing but Peri since she'd left him the day before. He knew the future was going to be hard for them, but he also knew that he could handle anything as long as he had her by his side. He'd completed his work for the morning ahead of schedule and had gone back to his small, two-room house to relax and dream for a while. He was stretched out on his lonely bunk, longing for Peri to come to him, when he saw her come up the steps to the porch and knock on the door.

"Philip?"

Philip nearly vaulted from the bed in his excitement. He flew across the room and threw the door wide open to let her in. "I can't believe you're here," he whispered, giving her no time to speak as he held her close and kissed her thoroughly. "I've been thinking about you all day . . ."

"And I've been thinking about you," Peri responded, returning kiss after abandoned kiss with equal enthusiasm.

When the first thrill of their reunion passed, they laughed with easy delight at being together again.

"You know, it's not wise for you to come here alone like this," he told her, pushing the door shut without releasing her.

"Why? Do you think people will talk?" Peri sounded like a conspirator, and her eyes were twinkling with happiness.

"Definitely," he answered, kissing her once more with hungry haste. "And it's important that we protect your reputation . . ."

"You're going to make an honest woman of me, aren't you, Mr. Montgomery?" she queried playfully.

The use of his alias stung Philip, and he wished he could be completely truthful with her. Circumstances as they were, though, he had to remain silent. "I'm going to marry you just as soon as possible."

"Oh, Philip, I can hardly wait . . ."

The thought of being together forever thrilled her, and she melted against him, seeking his lips in a passionate exchange that spoke of enduring devotion. Wrapped in each others' arms, they clung together, famished for a taste of true love. Philip alone had a shred of reason left, and he tried to control the raging need he had for her.

"Peri . . ." he murmured her name in between kisses. "Peri, we have to stop. You shouldn't be here, you've got to go before something happens . . ."

She looked up at him, her eyes aglow, a small smile

curving her lips. There was a fiery ache burning deep within her, and she instinctively knew that there was only one thing that could assuage it. "I was sort of hoping . . . that something might happen . . ."

He gazed down at her in wonder. "You don't know what you're saying . . ."

"Oh, yes, I do," Peri replied firmly. "I've loved you since the first day I saw you, and I'll never stop loving you. We're going to be married soon, aren't we?"

"Yes, but . . ."

"Philip, I need you . . . I need you now . . . this moment . . ."

Her sensual entreaty sent an electrical jolt of passion charging through him.

"Oh, God, Peri . . ." He clasped her to his chest, holding her as close as he possibly could. When they'd fled England he had thought that his life was over, but now this wonderful woman in his arms was offering him paradise. He wanted her and needed her, too. Every tempting curve of her perfect figure was pressed tightly to him, and he couldn't deny his arousal.

"Philip, please . . ."

Thoughts of waiting slipped away as he grew lost in the hazy mist of desire that enveloped them. Alone in the heat of the afternoon, they came together in rapturous splendor. Philip kissed Peri tenderly, then took her by the hand and led her to his small bedroom. With the utmost care he began to undo the buttons on her blouse.

Though not bold in her actions, Peri was without fear. Her eyes never left his as she reached up to help him. She loved this man. She trusted him with her life, and she wanted to share all the wonder of her feelings with him, to express the depth of her emotions physically.

Philip parted the soft material, and a tremor of need shook him as he gazed down at the beauty of her breasts beneath the semisheer chemise she wore. His touch was light, reverent, as he pushed the blouse from her shoulders and slipped down the straps of her chemise. The lacy edge caught at the crests of her breasts and he gave a groan at the seductive display. It seemed as if he was moving in slow motion . . . He dipped his head to press kiss after heated kiss along the tops of that satiny flesh.

"Oh, Philip . . . that feels so good," she whispered, arching to his mouth and in that movement allowing the chemise to slip completely free of her breasts.

His mouth sought the crest of one pale breast, and she couldn't stop the cry of ecstasy that escaped her. His caress was unlike anything she'd ever experienced before. Desire, hot and pulsing, throbbed through her. Settling low in her body, it created a driving need within her, the need to move, to get even closer to him, to feel the hardness of him against her.

Peri's eagerness nearly drove Philip out of his mind. He raised up to kiss her once more, then picked her up in his arms and carried her to the softness of his bed. He lay her upon it, brushing aside the tangle of blankets and following her down, lying beside her so he could gaze upon her loveliness.

"You're more beautiful than I ever dreamed . . ." he told her, his gaze warm upon her.

Peri blushed then for the first time. "I'm glad you think so." She smiled dreamily. "Kiss me . . ."

Philip bent to do her will, their mouths meeting in a flaming kiss that reduced any resistance that might have lingered in their souls to cinders. They both wanted this. There would be no holding back.

When the embrace ended, he shifted away only

long enough to help her finish undressing. Her outer garments were shed with haste, but he took his time and made erotic play out of stripping away the chemise. He traced a pattern of love on her skin as he drew the soft garment down her body. His lips lingered at her breasts, then her waist, and finally he kissed the sweetness of her thighs.

Anxious to be one with her, Philip paused in his lovemaking to partially undress. He came to her with his pants still on, for fear of distressing her. But though she was innocent, she was not an ordinary young girl.

"Philip . . . I want to know all of you, as you'll know me."

Her sweet acceptance encouraged him, and he wasted no time in discarding the last of his clothing. They came together in a blaze of glory. Heated flesh pressed to heated flesh. Philip's hands skimmed over her sensitive curves, cupping and molding her to him. Following his lead, Peri began to caress him with equal fervor. She explored the width of his powerful shoulders and the hair-roughed plane of his chest. His body was foreign to her, but she was eager to learn all the differences between them. They sought only to please each other. Each touch, each kiss, took them higher and higher, until they were no longer satisfied apart.

Philip moved to fill her with his love, breaching her innocence with the heat of his desire. Peri tensed, the pain of his possession momentarily sharp. But as he continued to kiss her, talking to her in low tones and telling her of his love, she relaxed and accepted him fully.

It was a blending of beauty, a rare and splendid loving. Philip began to move, but kept his pace slow so as not to hurt her any further. Though it was all new to her, Peri quickly understood what he needed from her. She matched her movements to his, wanting to give him pleasure. They gave to each other the rapture of passion's play. The joy of their union spiraling to heights of ecstasy they hadn't known existed.

The peak of pleasure burst upon them with explosive wonder. They clung to one another, gasping in surprise as wave after wave of rapturous delight washed through them. Each peak seemed to take them even higher than the last, until the crest was reached in a moment of breathless exhilaration that eclipsed anything they'd ever known before.

Caught up in the vortex of tempestuous love, they held tightly to each other until the storm of their desire calmed. Their bodies as one, they drifted on a sea of enchantment, oblivious to all but the glory of their joining and the truth of their love.

Long minutes later, awareness slowly returned. As they lay quietly together they had no regrets. Their lovemaking had been as special as they'd known it would be. With languid movements, they still touched and explored, but this time with gentleness and curiosity. It was a moment of intimacy, a bonding of hearts and minds.

"I'd better go . . ." Peri whispered, realizing how long she'd been away but making no real move to get up as Philip caressed the smooth curve of her hip.

"I know," he answered huskily, his hand moving to her waist and then to her breasts.

She gave a little whimpering moan as he cupped the soft mound and kissed the pert peak. Desire pulsed through her again as he worked his magic upon her flesh, and she was deeply disappointed when he drew away.

"I have to stop this. We might be discovered at any

minute," he confessed, kissing her tenderly. "But you're so irresistible to me . . ."

"I don't want to leave you . . ."

"Once we're married, we'll never be apart."

"I'm counting on that," she told him with a loving smile.

They rose together and helped one another dress, caressing and kissing with each garment that they were forced to don. Philip watched as Peri used his brush to fix her hair. He moved behind her as she stood before the mirror, and he slipped his arms around her, pulling her back against him and kissing the side of her neck. Peri purred with contentment and turned in his arms for one last, lingering embrace. When at long last they parted with the promise to meet again as soon as she could get away, her cheeks were flushed with happiness and her eyes were alight with the knowledge that she loved and was loved.

Charles came awake slowly in a fog of pain. The weight in his chest was oppressive, and he was having great difficulty breathing. He wanted to sit up, to do something to ease the distress, but he could barely muster the strength to move. All of his energy had to be used just to inhale. With agonizing clarity he realized what was happening. Soon the struggle to live would end. Soon the excruciating pain would be over and he would be able to rest in peace.

The thought of dying did not frighten Charles. The thought of dying without seeing his son again hurt him unbearably. There was little time left, and Charles wanted desperately to be with him. Dominic was his gift to life, his pride and joy. He needed him there. He needed to gaze upon him and know that he was a fine, strong man who would be all right alone.

"Nick . . ." he called his name, his voice a dry rasp.

Jordan had been standing at the window watching the bustle of plantation life and thinking how very strange it seemed that everyday things went on so smoothly when in reality the whole world was falling apart. The sound of Charles's strangled call pierced her downcast thoughts and brought her rushing to his bedside.

"Charles, It's Jordan, I'm here," she reassured him, taking his hand and holding it tightly in hers.

"Jordan . . ." he went on slowly, each word an effort as he fought to breathe. "I need Nick . . . Please, find Nick . . ."

Fear clutched at Jordan as she realized how terrible he looked, and she went cold with dread. "I'll get him for you, Charles. Please, I'll be back as soon as I can." She gave his hand a squeeze and, kissing his cheek softly, fled the room.

Peri had just entered the house, feeling light-hearted and happy, when she came face to face with Jordan as she rushed down the stairs.

"Peri! Thank God you're here—"

"Jordan . . . what is it?"

"Charles is much worse and he's asking for Nick. I've got to go get him. He's with Slater at that meeting," she quickly explained. "Can you stay with Charles until I get back?"

"I'll go right up."

Weddington had heard the noise in the hall and hurried forth to see what was wrong.

"Weddington, he's worse, and he's asking for Nick. I'm going to get him now. Have a horse brought around for me."

"A horse, ma'am?"

"I can't afford to waste time in a carriage. I'm afraid every minute counts."

"Yes, Miss Jordan. Miss Peri, I'll be up to help you just as soon as I take care of the horses."

Peri had already mounted the steps and was racing down the hall to her uncle's room. When she entered she found that he'd fallen back into a fitful sleep, the exertion of speaking to Jordan having taken a dramatic toll on what little strength he had left. As quietly as she could, Peri sat down in the chair by the bed to wait.

Within minutes, Weddington had a horse brought around front for Jordan. One of the stable hands mounted up to accompany her.

"It'll be safer for you to have him along."

"Thank you." Jordan gave him a heartfelt look. She knew that the butler loved Charles as much as the family did and that he was suffering, too. With Weddington's help, she swung up into the sidesaddle, and without pause the two riders headed off at speed for Mitchell's Tavern.

Julian Kirkwood was a heavy-set, middle-aged man who dressed with style and spoke with easygoing confidence. But his icy, beady blue eyes revealed the truth of his soul. Nick and Slater sensed immediately that he was not a man to trifle with or to take lightly. The three of them sat in a small back room at the tavern now, closing their deal over a drink.

"I appreciate your interest in my seagoing ventures," Kirkwood pronounced with robust authority as he sipped of the whiskey he'd ordered.

"When do you think we'll be receiving a return on our investment?" Nick pressed, trying to find out whatever information he could. Until now, Kirkwood had been amazingly adroit at avoiding giving specific answers to their questions, but now that he had their money, Nick figured it was time to ask for some hard facts.

"I'll keep you fully informed, but I should think you'll be seeing a payment within four months. Maybe sooner, if everything works out right."

"Good, the sooner, the better." Slater smiled wolfishly. Their whole pretense in meeting with him had been that they needed to make money fast, and they didn't care how.

Believing their ploy fully, Kirkwood had relaxed as the meeting had gone on. He'd had Nick and Slater checked carefully before meeting them and had found them both to be upstanding citizens. As far as he'd been able to discern, there was nothing in their backgrounds to give him cause for worry. Besides, now that he had their bank drafts in his pocket, it was too late for them to give him any argument against being involved in slave running, anyway.

"Right now, gentlemen, our flagship, the *Sea Demon,* is en route to Africa to pick up a very profitable cargo, if you know what I mean?"

Nick and Slater both went still at this first mention of the death ship they'd been trying to trace. Feelings of fury, followed closely by feelings of victory, surged through them. They were close now, very close. All they had to do was to notify some of Slater's government contacts, and when the *Sea Demon* came within territorial waters they'd snare the ship and its filthy, murdering, amoral owners.

"We know what you mean," Nick answered, smiling coolly. It amazed him that he could be so calm when all he wanted to do was take Kirkwood by the throat and strangle him. Still, it wasn't time yet. There was still Kirkwood's mysterious other partner to track down.

"You'll keep us posted at regular intervals?" Slater inquired easily.

"Definitely. Now that we're officially partners in this investment, I'll give you my address. That way, should you ever need to contact me for any reason, you'll know where to find me."

"Fine," they both agreed.

Kirkwood gave them the information, then they rose to shake hands, the meeting concluded. As they were saying their good-byes the door to the room suddenly burst open and Jordan came rushing in unannounced.

"Nick, I'm . . ." She stopped, frozen in place. Her face drained of all color and her voice failed her at the sight of Julian Kirkwood, an associate of Luther's she met once in passing in Luther's office many months ago.

Terror seized her soul, for she feared that he was there looking for her. She went cold and began to shake. Her heart was pounding and felt like it would burst in her chest. She wanted to run, but she couldn't seem to move. She stood poised like a doe in the midst of danger.

The men looked up at the unexpected interruption. Nick saw the terrible look of fear and distress on Jordan's face and immediately went to her.

"Jordan, what is it?" he asked earnestly as he took her by the shoulders in a gentle grip, his eyes boring into hers.

"It's Charles," she managed, maneuvering her back to Kirkwood's avid gaze and praying madly that he hadn't recognized her.

"My father . . ." Nick repeated, then glanced back at Slater. "Slater, I have to go . . ."

Slater waved them on, and Nick and Jordan

367

rushed from the room together. As she hurried back to her mount, Jordan's hands were shaking uncontrollably and her knees threatened to buckle. She was trembling so badly that only with Nick's help was she able to climb back in the saddle. Her nerves were stretched taut as she kept checking the door, expecting Kirkwood to come charging outside at any minute. When he didn't come after her she offered up a quick prayer of thanks, and then turned her thoughts to getting back to Riverwood as quickly as possible. Putting her heel to the horse's flank, she raced for home at Nick's side.

Understanding the urgency of their situation, Slater made their excuses to Kirkwood. He then left the tavern, intending to travel to Riverwood himself to be there in case Nick needed him.

After they'd all departed and he was alone, Julian frowned in thoughtful consideration. There had been something vaguely familiar about Kane's wife, but he wasn't sure exactly what it was. The look of shock and panic on her face had been disconcerting, but he assumed she'd been fearful because she'd dared to interrupt her husband's private meeting. Certainly, women had no right to intrude on such business affairs, but he supposed in a life-or-death situation it could be forgiven.

Dismissing the nagging feeling that he'd met her before, he patted the pocket that held the bank drafts and left the room. The day had been a most successful one, and he was pleased.

Chapter Twenty-eight

Jordan was terrified on the ride to Riverwood. At any moment she expected to find Kirkwood thundering up the trail behind them, ready to have her arrested for Luther's murder and shipped back in irons to England. With the passing of each mile, though, she slowly came to realize that he hadn't followed her. The nearly hysterical fear that had gripped her since leaving the tavern calmed a bit, and she was finally able to bring herself under some sort of control.

Jordan's thoughts were in turmoil as she tried to make sense out of what had happened. Nick and Slater had met with Kirkwood, but why? Nick had mentioned that it was a business meeting about shipping, and she wondered if that could be true. Logic told her it could. Luther and Kirkwood had both made their fortunes in shipping. Now that Luther was dead, Kirkwood was probably in need of new investors. Maybe that's what the meeting had really been about.

The thought that Nick and Slater might be investing in the illegal slave trade sickened her, but she had no time to worry about that. Just the knowledge that Kirkwood might have had another legitimate reason for being there with Nick sent relief swelling through her.

As they traveled toward home, moving farther and farther away from the tavern and the man who could send her to the gallows, Jordan managed to convince herself that he hadn't recognized her. Calming though that was, it was still not completely reassuring. She had met him once in passing in Luther's office many months ago, and given time and opportunity, she felt certain that he would eventually remember the encounter. Because of all the confusion and excitement at the tavern, he'd only gotten a quick glimpse of her, but if they ever met in more quiet surroundings, she was certain her life would be over.

Jordan was tempted to run away now and take advantage of the small headstart she'd have if she did, but her love for Nick and Charles held her bound. She had promised Nick that she would stay with him until the end, and she knew she could do no less.

Jordan told herself she would deal with it only if Kirkwood did come for her. Until that time, she would fulfill her part of the bargain. A fervent prayer was on her lips for the duration of the ride to Riverwood as she begged God to let things somehow work out, at least until Charles was resting in peace.

Peri heard the sounds of horses racing up the drive, and she rushed to the window to make sure it was Nick and Jordan returning. When she saw it was them, she ran from the room to meet them.

Nick paused outside only long enough to help Jordan dismount. Then, his father foremost in his mind, he ran inside and took the stairs two steps at a time in his haste to see him. Reaching the second floor hall, he found Peri standing outside his father's room. His heart constricted with fear, for he thought he was too late.

"Is he . . . ?" His question was choked with emotion as his eyes locked with his cousin's.

"No," Peri quickly reassured him.

"Thank God! I've got to see him . . ." Nick moved past her to enter the bedroom.

"How is he, Peri?" Jordan asked as she reached the top of the stairs.

"Jordan . . . I'm scared. He hasn't stirred since you left," she confided, glancing into the room toward Nick. "He can't breathe. He fights for each breath, but it never seems to be enough . . ." Her expression faltered. Uncle Charles meant a lot to her, and she hated to see him suffering so.

Jordan nodded and took her hand. "We'd better go in with Nick."

They entered the room to begin the vigil they knew wouldn't end until Charles had left them.

Nick had drawn the chair as close as he possibly could to the side of the bed and was sitting there, talking in low tones, trying to let his father know he was there.

"It's Nick. I'm here," Nick murmured, tears clouding his vision as he gazed down at his dying father. The harsh sound of Charles's shallow breathing seemed to fill the room, and Nick knew from what little the doctor had been able to tell him that his father didn't have long.

As if from a great distance, Charles heard the longed-for sound of his son's voice. Fighting his way up from the black well of unconsciousness, he opened his eyes to find Nick leaning over him.

"Dominic . . ." he gasped, groping blindly for his hand.

371

"I'm here," Nick repeated as he took his father's hand in his and held it firmly. There was no answering strength in Charles's grip.

"I'm glad . . ." he wheezed, fighting for air. "I needed . . . needed to see you again . . . To tell you . . ."

"Please, don't try to talk," Nick told him as he sat down on the bed beside him, not letting go of his hand. "Just save your strength . . . rest. I promise I'll stay right here with you. I won't leave."

Charles relaxed a bit, but his gaze never left his son. He drank in the sight of him, so tall and handsome and strong. "You were always a good boy . . ." He paused, straining for breath. "Where's Jordan? Is she here? And Peri?"

"We're here, Uncle Charles," Peri answered, coming with Jordan to the opposite side of the bed. "Both of us . . ."

"Good . . . Jordan?"

"Yes?" She bent over him so he could see her more clearly.

He took her hand in his feeble grasp, holding it with Nick's. "I want you two to promise me something . . ."

"Anything," Nick replied quickly, his throat tight, his eyes burning.

"Anything," Jordan added.

"Let your love be stronger than your troubles . . ." He closed his eyes for a moment. When he looked at them again, his gaze was burning in its intensity, mirroring the depth of his wisdom. "Trust one another completely and always be honest with each other . . . honesty is so important . . . You're partners in life now. Do everything you can to make your happiness last for eternity . . ."

His words pierced Jordan's heart like arrows. She

did love Nick with all her heart and soul, but he didn't love her. No matter how she wanted to pretend everything was fine, it wasn't. There were too many lies between them. After Charles was gone, she would lose Nick, too. Tears fell unheeded down her cheeks as she managed a trembling smile for the dying man.

"I love Nick, Charles. He's my whole life," she professed her innermost feelings in a quaking voice. She glanced up at Nick then, the truth of her emotions clearly revealed in her shining, emerald eyes. If in that moment Nick had but said the word, she would have stayed with him forever. But he' didn't, and she knew it was hopeless. She was dreaming. It would never be.

Nick's gaze met hers, and he saw the love reflected in her expression. A wild leap of emotion shot through him, but the realist in him cast it aside. He loved her, and he would have told her so right then and there, if he'd thought it would make a difference. But he knew the love she'd confessed before his father was a sham. He was sure that as soon as his father was gone, she would be gone, too. There was no point in making a fool out of himself. He knew the truth of how it was between them.

"Be happy . . . as Andrea and I were," Charles was saying. "Nick . . . your mother was so beautiful, and I loved her so much . . ." He turned his failing gaze to the portrait of his wife, and a serene smile curved his lips as he sighed her name, "Andrea . . . my love . . ."

In that moment of contentment and beauty, Charles left the agony of his weakened body behind to seek the glory of heavenly perfection. The pain faded away, lost in the swirling mist that had been his life. He was peace-filled at last, and he soared up-

373

ward toward the vision of light and purity. His heart was near to bursting with happiness as he sought the woman he loved. When he found her, their reunion was a starburst of eternal bliss, and they were united in spirit for all time. Freed from earthly concerns, his hand fell away from Nick's and Jordan's.

"Father . . ." The sorrow Nick had fought to control threatened to overwhelm him. The muscles in his jaw worked as he struggled to subdue the agony that filled his heart and his mind. "Oh, God, he's gone . . ."

He lifted his burning, tear-filled gaze to Jordan's, and she could see all the pain he was feeling etched clearly on his face. Jordan held tightly to his hand, her own sorrow and sympathy showing in her eyes. She wanted to comfort him, to ease the burden of his grief. The moment was interrupted by Peri, who went to Nick and hugged him. His gaze was torn from Jordan's, and he was forced to release her hand as he hugged his heartbroken cousin. He closed his eyes against the sight of his father's lifeless body and the one woman he loved, but could never have.

Jordan stood there, separated from Nick by more than the mere width of the bed. She felt the outsider. Watching the two cousins embrace, she knew the end had come. The charade was finished. The last act done. Charles had gone from them. Her role was finished.

Jordan waited just a little longer, a last fading hope and desperate prayer still echoing in her heart. Then, when the vestige of her dream had been reduced to dust, she quietly took one last look at the old man who'd been her friend and backed from the room.

In the hall alone, Jordan finally gave vent to her despair. Leaning weakly against the wall, she cried, drowning in a sea of sadness. Only the gentle sound of Weddington's voice brought her back.

"Miss Jordan . . . ?"

With all the dignity of the lady of the house, she drew herself up and wiped away the tears that stained her cheeks. "Oh, Weddington . . ." she half-sobbed, half-sighed. "Charles is dead . . ."

The butler remained standing rigidly, but his expression gave away his wretchedness. Tears spilled forth, and he didn't even try to hide them. "Yes, ma'am, Miss Jordan. Shall I see to the arrangements?"

"Please . . . I'm sure Nick would appreciate any help you could give him," she instructed.

Weddington went on into Charles's bedroom to speak with Nick, while Jordan started downstairs. The front door opening unannounced frightened her, but her fear was soon relieved when she saw it was Slater.

"Jordan, how is he?"

"Oh, Slater . . ." Her well of misery overflowed again, and she went to him, going easily into his supportive embrace. "It's over . . ."

"Where's Nick?"

"Upstairs . . . with his father . . ."

Slater pressed a soft kiss to her forehead, then hurried up the steps to console his friend.

It was very, very late, and Nick was very, very drunk. He sat alone on the steps of the gallery on the side of the house near the gardens. For once in his life, he had out-drunk Slater, but he was so far gone that he didn't even realize his friend had stumbled off to bed an hour before. In fact, when Nick looked up from pondering the mysteries of the life and death in his half-full glass of whiskey, it was the first time that he really noticed Slater wasn't there.

A snort of sad derision escaped Nick as he considered the state of his loneliness this day. First, his father had left him. Then he'd looked up and Jordan had been gone. And now Slater had deserted him too.

Nick took another slug of the liquor, hoping it would erase the terrible aching emptiness that filled him, but nothing seemed to be able to touch the place deep in his chest where his heart had once been. He tilted his head back and gazed up drunkenly at the moonless sky. Tonight he did not see the beauty of it. Tonight he did not see the myriad of twinkling stars that dotted the heavens and granted many a lover's wish. Tonight he only saw a vast, black, hollow emptiness.

Unbidden memories came to mind, memories of his mother, laughing and holding him close, whispering in his ear that she loved him and would never let him go. She *had* left him, though, he thought bitterly, and he'd needed her so desperately.

Nick took another drink. The image of his father's face when he'd first told him of his illness flashed through his mind, and Nick wished he could turn the clock back and relive the past months. He felt so utterly stupid, having wasted all those weeks courting women when he should have been at his father's side.

At the time, Nick had thought he was doing the right thing trying to find a wife to make his father happy. But what value did Riverwood really have compared to the priceless minutes he could have spent with him? Right now, he would have gladly traded all his wealth just to have his father back with him for one day, one hour, one minute . . .

Then there was Jordan. He chugged another swig

of whiskey, then threw the tumbler with all his might out into the darkness of the night. It crashed and shattered against some unseen, unyielding force, yet he took no satisfaction in the destruction. He felt only desolation and heartache, bitterness and misery. He was alone, and he would remain that way.

Grabbing one of the pillars, he jockeyed himself to his feet. He stood on the top step, swaying drunkenly, as he surveyed his domain. He owned everything as far as the eye could see, and yet right now it meant less than nothing to him. What good were riches if there was no one to share them with? What good was life without love?

Nick turned back inside, making his way through the rooms and halls he knew so well. His surroundings were familiar, but there was no warmth in them. Tonight everything seemed empty and meaningless. He mounted the steps slowly with unsteady tred, then made his way down the hall to his bedroom. He stood before the door for a long moment, then opened it and went in.

The curtains were parted, but the room was dark. Nick stared at his bed where his lovely wife rested in easy comfort, then turned away and sat down heavily on the sofa he had chosen for his own so long ago.

Nick leaned back and closed his eyes, but sleep would not come. Instead, his mind was filled with visions of Jordan. Tormented, he rubbed his eyes wearily, trying to erase her from his thoughts, but to no avail. Then, almost as if by miracle, he heard her call his name in a soft, desperate voice. Nick honestly thought he was dreaming. He sat still, listening, waiting, and finally her call came again. He rose, drawn magnetically by her siren's song to the side of the bed.

It surprised Nick to find Jordan asleep. Mesmerized by her beauty, he stood over her, watching her rest. He had never known feelings like the ones he had for her. The love he felt was twisted inside him with the hate and distrust he also harbored toward her. Like a mass of coiling venomous snakes, they roiled inside of him, leaving him hopelessly confused and embittered.

Drunk as he was, though, Nick's defense against his desire for her was weak. In a moment of overwhelming temptation, he couldn't resist touching her. With a gentle caress, Nick stroked the silken glory of her hair, then touched the softness of her cheek.

"Nick . . ." Jordan murmured his name again as her eyes slowly fluttered open. She had tossed and turned for hours before finally falling asleep. Hers had not been a restful sleep, but one filled with tormented visions of Luther and Kirkwood, Charles and Nick.

In her nightmare, she'd been trapped in a maze of horrors with no way out. Hands had clawed at her, grinning, leering faces had loomed over her, and taunting, laughing voices had resounded in her ears. Over and over she called out for Nick, wanting him, needing him. Finally she could see the way out of the maze and Nick was there waiting for her, his arms spread wide in loving welcome. As if in homecoming, she went into his arms and was enveloped in the warmth of his embrace. Jordan felt safe and secure, loved and protected. She lifted her face, wanting his kiss, and he bent toward her . . .

Half awake, half asleep, Jordan stared up at Nick with an expression of pure rapture on her face. She couldn't believe he was actually there, and she wasn't about to question the answer to her prayers. She loved him so . . .

Jordan knew that with the light of day she would

have to leave him, but for tonight she would know the thrill of his possession again and keep this memory alive in her heart for the rest of her life. Even if only for one night, it would be worth it.

"Oh, Nick . . ." she whispered his name. She turned to his palm to press a tender kiss there while her arms looped about his neck, drawing him down to her.

There was no resistance in Nick as he melded with Jordan. There was only need and passion. No words were spoken as they sought solace in one another's arms. His kisses and caresses told her everything she needed to know—that at this moment he wanted and desired her. Jordan knew she would have to be satisfied with that.

Giving herself over to the surging excitement his touch created within her, Jordan allowed herself only to feel. She gave no thought to tomorrow, she lived only for the moment, surrendering her innermost being to the glory of Nick's possession.

His kisses were drugging, his touch excruciating as he ripped her gown from her in his eagerness to bare her flesh. Her body seemed to vibrate with a life of its own as his hands sought out her most sensitive places and tormented her with knowing caresses. She was his, completely and wholly. She would never want another, there would be only Nick . . . Clinging to him, she sobbed his name over and over again as he brought her to the fullest of sensual pleasure.

Nick felt her body convulse with delight and knew complete triumph. With impatient hands, he discarded his own clothes, then moved over her temporarily sated body. He found her wet and warm and willing as he slipped deep within her womanly sheath. It seemed as if Jordan had been made for him and him alone. Held captive in the tightness of her love, he began to move.

Nick wanted to share the ecstasy with her. He began to kiss and caress her again in his eagerness to know the heights of their desire. Kiss after burning kiss left them both gasping for breath. His lips left hers then, trailing down the sensitive chords of her throat to her shoulder, then lower.

"Nick . . . oh, Nick, please . . ." Jordan cried, longing for the feel of his mouth upon her throbbing breasts.

Mindless with the driving hunger of his love for her, Nick suckled at that delicate flesh, drawing moans of ecstasy from Jordan. She began to move restlessly beneath him as he continued his sensual assault. Her legs entwined his, and she strained to get closer to him, to have him fill once more the fiery emptiness that seemed to grow unbound within her.

"Jordan . . ." Nick groaned. "You're so perfect . . . I love making you mine . . . I need you so . . ."

"Love me, Nick. Oh, please, love me . . ." she pleaded mindlessly.

Rising back up over her, he plunged deeper and deeper, his rhythm growing faster and faster. His thrusts were powerful as he sought love's ultimate release. When it came, like a bolt of lightning in the midst of a turbulent storm, he called out her name in a passionate plea. They were carried to the heights of desire on a wild wind, peaking and hovering in ecstatic oblivion, then plunging back to reality, their bodies joined, their limbs still clinging to one another.

Nick shifted away first. His passion drained away, he could no longer resist the whiskey's potency. A deep sleep claimed him.

Jordan lay perfectly still after he'd withdrawn from her and without a word fallen into his drunken slum-

380

ber. A silent tear streaked down her cheek, but she paid it no mind. Her thoughts were elsewhere, thinking about what had just happened between them and how it would never happen again. It was over. No matter how much she wished things were different, they weren't. Nick didn't love her. He never had and he never would.

Jordan drew a shaking breath and pushed herself up on one elbow to gaze down at Nick. She longed to touch him, to caress the hard muscles of his torso, to kiss him awake and tell him of her love, but she couldn't. It was finished. Now that Charles was dead the bargain had been completed. She would stay for the funeral, she owed Nick — and Charles — that much. But as soon as it was over she would leave. It was the only way . . .

Chapter Twenty-nine

It was a sunless day. The sky was a leaden gray, threatening rain, as the mourners gathered at the family cemetery to hear the priest say the final blessing. When Charles's body had been interred with his beloved Andrea's in the crypt, the man of God intoned his prayers, granting him peace and everlasting life.

Clad in black, Nick stood tall and straight as he listened to the priest's words. His handsome face was frozen into a stony mask as he fought with grim determination to master his emotions. He was refusing to think or feel. Later, when he was alone, there would be time for his grief and sorrow, but he would not, *could* not, face them now.

Jordan stood beside Nick, clothed in dark colors, her manner quiet, pensive, and subdued. The veil she wore hid her tear-ravaged countenance from the onlookers. Her heart was heavy with sorrow as she listened to the priest's prayers.

The priest was talking about being born to a new life, how the end of one was the beginning of another, and Jordan felt he was not only talking about Charles, but about her, too. She knew that when she left Riverwood she would be starting over. But where Charles had gone on to a heavenly existence with his wife, her next life would be a living hell, for she would be leaving her heart and soul behind, here with Nick.

Jordan let her gaze sweep across the crowd of friends and family who had gathered to pay their respects to Charles. Peri and Slater were there, along with her parents. The neighbors had come, along with Dr. Williams and Charles's lawyer, Aaron O'Neil. She recognized everyone and was glad that they'd come. But when a dark carriage drew up, its windows shrouded, she stiffened.

Her gaze was drawn to the mysterious vehicle, and she was glad for the protection of the veil that allowed her to watch without anyone knowing. Her heartbeat quickened as the door swung slowly open, and she waited with bated breath for the unknown occupant to step down. The minute Kirkwood appeared in the doorway of the carriage, Jordan recognized him. She swallowed tightly, again immensely grateful for the covering of the veil that hid her pale features from any prying eyes. Frightened, Jordan turned back toward the priest and began adding her own fervent prayers to his.

Now that Jordan was nervous, the service seemed as if it would never end. Her whole being was alive with the knowledge that Kirkwood was standing only a short distance away. Jordan believed she could almost feel his eyes upon her, ripping away protection of her veil and mourning clothes and revealing to all present the murderess who'd fled justice in England.

Jordan clasped her hands together tightly in front of her. It looked like she was praying, but in truth it was the only way she could control her shaking. A desperate voice inside of her begged God to let the service end so she could escape Kirkwood's loathsome presence and hide in the sanctity of the house.

As if in answer to her prayers, a low rumble of thunder echoed around them, drawing all eyes upward to the threatening clouds that now loomed overhead.

In his wisdom, the priest hurried his final words, and the service was ended. Sympathetic friends and relatives surrounded Nick and Jordan, embracing them and extending their condolences. Jordan held her breath as she caught sight of Julian pressing his way through the crowd.

"Nick, my sympathies at your loss," Julian said as he shook Nick's hand.

"Thank you, Kirkwood. It was good of you to come."

"Mrs. Kane . . ." He turned to her to take her hand, peering at her intently through the concealing veil. "Jordan, I believe it is? My heartfelt condolences on your loss."

Jordan couldn't help but tense at his use of her first name. "Thank you," she murmured, keeping her eyes deliberately downcast.

"I hope to be seeing more of you in the not-too-distant future," Julian said softly for her ears only, then let go of her hand and blended in with the crowd.

Jordan stood there frozen, immobile until Nick's call forced her to action.

"Jordan . . ." Nick said her name, drawing her attention back to him.

"Yes?" She glanced over at him sharply.

"I think we'd better go up to the house now."

She took his arm and allowed him to lead her down the path that led to the mansion. Most of the gathering followed them, but not Kirkwood. When Jordan glanced back, she saw him open the carriage door, climb in, and sit down. Before she looked away, she caught sight of a black-gloved hand carefully

384

parting the curtains for a moment, then letting them slide closed again.

A chill of pure horror wracked Jordan, for she knew it couldn't have been Kirkwood. He'd taken a seat on the opposite side of the vehicle when he'd entered it. Her thoughts were racing. She tried to imagine who would have accompanied him to the cemetery, then watched surreptitiously from the vehicle, never bothering to join the others. She kept coming up with the same dreadful answer—it had to be someone who was looking for her.

Panic seized Jordan, but she clung tightly to her self-control. *One more day,* she thought, *just one more day.* If she could just make it through today, then she could go. She could disappear again, just like she had from England, and Nick would be saved from the terrible embarrassment of finding out about her past.

Jordan clung to the solid strength of Nick's arm as they made their way toward the house. It felt good to hold onto him. She felt safe and protected as long as she was at his side.

Jordan cast a sideways glance at him. She could see how taut the line of his jaw was and knew he was fighting a desperate battle to maintain his mastery over his emotions. She ached to help him, to share his pain, but she knew it was impossible. Nick wanted nothing to do with her. He'd made that perfectly clear that morning when, after their night of loving, he'd barely spoken to her. She was certain that as far as he was concerned the bargain was complete. They were just going through the motions now until the time came when he could officially end the marriage.

As they started up the steps to the gallery, Jordan managed one last glimpse back toward the cemetery.

To her great relief, Kirkwood's carriage was headed down the drive away from the house. She was still safe, at least for now.

Philip had joined the group at the cemetery, deliberately staying near the edge of the crowd to keep a low profile. Knowing how Nick felt about him, he did not want the other man to see him. Peri had been standing with her parents on the far side of the gathering, and she had noticed him right away. Several times during the service her eyes had sought his, telling him with just a glance all he needed to know. He'd longed to be the one standing proudly by her side, but he knew for now he had to be satisfied with the way things were. Philip promised himself, though, that he would soon claim her for his own.

When the service ended and the mourners headed back to the main house, Philip slipped away from the crowd. As hired help, he wouldn't be welcome inside, and so he chose to watch the procession from a distance.

Philip's gaze followed Jordan as she disappeared inside with Nick, and he wondered how she was holding up. He knew how she felt about Nick, but judging from the conversation he'd had with Nick the other day, he honestly believed that the man did not return her more tender feelings. Jordan's love seemed hopelessly one-sided, and now that their bargain had been met, he prayed she would be strong enough to be able to walk away.

The thought of leaving Riverwood so abruptly troubled Philip. He loved Jordan, and he was bound to go with her when she did leave, yet he didn't know how he could ever bear to be separated from Peri. Philip knew he was going to have to have a long talk with his sister as soon as he could so they could make plans. His future happiness with Peri depended on it. Turning away, he slowly started to walk back toward his quarters.

"Philip!"

He spun around to find Peri running toward him. "Peri . . ." He took a quick look toward the house, and, seeing that they were unobserved, he caught her up in a warm embrace and kissed her hungrily.

"I'm so glad I caught up with you. I've only got a minute to talk . . ." she told him breathlessly in between quick, desperate kisses. "I had to tell you . . ."

"Tell me what?"

"I'm going back to New Orleans with my parents later this afternoon."

"Peri . . . why?"

"My parents thought Nick needed some time alone." She gave him a pleading look that begged for understanding. "Since I haven't been able to tell them about us yet, I couldn't give a reason for me not to accompany them."

Philip was disappointed, but he also thought her leaving for a while might really be a godsend. With Peri away, he would have time to help Jordan. "Don't worry. I understand completely."

"Good. I was afraid you might be angry."

"With you? Never," he vowed with a smile as he kissed her again. "I'll miss you, of course, but as soon as things settle down here, I'll come for you. Then we can be married. How does that sound?"

"Heavenly," she sighed, as content as she could be considering the unhappy circumstances. "I love you . . ."

"And I love you."

"I have to go before somebody notices I'm missing."

"I'll see you in New Orleans," Philip pledged, knowing that somehow he would find a way to go to her.

"I'll be waiting," Peri promised, and with one last fleeting kiss she hurried back to the house to be with her family.

The guests had long since departed. Except for a few low-burning lights, the house was dark and much too quiet. Weddington moved through the empty rooms, hating the oppressive silence and yet knowing that there was nothing he could do about it. Nick had disappeared into the study as soon as the last of the company had gone, and Jordan had retired to her room and asked not to be disturbed for the rest of the night. Weddington decided to check on Nick one last time before going to bed himself. He knocked on the study door and waited for him to invite him in.

"What is it?" Nick bellowed, annoyed by the interruption. He didn't want to see or talk to anyone. He wanted to be left completely alone . . . to drink and to think.

"Mr. Nick? Can I get you anything?" Weddington asked, stepping into the room.

"No, thanks," he replied curtly.

"How about something to eat? I can have the cook . . ."

"I'm not hungry, Weddington. Thank you. If I want anything, I'll let you know."

"Yes, sir." The butler knew when it was best to make a tactful retreat. He backed quietly from the room, leaving Nick by himself once more.

Nick slumped back in his chair once the servant was gone, the bottle of bourbon clenched tightly in his fist. Though he'd been drinking steadily since the last of the visitors had gone, the liquor had yet to really take effect. It aggravated him, and he stared balefully at the bottle, seriously considering switching to something different.

The knock at the door took Nick by surprise. He glowered at the closed portal.

"What do you want this time?" he snapped, thinking it was Weddington again.

The door swung slowly open, and he was amazed to see Jordan standing there. She was still dressed in her plain black mourning gown. She had pulled her hair back in a severe bun that morning, and she was still wearing it that way. She looked pale and fragile, and Nick knew a nearly overwhelming desire to take her in his arms and never let her go.

Nick refused to acknowledge his feelings for her, though. That morning when he'd awakened in his own bed to find her already gone, he'd known he'd made a terrible mistake. Then when she'd sent Weddington to check on him a short time later, he'd realized it was completely finished between them. They'd had very little to say to each other during the course of the day, and he couldn't imagine why she felt the need to talk to him now.

"You wanted something, my dear wife," Nick said with virulent sarcasm.

Summoning what little nerve she had left, Jordan moved farther into the room and pushed the door shut behind her. She had been upstairs in their bedroom, going over and over what she planned to say to him. It was important that she get this over with as quickly as possible. Kirkwood had discovered her identity, she was sure of it, and she had to get away from Nick and Riverwood while she still could. She didn't want to bring disgrace down on Nick. She cared too much.

"Why close the door, Jordan? I doubt you'll be staying that long," he snarled.

"I need to talk to you," she ventured simply.

"So, talk," he replied coldly. His dark-eyed gaze was resting on her with such insulting familiarity that she shifted uncomfortably.

Jordan gave a stubborn lift of her chin. She knew he didn't love her, but there was no reason for him to be so cruel. The way she saw it, he'd be glad to be rid of her. "I was hoping you'd give me my papers tonight, so I could leave Riverwood first thing in the morning."

Nick didn't know what he'd been expecting her to say, but it was certainly not this. His father hadn't even been dead thirty-six hours and here she was, already wanting to leave. His lips curled in disgust as he looked at her. Any hope that he'd ever had that she felt anything for him was wiped out in that moment. He took a deep drink as he continued to stare at her with icy regard.

When Nick didn't respond to her request, Jordan grew even more uneasy. She couldn't afford to stay any longer. She had to get away, now, before Kirkwood came back for her, and she knew he would—sooner or later. Although it was killing her to say these things to Nick, it was the only way.

"Nick, the terms of our bargain have been met," she pointed out logically, trying to keep her voice from wavering. "I played the part of your wife as you wanted me to, and now it's your turn to keep your part of our agreement."

"Ah, yes, our agreement," he sneered. "Well, you certainly proved yourself worthy of my investment. You had my father firmly convinced of your sincerity."

"I was sincere! I loved your father!" she countered,

390

not wanting him to belittle the feelings she'd had for Charles.

Nick wanted to scoff at her claim. She may have loved his father, but she'd never loved him . . . He found he wanted to strike out at her, to hurt her as she was hurting him.

"There are many words I'd use to describe you, Jordan, but *sincere* isn't one of them," Nick said caustically as he set his bottle aside and rose from his chair. He moved around the desk like an animal on the prowl, coming to stand before her.

There was a tremendous war of emotions raging within Nick. He loved her. There could be no denying it. Being in her arms, making love to her, was pure bliss for him. He remembered every sweet, succulent curve of her body and how perfectly the two of them seemed to fit together. Yet even as he loved her and desired her, he hated what she was. She had left him on their wedding night to go to another man. The memory of her betrayal still filled him with frustrated fury, and he knew he would never forgive her for it. Never.

"Nick, I don't want to get in a war of words with you. I just want to complete our bargain and go. That's all." Jordan did not retreat from his advance, but stood her ground. With a brave lift of her chin, she met his regard. His expression was so wooden she had no idea what his thoughts were.

"By all means, let's be done with this farce," he suddenly agreed, turning his back to her and returning to his seat. He unlocked his desk drawer and rummaged through it.

Jordan wanted to rush to him, to throw her arms around him and beg him to love her. She wanted to tell him that she didn't want to leave, that she loved him. But instead she held her tongue and stayed where she was. She knew it would do no good to humiliate herself that way. Nick didn't care for her. If he did, he surely would have said something about what had happened between them last night. Obviously their passionate lovemaking had meant no more to him than just drunken solace.

"Here we are," Nick announced, holding up the sheaf of papers that would mean her freedom. Without a second thought, he quickly signed over the document to her. Then he got out a bank draft and wrote it out for an amount far above what he'd originally promised her. He tossed the papers casually on the desktop near her. "There. Take them and go."

Jordan picked the documents up and glanced at them quickly before looking at Nick. "No, this is wrong. It's too much money."

"As accomplished an actress as you are, my dear, you deserve every cent. Please, take it with my compliments. Besides, it may take your Montgomery quite a while to find another job to support you."

She wanted to blurt out the truth, but she couldn't. She could only suffer in silence and bear his scorn without any attempt to defend herself. "I thank you for your generosity."

"What time do you plan on leaving in the morning?"

"As early as possible."

"Take everything with you. I don't want anything left behind," he told her coldly.

"All right, I will, thank you."

"Don't thank me. You've earned it all."

Her eyes filled with tears, but she quickly turned away before he could see them. She couldn't let him know how much his hatred hurt.

"Oh, and Jordan?" Nick's cutting voice stopped her.

"Yes?" she asked, without facing him.

"I'll take care of getting the annulment. Notify Weddington of where you'll be staying so I can forward the necessary papers to you when the time comes."

"I'll do that." With a calmness that belied her true feelings she walked out of the room.

The prospect of returning to the solitary confinement of the bedroom filled Jordan with misery. Instead of going upstairs, she left the house and ran all the way to Philip's quarters.

Nick heard her go outside instead of upstairs. He watched in embittered silence from the window of the study as she rushed off down the path to join Montgomery, knowing that as she went she was leaving his life forever.

Jordan was desperate to see her brother. She knocked on his door and called out his name, not caring at the moment who saw or heard her. It was over. What did anything matter any more?

"Philip!"

Her brother was there within seconds, throwing the door wide and taking her into a supportive embrace. "Jordan! What are you doing here now?"

"Philip . . . there's so much I have to tell you, but the most important thing is, Nick gave me my freedom tonight." She showed him the papers. "Now we can leave here first thing in the morning."

Philip heard the fear in her tone and wondered at it. "Why are you in such a hurry?"

"It's Kirkwood! He's here. He knows Nick and he's coming after me!"

"Kirkwood?"

"Luther's American partner. I met him once in London."

"And he knows Nick?"

"Yes. I don't know how it all came about, and I don't want to know. I saw them together the other day, and he was at the funeral today. I know he knows it's me, Philip. I know it!"

"If he recognized you, why hasn't he had you arrested yet?"

"I don't know, and I don't intend to stay around to find out. I just want to get out of here before it's too late."

She was so frantic that Philip held her close and began stroking her hair and murmuring softly to her. "All right, little one, just relax. We'll go, just like you want, but there's something I have to do before we can leave the area."

"What?"

"I want to go to New Orleans. I have to see Peri again."

"Peri?" She was surprised. She hadn't known that things had progressed between them.

"We're in love, Jordan, and we want to be married."

"Oh, Philip, that's wonderful. I'm so happy for you." She hugged him tightly.

"Thanks. I don't know how I can explain everything to her, but I'll think of something."

"I wish things were different."

"So do I, but they aren't. We'll just have to make the best of it."

"I hope Peri loves you enough to understand."

"I hope so too."

Philip walked Jordan back to the big house. He watched and waited until she was safely back inside, then he headed back to his own small house. Philip had been almost asleep when she'd first come to him, but now that he knew about Kirkwood, rest was the furthest thing from his mind. They had to get out of

394

there as quickly as they could. Any delay might cost Jordan her life.

By first light, Philip was completely packed and ready to go. All he had left to do was to put out the signal at the landing so the steamer would stop on its way downriver. He knew he wouldn't feel his sister was safe again until they were in the city, lost among the crowds.

Chapter Thirty

It was dawn. Jordan was already up and dressed. She'd packed most of her things herself and only now had summoned a servant to help her finish. A soft knock at the door signaled what she thought was the maid's arrival, and Jordan hurried to admit her.

"I thought you were the maid," she said, surprised to find Weddington there instead.

"I was already up when you rang, so I thought I would come and see what you needed," the butler told her. His gaze couldn't help but slide past her into the room, and when he saw that she was packing, his eyes widened. "Miss Jordan, what's going on?"

"Weddington," Jordan began as sternly as she could, "this is something I don't want to talk about. I'm leaving Riverwood this morning, and I called for the maid so she could help me finish packing."

As the head servant in the household, Weddington had always managed to maintain his dignity, but Jordan's departure shocked him so badly that he couldn't refrain from voicing his opinion. "But you can't leave!" he protested. "Mr. Nick needs you now. What would he do without you?"

At the mention of her "husband," Jordan stiffened. "Nick will do very well without me," she stated curtly.

"Oh, no, ma'am. He loves you, and if you leave him now, right after Mr. Charles has died, well . . ."

"Weddington." She put all the imperiousness she could manage into her tone. She couldn't discuss this with him. She couldn't humiliate them both. She would leave the explanations to Nick. They were his servants and he could tell them whatever he thought appropriate. All she wanted to do was go. "Trust me when I say that Nick is in full agreement with my departure. There is no point in talking about it. My plans are made, and I'll be leaving as soon as a steamer pulls in at the landing."

The shock on the butler's face turned slowly to sorrow as he realized he was helpless to dissuade her. "Miss Jordan, would it help if I said I didn't want you to go? Riverwood needs you."

The tenderness in his voice was unmistakable, and Jordan had to choke back the quick tears that threatened. She was standing with her back to him, folding the last of her garments, and her arms dropped wearily in a defeated motion. "Oh, Weddington . . ." she sighed. "I'm sorry. I really am, but this is the way it has to be."

He knew it would be best not to press, so he acquiesced. "Yes, ma'am. Shall I see your things down to the dock for you?"

"Yes, please." With an effort, she resumed her controlled demeanor. This was what she had to do, so she would do it quickly and get it over with.

It was only a short time later when Weddington returned to her room. A slave boy had run up from the cabins with a message for Jordan from Philip, and Weddington was relaying it.

"Miss Jordan, Mr. Montgomery has sent word that a steamer should be docking within the half hour." He was puzzled at Philip's involvement in her plans, but knew it was not his place to remark on it.

"Thank you. Have all my things been delivered to the landing?"

"Yes, ma'am," he answered respectfully.

"Good. I guess I might as well go on down there to wait . . ."

Jordan cast a longing glance around the room. She stared at the wide, comfortable bed and couldn't help but remember the hours of passion she and Nick had shared there. Jordan realized that she could have been happy here . . . if only things had been different. With a heavy sigh she turned her back on the bedroom and everything it stood for and walked away.

As Jordan made her way down the upstairs hall, she had to force herself not to pause before Charles's door. She missed him dreadfully. Squaring her shoulders in an unconscious gesture that nonetheless bolstered her flagging spirits, she descended the staircase.

Jordan's heart was pounding as she reached the main hall, for she feared a possible confrontation with Nick, but luckily he was nowhere to be seen. Her relief was tremendous. She strode from the house and with the waiting driver's help climbed into the small, open carriage Weddington had ordered brought around for her.

Struggling with all her might to keep from showing the heartbreak she was feeling, Jordan kept her gaze fixed straight ahead. She refused to look back at the house and she refused to think about never seeing Nick again. Weddington, however, was not about to let her go that easily. He had to say good-bye.

"Miss Jordan . . ." His deep voice was filled with poignant emotion as he came to the side of the carriage. "Miss Jordan . . . It isn't going to be the same without you."

Unable to resist his unspoken plea, she turned to take his hand. "Thank you."

"Yes, ma'am." He saw the glittering pain in her brilliant gaze and knew there was more to her leaving than he could ever hope to fathom. "Miss Jordan, if Mr. Nick needs to get in touch with you where will you be?"

"I'll be traveling to New Orleans first. After that, I'm not sure . . ."

The carriage started to roll. Weddington was forced to let go of her hand and step back. He watched her ride away, not understanding how Nick could just let her go without a word.

Jordan hadn't meant to let her emotions get the best of her. She hadn't meant to break down. But the pain of this final separation was so devastating that she couldn't help herself. She called out to the driver to stop, and she leaned out of the carriage to call to Weddington.

Thrilled, the servant rushed forward to see what she wanted. He hoped that she'd changed her mind, but his hopes were crushed.

"Weddington . . . take care of Nick for me . . ." was all she could say. Wiping away her tears, she ordered the driver, "All right, you can go on now."

With a slap of the reins, the carriage moved off, leaving the butler in total confusion. If she cared so much about Nick, why in the world was she leaving him?

Weddington stood rooted where he was for a moment, then turned and ran back into the house. Generally, when things were none of his business, he kept out of them. But this time was different. Something was terribly wrong, and he was going to talk to Nick about it right now. He raced into the house and went straight to the study, knocking loudly at the door.

"Mr. Nick, I need to talk to you! It's important," he spoke in a loud voice, for he knew Nick had drunk himself into a stupor the night before and would not be easy to wake up this morning.

Nick had been asleep in the chair, but at Weddington's summons he came awake with a start. His uncomfortable position, not to mention his pounding head, rendered him stiff and miserable. Noticing that it was daylight, he pushed himself into a semblance of an upright position, then he shouted out in annoyance for the servant to enter.

"What the hell do you want now? Didn't I tell you I wanted to be left alone?" he growled, glaring at the butler with bleary, bloodshot eyes.

"Mr. Nick," the butler began with urgency as he crossed the room to confront him. He paid no attention to his bad mood. This was too serious a problem to ignore. Something had to be done and quickly, before the boat showed up. "Miss Jordan's leaving, sir. You've got to stop her!"

Nick stared at him dazedly. It was really happening. She was actually leaving. After a moment, he snorted in disgust. "Is that what you woke me up for? Is that all you wanted to tell me? I could have told you that last night and saved you the trouble of worrying about it."

"But Mr. Nick! You've got to do something! You can't just let her leave!"

"The hell I can't!" he shouted, smashing his fist on the desktop. "Get out!"

Weddington was stunned by his reaction. "Mr. Nick, you mean you're just going to let Miss Jordan go? You're not going to try to stop her?"

Nick turned a frightfully threatening glare on him as he retorted, "I didn't stammer or stutter, did I? I said, get the hell out of here and leave me alone, and I meant it!"

Weddington couldn't imagine what was happening, but he did as he was told. "Yes, sir." As he reached the door, Nick called out to him.

"And Weddington."

400

"Yes, sir?" he asked, holding himself rigid as he turned to face him.

"I don't ever want to hear Jordan's name mentioned in this house again, do you understand me?"

"Yes, sir."

"Tell all the other servants, too."

"Yes, sir." With that he was gone.

Nick sat there, shaking with the force of the raw emotions he was trying to quell. Against his better judgment he got up from the desk and went to the window. He could see the open carriage with Jordan in it making its way down the landing road, and his hands clenched into fists of fury at his sides.

Nick watched until the carriage had disappeared from view and then turned away. On impulse, he started for the study door, intending to stop her, wanting with all his heart to bring her back. His hand was already on the doorknob when he brought himself up short. He tore himself violently away from the door, knowing he couldn't go after her. She didn't want to come back. She didn't love him. She wanted Montgomery. She had from the start, and the other man was probably waiting there on the landing for her right now.

In an uncontrolled fit of frustration, Nick slammed his fist against the wall with all his power. The plaster cracked beneath the force of his blow, but the pain in his hand was nothing compared to the piercing agony in his heart.

Ignoring his throbbing hand, Nick stalked to the liquor cabinet and snatched the last decanter of bourbon. In his need for a stiff drink, he didn't even bother with a glass but wandered out through the open French doors onto the gallery, drinking straight from the bottle. Nick stood at the rail, swigging the liquor and trying without success to force Jordan from his thoughts.

The steamboat gave a mournful whistle as it pulled

into Riverwood's dock, and Nick found himself staring off in the direction of the landing. A part of him wanted to run after her, to beg her not to go, but his pride held him immobile. He remained where he was. When he heard the steamer reverse engines and back out to mid-stream, he knew it was over. Jordan and Montgomery were gone. That part of his life was finished.

Nick stood there alone for a long time, then went back inside. He continued to drink uninterrupted for the balance of the morning as he wandered listlessly through the empty house. There seemed to be no point to anything any more. The future stretched bleak and empty before him. The more he drank, the more he searched for some meaning to life, some reason to go on.

By mid-afternoon — and after a half a bottle of bourbon — Nick finally realized that there was something he had to do. Before meeting Jordan, his driving motivation had been finding the owners of the *Sea Demon*. He would return to that grim goal now. It gave him a renewed sense of purpose.

Though Nick knew Slater's plan was to wait until the ship could be caught and then bring in some of his government associates to make the arrests, Nick didn't want to delay any longer. He knew who the rotten bastard was who owned the ship, and, as of the meeting with him yesterday, he knew right where he lived in New Orleans.

In a haze of drunken determination, Nick decided it was time to take some kind of action. He needed to feel as if he were in control of something in his life. He didn't want to wait any longer. He would go get Kirkwood and bring him to justice. Now.

Setting the half-empty decanter aside, Nick crossed the study to the gun case. Kirkwood was obviously a killer who would stop at nothing to achieve his goals, so Nick knew it would not be wise to face him unarmed.

"Mr. Kirkwood, sir, you have a visitor," the maid informed him.

Julian looked up, puzzled, from where he sat in his office going over some reports. "Who is it? I wasn't expecting anyone today . . ."

"A Mr. Dominic Kane, sir. He said it was important that he see you right away. Something about business . . ."

"Kane's here?" Now he was truly surprised, and he frowned, wondering what could have brought him into town today. "Send him in, please."

"Yes, sir. Right away." She hurried off to do his bidding.

Nick was quickly ushered into the office. The maid left immediately, knowing Kirkwood didn't like anyone eavesdropping on his private affairs.

"Kane, it's good to see you again. I hadn't expected to see you again so soon. Is there a problem?"

The ride into town had done nothing to clear Nick's head. If anything, he was even more convinced that he was doing the right thing. He was angry and frustrated, and he needed to do something about it. "You're the problem, Kirkwood," he answered succinctly.

"I am?" he drawled. "Well, this sounds interesting. Have a seat and let's talk," Julian invited, trying to gauge his mood and figure out what was bothering him.

"The only one of us who's going to do any talking, is you, to the authorities."

"Excuse me?" Julian tensed, his hand slowly moving to reach for the desk drawer where he kept a small derringer hidden.

"Don't bother going for a gun," Nick directed, drawing his own sidearm. "It's over. I'm taking you in for illegal slave running. I want to see you pay for what you've done."

Julian gave a low, threatening laugh as he realized that Nick had been drinking. "Come, come, Kane. What are you talking about? You're one of my prime investors. We have a business deal."

"That was all just a sham just to draw you out. MacKenzie and I have been tracking you down ever since we were passengers on the *Sea Demon* some months ago, when the captain was cornered by government ships. I saw what happened to the slaves on board. The orders that they be drowned to save the ship were yours. You are directly responsible for all their deaths, and I want to see justice done."

Nick was so intent on trapping Kirkwood he didn't hear the man come into the room behind him. The vicious blow to the back of his head took him completely by surprise. Defenseless, he collapsed unconscious on the floor.

"Well done, my dear Luther," Julian gloated as he rose from the desk. "You couldn't have come downstairs at a better time."

"You're right about that, Julian. After all these months, it seems my luck has finally taken a turn for the better. Yesterday I saw that little bitch for the first time, and today Kane walked right into our midst. If you only knew how hard I've been searching for Jordan. I've had detectives looking for her on two continents for months, and all this time she was right here . . ."

"I had no idea until yesterday, when you arrived so unexpectedly, that you were looking for her. Not that it would have mattered, though, for I'd only met her that one brief time in London, and I didn't even remember what she looked like. How did you find out she was in the area?"

"I have my ways," he replied elusively. "Sometimes it may take a little longer than usual to get the information I need, but I always get what I want in the end."

Julian smirked sharkishly. "That's why I like you, Luther. You always end up on top of everything."

"It's a shame Miss Jordan St. James isn't as smart as you are, Julian, my friend."

"You never did tell me what you wanted with her. What did she do to make you so angry?"

"I have a personal score to settle with the little slut." Then realizing that he sounded like a lover scorned, he quickly added, "She stole some important papers from my office, and I mean to get them back."

"Do you think she was working with Kane, helping him set this up?"

"No. She didn't even know him when the slaves were dumped. She was still in England then." He quickly dismissed the thought of her having any involvement in Nick's plans, for his sources had traced Jordan through the indentures to Mobile, where she'd met Kane, and that had only been a very short time ago. He wasn't quite sure how her relationship had evolved from hired servant to wife, and it didn't matter. All that mattered was that he'd found her, and now he was going to have her to himself.

"What about what he said about turning me in for the *Sea Demon?*"

"Don't worry about it. They can't do anything without proof, and if they'd had it, they would have arrested you before now. Besides, the game has changed. Now we've got Kane. I don't think anyone will be giving us any trouble, do you?"

They laughed together, heady with the power they wielded.

"What can I do to help you?" Julian offered.

"Let's get him tied and gagged and out of here."

"Right," he agreed, hurrying off to get some rope and a rag.

Jealousy filled Luther as he stared down at Nick. How dare Jordan refuse him, yet marry this man? He was going to make them both suffer, and he was going to enjoy every minute of it! Luther knelt beside Nick and took his pistol.

"Here, Julian, do something with this," he said when his partner returned. He handed him the gun and took the ropes from him.

In short order Nick was bound and gagged.

"Let's take him upstairs. There's an extra room that's never used."

Making sure there were no servants around, they carried him upstairs and left him there, locking the door behind them.

"Now that I'm sure Kane's not going anywhere, I know exactly what I'm going to do. I have a note I want to send . . ."

It was near dark when Weddington heard the call that there was a rider coming up the drive. He was half expecting it to be Nick returning home, and he went out with a lantern to greet him. The man who rode up to the house, though, was a scurrilous-looking stranger.

"This the Kane plantation?" he asked abruptly, not bothering with pleasantries. He did not even dismount, but remained in the saddle as if anxious to be gone.

"Who wants to know?" he inquired cautiously.

"That don't matter. I got an important letter here for a Mrs. Jordan Kane, and I'm supposed to deliver it to her myself."

Weddington had no idea what was going on, but he

wasn't about to let this lowlife know that Jordan wasn't there. "I'm Mrs. Kane's personal servant. I'll see that she gets it."

"I got to give it to her myself," the filthy messenger insisted.

"I'm sorry, but that's impossible. Mrs. Kane has already retired for the night. You can rest assured that I will see the note delivered, however."

The man wavered, and then, after considering the long ride back to the city, he agreed. "All right, here." He thrust the envelope at Weddington.

The butler glanced down at the missive and saw only *For Jordan Kane—Personal* written on the front. "I take it there's much urgency to this?"

"There sure is. Why else would he have hired me to ride all the way out here at this time of night?"

"Who is *he?*"

"Damned if I know. Some well-dressed fellow found me at the tavern and asked me if I wanted to make some easy money. I ain't one to turn down a fast profit, if you know what I mean."

"I know what you mean," Weddington replied with disdain, and he watched until the rider had galloped off into the night.

Turning his attention back to the letter, Weddington debated what to do. Had Nick been there, he would have given it to him, but in his absence, he knew he had to take charge. Since the note sounded extremely important, he made up his mind to go find Jordan and deliver the letter. He knew it might take a while to locate her, but he had to make the effort.

Weddington's guess had been right, but it was almost midnight before he finally located the hotel where Jordan and Philip Montgomery were staying. He was surprised to find that she'd signed in under her maiden name of Jordan Douglas. He told the desk clerk that he had a message for her, and he was made to wait while they checked to make sure that she really wanted to see him. When word came that she would see him right away, he hurried upstairs.

"Miss Jordan, a man came out to the house several hours ago with this letter for you," Weddington told her, handing her the missive.

Jordan stared down at the envelope, feeling a sudden sense of enormous dread. "Thank you, Weddington. I appreciate your taking the time to deliver it to me."

"Are you all right here? Do you need anything else?"

"No. I'm as fine as I can be, Weddington. Thank you."

He could tell she wasn't about to open the letter in front of him, so he bid her farewell and departed, hoping he'd done the right thing.

Jordan closed the door and locked it before going to sit on her bed and open the letter. Her hands were trembling as she slipped the two sheets of paper out and read the message written there:

My Dearest Jordan—
   The search has been long and hard, but at last I've found you. Did you really think you could get away from me that easily after what you did? If you want to see your husband alive again, bring the papers you stole from me and meet me at Julian Kirkwood's house at 2700 St. Charles St. right away. I will be waiting for you. It's been a long time—

Luther

Chapter Thirty-one

Luther was alive . . . Luther was alive . . . Jordan's head was spinning, and terror unlike anything she'd ever experienced before seized her. Icy tendrils of fear crept up her spine as she read the note again, memorizing the address. She found herself shivering in spite of the heat.

Jordan didn't know how Luther had managed to track her to Louisiana, and it really didn't matter anymore. All that mattered was that she go to him as quickly as she could. She had to help Nick. She couldn't let Luther harm him in any way. He had nothing to do with any of this. It was a personal vendetta . . . something just between Luther and her.

Jordan was so numb with disbelief that she didn't even notice Luther's letter fall to the floor as she got up and started into Philip's connecting room. She was glad Philip had gone to see Peri and her family for the evening, for she didn't want to involve him in this ugliness. His future was with Peri, and hers would now be with Luther.

Going into Philip's room, she sought out pen and paper and wrote him a short note. She told him that she was leaving to go out on her own. She tried to convince him that it would be better if they went their separate ways now, that she would be fine, and that he shouldn't worry about her. She left it on his dresser where he would easily find it and then quickly hurried from the room.

Philip stood up and shook hands with Peri's father. "Thank you, sir. I promise I'll do everything in my power to make her happy."

"It's obvious my daughter loves you, Philip, and that's all I care about," Randall Davidson replied, his eyes warm upon Peri and the man she'd chosen to be her husband.

"Oh, Papa . . ." Peri went to her father and hugged him. She hadn't known how her parents were going to react to her engagement to Philip, and she was thrilled that everything had gone so smoothly. "I'm so happy . . . Thank you . . ."

"You're welcome, darling," he told her as he kissed her on the forehead. "As far as a job is concerned, let me make some inquiries among my banking friends. There just might be a position open that would be perfect for you."

"I'd appreciate it, sir." Philip put his arm around Peri as she returned to his side.

Marjorie smiled happily as she watched her daughter and future son-in-law. "This is so exciting. We'll have to start planning the wedding right away. There's just so much that has to be done . . ."

"We can start first thing in the morning," Peri announced with delight, gazing up at Philip adoringly.

"For now, though, I think I'd better call it a night," Philip said. "Thank you for everything. Dinner was delicious."

"We look forward to seeing more of you," Randall and Marjorie told him.

410

"Good night, ma'am, sir," he bid as Peri led him from the room to the privacy of the front hall.

Before Philip could say a word she was in his arms kissing him. When they broke apart, he smiled down at her.

"I can hardly wait to make you my wife . . ."

"I can hardly wait to be your wife, Mr. Montgomery . . ." she whispered, pulling him down for another quick kiss.

Philip longed to tell her his real name and confide in her about everything, but it wasn't safe yet. He wondered despondently if it ever would be.

"I'd better go . . ."

"Will I see you tomorrow?" Peri asked eagerly.

"I think that could be arranged . . ." He gave her one last tender kiss and then left the Davidson's mansion in the American section of New Orleans. Hailing a cab, Philip started back to the hotel, intent on telling his sister his good news.

Jordan kept her head held high as she knocked on the door at the address Luther had given her. Inwardly she was quaking. It devastated her to concede that Luther had won, but there could be no denying it now. He'd backed her into a corner, and there would be no escaping him this time. He had Nick, and she had to do whatever she could to save him. Jordan swallowed nervously as the door slowly opened, and she found herself facing Julian Kirkwood.

"Well, well, if it isn't the wife of one of my investors. Come in, Jordan. It's a pleasure to see you again, believe me." He smiled widely at her, but his eyes were cold and calculating.

"Thank you." She stepped inside the foyer. When he shut the door behind her, she felt like a fly trapped in a

411

spider's web.

"Right this way, please," he told her, ushering her down the hall. "There's someone here who's very excited about seeing you again." He stopped before the parlor doorway, and with a sweep of his arm directed her inside. When she'd gone in, he closed the door behind her, leaving them completely alone.

Luther was standing by the fireplace, one arm braced on the mantel, sipping from a snifter of brandy when she walked into the room. He looked coolly composed and very debonair, but when he looked up at her, his eyes locked on her with burning intensity.

"Hello, Jordan," Luther greeted her.

His tone was so soft and so deadly that she held her breath. She waited breathlessly to see what his next move would be, just as the doomed fly watches and waits for the spider's inevitable attack.

"Good evening, Luther."

"You look very beautiful tonight, Jordan. Married life must agree with you . . ."

"I didn't come here to discuss my marriage with you."

"My, my, how very cool we sound," he drawled sarcastically, moving away from the mantel to come stand before her. "Why is it I have the feeling you're not quite as sure of yourself as you sound?" He lifted one hand to caress her cheek with a single finger.

Jordan couldn't prevent the shudder that wracked her, and she dodged away from his touch. "Where's my husband? I want to see Nick," she demanded.

"Ah, the beloved spouse," he sneered. "Don't worry about him. I've got him safely tucked away upstairs, and you will be seeing him soon. But first I think we have to have a little talk. There are a few things we need to straighten out between us."

"Like what?"

412

"Like where are the papers you stole from my office? I want them now."

Jordan didn't hesitate. She withdrew from her purse the damning packet of documents she'd so carefully guarded all these months and quickly handed them over.

Luther looked through them carefully, then gave her a pleased smile. "Very good. They're all here. It looks like you finally might have learned a little bit about what it takes to satisfy me — such as total obedience to my commands."

"You have the papers. I'm here. Let Nick go."

"Not so fast, sweet." Tossing the packet carelessly onto the sofa, Luther snared Jordan by her wrists and dragged her forcefully to him. "Do you have any idea how hard I looked for you? Do you?" His mouth descended to ravage hers in insulting domination.

Jordan wanted to fight him, but she didn't dare. Not now. Not until she was sure Nick was safe.

Luther lifted his head to gaze down at her. "So you really have learned to be submissive, have you?" He chuckled. "Good, very good. Then what I have planned for your husband will work quite well."

"What do you mean?" Jordan was suddenly terrified for Nick's safety. "Nick has nothing to do with what happened between us."

He laughed again, this time in victory. "I was right. You don't have any idea about his activities, do you?"

"What are you talking about?"

"Obviously you knew he had a business deal with Julian."

"Yes, but I only found out about that a few days ago when I saw him with Julian for the first time. When Julian didn't seem to recognize me or come after me right away, I thought that Nick really was working out a shipping arrangement with him."

"Just as I suspected. You were totally ignorant of your husband's real motive."

"What real motive?" She eyed him suspiciously.

"Your husband was plotting with MacKenzie to see the owners of the *Sea Demon* arrested and hung for their part in the murder of a shipload of slaves a little over seven months ago."

"What?" Jordan was completely shocked.

"Interesting that he never confided in you, since you could have been so helpful to him. I mean, after all, my dear, you and your brother are the ship's owners, aren't you?"

"Why you—"

"You see, your husband and his meddling friend were on board the night the ship was forced to dump cargo. He didn't like the idea, and he decided to find the real culprits, the owners who would order such carnage, and see them pay for the crime. So you see, Jordan, while he was so busy trying to track down the owners, he had the real criminal right in his bed."

Jordan gasped at the revelation and went pale.

"I think Kane's really going to enjoy finding all this out, don't you?"

"Just let him go. I'll do whatever you want."

"Oh, it's far too late for that, my dear girl. You're going to do whatever I want regardless. You're hardly in a bargaining position any more." He crushed her to his chest once more and kissed her hotly as he fondled her with open enjoyment. Her silent acquiescence thrilled him. He had tamed her, but he was not done yet. He wouldn't be completely satisfied until he'd humiliated both her and her husband.

"What do you want from me? What do you want me to do?" she asked as he shifted to press wet, slobbering kisses to her throat.

At her questions, Luther immediately withdrew his

attentions. There would be plenty of time for that later. Right now he wanted to see both Kane and her suffer for a while.

"We're going to go upstairs and pay your husband a visit. From what I understand, yours was a very loving marriage. I want you to convince him that I'm the one you want. That you only married him for the convenience of it. I want you to be so believable that the man will never want to lay a hand on you again. Understand?"

She was sickened by the thought but she agreed. "Anything else?"

"I don't think so. Once I give him my version of why you're here with me, I think my point will have been made. But remember, Jordan, actions speak louder than words. If you want him to live, you'll go along with everything I say and do. You might even be a little aggressive to make our point."

"All right."

"Let's go . . ."

Philip reached the hotel in short order. He was anxious to share his good news with his sister, but when he saw no light coming from under her door he decided she had gone on to sleep. Disappointed that he couldn't tell her right then, he went on into his own room, prepared to wait until the following morning.

Philip unlocked the door to his room and made his way in the dark to the dresser. It took him a minute of fumbling to finally light the lamp on the dresser. When he turned up the lamp, he saw the short note she'd left there for him.

Philip read it with a sense of growing disbelief. When he'd left Jordan earlier that evening she'd been fine. But now she was telling him that they had to go their separate ways and that he shouldn't worry about her. What could account for this sudden change?

Philip knew Jordan was a very capable woman, but the world was a very dangerous place. He had no intention of letting her disappear like this. He charged through the door that separated their rooms and lighted her lamp so he could look around. Her bed had not been slept in, but what surprised and puzzled him more was that most of her things were still there. Wherever it was she'd gone, she'd gone practically empty-handed.

In desperation, Philip began a frantic search of the room, hoping to find some small clue to her disappearance. He found the forgotten letter lying halfway under the bed, and he read it in utter horror. *Luther had found them. He'd taken Nick hostage in order to lure Jordan to him!*

Though Philip loved Peri, he wouldn't be able to live with himself if he didn't do something to help his sister. Jordan was his own flesh and blood. He had no intention of letting her sacrifice herself to the altar of Luther's perverted lusts.

In a rage, Philip headed for the door, ready to face down Radcliffe himself. As he was about to open it there came a solid knock that startled him. He threw the door wide in his anger and found himself face to face with Slater.

"What the hell are you doing in Jordan's room?" Slater demanded before Philip could even say a word. He pushed past him to step inside Jordan's bedroom. "Where is she? What have you done with her?"

"That's none of your damned business," Philip bristled.

"Well, I'm making it my business!" Slater threatened.

"Why? What are you doing here?" Philip demanded

416

in return, not about to be bullied by him when Jordan was in so much danger.

They eyed each other suspiciously for a minute like two wary beasts.

"Weddington came by to see me tonight. He said there was some kind of terrible trouble brewing. He told me Jordan left Nick this morning and came here with you. Then he said that Nick had disappeared this afternoon and he hadn't seen him since. He insisted that I come here and talk to Jordan to see if I could find out what was going on. Since I care about the both of them, I decided I'd better do what he said."

"There's trouble, all right," Philip confessed.

"Like what?"

Philip didn't say a word, but held out the letter to Slater. He took the proffered missive and read it quickly, then looked up, frowning.

"What is this all about? I want to know the truth, and I want to know it now. What's going on?"

Philip knew he had to have help to deal with Luther, and so he began to relate everything that had happened, hoping he would be able to trust Slater once the entire truth was out. "To begin with, my name isn't Montgomery. It's St. James, Philip St. James, and Jordan's name isn't Douglas. Hers is St. James too."

"My God! You two are married?!?" Horrendous thoughts of bigamy raced through his mind.

"No, we're not married!" Philip quickly denied. "Jordan's my sister!"

"Your sister?!" Slater repeated in fascination, then gave a small laugh that sounded almost delighted when he thought of how Nick was going to react to the news. Montgomery was Jordan's brother. No wonder she acted like she loved him. She did love him—like a brother.

Philip gave him a black look. "The situation is far

417

from humorous."

"Sorry, go on," he was quick to apologize. "Why all the subterfuge? Why the lies?"

Philip began at the beginning, telling him everything—from his bad judgment in investing with Luther to the fateful night when Jordan thought she'd killed him.

"Obviously he wasn't dead, but for all these months she's believed she was a murderer."

"Dear God . . . no wonder she couldn't tell Nick the truth."

"Indenturing ourselves was the only way we could escape. We had no money, and since we didn't want to be found, we changed our names. Then we met you and Nick, and we thought that maybe things would work out. Everything got complicated, though, because Jordan fell in love with Nick. She'd hoped Nick would fall in love with her, but then she saw you two with Julian at the tavern. She thought Julian was tracking her down for the authorities."

"So that's why she looked so stricken . . ."

Philip nodded. "And that's why we had to leave Riverwood. She didn't want to go, but she didn't want Nick to find out the truth about her. She didn't want to bring any embarrassment or humiliation down on him."

"If only she'd known what Nick and I were up to, she wouldn't have panicked."

"What are you talking about?"

"There's more to this than you know. Nick and I had the misfortune of being on the fateful voyage of the *Sea Demon* when they killed all the slaves. We vowed to find the ship's owners and have them arrested for their viciousness."

"According to Luther's documents, Jordan and I are the owners."

418

"Yes, but we both know the truth, and documents are easily forged." Everything suddenly came together for Slater. "How long ago did Jordan leave here?"

"I don't know . . ."

"We'd better hurry then. We don't have a minute to waste. There's no telling what Radcliffe and Kirkwood might do to the two of them. They're deadly men, Philip, very deadly men."

"I know," he answered.

"Do you have a gun?"

"No."

"Here, take my derringer," Slater slipped the small weapon out of his inside coat pocket. "It's not much, but it's better than nothing. I've still got my sidearm."

Philip took the gun from him, and they raced from the room to save Jordan and Nick from Luther's evil designs.

Chapter Thirty-two

Nick came awake slowly. The room was strange and dark, and for a minute he was disoriented. His head throbbed from the wicked blow that had laid him low and from his overindulgence in bourbon. He tried to move, to right himself and get comfortable, and was shocked to find that his hands and feet were bound. Fury filled him and he fought to be free, but the struggle was a useless one. Trussed up and gagged as he was, he was as helpless as a newborn babe, and he knew it.

Lying on his side on the hardwood floor, Nick silently cursed himself for trying to take Kirkwood alone. He should have known that bastards had partners. He should have remembered to protect his back. Nick prayed that he would get a second chance to face him, but this time on more even terms.

Nick heard the sound of footsteps in the hall followed by a low murmur of conversation. He looked up just as the door started to swing open.

Luther had grabbed Jordan by the arm just as they were about to enter the room. He jerked her around to him, a leering conqueror's smile on his coldly handsome face.

"I want to see some emotion out of you in there," he commanded.

"Don't worry, Luther. I'll do what you want," Jordan promised.

"That's what I like to hear, but just remember that your husband's life hangs on your ability to convince me that you love me. If you're even a little less than believable, Kane won't live to see daylight." His hand tightened on her to emphasize his point, his jealousy of Nick a living, breathing thing. He hated Nick for his investigation of the *Sea Demon,* but he despised him for having taken Jordan. He would have his revenge! "You're mine now, Jordan, and I want him to know it."

"I understand." Jordan didn't want to do this. She hated the thought of even being near Luther, let alone acting like she loved him, but she had to go through with it. Nick would die if she didn't.

Nick . . . the thought of humiliating him this way sent pain shooting through Jordan. Though she knew he didn't love her as she loved him, Luther's plan was still vicious. The only thing that gave her the strength to go on was the knowledge that she was saving Nick's life.

"All right, let's see what kind of an actress you really are." At her nod, Luther opened the door. With a firm hand on her elbow he escorted her inside.

The bright light of the hall put Nick at a disadvantage as he tried to see who had come into the room. He could only make out the silhouette of two people, a man and a woman, standing in the doorway with the light at their backs, but somehow he knew the woman was Jordan. He knew it as he lived and breathed. He knew it as he knew his own mirror image.

Horrible thoughts and desperate concern for her safety wracked Nick. He wondered what twisted, devious plan his tormentors had in mind if they'd kidnapped her and brought her here to use against him. He wished she were out of there. He didn't want her to see him this way. He wanted her safe and protected. His worry about her consumed him as he waited tensely to find out their deadly plan.

It was then the unknown man moved into the room to light the lamp, and it was then that Nick's life turned to pure hell. There before him stood Jordan, just as he'd known she would be, but instead of being forced to accompany the stranger, the man at her side had his arm draped around her waist with possessive familiarity.

"Nick . . ." Jordan couldn't help but gasp his name, seeing him bound and gagged this way. Her heart wrenched. She wanted to run to him and free him, but Luther's promise to kill Nick held her still. She could only stand there with a benign smile on her face, looking to all the world like she was enjoying herself.

"It's good to see that you've finally come around, Kane," Luther began robustly, feeling completely in control and loving every minute of it. "I was beginning to think that maybe I'd hit you just a bit too hard." Luther gave a soft, menacing chuckle. "Allow me to introduce myself. I'm Luther Radcliffe, Jordan's longtime partner and friend." He ran his hand up Jordan's arm to caress her shoulder with a knowing touch. But even as he caressed, his eyes were on Nick, watching for and rejoicing in the flash of anger and pain he saw in his eyes.

Nick didn't understand. Jordan's partner? The other man's touch grew more and more bold, and he found himself straining at his bonds, trying to get loose, wanting to throttle him for touching her. Suddenly it dawned on him that Jordan wasn't trying to resist him at all. If anything, she seemed perfectly content to have his hands upon her. Hell, she was even smiling!

"Your wife is quite a woman, Kane, but I'm sure you

knew that already," Luther said with a confident, gloating smile.

Nick wanted to rip the man's throat out. Jealousy, worry, and confusion were all mixed up within him as he tried to understand what was going on. The only thing that was clear to him was that no matter how hard he'd fought it, he loved Jordan with all his heart. It was desperately important to him that he keep her safe from this man.

"Of course he knew that. He married me for love, didn't he, Luther?" Jordan turned toward her tormentor, pressing herself to his side and taking care to keep her expression affectionate.

"That he did."

Nick wondered at her statement. Jordan of all people knew the real reason why they'd married. His confusion began to grow. Why would she lie to Radcliffe if, as he said, they were so close? Was she being forced to act this way? His suspicion that she might be innocent was just beginning to grow when she reached up to kiss the other man. Anger consumed him, and he thrust his doubts aside. His expression turning to one of pure loathing as he growled his outrage.

Luther looked decidedly amused over Nick's discomfort. "Yes, we do have a lot to talk about. Let's make things a little easier, shall we?" He left Jordan's side to untie the filthy rag they'd stuffed in Nick's mouth earlier. "Much better without it, isn't it?"

"Go to hell, you bastard! You keep yours hands off my wife. This is between you, Kirkwood, and me. Let her go. Get her out of here."

Luther threw back his head and gave a loud sarcastic laugh. "Why should I let her go when I've waited so long to be with her again . . . to touch her and kiss her . . . ? It's been a long time, Jordan . . ."

"She's an innocent in all this, Radcliffe . . . Leave

her out of it," Nick argued.

"You're such a fool, Kane," he sneered coldly. "There's no way to leave Jordan out of this. She's been involved with the *Sea Demon* since the very beginning."

Jordan blanched at his revelation, but said nothing. She knew if she did anything or protested in any way, Luther would kill Nick without a second thought. She fought to maintain a calm outward demeanor, but she had to clench her hands into fists at her sides to keep them from shaking.

"I don't know what you're talking about. I just want Jordan out of here," Nick said, his dark gaze going from the arrogant smuggler to his wife, who was standing next to the man looking perfectly content. He studied her face, trying to read her expression. She was a bit pale and there was a trace of something — worry, maybe? Or guilt? — mirrored in her eyes, but he couldn't be sure. A trace of doubt entered his thoughts. "Jordan, please go."

"No, Nick. I don't want to leave. This is where I really belong," she replied easily, leaning even more intimately against Luther.

The businessman gave a soft laugh. "She's happy here with me. Why would she want to go? We're old friends. Aren't we, love?" He moved to hold her close, tilting her chin up with a finger and pressing a soft kiss on her lips.

"Jordan . . ." Nick couldn't believe what he was seeing. "What's this all about?"

"You see, Kane, Jordan may be your wife now, but back in London she was my partner . . . and more." He drew her close and kissed her hotly. Jordan gave a good imitation of being caught up in the heat of it. "Jordan made quite a few wonderful investments with me, and one of them was the *Sea Demon*. She was

424

quite pleased with the profit the ship was turning, until that fateful day when the *Demon* had to dump cargo in the Gulf. Of course, you know all about that debacle, don't you, Kane?"

"He does?" Jordan asked, suddenly not understanding what Luther was talking about.

"Oh, yes, my dear, this is all quite entertaining when you think about it. Let me fill you in on the whole story. You see, your dear husband has been trying to stop the *Sea Demon* from smuggling slaves into the country. He's been searching for you, her owner, for months now, and all the while you were right here in his hands, so to speak. It's too bad you weren't more astute in your checking, Kane. You could have saved yourself a lot of trouble. Too bad, the way things worked out for you. But that's the way it goes sometimes," Luther taunted with open delight.

Jordan felt sick as it all became clear to her. The real reason why Nick and Slater had been meeting with Julian was to trap him! If only she'd known, she could have helped Nick to catch him. Instead, she was now being forced to act the part of the satisfied owner, when in reality she'd despised everything about that investment.

Jordan managed a light laugh, though it nearly killed her to do it. "You're right, it is quite funny. Maybe Nick should give up trying to be an investigator. He seldom recognizes the reality of things, he only sees what he thinks is the truth." She was cloaking her words in sarcasm, but in reality she was desperately trying to reveal the truth to him.

Nick was too caught up in the pain of Luther's revelations to understand. Her words were like a physical blow to him, bloodying his heart. Nick was miserable. A bitter pain that he feared would never ease surged through him. He stared at her through a red haze of agony, and he silently damned her lying, deceiving soul to hell.

Luther could see the play of emotions on Nick's face, and he was pleased. If there had been any love in the marriage, he'd managed to destroy it. He felt victorious and invincible. He'd won. Now, all that was left to do was to claim the final prize.

Jordan sensed all that Nick was feeling, and it left her devastated. She had deliberately set out to destroy any kinder feelings he might have had for her, and she'd done it. Though her motive had been to save him, it didn't ease her own misery to know that in saving him she'd left him despising her. She told herself to be strong, that this couldn't go on much longer. Soon she'd be away from Nick, and she would never have to suffer his condemning gaze again. For some reason, though, that thought did little to soothe her.

"Well, my darling, now that your beloved knows the full truth, shall we allow him his privacy?" Luther suggested. He was hot for Jordan, and he meant to have her now.

"Of course, let's go," she agreed, eager to be gone from Nick's sight.

Luther turned her in his arms and casually toyed with the buttons at her bodice, loosening four so that her bosom was bared to the top of her chemise. "You have such lovely skin, Jordan. I can hardly wait to touch you again . . ." He pressed a kiss to the soft flesh.

Nick turned his head away so he wouldn't have to watch, but his avoidance only drew another triumphant laugh from Luther.

"So, you're not a voyeur, eh, Kane?" He thought of forcing the issue, of taking her right there before him, but decided against it. This was their first time, and he had a lot he wanted to teach Jordan . . . a lot he

426

wanted to punish her for. Later, he decided, he would wreak that ultimate revenge, but for now, having her to himself was enough. He crushed her to him, kissing her again.

"I've missed you all this time," she cooed, hoping her lie would save Nick.

"I'll just bet you have, Jordan, and I've missed you, too. That's why I came after you. I want to make up for the little misunderstanding we had in London."

"I'm glad you did," she answered, nausea threatening.

"So am I," he kissed her again, deliberately touching her breasts, all for Nick's benefit.

A moan of disgust escaped Jordan as Luther's hands moved boldly over her, drawing Nick's attention. Instead of thinking she was hating it, though, Nick thought hers had been a moan of desire. The abhorrence and loathing he was feeling was so powerful it sickened him.

"Come, my dear, we don't need an audience . . ." he breathed to Jordan as he cast Nick a smug look. "Let me gag him again, and then we can go where we'll be completely alone . . ."

Jordan managed a murmur of agreement. At that moment, she would have agreed to anything Luther wanted just to get away from Nick's damning gaze. Tears burned her eyes as she realized that she would probably never see him again. He would forever believe the worst of her, and there was nothing she could do about it. Her heart was all but destroyed, but then, what did she need a heart for? She walked from the room on Luther's arm, feeling the heat of her husband's hate-filled regard on her back.

Only when she was outside in the hall did she allow her defeat to show. Her shoulders slumped wearily. She felt jaded and dirty from having had Luther's hands upon her, but what troubled her most was what she'd done to Nick—and what she knew was yet to come.

"Now, Jordan, let's finish what we started all those months ago . . ." Luther said with relish. "Julian has prepared a very private room for us to share tonight."

"What about Nick? You said you'd let him go . . ." she argued, wondering why Luther had taken the time and trouble to lock the door after them.

"All in good time, my dear. All in good time. I'm not about to set him free until you've performed everything I want you to do to my satisfaction."

"You're loathsome . . ."

Angered by her words, Luther grabbed her and slammed her against the wall. "If I were you, I'd watch myself. Who knows? I just might change my mind about letting your precious husband go."

"You wouldn't . . ."

"There's nothing I wouldn't do, Jordan. Remember that. Ever since that night in London I've been determined to find you and finish that evening. No one does to me what you tried to do and gets away with it. You're going to make it all up to me, and you're going to start right now."

His words sent terror through her, and she began to tremble in spite of her determination to stay in control. Luther chuckled again, seeing the fear in her eyes.

"I'm glad you're frightened. You damn well should be. Now, let's go before I decide to take you here in the hall and let your husband listen to your screams of ecstasy!"

He kept an arm around her, his hand splayed familiarly across her ribs resting just beneath the swell of her breast, as he led her off toward the staircase to the third floor. It was there that Julian had created the perfect setting for him to wreak his revenge upon her. He hoped Jordan enjoyed what he had in mind for the night, but he really didn't care if she didn't . . .

When they reached the top of the steps, Luther guided her forward to a door at the far end of the hall. He threw the door open and smiled at what he saw.

Several lamps lit the windowless room, and Jordan noticed right away that there was only the one door. As her gaze fell upon the bed, she knew she'd met her fate. It was wide and covered with satin sheets. There was also a small table and two chairs spread with a sumptuous array of foods and a bottle of champagne in an ice bucket.

"What do you think, my dear? I have a feeling that we won't be needing anything all night, so we won't be interrupted." He gave her a little push to get her to move into the room.

It was only then that Jordan saw the shackles attached to the bed's headboard. She let out a cry of fright and tried to turn and run from him. Luther was too quick for Jordan, though. He snared her arm and swung her forcefully around to face him. With great pleasure, he slapped her, snapping her head with the strength of the blow.

"This could have been a wonderful night for us, Jordan, but it's obvious to me that you aren't *really* willing. Perhaps force is the only thing you understand. Did Kane have to beat you to get you in his bed?"

"No, I love Nick."

"Well, he doesn't love you, not any more. Did you see the hate in his eyes when I kissed you?"

"Nick never had to force me to do anything. I gave him my love freely." Defiance was the only weapon she had left, but it was useless against his superior strength.

Luther's eyes darkened with anger at her words. "It doesn't matter to me if he did or not. It's not your love

I want. I only want your body. Now get over there and take off your clothes. I'm tired of trying to be nice to you, and I'm not averse to using pain to get what I want. Sometimes it can prove to be the perfect aphrodisiac."

"No! Let me go!" Jordan began to fight against him, trying to break free.

"You're a fool, Jordan. Even if I did let you go, which I won't, you have absolutely no place to run. Certainly your beloved husband doesn't want you back. He believed everything I told him about us," he reminded her heartlessly, wanting her to know that she was at his mercy. "And I'm sure the authorities here would be very interested in your connection to the *Sea Demon,* don't you think? So, you might as well relax and enjoy the time we're going to spend together. And trust me, we will be spending a *lot* of time together, right here in this room. I've waited longer for you than I ever have for anything or anyone in my life, and I intend to slake my desire for you fully."

Jordan's eyes rounded with terror as she saw the unadulterated lust in his eyes. When he reached up and grabbed her dress by the neckline and ripped it viciously open down to the waist, she began to tremble uncontrollably.

"Ah . . . you're so gorgeous . . ." he muttered, staring at her bared breasts. "It's a pity Kane got you first, but I'll be the one to have you last . . ."

Luther was practically drooling as he dragged her to the bed and threw her down on it. With open delight he picked up one of the shackles and fastened it about her wrist as she squirmed, trying to get away. Her fear pleased him, and he was sorry he didn't have any bonds for the foot of the bed, too. That would have made the evening really interesting.

"You know, Jordan, I wouldn't have had to resort to

this had you not attacked me the last time. But I fully intend to have you tonight, and nothing and no one will stop me!" Luther was talking quite coolly as he finished chaining her to the bed. That done, he eagerly tore the rest of her clothes from her body and then moved away to undress himself. His excitement was growing with each passing minute, and he could hardly wait to sink himself into her hot depths.

Chapter Thirty-three

Slater and Philip made record time racing to Julian's house. They scouted the grounds, searching for some sign of Jordan or Nick, but found nothing. Everything seemed quiet. The only room with a light burning was Julian's office.

"We're going to have to break in."

"Right," Philip agreed, trying not to let his nervousness show. He had recognized early on that Slater seemed particularly adept at this kind of thing, so he had acquiesced to his leadership.

"There's a side parlor window open; we'll go in through there. Only use the gun if they give us no other choice," Slater instructed carefully.

Philip nodded and then followed Slater's lead through the window and into the darkened room. They made their way quickly through the maze of furniture to the hall door. Philip was on edge. It seemed every sound was magnified a thousand times. His heartbeat was thundering in his ears and his breathing sounded loud—harsh and rasping. He wondered how Slater could remain so cool under such dangerous circumstances.

Though Philip thought Slater confident, it was far from the truth. Slater was tense too. He was very aware of the kind of men with whom they were dealing. Human life meant nothing to them, and the nagging fear hounded him that they might be too late to save Jordan and Nick. Still, Slater knew he could do no less than his best to try to rescue them.

Motioning for Philip to stay back, Slater pressed himself tightly against the wall as he crept toward the door. He glanced out into the shadowed hall to check for signs of activity and discovered to his relief that it was deserted. Knowing that time was of the essence, he boldly led the way out of the parlor and down the hall to the closed study door.

"Stay here and keep watch for me," he whispered, and then drew his gun, gesturing for Philip to do the same. Armed and ready, he slammed the door open and charged into the room alone to confront Julian at his desk.

Julian was shocked by the intrusion and started to go for his gun, but Slater was too fast for him. Looming before him, he aimed his pistol straight at his heart.

"I wouldn't do that if I were you, Kirkwood," Slater threatened in a voice that left no doubt about his intentions.

Julian could tell by the menacing glint in his eyes that he was serious. He judiciously brought both hands into full view on the desktop. "MacKenzie . . . this is a pleasant surprise."

"Where are they?" he demanded, not wanting to waste time.

"Who?"

"You're well aware who I mean. I'm here for Jordan and Nick."

"They're not here."

Slater showed him the letter. "Somehow I find I don't believe you. Now, are you going to take me to

433

them or am I going to take you and this house apart by myself, piece by piece? It doesn't matter to me which you choose. Either way, I'll find them. Which one will it be?"

Julian wanted to stall for time, but he knew he wouldn't be getting any help from Luther. He'd heard him disappear upstairs to the private room, and he knew he wouldn't be back down until sometime the following day. His servants, too, had retired for the night, and their quarters were in a separate building at the back of the house. The only thing he could hope to do was try to convince MacKenzie that he was cooperating fully and then distract him so he could go for his own gun.

"It seems I have very little choice in the matter, doesn't it? I'll take you to them . . ." he acquiesced.

"That's a very wise decision on your part, Kirkwood. Let's go." He waved Julian in the direction of the hall.

In one smooth, deceptive motion, Julian rose to his feet, and at the same time grabbed a sheaf of papers off his desktop and heaved them at Slater. He'd hoped to catch him off guard and give himself time enough to get his own gun, but he hadn't counted on Slater's lightning-fast reflexes or expert marksmanship.

Years of working undercover had taught Slater to be constantly on the alert for the unexpected. As the other man reached in his desk drawer for his gun, Slater fired. His bullet slammed into Julian's chest. He collapsed to the floor, dead, his own pistol falling from his lifeless hand. Slater ran to his side to make sure he was dead, then picked up the gun to take along with him, just in case.

The sound of the shot brought Philip into the room at a run, his gun ready. He was immensely relieved to find that Slater was unharmed. "Thank God you're all right!"

"Come on, we've run out of time. There's no telling who heard the shot. We've got to search the house and fast!"

Slater charged into the hall and up the staircase with Philip close on his heels. They systematically began searching each of the multitude of rooms on the second floor. It surprised Slater that there was no immediate rush of servants to check on Kirkwood, but he was glad for the reprieve.

Slater couldn't help but wonder where Radcliffe was, though. Surely, if he'd heard the shot, he would have come out to check. He felt almost certain that the other man wasn't in the house, but he didn't want to voice his opinion and worry Philip needlessly until they'd finished searching. They approached the last room, and Slater knew they were on to something when he heard a thumping inside and found the door was locked. Luckily, the key was in the lock. Slater quietly unlocked the door and cautiously pushed it open.

The light from the hall was just bright enough to enable him to see Nick.

"Nick!" He holstered his gun and rushed inside. "Philip, light the lamp so I can see something!" Slater dropped to his knees beside his friend and worked at the gag and the ropes.

"What the hell is he doing here with you?" Nick demanded with open hostility the minute the gag had been removed.

"He's been helping me find you and Jordan. Where is she? Do you know where they've taken her?"

"What do you mean 'taken her'? She went with the bastard of her own free will," Nick sneered as Slater

435

untied his wrists. Nick began untying his own ankles, eager to be out of there.

"Like hell she did!" Philip countered angrily, coming to stand near them.

"Go find her yourself, then, if you don't believe me. You'll see how much she's fighting Radcliffe, and you'll be in for one big surprise. You've already been replaced," Nick told him sarcastically, his bitterness fueling his anger. He got to his feet and faced Philip squarely. "They may not appreciate your interrupting them, though. They could hardly wait to get out of here so they could be together . . ."

"You stupid bastard!" Philip lunged for Nick, ready to beat him within an inch of his life.

Nick was ready for him. The turmoil of his emotions had him ready to hit out at anything or anyone that gave him cause. At that moment, there was nothing he would have liked better than to throttle Philip.

Only Slater's quick thinking prevented a major fracas. "Stop it! Both of you!" he ordered, throwing himself between them. "There's a lot you don't know, Nick, and it's time you found out."

Nick gave his friend a skeptical look. "Found out what? That Jordan is the owner of the *Sea Demon?* That's she involved not only with Montgomery here, but also Luther Radcliffe?"

"You're damned right she's involved with me!" Philip retorted furiously, still longing to hit Nick for all the heartache he'd caused Jordan. "She's my sister!"

The change of expression on Nick's face would have been ludicrous if the situation had not been so serious. "Your sister . . . ?"

"It's too complicated to go into just now. You'll have to trust me on this, Nick. They blackmailed Jordan into coming here by threatening your life," Slater explained.

"She came here to save you," Philip told him scathingly. "She loves you enough to sacrifice herself to a man like Radcliffe! Doesn't that mean anything to you?"

"She loves me?" Nick repeated, astounded.

"Why else would she come here and give herself to the man she ran away from months ago? She's loved you for a long time, but you were too blind to see it."

"I thought she loved you . . ." he replied lamely in his own defense. "Damn! It was all an act . . ."

"What was?"

"The way Radcliffe was treating her—and the way she was responding. It was almost as if she was his own personal property . . ."

"Of course it was an act. She hates the man! We've got to find her!" Philip insisted. "The man's a fiend. If he hurts her—"

"If he's hurt her, I'll kill him . . ." Nick vowed, his visage grim with a terrible resolve. "Give me a gun . . ."

Slater handed him Julian's weapon. "How long has it been? Do you have any idea where he took her?"

"It's been less than half an hour," he answered, starting from the room. "I heard them move off down the hall, but not toward the front staircase. They went this way . . ."

Philip and Slater chased after him as he sprinted toward the steps to the third floor.

Luther had been toying with Jordan, playing upon her fears to make her cower with terror before him. His sole purpose in finding her had been to conquer her and break her spirit completely. He wanted her bent to his will. He wanted her groveling before him, begging for his favors. Only then would he feel she'd paid for her attack on him.

Jordan watched as Luther approached the bed wearing only his pants. She kept her features totally blank, but it was becoming more and more difficult to do. She found his nearness and his touch so revolting that it was next to impossible to appear unaffected. Time was running out. She knew it wouldn't be too much longer before he got tired of tormenting her and actually took her, and she wondered if she would live through it.

"Well, Jordan, have you come round to my way of thinking yet?"

"I'll never want you, Luther! Never! You may be able to take my body by force, but I'll never be willing!"

"Ah, ever defiant, ever stubborn, ever foolish . . ." He sat down beside her on the bed and reached out to caress her. "You know, sometimes you speak before you think. Have you forgotten that I hold your husband?"

"No," she answered in a hushed voice.

"I thought not." His touch turned from gentle to harsh, biting into her tender flesh and causing her to whimper and squirm. "As I told you before, I don't care if you're willing or not. It doesn't matter to me at all. All that's important is that I own you body and soul. Do you like it when I touch you this way?"

"No!" she cried, unable to hide her agony any longer.

"Good," he said with a smile, increasing the pressure of his hands, wanting to hear her scream out loud and beg him to stop. "It's never been my intention to pleasure you. I only want to please myself, and hurting you pleases me very much . . ." His eyes were glazed with sadistic excitement. "Do you know how long I've waited for this moment?"

"No . . ." Jordan could only manage a tight whisper. He was being so hurtful that she tried to dodge away from his hands, but the bonds at her wrists kept her pinioned to the bed. She brought her knees up in an effort to shield herself, but the action drew his immediate ire.

"You will lie perfectly still, do you understand me?" He stood up and drew his belt from his belt loops. Doubling it up, he struck her with it on her thighs.

Jordan tried to keep from screaming, but his lashing was so painful she couldn't prevent the cry of pain that escaped her. She realized then that he was a madman and that there could be no reasoning with him.

Defeat seared her soul. There was no use in fighting. There was no one to come to her rescue. Philip would have no idea where to look for her. Since she'd left him that note, he would think she'd gone off on her own somewhere . . . he might not even worry. And Nick would leave here believing she was happy with Luther. There would be no one to care if she lived or died. She was totally alone, completely helpless . . . Tears slipped from her eyes and trailed down her cheeks.

Luther saw the tears and tasted victory. He'd beaten her. Now he would slake his lust on her defenseless body. Now he would know the glory of possessing her fully. His body was hot and throbbing and ready. He cast the belt aside and reached down to unfasten his pants.

Nick had just reached the top of the steps when he heard a very faint cry coming from the room at the end of the hall. It sounded like Jordan, and his jaw clenched in anger. Murder was on his mind as he raced toward the room. He crashed against the door with all his might, breaking through on the first try.

Luther had been just about to drop his pants when the door to the room was smashed open. Shocked by the interruption, he turned to find Nick barging into the room.

Nick paused only long enough to see Jordan naked, tied to the bed. That one quick look told him all he needed to know.

"Nick!" Jordan cried his name out loud. She couldn't believe he'd come after her!

Enraged by Luther's attack on Jordan, Nick was beyond rational thought. He tossed his gun aside and bodily tackled the amoral opportunist who stood over her. Bloodlust filled Nick. A red haze colored his vision. He wanted to kill Radcliffe with his bare hands. He wanted to choke the life from him and beat him beyond recognition. He had no other thought in his mind than to kill.

Nick's assault knocked Luther to the floor. Having the element of surprise on his side, Nick had the immediate advantage over him. They grappled together, but Nick's fury gave him superior power. He took him by the throat, both of his hands closing around his neck with lethal force.

Philip and Slater came running into the room to help.

"Take care of your sister," Slater told Philip, before going to Nick's aid.

Philip hurried to the bed, and after locating the key on the nightstand, quickly unfastened the shackles.

"Thank God you came!" Jordan sobbed as she threw her arms around her brother's neck and buried her face against his shoulder.

Philip held her close, grabbing up a sheet and wrapping it around her as best he could. "I was so worried . . ."

Luther's face was turning purple and Nick took pure animalistic delight in his suffering.

"Nick!" Slater came to him. "Nick, stop now! Don't kill him! Don't sink as low as he is!"

"Get away from me, Slater!" Nick's voice didn't even sound like him as he warned his friend away.

"Nick! Jordan needs you! Go to her. Leave Radcliffe to me . . ."

For the first time since entering the room, Nick's sanity returned. He loosened his hold on Luther as he glanced toward his wife. She was huddled on the bed with her brother, wrapped only in a sheet. Nick dropped his hands from Luther's neck as he slowly got to his feet. Luther began to choke and cough as air once again made its way down his bruised throat.

Nick felt all the fury drain from him. He walked slowly across the room toward the woman he loved, his gaze focused only on her. There was so much he wanted to tell her, so much he had to say to her, and he wasn't quite sure how to begin. He stopped next to the bed, his eyes meeting hers for the first time without any lies or deceptions between them. Only the light of his love shone in their depths.

"I love you, Jordan," was all he could think to say. It was said with heartfelt simplicity and the utmost sincerity, and it touched her as nothing else would have at that moment.

"Oh, Nick . . . I love you, too!" Jordan's tears spilled forth as she began to cry in earnest, but this time her tears were happy ones. She let go of Philip, moving out of the safe haven of his arms and into her husband's protective, adoring embrace.

Nick kissed her softly, then swept her up in his

441

arms and started to carry her from the room. Jordan linked her arms about his neck and rested her head upon his shoulder. There would be time later for questions and answers. All that mattered now was that he loved her and that they were going to be together.

Luther was coming around, and he looked up to see Nick leaving with Jordan. Unable to accept that he'd lost her, he came to his feet with the roar of a maniac.

"She's mine, Kane! She belongs to me!" He went for the gun Nick had discarded earlier, and, getting a hand on it, turned and fired wildly.

The bullet went wide, missing Nick and Jordan by inches as they dove for cover. Slater hadn't expected Luther to try anything, but when he went for the gun, Slater had fired. His shot was accurate and deadly, and Luther joined his partner in death.

"Are you all right?" Slater asked worriedly as he ran to Nick and Jordan. Philip was right behind him.

"Jordan?" Nick looked down at his lovely wife. He had covered her body with his own in his effort to protect her from Luther's shot.

Jordan gazed up at him, fear leaving her eyes to be replaced by shining adoration. "I'm fine, as long as I'm with you . . ."

"Jordan, let's go home . . ." Nick said hoarsely.

"You two go ahead," Slater agreed. "Philip and I will call the authorities in and tell them what happened. We'll meet you at Riverwood tomorrow . . ."

"Make it the day after," Nick said without looking at his friend.

"You'd better take my jacket . . ." Philip suggested as he quickly stripped it off and handed it to Nick.

"Thanks." Nick slipped it around Jordan, covering her protectively.

442

"You know Philip's my brother?"

"I know," he answered, smiling tenderly.

She returned his smile. Nick picked her up then and carried her from the room. He wanted to take her away from all the ugliness.

Riverwood was where they needed to be. At Riverwood they would talk and love and start to build a new life together, so that in time true paradise would be theirs forevermore.

Epilogue

Nick cradled his wife in his arms as they lay together in the comfort of their own bed, the terrible events of six months ago forgotten in their bliss.

"Didn't Peri look absolutely beautiful today?" Jordan sighed, thinking of how lovely she'd looked in her wedding dress earlier that morning.

"I don't think I've ever seen her prettier or more excited. I hope they're going to be happy together," Nick answered as he kissed Jordan softly.

Her eyes were glowing as she gazed up at him. "If she loves Philip one-tenth as much as I love you, they should be ecstatic for all eternity. I love you, Dominic Kane . . ."

"A few months ago I thought I'd never hear you say those words," he murmured, nuzzling the sweetness of her throat.

"A few months ago I thought you never wanted to hear them. I thought you only wanted your freedom. You'd made it so plain to me the first night we met that ours was to be a marriage in name only that I held out little hope of ever winning your love. And then I had to worry about being hunted down as a murderer, too . . ." Jordan shivered as she remembered those terrible times.

"Easy, love," Nick soothed, "everything's fine now. You'll never have to worry about any of that ever again. Slater, Philip, and I worked with the authorities, and both your names have been cleared of all involvement with the *Sea Demon*. I want you to put it from your mind now and concentrate on this instead . . . I love you more than life itself, and I'll do whatever I have to to keep you safe."

Jordan drew him up to her for a flaming kiss. "I love you that way, too, Nick. When I thought Luther was going to hurt you that night I was so afraid . . ."

He kissed her again, wanting to distract her thoughts. "He's dead now, he can never hurt either of us ever again. We've got our whole lives ahead of us . . ."

"Do you think anyone is as happy as we are right now?" Jordan sighed dreamily.

"I'd like to think so . . ." Nick answered, but his tone left a question unasked.

"Who are you thinking about?" She knew him well and knew when something, or someone, was on his mind.

"I was thinking about Slater," he replied slowly, remembering all his friend had been through. "I'd like to think that he's found some measure of contentment."

"I do too. He's been a good friend to both of us."

"He's a very special man."

"He's a lot like you . . ."

"You think I'm special, do you?" Nick shifted his body over hers, bracing himself on his elbows above her as he fitted his hips intimately to hers, his flat stomach pressed to her slightly rounded one.

"Very," she replied huskily. Then, with a laugh in her voice, she asked, "How much longer do you think we have until we can't lie together like this anymore?" Jordan's smile was impish as she thought of the baby she

445

carried deep within her . . . Nick's child . . . Charles's beloved grandchild . . .

Nick slipped a hand between their bodies to caress the soft beginning swell of her growing abdomen. "I'm not sure, but I think we'd better take advantage of what time we do have, don't you?"

"Absolutely . . ." She put her arms around his neck, pulling him to her, her lips seeking his with reckless abandon.

Their unending desire for each other flared to life again. Each kiss and touch led to another and another as their insatiable hunger grew. Their mouths met as their bodies fused into one. Nick's passion fanned the flames of Jordan's excitement until the heat of their joining ignited in a fiery explosion of ecstasy. Consumed by the wonder of their loving and giving, they reached ultimate rapture together. In breathless delight, they clung to one another, knowing that their strength lay in their mutual love and that their love would last forever.

In his bedroom on his plantation north of New Orleans, Slater MacKenzie lay alone on his solitary bed. He had celebrated Philip's and Peri's wedding that morning; what a perfect couple they made! He had spent the day with Nick and Jordan, marveling at their enduring love. But when he'd come back here to his home and found himself alone, memories of his own true love kept surfacing.

Slater didn't want to think about Françesca. It hurt him too badly to remember the wild, passionate love they'd shared and to acknowledge that he would never know her kiss or her touch again.

The way she'd died still haunted him. Sometimes he almost wished it had been any other way, so he could have been with her, loving her until the very end.

A restless misery filled Slater. He rose from the bed and went to the window to stare out at the night-shrouded fields. His view was to the East . . . toward Cuba.

Slater suddenly realized that he would have no sense of inner peace until he'd found out the complete truth about Françesca's death. Only then would he be able to say his final good-bye to her. Turning away from the window, Slater grimly decided that now the time had come.

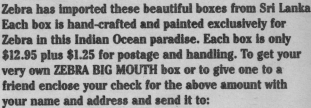